Author's Note and
Content...

Dear Reader,

Writing *Husband of the Y...*
for me, and I hope the love and care I put into it resonates
with you.

Marvin and Olan were my first couple and will always
hold a special place in my heart. Building this universe
around them has changed my life, and it was important to
me to give them and all the other characters the finale they
deserve. I hope I've done that and you enjoy this series finale.

Sheldon, Theo, Vincent, and Kent all return to help
Marvin and Olan tie the knot, but other characters from
the first three books also appear. There are lots of little
cameos and mentions of favorites. May you find as much
joy with them as I have.

Of course, I'll thank more folks in the acknowledgments after the story, but please know, from the bottom
of my gay heart, none of this could happen without you –
my dear readers. Thank you. Thank you. Thank you.

Husband of the Year is an open-door romance intended
for mature audiences. The characters in the story are
consenting adults, and there is explicit, on-page sexual
content, explicit language, and adult situations.

While *Husband of the Year* is a love story, there are serious issues.

Within recovery spaces, individuals typically use the term 'alcoholic' to describe those in the process of overcoming alcohol dependency. While I'd prefer to label the illness and not the person, phrases like 'person with an alcohol problem' or 'person with alcoholism' aren't commonly used within the recovery community.

Here are the content warnings if you need them:

Themes of addiction and recovery (including descriptions of being a child of an alcoholic, substance use, and rehabilitation facilities), discussions of death from an overdose (not of main characters and before the story takes place), and discussions of foster care and adoption due to parental substance use.

All my best,

M.A. Ward

I

'Adorable.'

One word.

No matter how many times Olan has said it during our nearly two years together, hearing it from his beautiful lips never loses its magic. It's incredible how a single word can bring such a profound sense of peace to my soul. It applies temporary brakes on the overthinking, anxiety-riddled train barreling through my brain. It calms the nerves that rattle through my veins like an unattended city fire hydrant on a hot summer day. With one word, Olan Stone grounds me.

I close my eyes and say a quick prayer that he calls me adorable for all eternity. When we're old and gray in rockers on our front porch, I want to hear that simple word from his beautiful lips. It doesn't hurt when he utters it in a deluxe room of a resort on a tropical island far away from the responsibilities and stresses of adulting. Or that his index finger traces my bottom lip as his deep brown eyes lovingly scan my face. Or that his not-too-small, not-too-big, but perfectly sized Goldi-cock thrusts deep inside my ass. My head pushes back, sinking into the pillow as he fills me up.

Taking a short five-day vacation during the school's February break to Isla Mujeres, a small island off the coast of Cancún, was Olan's idea. I would never dream of flying off to sun-filled sandy beaches to escape the harsh Maine winter and all of life's adult obligations. And leaving his daughter and my cat for more than a day or two always leaves me feeling uneasy. The variables of what could go wrong seem to multiply each day we're away – it's like anxiety math threw a party and invited all the worst-case scenarios.

'You need a respite,' Olan informed me two days before we left. 'And not the sit-at-home and worry about everything kind. I'm taking you away.'

Learning that the island's name means 'Island of Women' left me perplexed. When I asked Olan why he chose it, he gave me a sheepish smile, a hint of that tooth gap that makes my insides simmer, and said, 'Trust me.'

And I did. And I do.

Because my homeostasis lives in the land of worry, instead of relishing my gorgeous fiancé whisking me away for a romantic getaway, I immediately spiraled. Here's the thing about seemingly getting your life in order: there's always something new to obsess about. Win the lottery? Taxes. Scams. Drifters. My therapist, Erika, was like my anxiety GPS, masterfully guiding me through the potholes of life. Then she retired and left me feeling like I'd just been handed an old-school paper map with no 'You are here' dot. I still haven't found a replacement.

Olan's ex-wife, Isabella, assured me both Illona and Gonzo would be fine. Since she moved to Portland nearly a year ago, our relationship has gradually evolved into a friendship. She lives downtown in a beautiful, impeccably decorated loft, but with all of us heading over to the mainland for work and school and Illona's every other weekend with her, we've fallen into a lovely rhythm of co-parenting together. Being friends with the ex-wife isn't something most people recommend or understand, but we all simply want the best for Illona – and as little family drama as possible in our day-to-day lives. It's one thing I don't fret about.

Because Gonzo doesn't travel well, on the rare occasions Olan and I take a trip, Isabella stays at our house on Peaks Island. Jill was mortified the first time it happened. 'His ex-wife. In your space. Without you there? What if she finds . . . *things*?' Being a plane ride away, the peace of mind of having Illona's mother with her and Gonzo overrides any fear of her discovering . . . things.

But wait. Did I put the . . . things in the back of the dresser and cover them with clothes? Is the lube adequately hidden in the drawer of the bedside table? Did I remember to push it toward the back and place wholesome self-help books in front of it? What would Isabella think if she found it? Surely she knows we have sex. And need lube. Lots of lube.

'Babe, you okay?' Olan asks.

With my legs securely wrapped around his waist, Olan's heavy, warm breath lingers in my ear. Marvin Gaye croons 'How Sweet It Is (To Be Loved By You)' from the portable speaker Olan brought so he could continue teaching me the ins and outs of Motown essentials. I remember it was produced by Holland and Dozier, who are the team behind some of Motown's biggest hits. There's a James Taylor version that makes Olan's face squish up like he's just eaten the world's most sour lemon. I also know it's no accident one of his favorite artists (and quickly becoming one of mine) is named Marvin. His 'Motown Lessons' have become something fun to distract me from the stresses of planning our wedding – and life in general. Whether or not intentional, they have a way of pulling me out of my incessant thoughts.

'If you're marrying me, this is critical knowledge,' he said after my first lesson.

And I'm an excellent student. There's often dancing. Singing. And sometimes sex. I love those lessons best of all.

The island's warm, humid air is a dramatic switch from the chilly, snowy Maine winter. The air conditioner on the wall in our room runs constantly but isn't quite able to keep the tropical dampness at bay. Or maybe it's Olan's sweaty body on top of mine. My fingers trace the small of his back, and he's definitely wet. There's a ripeness to him when he's worked up that somehow turns me on even more. As he lets go and immerses himself in the passion of sex, I am privileged to witness a side of him that is reserved only for me.

Our days on the island have been spent walking the beaches, swimming, eating, and taking naps – naps that always include sex. Olan calls them 'play naps,' and every time he says it, a tiny ember in my belly rekindles. We cuddle, kiss, and grope, which escalates to lovemaking

PENGUIN BOOKS

Husband of the Year

Writing as M.A. Wardell, LAMBDA Literary Award nominee Matt writes spicy queer rom-coms. His goal is to tell adult gay love stories with a diverse representation of flawed and damaged characters who find healing through love. Matt loves rom-coms and has always wished for better representation, so he's writing the stories he wishes existed. The queer men in his stories are flawed and messy. Helping them find their HEA is his passion. Matt lives near the ocean with his husband and cats. When he isn't writing, he's snuggling those cats, reading all the rom-coms, walking to unravel plot points, and taking long, hot baths.

Husband of the Year

Teachers in Love: Book 4

M.A. WARDELL

PENGUIN BOOKS

PENGUIN BOOKS

UK | USA | Canada | Ireland | Australia
India | New Zealand | South Africa

Penguin Books is part of the Penguin Random House group of companies
whose addresses can be found at global.penguinrandomhouse.com

Penguin Random House UK,
One Embassy Gardens, 8 Viaduct Gardens, London sw11 7bw

penguin.co.uk

First published in the United States of America by Hachette Book Group 2025
First published in Great Britain by Penguin Books 2025

002

Opening and closing illustration by Ian Leone. Inside illustrations by Mayhara Ferraz
'The Blue Rose' poem reprinted by permission from A.M. Johnson

Set in 12.5/14.75pt Garamond MT Std
Typeset by Six Red Marbles UK, Thetford, Norfolk
Printed and bound in Great Britain by Clays Ltd, Elcograf S.p.A.

The authorized representative in the EEA is Penguin Random House Ireland,
Morrison Chambers, 32 Nassau Street, Dublin D02 YH68

A CIP catalogue record for this book is available from the British Library

ISBN: 978-1-405-97938-2

Penguin Random House is committed to a sustainable future
for our business, our readers and our planet. This book is made from
Forest Stewardship Council® certified paper.

To Dave – husband of the millennium

and concludes with more cuddling, kissing, and, eventually, sleep. It's been heavenly.

'Yeah, I'm good. No, better than good. Amazing.' I reach lower, grab Olan's firm ass, and draw him closer. His cock plunges deeper like he's trying to find hidden treasure, rearranging me from the inside out. 'Will you kiss me? Please?'

'Marvin Block, you never have to wonder about that.'

His lips brush mine, the faintest hint of his cherry ChapStick sweetening the kiss, and I attempt to center myself in the moment. Thoughts of children, ex-wives, cats, the hustle and bustle of school, and the freezing temperatures are all banished from my mind. Away with you, monkey brain! My eyes lock on to the ceiling fan, and I stare, watching the blades blur as Olan nibbles on my lower lip.

'Babe?' He's completely still – the only movement his dick throbbing inside me.

'Thank you for this.' I kiss him, doing my best to convey my deep gratitude. Yes, for the trip, but mostly for him.

'You needed a distraction from ... well, everything. And it's going to be even more hectic once we return. We have to get moving on planning the ...'

My hand covers his mouth, his luscious lips vibrating on my fingers. Talking about the wedding will simply send my anxiety into overdrive.

'Not now. Not yet. One more day of ...' My fingers find Olan's butt and squeeze the firm muscle.

'Yes, sir. My adorable fiancé.'

He smiles, and that's it. His sweet lips part, revealing that sexy tooth gap, and his words flip a switch in my brain.

I'm present. In the hotel room, the light, warm weather comforter neatly folded and placed on a sitting chair, getting railed by the most beautiful man in existence.

My head dips back, and Olan's tongue finds my neck, licking and sucking, and I don't even care if he leaves a mark. He brought me here for this. For a reprieve. Between the rest of the school year and our impending nuptials, it's going to be ... a lot. This is our last escape before the chaos descends. But now, I focus on him. His breath. His heartbeat. His weight on me. His honeyed lips attempt to taste every bit of my skin. His dick darts in and out of me. The moans and gasps he's making signal his pure delight.

'Olan?'

'Yeah?'

His fingers comb through my curls.

'Can I ride you?'

He chuckles. The sweat on his brow glistens under the sunlight coming from the window, and I'm grateful for a room on the top floor overlooking the private beach. We haven't closed the curtains once, and there's something magical about sleeping and fucking with the waves crashing outside.

'Of course. Whatever you want.' Olan rolls over and puts his hands behind his head. He's simply getting comfortable, but as his muscles flex, I stare for a moment, once again in awe that I get to spend my life with someone so beautiful – inside and out.

Olan reaches down and pushes his cock, thick and hard, so it's standing straight up. I'm not sure if he's admiring it himself, putting on a show for me, or a bit of both, but my eyes are certainly enjoying the show.

'Like what you see?' he asks as he wiggles his eyebrows.

The words should make me cringe, but they don't. Because coming from Olan, with his sweet soul and kind heart, everything comes off as completely sincere.

I nod and take over, holding his dick up. It's still slick with lube, but I take the intermission as an opportunity to apply more to both of us.

'Never enough,' he says, repeating our little inside joke.

And he's right. The more we use, the more unhinged we become. Because when everything is greased up, the experience gets a major upgrade.

'Now,' I say, setting the cheap bottle of lube we bought at the bodega a few blocks away on the bedside table.

'I'm going to ride your cock.' I straddle him.

'And you're going to pound me.' I lower myself.

'Sound good, Mr Stone?' My fingers position his tip right at my hole.

A smile overtakes Olan's face. What I call 'the big one' spreads from cheek to cheek, every tooth showing. It appears whenever he's overjoyed – watching Illona sing and dance, licking soft-serve ice cream with sprinkles in a waffle cone, or when he's completely engrossed in pounding my ass into oblivion.

Olan nods and slowly pushes back inside me. I'm open and ready for him and my eyes close with the complete ecstasy of his cock filling me up.

'There we go,' I say, finding a rhythm on top as he grins up at me.

My thumbs find their way into my mouth, and I wet them before attending to his chest. As I massage Olan's firm pecs, my slick fingers giving his nipples attention, his face twists with pleasure. With the first swipe, he thrusts inside me, his cock becoming even harder.

'Now, fuck me.'

Olan moves his hands to my waist, holds me in place and guides me up and down at a faster pace. Even though I'm on top, he's plunging up as I descend, sending frissons of delight through me as his dick hits all the right spots.

'Olan. You're rocking my world.'

He smiles, and it erupts into a laugh, his deep chuckling echoing in the room against the sound of our bodies slapping together. It's a familiar symphony my ears have grown to relish.

'Happy to rock it,' he says, and again, his dad-level humor tickles the cockles of my heart.

Olan grasps my dick, stroking, and I keep a hand on his left pec, flicking and pinching his nipple, while the other reaches back and begins massaging his balls. The only thing Olan loves more than fucking me is having his ass played with while he's doing it. My fingers catch some lube from my ass as he's fucking me, and I add a little pressure under his sack, eliciting a deep moan from Olan's lips.

'Is your hole horny?' I ask. Olan's eyes lock on mine, and he nods slowly as he rams his cock inside me.

I maneuver my index finger to his opening, and yup, he's ready to roll. He stops fucking me for a moment while I slip the tip in. A low, deep noise escapes his lips. Having me finger-bang him while he fucks me will send him over, and I'm ready to watch him come undone.

'You good?' I ask.

He welcomes my finger, and there's clearly room for

another, but Olan and I always check in with each other. It's kind of our thing.

'Yeah. Good. Great. Another.' Olan's strong fingers grip my cock, and he pumps, taking care to massage under my balls. He reaches under, caressing where his dick stretches me open, and then returns to stroking.

I add my middle finger to the first, and Olan shifts, opening his legs wider and lifting his knees, giving me better access to his warm hole.

'Another.' The word leaps from his lips, and now I'm grinning like I've just won the lottery. At home, I'd grab a toy and fuck him properly, but on vacation, we'll have to make do with finger-banging.

Since we began dating, Olan has continued to defy expectations. Refusing to label his sexuality as bi, pan, gay, or anything really, he's also rebuffed designations in the bedroom. Technically, we're versatile with each other, but Olan avoids defining it explicitly. *Why does everything require a label? We're not clothes.*

The longer we're together, the more we take turns, and while I'd be happy with either role, being inside Olan while having him inside me is perfection to a tee.

With three fingers he finally seems satiated. He plunges into me while stroking my cock as I go to town on his ass. My thumb glides between his opening and balls, adding pressure and Olan's hips shake. Deep dicking me while being fucked by a trio of my fingers does the trick. He's close.

'Marvin . . .'

'I know. Go for it. Fill me up.'

I squeeze his firm nipple a little harder, and his cock

unloads. Throbbing. Pulsing. Shooting inside me. My fingers push deeper, burrowing and stretching until I can't go any further. Olan's entire body trembles as he lifts his pelvis, breeding me.

'Fuck. Holy fuck, Marvin.'

Olan's gaze glues to mine, and he's quiet while the last spasm explodes inside me.

He jerks me faster, determined to make me come. Olan's fingers gently graze my chest, finding my nipples and reciprocating the attention I just gave him.

'I'm close,' I say, feeling my orgasm knocking.

'Right here,' Olan replies, nodding at his chest as he thrusts up. 'Hit me with your best shot.'

I laugh at his unintentional nod to Pat Benatar, and then it happens. As he remains deep within me, my pulsating cock surges with pleasure, releasing a torrent of scorching cum onto Olan's glistening chest. It pools in the little dip between his sturdy pecs, and I'm grateful for the extra washcloths we requested from housekeeping.

We're both still. His fingers still wrapped around my cum-coated cock, Olan whispers, 'God, I love you.'

I lean forward, and his dick slips out as my lips find his. My ejaculation, mixed with our sweat, smooshes in between our chests, and there's something incredibly hot about being covered in the fruits of our labor. I nibble the ChapStick from Olan's lower lip before reaching up and grabbing at his thick hair.

I deliver a slow, steady kiss, my fingers getting lost in his curls.

'You. Are. My. Favorite.'

Olan laughs and replies, 'That makes me very pleased.'

'Now . . .' I say.

'I know . . .' Olan kisses my nose. 'My guy is hungry.'

'No.' I nip at his chin. 'Starving.'

'Let's get some food.'

I stand to grab a washcloth from the bathroom, and Olan leans over and slaps my ass. I try to give my best annoyed face, but my mouth just ends up looking like it's trying to whistle with a mouthful of mashed potatoes. He's clearly not buying it.

'Adorable.'

2

'Do you want another margarita?' I move my thumb along the vein I've become so fond of, tracing its path on Olan's forearm. One major benefit of heat and humidity – short sleeves.

We're sitting at the hotel bar, waiting for a table. The bar itself is a stunning centerpiece, crafted from polished mahogany and adorned with gleaming glass shelves displaying top-shelf spirits and exotic liqueurs wasted on us. We eat at least one meal a day here simply because it's the closest available sustenance to our bed. And they make mean fish tacos. They put slices of avocado on each one, and then smother them with a spicy crema. I could eat them for every meal. We've turned our beach strolls into a full-blown taco tour, diving into every tiny local joint we stumble across, all in the name of finding the island's best fish tacos. The plot twist? They're all so ridiculously good, we're starting to think the tacos have joined forces to make sure we never leave the island.

'Virgin.'

'Excuse me?' My head tilts. 'Not even close. You were literally just inside me.'

'No, I mean a virgin margarita,' Olan says.

'Of course.'

I nod to grab the waiter's attention, and Olan's cell, resting on the turquoise-tiled table, buzzes. When we arrived four days ago, I was told to stash my phone in the in-room safe and forget about it. The only person who'd need to reach us here is Isabella, and she has Olan's number.

'Maybe Gonzo isn't eating. He does that sometimes when he misses me.' Worry coils within me, tightening its grip. 'Let me talk to her. I can give her some tips. And talk to him. Tell her to put me on speakerphone. He might just need to hear my voice.' I reach for Olan's phone, but he pulls it away.

'It's my mother.' Olan's lips purse as he blinks rapidly a few times. I open my mouth, but I'm not sure what to say. 'I should take it.' He stands. 'I'll be right back.'

His brow wrinkles as he heads for the hallway leading toward the beach exit.

Olan's relationship with his family is complicated and, honestly, I can empathize. They talk on the phone every few weeks, but on my end, all I hear from Olan are a lot of ums, yeahs, and okays. When I've tried to push him for more information on Rebecca and Erik Stone, his willingness to offer anything beyond surface-level facts remains minimal. I know they still live in the south side Chicago home where Olan and his brothers were raised. They're retired, but Rebecca managed caretakers at a nursing home, and Erik was a city bus driver.

Communication with his brothers is even more sparse. Gabe, two years older, is married, with two boys slightly older than Illona. He sells huge industrial cooling units, which requires him to travel often. Then there's Liam. The youngest. I know he struggles with drinking, but Olan has never filled in the details. They don't talk often – maybe once a year since we've been together, but he gets sporadic updates from his parents.

Olan usually calls his mother. Why would she be calling him? And while we're in Mexico. I wonder if something's wrong. Did something happen to his dad? Olan exits the building, and I'm momentarily mesmerized by the twinkling lights hanging above.

My mind wanders to my mother. Crap, when was the last time I called her? I didn't even inform her about this trip. She'd worry. And want every detail about flights, hotels, island dynamics, and hotel safety protocol. Chances are she's seen a *Dateline* about someone being murdered on an island and that's all I'd hear about. I'm certainly not calling her now. Or while we're here. Maybe from the airport. Maybe when we're back. I'll tell her all about it after. Once I'm safely home.

'Is this seat taken?'

Blinking out of my mini-spiral, a white woman, probably around the same age as my mother, smiles at me with ruby red lipstick. She has bright orange hair, and I admire both the tenacity and effort it must take to keep it so vibrant.

Before I can tell her, yes, the seat is taken by my gorgeous fiancé and he will be right back, she's hanging her purse on the back of the chair and sitting.

'Elise.' She extends her hand, and I instinctively take it. But she doesn't want a shake. She uses me to steady herself, while her other hand grabs the bar as she hoists herself onto the stool.

'Marvin,' I say.

There's some wobbling as Elise sits, and I do my best to clasp her hand firmly until she settles.

'Marvin.' She repeats my name, pursing her lips, mulling over the sounds or perhaps considering it before nodding her approval.

'And what's a handsome man like you doing here all by yourself?' Elise taps the wood counter, and the bartender appears. 'Chardonnay, please.'

The bartender nods. His long hair, pulled back into a ponytail, has a few stray wisps that tickle his face.

'Did you want anything?' Elise asks.

'No, I'm good.' I raise my seltzer, the lime hanging on the rim for dear life. 'But thank you. Wait. Yes. A margarita. Virgin.'

'One virgin margarita,' Elise repeats, and the bartender nods and busies himself making our drinks. 'Now, tell me why you're here alone.'

'I could ask the same of you.'

A wide smile cracks Elise's face in half as her head tilts back, and a loud, shrill cackle takes over the entire bar area.

'Me? I've been coming here for years.'

'By yourself?'

'Well, for the last . . .' She looks to the sky, searching. 'Six years, yes. Since my husband passed. Richard and I honeymooned here over thirty years ago.' Another smile spreads on Elise's face. 'He brought me back every February for our anniversary, and I figured he'd want me to keep up the tradition. So here I am.'

'Wow. That's so sweet. And thirty years.' I press my lips together, and a gentle smile slowly curves onto my face.

'Now, what's your excuse?'

'Excuse? For what?'

'For being . . .' Elise motions around us. 'In paradise. Alone.'

'Oh, I'm not alone. My fiancé is taking a call.'

'Of course. You're engaged. And what's the lucky lady's name?'

'Well, his name is Olan.' I smile. My stomach stills waiting for her reaction.

'His. Of course. My apologies for assuming.'

'No worries. And speak of the angel.'

Olan returns, his white linen shirt billowing as he walks and stands near us. Attempting to understand the purpose of his mother's call, I study his expression, only to be met with his expertly maintained poker face. My eyes find his, searching for a clue, but there's nothing. When he sees Elise perched on his stool, he quickly snatches a free one from the end of the bar. He positions it between us, distancing himself further from the counter, forming a triangular arrangement perfect for conversation.

'And you must be Olan,' Elise says, extending her hand.

'Ma'am.' Olan shakes it and does a small bow. I'm not sure if he thinks she's royalty, or he's just showing extra respect, but it's possibly the cutest thing I've ever seen.

'Elise, please. And thank you for letting me steal your lovely fiancé for a few minutes.'

'No, thank you for keeping him company while I was occupied.'

Olan and I exchange a glance, my eyes filled with unspoken encouragement.

'It's my pleasure. I hear you're engaged. Regale me with the details of your impending wedding.' The bartender delivers our drinks, and Elise takes a sip of her wine. 'No, wait. Start at the beginning. How did you meet?'

I clear my throat. 'I was his daughter's kindergarten teacher.'

Elise's eyes bulge and a mischievous grin appears on her lips. 'Scandalous.' She takes another drink, this time a large gulp. 'I love it.'

'It wasn't egregious.' Olan lifts his mocktail, and my eyes hone in on his lips. A flash of that first kiss in my tiny apartment. My surprise at his interest and overall enthusiasm for kissing floods back. Being pushed against the wall, as he tasted, nibbled, and devoured my mouth. Our midsections rutted against each other near my old apartment's front door while Gonzo looked on in horror. A quick shiver scurries up my spine. 'It's not like I gave her any special treatment because her dad was . . .'

'In your pants?' Elise laughs, and again, nearby patrons glance to see what the commotion is all about.

'I was going to say "interested in me", but you're not wrong.' I sip my seltzer quickly, attempting to moisten my parched mouth.

Olan pats my knee. As his fingers linger, squeezing and rubbing, my chest releases a tiny bit of the building tension.

'A gorgeous father of a student,' Elise says with a wink. 'A secret affair. I'm impressed.'

'It was only a secret for a few months,' I say.

'I couldn't keep things hidden for long.' Olan's fingers wrap around my chin, his thumb coming close to my bottom lip. 'Look at this adorable face.'

My shoulders lift in amusement, and a soft laugh bubbles up. I meet Olan's gaze, and I find myself captivated by his mesmerizing brown eyes – my future stares back at me and I'm still amazed at how my love for him continues to flourish.

'We've been together for almost two years now,' Olan says. 'Living together, planning a wedding. This one . . .' Olan's hand migrates to my shoulder. 'Needed an island getaway.'

'Well, you couldn't have picked a better one,' Elise says. 'The food, the people, the drinks.' She lifts her glass. 'My Richard loved the quiet beach on the west side of the island. The tourists don't venture that far, and it's usually quite empty. He'd pack us a picnic, and we'd spend the day reading, swimming, and grazing on his makeshift spread from the bodega. On our honeymoon, he convinced me to go skinny dipping, and we continued the tradition every year after.'

'He sounds like a special man,' Olan says.

'He was.' A nostalgic smile takes over her face. 'He was my blue rose.'

Olan's eyebrows scurry together. 'Your what?'

'My blue rose. Rare. Special. Unattainable. There's a poem I read once by . . .' Elise's eyes scan the sky, searching. 'Someone thoughtful. People search their whole lives for that special person – a soulmate. Their blue rose.' A contented smile blossoms on her face. 'Richard was mine.'

The love radiating from Elise's face catches me off guard, and my heart aches for her loss. But I'm also grateful for the joy they shared. 'And you were his.'

Elise nods, pulling her lips in, her eyes exploring, perhaps for another cherished memory of her husband.

'And you two. You've found your blue rose.'

'Absolutely,' Olan says, taking my hand in his. 'He's never getting rid of me.' Olan kisses my cheek softly, the smell of linen, coconut, and cherry swirls as he whispers into my ear, 'You're stuck with me.'

'Happy to be stuck,' I say and take a deep breath, attempting to capture as much of this feeling as possible and bottle it up. Since the moment his lips landed on mine two years ago, Olan has done something to my body's chemistry. Sure, the erections are plentiful and often unyielding. But he's somehow managed to both excavate and nurture my heart in a way I never knew possible. All my life, I'd heard the word bashert and wondered if it was a crock of shit, but nope, I just hadn't met my . . . blue rose.

'Well, let me leave you two to your night,' Elise says, standing and setting her almost empty glass on the bar.

'Why don't you join us for dinner?' I ask, knowing Olan would be more than happy to continue our conversation with Elise.

'No, no. I have . . . a late-night swim waiting.' She winks, grabs her purse, and stands. Olan and I promptly rise to our feet.

'Take care, boys. And maybe I'll see you back on the island sometime.'

'Good night,' Olan says. We both wave, and Elise heads

toward the exit, the fringe on her shawl shaking with each step as she departs.

'What a lovely lady,' Olan says, taking my hand and we sit.

'So sweet,' I say as I run my finger along his forearm.

'Just like these.' Olan's lips land on mine, and his kiss, like everything about him, makes me feel like the most precious, cherished treasure – his blue rose.

After a long stroll along the water, we end up at the small beach on the west of the island. Elise was right; there's nobody here except us and a few stray seagulls. The shoreline is a crescent of pristine, powdery sand, gently curving around water that sparkles like jewels under the moonlight. The beach is framed by lush, emerald-green foliage that provides natural privacy and a sense of seclusion.

With his convincing smile, Olan persuades me to take a quick dip in our underwear. The warm water and night sky dotted with stars provide a peaceful backdrop for our swim.

We're able to stand, the ocean up to our chests, and Olan wraps his arms around me, pulling me close. Water beads on his skin and when he kisses me under the sparkling sky, it seems as if the entire universe has converged to create this perfect moment for us.

'Mmmmh. Tasty.' He takes a quick lick at my mouth.

'I love you,' I say. 'Thank you, again. For bringing me here.'

'Anytime.'

Another kiss lingers on my lips as Olan intertwines his fingers with mine, his touch sending a gentle electric current through my body. With a tender tug, he pulls me toward the shore. The sand beneath our feet shifts and molds with each step.

We're soon lying on the beach in our wet underwear, waiting to air dry enough to put the rest of our clothes on.

'What is it about the ocean?' I ask, taking in a deep breath.

'The fish? The salt?' Olan tilts his head in thought. 'The gravitational pull of the moon creating lapping waves and the tidal current?'

I prop myself up on an elbow and lean over to kiss his chin. Lips. Nose. Forehead. Finally, skirting back to his mouth, and taking a small bite of his lower lip.

'You are such a nerd.' Another kiss. Longer. Deeper. My tongue skates over his mouth. 'Fuck, I love it. You. Being nerdy. All of you.'

'Yeah.' Olan's arms encircle my torso, pulling me on top of him, our damp skin clinging together like two magnets. 'I kind of got that.'

'But the beach. The oceans. All of them. The Atlantic. Pacific. Indian. Even the Arctic. They're all so magical.'

'Scientists have given names to the different oceanic regions, but technically, they're all one body of water. The sand, too. Every grain is connected. The sand we'll stand on in Maine to take our vows could've been here at some point.' He reaches down and picks up a handful, letting it cascade over his fingers and return to the beach. 'And the stars.' He glances toward the heavens. 'Same stars we'll get married under thousands of miles away.'

My teeth land on Olan's chin, and I bite down hard enough to elicit a small 'ouch' from him.

'What was that for?' he asks.

'For being such a . . .'

'Nerd. I know.' Olan points to himself, and I nestle my face into the crook of his neck.

'My nerd. My fiancé nerd. Future husband nerd.' My hands travel to his chest, delighted by the firmness of his pecs. 'Nerdy love of my life, nerd.'

Olan captures my lips in a tender, fervent kiss, the lingering taste of the ocean salt still vivid between us. We lie side by side beneath the vast, twinkling expanse of the night sky, each star a distant witness to our closeness. The gentle rhythm of our breathing and the whisper of the waves create a serene backdrop as we bask in the cocoon of our love and the promise of our future together.

3

Some people say the bigger seats, stream of drinks and snacks, and constant doting from the flight attendants in first class are nothing more than an overpriced, unnecessary luxury. Those people are wrong.

As a teacher, I've never had much disposable income for flying. And when I do, I'm typically in the back of the plane – near the bathroom and galley, where the flight attendants sit and make small talk with each other. But Olan insisted I'd enjoy first class. There's a dedicated flight attendant, and it appears his only job is our comfort.

Staring out the window, a blanket of clouds covering the ocean below, my mind swirls with thoughts of the plane. How does a giant hunk of metal filled with people and all their luggage stay up in the sky? Exactly where are the rafts if the plane goes down and manages to land on water? Is the flotation device I'm supposed to use under my seat, or is it my actual seat cushion? Do I blow into the tube to inflate it inside the plane or wait until I'm drifting on the sea full of ravenous sharks? How will the flight attendant get an infant life vest to the poor woman sitting in the back of the plane with her newborn?

Olan gently takes my hand. His strong fingers squeeze mine, and he pulls it toward his lips for a kiss.

'You okay?'

'Fine. Totally fine,' I say, biting my lower lip.

'Marvin. Look at me.'

I do as I'm told, and yup, the mere sight of his face puts me at ease.

'Take a deep breath with me,' he says.

I watch his face and follow when he purses his lips, pulling air in and then pushing it out slowly, all while never letting go of my hand.

'Better?' he asks.

I nod and offer a small smile.

'Illona will be excited to see us,' he says.

'Not as excited as Gonzo.'

'Nobody will be more excited than Isabella,' Olan says, and we both laugh. She loves the bonus time with Illona, but she's purely a good sport about taking care of Gonzo. There's a reason Olan and Illona never had animals. Isabella Stone is not a pet person.

'Close your eyes. I'm right here.' Olan lifts my hand and tugs it close to his chest. The thumping of his heart beats against my fingers, and my eyes shut. As long as we're together, I'll be okay. He's got me.

Apparently, when you return to the United States, the government has intricate forms for you to fill out. And questions to ask. And people to ask them.

Olan and I stand in line at Boston's Logan Airport, waiting our turn to clear customs. We each have a duffel slung over our shoulder, the only luggage we brought because Olan assured me we'd be naked or in our bathing suits most of the time. He was correct. As the line moves, we get closer to the agent, and there's something about his face that throws me. He's a young white man, maybe in his mid-twenties, with a buzz cut and a clean-shaven, severe jawline. The TSA uniform hugs his muscular body, and in the time I've been watching him, I've yet to see even a hint of a smile on his face.

'Do we go up together or on our own?' I ask Olan when there's only one person in front of us.

'Together.' Olan shifts his bag and throws his shoulders back. 'They speak to the entire party that's traveling together.'

'Oh. Okay.'

I'd noticed families going up together, but Olan and I aren't family. Yet. We're not married. And there's the fact that we're two men. Even once married, would everyone consider us family? Does the agent know we're gay? Does he care? Does it matter? Of course, the minute we walk up to the agent together, he'll know. Won't he? There's no way Olan and I are brothers. We could be friends. Or work colleagues. Traveling together. From Mexico. Yeah, not likely.

It's our turn. We walk up silently, and Mr TSA says, 'Passports, please.'

Olan hands him our documents and I stand slightly behind, letting him take the lead. It's one in a long list of my favorite ways Olan takes care of me.

'Traveling together?' The agent's eyes don't leave our passports and the paperwork Olan handed over.

'Yes, sir.' Olan's voice comes out louder than I'm used to.

'Where are you flying from?'

'Cancún, Mexico.'

The agent's eyes dart up, scanning Olan, me, and back to Olan. I'm not sure what he's looking for, but my skin crawls as he studies us with his slightly squinted eyes.

'How long were you out of the country?'

'Five days.' Olan's never a man of many words, but my throat constricts with his particularly clipped answers.

The agent scours us with his eyes. Then, back to the paperwork. He types something on his computer without returning his gaze to us.

'Sir. Mr' – he reads my passport – 'Block. Welcome home. You can wait over there.' He nods to a cluster of metal benches. 'Mr Stone, come this way.'

There are two more agents. I'm not sure where they came from – they seem to have materialized out of thin air.

'Keep your bag with you,' one of the new scary agents says. Her hair is pulled back into a tight ponytail.

'Should I come –' I begin, but Olan interrupts.

'Marvin. Wait there. I'll be right back.'

I walk to the bench, a knot tying in my stomach, as I watch Olan escorted by two of the agents. They turn a corner and he's gone.

My hand wanders into my pocket and checks for my phone. Yup, it's there. Maybe I should call Isabella. No, Jill. She could be here in an hour if she drove fast. Jill Kim will know what to do. She's not only my work wife and best friend, she knows how to handle the toughest situations at school. If you can manage a kindergartner refusing to come down from the jungle gym, you can handle two menacing TSA agents. Why did they take him and not me? What do they think we were doing in Mexico?

I'm staring at the contacts on my phone. Isabella. Jill. Sarah Block. Yes, I have my mother's full name instead of 'mom' in my contacts. What if I call someone and they come for me? What are they asking him? Doing to him? My head feels light and I take a deep breath and remind myself I'm safe. Olan needs me to be calm. Cool. Collected. Fuck. I'm none of those things. Ever.

Olan drove us here in his fancy James Bond car and, even though I'm a capable grown-up, I'm not sure I could get the damn thing started. And the parking garage ticket is in his wallet. Would they let me out of the lot without it? Of course they would. They're not going to hold me hostage in Olan's fancy-pants Aston Martin for all eternity. But I'm not driving back to Portland without him. No way. He's driving. He has the ticket. And the car keys. And he's . . . Olan. Fuck. Tears sting the corners of my eyes, and I close them, breathing deeply. My fingers reach for my temple and, using my index and middle fingers, I tap quickly the way Erika showed me. Five taps near my eyebrow. Five under my eye. Five on my collarbone. Combined with deep breathing and my anxiety might lower a notch. If not, I'll repeat. Erika truly was the ideal therapist for me, a perfect match. Why'd she have to go and retire? Didn't she know it took me my entire life and four failed therapists to find her? She knew. Because I told her.

Counting to twelve, I move to my clavicle and repeat.

Am I calmer? Marginally. Another deep breath, in through my nose and out through my mouth, and I open my eyes.

And then I see him. Olan. Alone. Walking toward me like nothing happened. His lips pulled in, but a hint of a smile on his gorgeous face.

'Are you okay?' I leap to my feet and wrap my arms around his torso, pulling him close, wanting to check him for any harm.

'What happened? What did they want?'

'Marvin. Babe. I'm fine.'

'What happened?'

'They just had a few questions about what we were doing in Mexico.'

'We were on vacation. Fucking. Daily. Did you tell them that?' A fire ignites in my belly now that he's safe with me. 'Why didn't they ask me? Why only you?'

'It's random.' Olan's gaze darts up for a split second and he shrugs. 'They're just doing their job.' He takes my hand, pulling me toward the exit. 'I'm used to it.'

'Used to it? Used to what?'

'Marvin. Please. Not now. I'm tired. Let's go home.' Olan's eyes find mine, and a pleading stirs behind them.

'Okay.' I take his hand, right in the middle of Logan airport, and I hope the agent sees. Olan walks a half step in front of me, an eagerness to leave propelling him toward the parking garage.

As soon as we're on the highway, Olan flips a switch on the steering wheel, and 'My Girl' blasts through the speakers. There's no lesson. No information about the artist, songwriters, or chart history from him. I simply listen as I stare out the window. Clouds stretch across the sky, casting a shadow, but The Temptations insist there's sunshine behind the overcast sky, and a bittersweet atmosphere lingers as we drive home in silence, accompanied only by the comforting sounds of Olan's Motown playlist.

4

'Daddy!'

As soon as we walk through the front door, Illona, in her favorite pajamas adorned with purple unicorns, rushes into her father's waiting embrace. Every few days, I have to wash them first thing in the morning so they're ready for bedtime because, for some reason, currently, no other pair will do. Olan says not to fuss; she'll manage with another pair, but it's such a small thing to do for her. Why not let the child be happy in her purple unicorn pajamas? She's almost seven now, and I keep waiting for him to tell her she's too big to be picked up like this. But he hasn't. And I don't suspect he will for a while. He gets to pick her up and I get to wash her favorite PJs.

Olan was still quiet on the ferry ride, but it's been a long day of travel, and it's almost our bedtime, let alone Illona's.

'What are you doing up?' Olan squeezes his little girl, and she buries her face in his neck before answering.

'Mommy said it was okay.'

'No sleeping was happening until you two were home.' Isabella walks toward the entry, a chunky white cable-knit sweater wrapped around her thin frame. Even when she's relaxed and comfortable, she manages to appear like she's just stepped out of a fashion magazine. 'She's been waiting patiently.'

I wrap Olan and Illona in a hug, and she leans over and kisses my cheek. She smells like bubblegum and jasmine, the latter remnants of her mother's perfume. I love traveling and seeing unknown places, but nothing beats coming home.

'And where's my kitty boyfriend?' I ask.

'Gonzo had no trouble falling asleep,' Illona says. 'He's in my bed.'

'He slept with her every night you were gone.' Isabella brushes a loose strand of hair from her face. 'It was like he was watching over her.'

'And missing his dads.' Illona kisses Olan and then yawns. It's well past her bedtime, and now that we're home, her body revolts against her insistence on waiting up for us.

'Let's get you to bed.' Olan's hands smooth Illona's hair as he carries her up the stairs, leaving us in his wake.

'Did you have a fun trip?' Isabella asks. She moves toward the living room, where I see her travel bag, presumably packed and ready to head out.

'Oh yeah. It was beautiful. Very relaxing.'

'And Olan. He seems more quiet than usual. Is he okay?'

Two years ago, Isabella asking me this would have sent my anxiety into overdrive, but we've become friends. Jill will never stop ragging me about befriending the ex-wife, but really, having her move to Portland has been a blessing. She knows Olan better than anyone and Illona has thrived even more having her mom so close again.

'I think so?' I sit on the couch and Gonzo, presumably woken by having his bed intruded on, saunters down the stairs to investigate.

'There's my guy,' I say as he leaps onto my lap, immediately headbutting my chest as his loud purr provides a soothing score.

'This one barely ate while you were away. I had to resort to cans of tuna.'

I run my fingers over Gonzo's coat, feeling the smoothness beneath my touch, confirming his frame hasn't drastically changed.

'Your dads are home. Normal eating may resume,' I say.

Isabella's eyebrows draw together. 'Maybe Olan's just tired.'

'Something happened.' I bite my lower lip. 'At the airport.'

'In Mexico?'

'No, Boston. At Logan.'

Isabella's eyes open wide and I take a breath.

'When we came through customs, they took Olan away. It was only for a few minutes. He says they just asked him some questions, and that it wasn't a big deal. And he doesn't want to talk about it anymore.'

'Oh.' Isabella's fingers rub her chin. She knows something. I can tell. Or at least has a thought.

'What? What is it?' I ask.

She reaches over and takes my hand. Her fingernails are a deep burgundy, and the polish is smooth like glass.

'Damn microaggressions.'

'Because we're two men?' I ask.

'No. I mean, maybe that's part of it.' A slight frown appears on Isabella's face. 'Yes, you're two men. But one of you is . . .'

My head spins and the word gets stuck like thick glue, and I clear my throat before it comes out.

'Black.'

My heart races and my mind unravels. I should have said something more at the airport. Or called for help.

'It happens. Often. And a Black man and a white man together. Or even worse, a white woman.' A knowing look overtakes her face. She and Olan were married for years. Of course she understands this.

'Some people are . . .' She contorts her mouth, trying to find the right word.

'Hateful,' I say.

'Yes. Exactly.'

In bed, Olan gives me a quick kiss and turns the lights off. He hasn't said a word since he came upstairs and put Illona to bed. Before she left for the last ferry of the night, Isabella reassured me the best thing for me to do was be here for him. Comfort him. She assured me if he wanted to talk more about it, he would. When he's ready.

'Olan?' I prop myself up on an elbow. He's got soft music playing, his endless playlist that he keeps tweaking for our lessons. I'm aware of the immense joy these songs bring him, so I'm glad he's playing them, their familiar tunes creating a comforting atmosphere as we settle in for the night.

'Mmmh.' His tone is low and a sudden swell of wetness overtakes my eyes. The current song fades out and one I'm not familiar with plays. A woman, with a sweet alto, belts, instructing me.

'C'mere.' I open my right arm, inviting him in and he cuddles into my chest.

'Kim Weston,' Olan says. '"Take Me in Your Arms (Rock Me a Little While)". Completely underrated.'

With a faster beat than the mood calls for, the music softly fills the room, and listening to Ms Weston, I do my best to rock Olan softly.

'You know what?' I ask. In the comfort of our bed, we sway to the soothing melody. When I catch a whiff of Olan, with his distinct special sweetness, my heart swells with affection.

'What?'

'I love you.'

I kiss Olan's hair, pressing in to reach his skull through his mountain of coils.

He tilts his head up, and I'm able to brush my lips on his forehead.

'I love you.' I blink, saying each word quietly, like a peaceful promise. 'And I can't wait to be married to you.'

Olan doesn't speak. He answers by adjusting himself so we're able to kiss properly. Olan's fingers find my cheeks, holding me in place as he presses his mouth on mine. There's an urgency. A longing. There is nothing I desire more than for him to fully grasp the extent of my love.

He lies on his back, staring at the ceiling, and speaks softly. 'I'm an engineer. I have more money than I know what to do with. I'm a good father.'

'Amazing father,' I say.

'I know I'm a good person. But I can't change the way others see me.'

There's nothing I can say to make this better, so I simply lean in and press my lips against his, and whisper, 'I love you.' I hold his face with my hands, and the need to say it again consumes me. 'I love you. I love you. I love you.'

With each phrase, I dot the landscape of his face with my lips, treating every spot of skin like a canvas in a masterpiece.

'I know.' He kisses me gently as his hand moves up and gets lost in my mop of curls. 'I love you, too.'

We cuddle and kiss, our hearts beating in unison as we revel in the closeness, pausing only to whisper 'I love you' to each other, the words imbued with a warmth that seems to deepen with each repetition. The soft sounds of Detroit's finest record label fill the room, their melodies weaving through the air like a gentle caress, blending seamlessly with the warmth of our affection, finally lulling us to a peaceful slumber.

5

From her window seat, Illona fixes her eyes on the view outside, captivated by the sight of the island slowly fading away while we make our way toward the mainland. This is our quiet time together before we both plug in on the bus. We sit. Sometimes in silence. Sometimes not. But I cherish this one-on-one time with her.

'I'm really glad you and Daddy are home.'

She leans her head on my shoulder but keeps her focus on the waves outside.

'Me too.' I lay my hand on the side of her head. Olan pulled her hair back into two low braids and I'm careful not to disturb them.

This morning, Olan woke me with a kiss and coffee. He seemed much more himself than last night. Maybe it was the kissing and cuddling and relentless I love yous but I was happy to see the small gap between his front teeth when he leaned over to wake me after his early morning basement workout.

I know what happened isn't something that Olan can simply 'sleep off', but I'm also not sure he wants to talk about it. With me, anyway. He isn't particularly close to his family. He has a weekly phone call with his parents, but they're so far away. I wish he had more friends for support. Even after two years here, most of the people he knows are from AA and, well, they're mostly white.

Scanning the ferry, there's not a single person of color besides Illona. And she's with me. A white man. What do people think? What if it was Olan? With a white child? My heart momentarily gallops and I squeeze Illona a little closer, kissing the top of her head.

'Are you getting excited about the wedding?' Illona's sweet face turns toward me. How do I have such a deep love for a little girl I've only known a short time? If I had a nickel for every time someone has told me I'd be a wonderful father, I'd be as rich as . . . well, Olan. Sometimes I think I want kids of my own. But I'm not sure Olan wants more. Or even if I do. When the one you have is pretty perfect, why tempt fate?

'Yeah. We need to start planning the details. August will be here before we know it.' I don't know much about planning a wedding, but I know there's a lot of moving pieces. Olan and I are meeting with the coordinator at The Ocean Inn soon to get the ball rolling.

'Any ideas about flowers yet?'

I'm not sure if Illona's more excited about us getting married or the opportunity to be the flower girl. She's determined to match her dress to whatever the flower theme is and Isabella has promised to make that happen.

A flower theme isn't anything I've heard of, but Illona assured me it's real.

'You know, your dad and I haven't talked about flowers, but maybe . . .' Elise's bright orange hair and red lipstick flash in my mind. 'Roses.' Illona's eyes open wide. 'Blue roses.'

'You went swimming? In the ocean? Naked?' Vincent's voice fills my headphones as Illona and I ride the city bus headed for school. Taking the car back and forth on the ferry is an ordeal. My car stays at our house on the island, and Olan leaves his in the ferry parking garage. He needs it to drive to work, and luckily, the Portland city buses, while not extensive, have enough routes to get us from the dock to school on a single bus. The commute has become our time together – and right now, Illona is also plugged in, watching an animated show about magical rainbow fairies on her tablet.

Just over two years ago, Olan and I had just started connecting. A month before that was the day we met. Wait, was that an anniversary we were supposed to celebrate? What do you get someone for the day-we-met anniversary? A card? Candy? A blow job? There are so many firsts. The day we met. Our first kiss. The first time we were naked together? The first time he fucked me. The first time I fucked him. When we decided to make things work after the brief breakup caused by my overthinking brain. The day we moved in together. Soon, we'll have a wedding anniversary. I'm going with that. Although a first kiss anniversary celebratory blow job might be on the cards.

'Marvin? Did I lose you?' Vincent asks. I'd almost forgotten he was on the line.

'No, I'm here.' I check Illona, and she's engrossed in her show, but I still default to camouflaging my words.

'Aked-nay.' A peek of a smile appears on my lips because even though she's not listening and she's mostly figured out pig Latin by now, Vincent and I love using it to talk about adult subject matter around her.

'In the water,' I continue. 'And then . . .' Illona's head dips down, eyes locked on her screen, a smile on her beautiful face reacting to whatever the green fairy is saying. I've watched the show with her enough to know the green one has the best one-liners.

'Ucking-say. Ucking-fay.'

'In the water?' The horror in Vincent's voice makes me wince. He's not a fan of swimming. Or public nudity.

'No. Not in the water.'

'On the beach? Marvin Block. Do you know how filthy beaches are?' Or germs. 'Sand in your . . . ass. Are you kidding me?' Or dirt.

'We had a towel. And if you're really curious, most of the . . . ex-say happened in our hotel room, which they kept spotless. I even commented to Olan, "Vincent would love this place. You could eat off the floors."'

'As if.'

After our notoriously horrible first and only date two years ago, Vincent and I stayed in touch. There might not have been romantic chemistry, but he couldn't have been more of a gentleman. He seemed like he could use a friend. And since my friendships comprised of Jill, Gonzo, and a few other female acquaintances I had at school, I figured maybe a male friend might be good for me, too. Vincent and I became close quickly – he's like my little brother. Except he's older than me. But age can't account for gay-sibling dynamics.

'It's a figure of speech,' I say, doing my best to assure him. 'Nobody's eating off the floor.'

'Except the ants and roaches.' The sarcasm in Vincent's voice makes me smile. I love teasing him, and he lets me. Yup, definitely brothers.

'How are things with you?' I ask, attempting to shift the focus away from floor-feasting fiends.

'Excellent. I'm having the kids build dams with LEGO to see if they can control the water flow on an inclined surface.'

'Oh, they'll love that. LEGO. Water.' I peek out the bus window and see we're about five minutes away from our stop. 'And let them get wet. That's part of the fun.'

'I have a plethora of paper towels,' Vincent says. 'I got special permission to purchase the good ones. Not those brown ones that require an entire roll to clean up a table-spoon of liquid.'

'Special permission?'

'Yeah, I know the principal.'

'How is Kent? Still amazing . . . ock-cay?'

Vincent coughs. Or chokes.

'Are you okay?' I ask.

'Fine, yeah, fine. Um, he's fine. And yes. Still amazing.'

Vincent finally found his person. Kent has to be the most patient and kind human on the planet. When they first began dating, of course, I was more than encour-aging, but inside, I wasn't sure things would work out. Vincent has a lot of quirks. I knew it would take a special person to appreciate him, and Kent has proven he cherishes all Vincent offers.

'And things at Lear?'

'Fine. Honestly, Kent is so busy I rarely see him unless he's stealing me into his office for a quick kiss, which is fine. We see each other at home all the time.'

'And Sweetums?' I ask, knowing Vincent and Kent's cat have a complicated relationship.

'He's . . . alive.'

I grin. 'Well, that's setting the bar high.'

'He's fine,' Vincent says. 'He's either napping, demanding belly rubs, or plotting his next mischief.'

'Yup. Sounds like a cat.' Gonzo's chubby face flashes in my head, snuggled up, purring, pawing at my hand if I stop petting him, but also chewing on the cords in Olan's office for no apparent reason.

'We have an understanding.'

'That he rules the roost?'

'Yeah. That.' Vincent cohabitating with a cat isn't something I thought would ever happen – a true testament to his bond with Kent.

'Listen, we're almost at Pelletier,' I say, spotting the school a few blocks away. The city was kind enough to plan a bus stop right outside the building.

'I'll see you Friday for dinner,' Vincent says. 'You're finally going to meet Ruth. She's bringing her new girlfriend. Well, technically, they used to date and are back together. So . . . recycled girlfriend?'

'The infamous Ruth. I can't wait.' I glance at Illona, imagining her weekend adventures with her mom. 'Okay, gotta run. Text me!'

41

I gently shake Illona, drawing her away from the glow of her tablet, and nod toward the school in the distance. Her eyes shift with a moment of realization, and she swiftly gathers her things, her movements tinged with a mix of urgency and excitement. With a shared glance, we rise from our seats, ready to step off the bus and embrace the day ahead.

6

> Marvin: We're here.

Olan: Thank you for letting me know. Please give Illona another kiss for me.

> Marvin: Will do! 😊

Olan: I love you. My blue rose.

'My favorite two humans on the planet.' Jill's hair, now shoulder-length and currently pulled up into a messy ponytail, bounces and sways as she pings around her classroom, preparing for the day.

I dip my head, knowing she's full of it.

'That I don't live with,' she clarifies.

'Nick and Maria will be glad to hear it.'

Maria is almost two, and she's talking up a storm. With her growing vocabulary, she's speaking three-word sentences. And Nick is the . . . Nickest. He's a wonderful father, which, of course, makes Jill and me swoon over him even more, and when we all get together, he and Olan bond over daddy/daughter shenanigans.

'You survived Mexico, I see – still pale as a ghost.' Jill lifts my chin, inspecting my face. 'Did you even *try* to get any color?'

'He enjoys being pale,' Illona says as she drops her backpack and stands by the door.

'No, this' – I point to my chin – 'is about skin care. And safety. The sun ravages your skin.'

'When you have no pigment,' Jill says, dropping my chin and moving toward Illona. 'Us beauties,' she says, taking Illona's face in her hands, 'know how to handle the sun.' She turns and gazes down at Illona and adds, 'But a good sunscreen still helps.'

Illona clutches her backpack to her chest. 'Noted. May I go write now?'

'Yes, sweetie. I'll be right over,' I say. Olan's rule is no tablet once we're at school, and Illona prefers to write and draw in her journal while I prepare for the day.

Shutting the door so it's only open an inch, Jill whispers, 'So, how much hotel sex did you have?'

'Excuse me?'

'Vacation sex. Hotel sex. No kids to worry about interrupting you. With crying. Diapers. Wanting something from you.' Jill's gaze wanders out the window. 'No responsibilities. No adulting required. Just the two of you. Far away.'

'You know, Olan and I are happy to take Maria for a night. Even a sleepover. We have all those extra rooms, and you know how Illona feels about her.'

'Really? You'd do that?' A glimmer in her dark eyes

sparkles. 'Nick would never. I mean, really? Maybe. Let me talk to him.'

I take Jill's hand and offer a supportive smile. 'Of course I mean it. I wouldn't offer otherwise. We love Maria. And Olan is always going on and on about Illona growing up too fast. He'd love a weekend with a baby.'

'Maria's not a baby. She's almost two. They don't call it the terrible twos for nothing.'

'We can handle her. Talk to Nick. Let us take her for a night.'

Jill's family calls the picturesque state of California home, while Nick's dad is occupied with his second-shift duties at an Ohio glass factory. They don't have much of a support system here in Portland other than, well, us.

'If we take Maria on a weekend we have Illona, she can help. Honestly, if we took her on a weekend Illona was with her mother, she'd be upset about missing her stay.'

'Okay, okay. I'll talk to Nick.' Jill hugs me, and the faint scent of her perfume, with hints of vanilla, comforts me. 'Thank you.'

'So.' Jill pulls away and resumes her pre-day rituals. 'Hotel sex?'

'Amazing. But also there was . . .' I lower my voice, even though we're alone. 'Beach sex.'

'Yeah, there was.' She walks over and holds her hand up. Despite the juvenile locker-room shenanigans, I can't help but relent and give her a high five, the sound echoing through the room. 'And now, back to life,' she says.

'Back to reality.' The chords and melody swirl in my head, but I quickly shoo them away. 'It's almost March. The wedding is in . . .' I quickly count up to August, putting a finger up for each month. 'Five months. We haven't done much. I mean, we've picked the venue. And The Ocean Inn seems to do most of the work. I think. We need to go back and meet with them at some point. Pick the dinner choices. That sort of thing. I'm not sure when. I think I have it . . .' I pull out my phone and open the calendar app, searching for the appointment. I know I put it in here. Or thought I did. Maybe it was Olan who put it on his phone. I should text him and ask. And tell him I love him. And miss him. After all that . . . hotel sex.

'Well, I'm here if you need anything,' she says. 'Emotionally. I'm not actually able to do much. With the baby. And full-time job, and all.'

I laugh because gender stereotypes be damned – Jill Kim is going to be my best man. Although we haven't quite settled on what to call her yet.

'Spoken like a true Best Person.' Jill's face contorts like I've just told her the district is moving to a year-round calendar. 'No? Best Person?'

She shakes her head. 'Too generic.'

'Best Gal?' I ask. Jill cocks her head, contemplating before her cheek twists up and her eye squints. 'Groomsperson? Groomslady?'

'We'll figure it out,' she says. 'Whatever you want to call me – I'll be there. And if you want a banger bachelor's party . . . complete with strippers, I'm your woman. Maybe a cowboy. Oh, a hockey player – those are very in right now. I bet Nick knows someone.'

'Best woman!' I shout.

Jill nods slowly, her lips pulled in. 'Hmmm. I am the best. I am a woman. A definite possibility.'

Leaving Jill to contemplate her wedding-role moniker, I join Illona in my classroom. Knowing I'd be coming back after not only break, but being away for a few days, I planned ahead, the entire week's activities copied, collated, and clipped neatly on the kidney table I use as both a place for small groups and my desk.

'So organized,' Illona says, looking up from her writing. The girl loves school, but writing is her favorite. She typically writes stories about fairies, unicorns, and kittens – sometimes all of them – and then peppers the margins with cute doodles. Lately, she's been less keen to share her work. Another sign she's getting older.

'I'm trying,' I reply. And I am. At least in small doses.

Ironically, winning Teacher of the Year was a wake-up call to reevaluate my work–life balance. What I quickly realized was the work portion of the pie was taking up a lot more than the life portion. I suppose having Olan be a part of the home category hasn't hurt. No, definitely hasn't hurt.

My reign as Maine's Teacher of the Year was fun, but also more work than I realized. Besides my regular teaching duties, I traveled across the state visiting with teachers and students and advocating for education. I walked in parades in tiny towns I'd never heard of and attended a function at the State House with the governor. The highlight of the year was a trip to DC to meet with the other state nominees and attend a ceremony where the national winner was announced. Sadly, there was no sash. Or crown. Or year's supply of Anastasia of Beverly Hills Cosmetics.

As Olan told me, I had a one in fifty chance. Contrary to expectations, the trip became even more enjoyable when I didn't advance to the final round. Olan and I spent time sightseeing, and the official events were more social than competitive. Plus, we got to spend a few days away in a hotel where, yes, the best sex takes place.

Being named Maine's Teacher of the Year was an incredible honor, but the real joy comes from the daily interactions with my students.

The clock above the door does its ritualistic three loud clicks and a soft buzzer sounds, alerting staff that children are en route.

'Okay, Miss. Time for you to head up.'

Illona folds up her journal, tucks it under her arm, and walks over to tug at my cardigan.

She points at her cheek, tapping.

'Yes, ma'am.' I kneel in front of her and kiss her face. She turns and I kiss the other cheek. 'That one is from your father.'

'Thank you,' she says.

'Have a wonderful day.' I give her a quick squeeze and when I pull back, she kisses me, right on the lips, and even in the hubbub I can hear approaching down the hallway, my chest swells at the love we've cultivated in a relatively short time.

'You too.' Illona tosses her backpack over her shoulder and heads for the hallway. 'Don't forget who's in charge.'

'The kids!' I yell after her.

'Exactly,' she shouts back, and she's off to Mrs Day's second-grade class upstairs.

Our school isn't huge and there are days we see each other passing lines in the hallway or when I'm grabbing copies while my class is at a special and Illona's on her

48

way somewhere. But more often than not, our paths don't cross until I return from taking my pickups to the cafeteria and she's patiently waiting for us to head home together.

Come to think of it, having Illona with me has helped with the old work–life balance as well. Sure, she's happy to sit and write while I do my planning and prepping before or after school, but I do my best to get most of my work done when my class is at specials and lunch so we can get home. Of course, it means Jill and I don't get as much time to kibbitz together at school, but she's typically itching to leave as soon as possible to pick Maria up from daycare. We make up for it with evening texts and weekend visits. Our strawberry donut dates remain a cherished tradition, thanks to the amazing dads who eagerly embrace one-on-one time with their daughters.

'Mr Block!' Alex crashes into me, wrapping his tiny arms around my waist, and the pressure from his squeeze reminds me to breathe. Deeply. In the world of kindergarten, hugs are big, and emotions are even bigger.

'Good morning, Alex.'

I extend my hand, and he reaches out with his tiny fingers, grasping mine with a gentle, trusting hold. Together, we head into the classroom to begin our day together.

7

Sitting crisscross applesauce on the rug, surrounded by my class – their sweet faces staring at me, waiting for me to begin our morning meeting routine – I take a breath and center myself. Vacation is over. They've missed me and while I was thrilled to be off with Olan having fantastic hotel and beach sex, I'm genuinely glad to be back with them.

'Friends, I hope you all had a wonderful break. You're all so much . . . bigger. Taller.'

It's amazing how much they appear to grow in only ten days. I scan the room, silently saying their names in my head. Of course, I haven't forgotten them, but also, when the classroom-placement gods (also known as our principal, Dr Knorse) give you eight children with names that start with *A*, after any time apart, you need a refresher.

'Let's go around the circle and share one fun thing we did while on break. It might sound like this: One fun thing I did on break was . . . I'll go first. One fun thing I did on break was . . .' Images of Olan and me flash in my head. His legs wrapped around my waist in the hotel bed as I slammed into him. My tongue lapping at his balls on the beach towel as the waves crash onto the shore. Riding his perfect cock on the ottoman in the hotel room that seemed to be placed there for that exact purpose. '. . . swimming in the ocean.'

'In Mexican?' Andrew asks, his shaggy blond curls bouncing as he tilts his head.

'Mexico. Yes. In Mexico.'

'Were there sharks?' Alex asks, genuine fear on his face.

'No, no sharks.'

'I'd be afraid of sharks,' Alex says.

'Olan was there. He'd protect you,' Austin says.

'Yes, Olan was with me. And I'm pretty sure sharks would be scared of him.'

'But not Illona,' Audrey adds. She always remembers the details. 'She stayed home with her mommy.'

'And Gonzo,' Amanda adds. 'How's Gonzo?'

'He's fine. He missed me terribly, but he was well taken care of, and now we're all back together.'

Kindergarten students want to know everything about their teacher. And Gonzo is the star of most of my stories, so they're always curious about his antics and well-being.

Realizing that my quick model share is going off the tracks, I attempt to regain control of the train.

'Ben, why don't you start?'

I decide to pick someone who's not on the A-Team, the nickname I've given the group of *A* friends, which gives me half the class as an option. 'One fun thing I did on break was . . .' I remind him of the sentence starter.

Ben smiles and, before I can comment, says, 'One fun

thing I did on break was losing a tooth.' The *s* whistles in the void in the front of his mouth.

'Oh, we need to add that to our tooth graph at calendar time. Don't let me forget,' I say.

Ben nods quickly, and I know he and the other children will remind me.

I acknowledge the next child, and they soon take over, regaling me and each other with stories of snowmen, puppies, siblings, and movies. Miraculously, I don't flub any of the A-Team's names, and after reconnecting through sharing and a quick song about letter sounds, we're ready to start our day.

'I thought since we only have a few months left of kindergarten, we could talk a little about resolutions we have for the rest of the school year.'

Immediately, confused faces stare back at me, and I continue. 'Remember, a resolution is kind of like a promise you make to yourself. We made them back in January. It's a goal you set for yourself.'

The sea of faces becomes slightly less confused.

'Well, that's the idea anyway,' I say. 'Some people try to exercise more. Or eat less candy.'

'I want to eat *more* candy,' Brian shouts, and the children giggle.

'Well, yeah, more candy sounds good to me, too,' I say. 'But we're going to focus on school. What's something we want to do better at school?'

'Like getting across the monkey bars?' Riley asks.

'Exactly,' I say. 'You've been trying all year, right? And you're almost able to get across on your own. That's something you want to achieve.'

Some children nod slightly, and I smile, knowing they're grasping the concept.

'It could be something on the playground – like the monkey bars – or something in the classroom. Like reading or writing.'

'Or counting,' Danny says.

'Yes, or counting.'

'I wanted to count to twenty,' Danny says.

'Right!' My face lights up. 'And you can count past that. So, now you can set a new goal.'

'Four billion!' Danny shouts.

'Maybe we can try for . . . one hundred,' I offer. 'That would be a perfect resolution.'

I can see the wheels turning in their little heads and decide a quick turn and talk might help solidify their thoughts. 'Let's turn to the person next to us and tell them an idea we have for our resolution. It would start like this: My new resolution at school is . . . Go ahead.'

I listen in as they take turns and hear lots of ideas about reading bigger books, writing more pages, and counting higher. First day back, and we're already rolling in the right direction.

As I call them back together, I grab the paper with the 'My new goal is . . .' prompt I prepared before the break. I show them how to write their resolution on the line and send them off. Not only are they bigger, taller, more grown up, with fewer teeth, but they also remember the routines of school and only need a few gentle reminders.

As they finish writing and coloring, I staple their papers to the bulletin board, and they proudly read each other's, sharing the promise they're making to better themselves.

'Mr Block, what's your goal?' Katherine asks. Her long, straight brown hair falls to the middle of her back. She can be quiet and I'm pleased to hear her voice, although I hadn't thought of a resolution to share.

'Hmmm . . .' My mind races. Worry less. Be more organized. Try to be more present. Attempt to get a toy inside me while Olan's fucking me. I grab a blank piece of paper and begin writing on the line. 'My new goal is to help my students learn even more.'

'But you already do that,' Katherine says with furrowed brows.

'More. I can always do more. Better.'

Katherine nods like it makes perfect sense, gives me a quick hug, and heads back to her table with a smile.

> Marvin: On the ferry.

> Olan: Can't wait to kiss your face.

> Marvin: It can't wait to be kissed.

> Olan: I've been thinking about you all day. I'm worked up.

> Marvin: Really? The rest of me can't wait to get some attention too.

> Olan: Dinner. Then bed. ☺

We walk through the front door after a twenty-minute bus ride and twenty-five-minute ferry ride, and Illona jets upstairs. Presumably to pee, which is what I need to do after that commute. Music fills the living room, and Olan stands at the kitchen island, stirring something in a large pot.

'The Four Tops?' I ask, walking over for a kiss.

'Yes. And the lead singer is?' Olan asks, his lips lingering near mine.

'Um . . . Wait. Don't tell me.' I rack my brain. Olan told me this. The Four Tops. That gravelly voice. Gravel. Like what you might work on if you were wearing jeans. 'Levi Stubbs!' I shout.

Olan grabs me close, kissing me deeply. The music swells under Levi's deep baritone, along with my cock in my pants.

'Can I ask a silly question?' I ask.

Gonzo lazily strolls in, purring softly as he rubs against my shin, and I bend over to scoop him up in my arms.

'No such thing.'

'Why isn't the song called "Sugar Pie, Honey Bunch" instead of "I Can't Help Myself"?'

'Technically, "Sugar Pie, Honey Bunch" is part of the title. It's just in parentheses after the title.'

Olan tenderly pets Gonzo, before planting a soft peck on the top of his head.

'Well, it shouldn't be confined to parentheses. It deserves to stand on its own.'

Olan's lips capture mine, the background vocals and strings creating a wall of sound as his hands land on my hips and we gently sway to the music. Gonzo takes this as his cue to leap from my arms and bolt upstairs.

'Who's the nerd now?' Olan asks.

'My friend, nobody out-nerds you.' My hands travel behind him, grabbing his firm ass through his fleece joggers.

Olan's company, GreenSpace, allows him to work from home three days a week, and Mondays are typically an at home day. Some weeks, he goes in more, some less, depending on his schedule, but I'm constantly envious. Why can't teachers have the option to work from home?

'I missed you.' His fingers brush my bottom lip. 'And these.'

We've only been apart for ten hours, but coming back from vacation, even a short one, and all the . . . hotel activities. Yeah, I'd rather be back on the beach lying on his chest before riding his dick.

'Me too,' I say. 'Missed you, I mean. And this.' I squeeze his butt, a flash of heat surging up to my core until we're interrupted by Illona's voice.

'Child entering. Hands where I can see them,' she says, marching down the stairs, cradling Gonzo.

'Princess, how was your day?' Olan resumes stirring the pot, which I've surmised is beef stew – his favorite. This morning, he informed me that returning from a tropical paradise to the deep freeze of Maine required soup – or at least stew. Another perk of Olan's work-from-home days – he cooks.

'Good. I wrote another chapter in my story.'

'For school or for pleasure?' I ask. Illona loves writing so much she's started her own stories at home in addition to the themed writing required at school.

'Both. Well, almost finished the opinion piece at school. I finished the fiction chapter in my free time.'

'Nice.' Olan leans down. Illona carefully puts Gonzo down, wraps her arms around his neck, and they exchange kisses. 'What's the opinion piece about?'

'Why three parents are better than two.'

'That's my girl,' Olan says.

'How long until dinner?' she asks.

Olan stirs and then tastes his stew as Gonzo resumes rubbing on my shin. 'I'd say about fifteen minutes.'

'I'll be in my room writing.' She heads back upstairs and stops halfway at the landing. 'Behave.'

'Yeah, behave,' I say, kissing the back of Olan's neck as he covers the stew.

'Oh, I have a present for you,' he says.

'For me?' I grab Gonzo and sling him over my shoulder, kissing his belly as he settles. 'But you were home all day working? When did you buy me a present? In Mexico? Did you forget to give it to me?'

'No, silly. I took a walk at lunch and . . .' Olan opens the fridge and pulls out a small bundle of tissue paper inside clear plastic wrap.

'What's this?'

'Open it.'

I peel back the plastic and paper, and the crinkling sends Gonzo running upstairs. My heart pauses when I see it. The most precious, tiny white rose.

'Olan. It's beautiful.'

'I was at Hannigan's picking up items for the stew and saw it in the floral section.'

Hannigan's Island Market has become where we do the bulk of our shopping. Since my car stays on the island, we use it for bigger trips, but typically, Olan straps on his backpack and picks up a few items daily when he takes his lunchtime walks. Their floral department isn't much more than a few flowers in buckets, but in a pinch, there are blooms to be had.

'And since blue roses don't exist in nature,' Olan continues, 'I figured this was the next best thing.'

He moves behind me, wrapping me in his arms, staring over my shoulder at the soft petals in my palm.

'Wait, blue roses don't exist?'

'It's a lovely idea, but negative. I did some investigating, and Japanese researchers produced a rose with blue pigment petals through genetic engineering. It took them fourteen years, but they're not mass-produced. So, when you see a blue rose, it's typically . . .'

'Fake.'

'I was going to say dyed.' Olan's lips pepper my neck, snaking up right behind my ear.

'Maybe we can get blue ones for our wedding.' I lean in, letting the warmth of his breath send shivers down my spine.

'Perhaps.' Olan spins me around, and his lips brush mine. Sometimes, I wish I could hit pause on the world. Dinner cooking on the stove: pause. Illona upstairs waiting for dinner: pause. Planning our wedding: pause.

My tongue finds the gap between Olan's two front teeth, and the excitement in both our pants becomes palpable.

'We're going to bed early tonight,' he whispers in my ear. 'Tuck Illona in, and then . . .' Olan reaches down and rubs his thumb against my tented pants. 'Take care of this.'

With no actual pause button for life, the timer rings. Olan resumes stirring the stew instead of my insides, and I head to the bathroom as Illona comes skipping down for dinner.

8

Illona dries the dishes as Olan scrubs the stew pot. Our kitchen has a fancy dishwasher with lights and buttons and beeps I still don't quite understand. Thankfully, Olan prefers to hand wash and dry. When I asked him why, he simply flashed his intoxicating smile and said, 'It's more family time.' And how am I supposed to argue with that?

I've packed the leftovers in a large plastic container, and Gonzo sits on the counter, staring at his humans, hoping there's a spill for him to help clean.

'That's a pretty flower,' Illona says, nodding toward the rosebud. It sits in a small juice glass on the windowsill, next to a ceramic chickadee Olan bought at a quaint craft store near the ferry, not knowing it was Maine's state bird, but simply because it was cute.

'Your dad got that for me,' I say, snapping the lid on the leftovers.

'I'm thinking roses for the wedding.' Olan dries his

hands on a dish towel and plucks the flower from its nest, handing it to Illona. 'What do you think?'

'White roses?' Illona asks. She's holding the flower like a tiny baby bird, careful not to ruffle its petals. 'Marvin mentioned blue.'

'Yes, I think blue.' Olan places his hands on her shoulders, rubbing. She leans back into him, and my heart melts watching the two of them.

'Blue roses sound lovely. But I've never seen a blue rose.'

'A florist would have to dye them.' I nod toward the flower in her hand. 'White ones. They dip them in blue dye.'

'Ohhh.' Illona hands me the rose, turns around, and squeezes her father. 'I want a blue dress then. With blue roses. Or a white dress. With blue roses. Pink with blue roses?'

'Your mother will help you,' Olan says. 'She's already offered to be your stylist.'

'Perfect. Maybe we can look this weekend.' Illona steps back from Olan and opens her arm, inviting me into their huddle.

The three of us embrace in the kitchen and, not wanting to be left out of the love fest, Gonzo saunters over. His tail curls into a question mark as he weaves in and out of our legs, rubbing on us.

'Blue roses,' Illona says. 'Even Gonzo approves.'

I can't help but be overwhelmed by the sense of calmness and contentment that washes over me as we nestle into each other. These two have welcomed me into their family with so much love. Honestly, Isabella has too. She moved to Portland to be closer to Illona but has made it her business to include me in their family structure.

The voices of colleagues and parents echo in my head.

You'd be a wonderful father.

You're so natural with children.

It's a shame you don't have kids of your own.

Illona's arm wraps around my waist, her face moves from being smashed into Olan's stomach to being smashed into mine, and my heart knows, this is what I'm meant for. A new purpose for my life. As I prepare to take on the role of Illona's stepfather, I contemplate the importance and impact it will have on both of our lives.

Lying in bed, Gonzo snuggles between my legs, ready for sleep. He often vacillates between Illona's bed and ours, and we've grown accustomed to his routine. If he's not with us, I know I'll find him cuddling with his favorite small human.

Olan walks into the bedroom, a dark gray towel wrapped just below his waist, the taut muscles on his stomach glistening from the shower. Bathing before bed? There's a glimmer in his eyes, and I know what he's contemplating.

'Are you exhausted from your first day back?' he asks.

'A little. Isn't that why you wanted to go to bed early?' I muster up a fake yawn.

'Not exactly.' Olan drops his towel, and his beautiful cock, already semi-hard, points toward me. The sight of him aroused, his dick stiffening as he stands before me, makes my mouth water. This is exactly why we retired to the bedroom immediately after tucking in Illona.

Sure, I'm worn out. Teaching kindergarten is a little like running a marathon. Not that I'd know anything about organized exercise. Last year, I ran in a relay race as part of kindergarten field day and dropped the baton, losing the race for my class. They still cheered for me because five-year-olds are forgiving like that. As tired as I am, it's just after eight, and we rarely go to bed until at least nine. Or nine-thirty if I've fallen asleep on the couch and Olan lets me sleep a little before stirring me to head upstairs.

He presses a few buttons on his phone, and the speakers come to life, filling the room with thumping bass and strings. When Marvin Gaye's smooth voice joins the music, a lighthearted grin spreads across my face. I know this one.

'"I Want You,"' I say with a smile.

'Good. I want you, too.'

'No, the song. Marvin Gaye. From the album of the same name. On Tamla, which became Motown.'

'You remember,' Olan says, crawling next to me. 'You're such a good student.' He kisses my cheek. 'But it's a subsidiary label, so it counts.'

'Does it?' My hands grab at his ass. He's still damp from the shower, and my fingers glide over his skin.

Olan nods. His lips brush against mine, and because he keeps a tube in every room of the house, they're coated in cherry ChapStick. He takes my lower lip between his teeth. 'Oh yeah. It does.'

Sensing what's about to happen, Gonzo quickly scurries under the bed, seeking refuge.

'Somebody . . .'

'Wants you,' he says. Olan takes my chin in his hand, locking his gaze with mine as his fingers dance down toward my boxers, palming my hard-on. 'Inside me.'

Two years isn't a very long time. If my math skills

were better than a kindergartner's, I'd double 'Seasons of Love's' five hundred, twenty-five thousand, six hundred minutes and come up with an impressive number. I'm estimating it would be just over a million minutes. And in that time, Olan has become much more comfortable asking for what he wants. There's way less blushing and shyness around his desires. Time and experience have bred an ease between us, and remarkably, the sex has become even hotter.

This isn't Olan's playlist, it's the entire album. He calls it Marvin's 'sex album' and while I understand he means Mr Gaye, it has also become my sex album. The bass. The synths. The strings, coating over everything like warm honey. I tilt my head back and he kisses my neck, peppering the skin, nibbling, and licking. I'm not really in the mood for a hickey the first week back from vacation. But fuck, it's February – time for turtlenecks! Totally worth it, right?

My hand moves between our bodies, reaching for his hard dick, and I slide my fingers over the tip. It's wet, either from the shower, precum, or both.

'Let's get these off you,' Olan says, and he tugs at my boxers. With a gentle lift of my hips, they're off and my cock slaps against my stomach. Olan grips me, and we're thrusting into each other's palms as his lips return to my neck, this time hovering near my ear.

Olan straddles me as Marvin Gaye croons softly, the earthy guitar strums with horns and strings creating a symphony of sound as he reaches over and opens the nightstand drawer. I move my hands to his solid pecs, rubbing and holding him up as he applies lube to himself and finally my dick.

'We're having dinner at Vincent and Kent's Friday,' I say.

'Mmmh. Nice.'

'Vincent has been itching for us to meet Ruth. Kent's work wife. She's a PE teacher.'

'Marvin.' Olan's finger, slick with lube, covers my mouth.

I chuckle, because yeah, I need to focus on the task at hand. In my hands. Olan's beautiful chest. My thumbs pilfer some lube from his palm and give his nipples some attention. As I touch them, they perk up beneath my fingertips, causing Olan to release a gentle moan.

The songs on this album aren't necessarily hits. I don't recognize most of them, but the entire piece sets the mood – for lovemaking. My hand moves under Olan's balls and reaches for his hole. The moment my finger enters, Olan lowers himself, his hips rocking slowly, easily taking it all the way to my first knuckle.

'Fuck, Olan.'

'I missed you today.' He leans over and kisses my lips tenderly. 'You left me home alone, and all I could think about was . . .' He reaches back and strokes me. 'This.'

'That's all you thought about all day?' I poke my cock at his hole, my finger carefully pulling out. 'No meetings? No work? Wow. A day of only thinking about my dick.'

Olan laughs, a tiny bit of saliva gathering in the corner of his mouth, and I pull him down to suck it off.

He pulls back, keeping his face close. 'Now, can you pound me? Please?'

'Always such a gentleman, Mr Stone.'

Olan sits up, positioning my cock at his entrance and gently guides me inside his welcoming hole. My shoulders drop as my dick enters him fully. The physical pleasure marries the emotional connection and yup, fucking Olan is right up there with . . . being fucked by Olan. Our bodies become one, moving in rhythm as the music swells, urging us on.

'You really missed me,' I say, thrusting up as he moves down. 'You're so . . .'

'Open.'

'I was going to say horny, but yes, open works.'

I chuckle and Olan slips a finger into my mouth. As I suck it, teasing the tip like what I wish I could do to his cock as it flaps with each bounce, his voice, low and deep, says, 'I'm addicted to this. You.'

With my lips wrapped around his finger, tasting his sweet skin, I'm unable to reply, but I'm thrilled to be his only addiction. If only I studied gymnastics instead of teaching, maybe I'd be flexible enough to suck Olan while fucking him. Maybe that should've been my new goal.

We quickly find a rhythm, and the sensation of being buried inside Olan somehow awakens a raw vulnerability within me. I reach up and he weaves his fingers with mine, and I take a deep sigh, wishing we could stay like this forever.

'Okay, I need a respite.' With a heavy breath, he falls next to me, and I immediately turn and kiss his brow, damp with sweat.

'Respite.' The word comes out of my mouth as an echo, and I'm not sure Olan Stone could be any more of a sexy nerd if he tried.

He takes my slick cock in his hand and strokes it as his lips find my chest, sucking and flicking his masterful tongue on my nipple. He knows how hard it makes me and he's quickly applying more lube to my dick, speeding everything up.

'Wait. I want to fuck you more. Is that okay?'

Olan's head pops up like he's just heard the starting whistle at a race.

'Yes. Absolutely. Affirmative. How?'

'Why don't you get on all fours? Does that sound good?'

'Nope. Not good.' He springs up and positions himself, wagging his plump ass to spur me on. 'Fantastic.'

'Who's adorable now?' I ask.

The horns and strings on an alternate instrumental mix of 'I Want You' provide the perfect soundtrack for what we're about to do.

Moving behind him, I spread him open, taking in the view. Olan's love for bottoming was not something I ever expected. Especially that first day we met in the conference room at school. Although when I saw his ass in those khakis, stretching and taking up every inch, I certainly fantasized about this exact situation. A flush of heat shoots up from my core, spreading through my chest. While I know our bedtime is looming, right now I'd like nothing more than to sit and stare at Olan's beautiful ass for all eternity.

'Your hole is spectacular,' I say. 'Would you like me to take a picture and show you?'

Olan chuckles and says, 'I'll take your word for it.'

I lean over, spit, and use my fingers to spread and push it into him, adding to the slickness of the lube.

'Do you need more?' I ask.

'Fucking? Please.'

'No.' I laugh at his concreteness. 'Lube.'

'Oh. No, I think there's a sufficient amount. Go for it.'

'Let's just make sure you're ready,' I say, and ram my tongue inside him. The warmth of his body takes me in as he relaxes, allowing me to taste the sweetness of where my cock was a few minutes ago. What if my dick could taste? Jill convinced me to read a monster romance once and there was a Kraken who could taste with his arms. All eight of them. Which he also used to fill every orifice of his partner. Who knew tentacles could be so hot? Jill. She always knows.

My hands pull his cheeks further apart, allowing me to plunge deeper, and I reach under to stroke his cock. He's slick from lube and precum and I can't wait to taste all of him. Olan pushes back, a subtle hint he's ready for more. Focus, Marvin.

'I'm ready,' he says.

'Okay.' I move into position, placing my dick at his entrance, waiting, and he gently glides back, taking my entire shaft in. Balls to the wall. Yup, he's more than ready.

I slowly begin fucking him, watching his perfect ass stretch around my cock as it slides in and out.

'Fuck, yes. Use my hole.' He moans a little and then adds, 'Please.'

My lips curl into a smile at his marriage of crassness and politeness.

'You tell me if it's too much or you need a break.'

'Will do. But right now, please pulverize me.'

And with that, I grasp his hips, my fingers digging in until I feel bone, and thrust myself inside. Plunging over and over, I find a rhythm, doing my best to match the seventies cadence coming from the speakers. Our bodies create their own percussion, slapping together as low grunts come from Olan's lips.

'You like that?' I ask.

'Yes. So damn much.'

My thumb grazes the perimeter of his hole as I plunge inside, desperate to experience more of him.

'Does it feel good?'

'Amazing. Keep fucking me. Just like that.'

Continuing my pace, I glance down, watching my cock boning Olan. Desperate to make it more real, I slide a finger in, stretching his hole slightly. My skin delicately senses the point of our connection, and a yearning arises to experience it with my tongue as well – taste my cock inside him. I really should look into acrobatic classes.

'Can you come like this?' I ask, knowing the answer.

'Yes, but, wait.' Olan stops and flops over onto his back, thrusting his feet in the air. 'Like this.'

I move between his legs, bend over his torso, and kiss his chin. My mouth dances up to his lips, and I brush my tongue against his.

'I love you.' My voice, deeper than usual, reverberates against his chest and I close my eyes and sigh, grateful for another bond.

'Fuck me like you love me.'

My eyes spring open and Olan hurries to add, 'Please.'

Lifting myself, I grab onto his ankles and plunge inside. Olan's horny hole welcomes my return, and I immediately move a hand to his cock, already dribbling more precum.

Now, jerking Olan while fucking him isn't easy. It's akin to chewing gum while patting your head and rubbing your stomach. But to have him this way, both arms behind his

68

head, eyes rolling back as he turns to bite at the pillow all because of me, it's more than worth the effort.

'You like that?' I ask, crashing my dick inside him. He's mostly still, but I can feel his cock thrusting into my grip, eager to come.

'I love it. Love you.' As he opens his mouth, I gently slide my index finger inside and he eagerly begins to suck. 'Mmmh.'

Here's what the guys on the hookup apps are missing. When you know your partner well, there is a deep and powerful intensity that emerges – including knowing their sexual tells. When Olan's hips tremble, ever so slightly, sometimes he moves a hand to my back, pawing at my ass, but not tonight. There's only the slight vibration of his hips, the parting of his lips, and his tongue just barely pokes out. He's on the cliff, about to freefall.

'Come for me. Please.' My thumb teases his tip, stroking faster, fucking deeper, doing my best to give Olan the best possible orgasm.

He nods, the pillow trapped in his bite, and with a powerful thrust from me, his hole clenches around my cock as the first blast of cum covers his lean stomach.

'There we go,' I say. 'I'm fucking the cum out of you.'

With a swift motion, I swipe at a drop nestled in the crevice of his abs, savoring the taste as I pop my index finger into my mouth.

'Delicious,' I say, licking the tip of my finger. 'You did miss me.'

There's more shooting, and Olan's abs catch his release like a gutter, draining it down toward his neatly trimmed pubic hair. He is meticulous with everything. But now, under me, with Marvin Gaye serenading us through it, he's come undone, and it makes my entire soul levitate.

'I did. So much.'

When he finishes, I pause, but don't pull out.

'Give me a second.'

He covers his face in the crook of his elbow, but I can hear him panting, and it's so damn sexy.

'Olan, you can have all the time in the world.' I glance at the clock. 'It's only eight forty-five.'

Olan laughs at my time check, but hey, we have to get up early tomorrow.

'Okay. I'm good.'

Unlike me, Olan is perfectly happy to keep getting fucked once he's come. When he's topping, if I come first, it's all over. But not him. He loves it. And who am I to say no to that handsome face?

'I'll be quick,' I say, lifting his legs and taking a peek at my cock, still lodged inside his hole.

'Take your time.' Olan moves his hands behind his head like he's lying on a blanket in the park about to watch fireworks dance across the sky. My fireworks. Blasting inside him.

'Can I just . . .' I pull out of him, move back, and pop his dick in my mouth, sucking the cum off, licking and cleaning him with my tongue. The sensation of him inside my mouth, even for a brief moment, sends a surge of pleasure through my body. My cock becomes even harder as my impending orgasm approaches.

'Now . . .' I gingerly turn him over, and Olan, knowing what I want, arches his back, exposing himself. 'I'm ready for this.'

I lightly slap his ass cheek, and Olan chuckles. 'I kindly request the return of your dick . . .' He reaches back and points to his ass. 'Here.'

A quick laugh escapes my mouth and I brace myself on the bed, leaning over him, and guiding myself back inside. Now that he's come, Olan's attention shifts solely to my pleasure. With a wide grin on his face, he reaches back, pulling and tweaking at my nipple.

'There you go,' he purrs, grinding back onto my dick. 'Fill me up like you love me. Give it all to me.'

This chatty-during-sex Olan makes the fire in my belly ignite and, at this angle, I'm able to slam into him. His voice. His hand. His ass. All of him. My orgasm prickles, and I pull out because today, I'm in a marking mood.

'Babe. Oh yeah. Plaster me.' Olan's fingers crawl under my cock, massaging my balls and intensifying the pleasure until I can't hold back any longer, and I explode, painting his back with my release. 'Whoa. I guess you missed me too, eh?'

'Olan . . .' I collapse next to him and kiss his shoulder. 'I miss you every second we're not together.'

'Come here.' Not wanting to turn over and get the bed messy, Olan points to his mouth.

Our lips brush, and I sigh into him.

'Let's get you cleaned up.' I reach for a washcloth in the nightstand drawer.

As soon as I turn away, Olan says, 'I can't wait to marry you.'

I carefully wipe him clean, taking pleasure in attending to his care. 'Me too.'

'Now, let's get some sleep.' Olan rolls over, opens his arm, and pats his chest.

With my head nestled against his shoulder and a smile painted on my face as we drift off to sleep, our bodies buzz with the euphoria of the mind-blowing sex we just shared. I can't believe I get to marry him. It's a dream come true.

9

The first week back after break flies by in a whirlwind. By Friday afternoon, it seems impossible that Olan and I were in Mexico only a week ago. This is what nobody talks about when it comes to vacations. The weight of reality smashes to bits any relaxation points gained.

I sit in a chair, surrounded by the class who are bundled up like little dumplings, waiting for dismissal. 'Let's start the weekend off right by sharing any plans we have,' I say.

'I'll go first. This weekend, I'm having dinner with friends. Amy?' I nod toward her to begin.

'I'm Amanda.'

'Oh, sweetie. I'm so sorry.'

This is what happens when you have eight A names. After the first week of school, I thought about asking them to continue wearing their name tags but didn't want them to feel like they were burdened with the dreaded Scarlet Letter. I make a sincere effort to get them right.

'Amanda. This weekend . . .'

'This weekend, I'm going to play ponies with my cousin.'

'Real ponies?' Michael asks. He's tugging on his hat, attempting to wrangle his thick curls inside.

'Toy ponies. I got a pink one for Christmas,' Amanda says. 'But sometimes we just pretend we're ponies. That's the most fun.'

'Way more fun,' Riley says. 'You should try unicorns.'

'Or one of you could be a pony and the other a unicorn,' Alex adds.

Usually, when a conversation goes off the tracks, it's my job to right the train, but in this instance, at dismissal, during a share, their desire to converse, participate, have one last grasp of time together before the weekend, I try not to interrupt and only intervene with a gentle nudge if things spiral out of control.

'I love that,' I say. 'You can play with toys, but sometimes your imagination is even more fun. And if you have more than one idea, you can combine them. Ponies and unicorns. What could be more fun?'

The kids nod as I summarize their conversation, and Jean, the sweet school secretary, booms over the intercom, announcing the start of our dismissal process.

Adults come and go, picking up children for buses, and at some point, Illona enters the classroom. On days when I have a staff or parent meeting, she sits and waits for me, and then we start our journey home together.

'Your mom will be here in a few,' I say.

It's an Isabella weekend and Illona skips over for a quick hug.

'She texted me a few minutes ago. She's just parking.'

'Okay.' Illona sits at a table and takes out her journal and a purple pen.

'Danny, Austin, let's go.' I put my hands out, and they each take one, and we head down to the cafeteria.

I walk about halfway into the giant space, tables set up with notebooks and lists, and the boys run over to their adults. Just over two years ago, Olan was standing in the sea of parents, looking like a snack in his baseball hat and doing his best to fly under the radar. If you'd told me I'd be marrying him back then, I would have laughed in your face. The kind of laugh where a tiny bit of snot flies out. Yes, I fell for him the minute I saw him in the conference room for Illona's transfer meeting, but I was sure it would be nothing more than a silly crush.

'Mr Block.' Dr Knorse smiles and offers a wave.

'Dr Knorse.' I return her gestures.

As I smile, I can't help but remember when I was so sure she'd fire me if she found out I was shtupping a parent. To my surprise, she'd been understanding and kind. The fact that Olan and I are now getting married doesn't hurt. This wasn't some torrid affair. There's going to be a wedding.

'Have a good weekend, Marvin.' She pulls her lips in and gives a terse nod.

'You too.'

She's distracted by a confused parent. The woman appears lost. It's probably her first time picking up, and Tori guides her through the process of finding her child's name, showing her ID, and signing. Dr Knorse loves running a tight ship, but there's a softness underneath her armor. I mean, it's deep down – Mariana Trench deep, but it's there. You just have to send an exploratory deep-sea submarine to find it.

When I arrive back in my classroom, Isabella stands near Illona, waiting.

'Hey, sorry, just taking the pickups down.'

'No worries. We're fine.' Isabella's long, puffy coat, much more practical than her typical wardrobe, still looks trendy on her. Isabella Stone could make a garbage bag fashionable.

'How are you?' I ask, kissing her on the cheek.

'Wonderful.' She unzips her coat to her waist, exposing a beautiful soft lavender sweater. 'Sweetie, bathroom.'

Doing as she's told, Illona skips away to use the bathroom before they leave.

'The shoot was a success, and the chef's spread of summer rolls tasted as delicious as they looked.'

Isabella works as the associate editor for a captivating foodie magazine, with glossy pages that catch your eye as you stand in line at the grocery store. I'm pretty sure with the money they made from selling their business, she doesn't need to work, but she loves being around the glamour of photo shoots . . . and hunky tattooed chefs.

'Did anyone say it?' I ask.

'Say what?'

'The name of the magazine?'

Isabella rolls her eyes. 'Eat Maine. It's Maine, Marvin.'

'No, the magazine is called Eat Me. *Me*.'

'The ME is capitalized. It's an abbreviation and pronounced Maine.'

'Whatever you say.' I give her a wink. 'But it's not nearly as fun that way.'

'All good.' Illona returns, her hands up. 'And yes, I washed my hands.'

'All right, sweetheart,' Isabella says. 'Let's get going.'

'Have a fun weekend,' I say to both of them.

'We're going to get our nails done.' Isabella pats Illona's back. 'And your dad tells me there's a flower girl dress to search for.'

'Yes! Blue roses. Or blue with roses. Any color. Maybe pink roses? On blue. Would that look pretty?' Illona rubs her chin. 'I'm not sure.'

'Sweetie, we'll find something. I promise.'

Illona walks over, and I kneel and open my arms.

'This hug has to last me all weekend,' I say. 'The only planning we've done beyond the venue is your dress. And that's only because your mom is on it.' My chin rests on Illona's shoulder and I smile up at Isabella.

'Marvin, planning a wedding is a lot. Have you considered finding someone to help?'

'With the planning? I mean, Olan will help. He agreed on blue roses.'

Isabella pulls her head back, her eyes bulge open, and the loudest laugh I've ever heard from her bellows from her pink lips.

'Olan? Help? With a wedding? Marvin. Marvin.' She puts her hand on my shoulder. 'Marvin. Olan is an amazing father. A phenomenal cook. He'll be a wonderful husband. He can plan a lovely vacation. Date night? He's your man. But a wedding . . . that's on a whole different level.'

'Oh.' My head spins a little because I can vividly picture it. Olan and I on the beach in our suits. Not matching, that would be tacky. We're not groomsmen. But coordinating colors. Maybe blues and tans. A splash of color here and there. Our friends and family gathered on chairs as the ocean breeze blows the fabric on Jill's and Illona's dresses. Our families will sit in the front. Sarah will put Rebecca and Erik at ease with embarrassing stories about me. Mother, nobody wants to hear about the time I had a terrible fever in preschool and you had to take my temperature in the tushy. Oy.

'Don't you know anyone who could help?' Isabella asks. 'Someone organized. Someone who knows about weddings.'

'I don't think so,' I say. 'But we'll figure it out. Or find someone.'

'Okay, let's go, peanut.' Isabella taps Illona's shoulder and they head out.

As I grab my bag, my mind races with thoughts of everyone I know. Surely someone must have experience with weddings – or at least know someone who does. The picture of Olan and me on the beach returns, and I'm determined to make it a reality.

'This is the original version.'

Drums, cymbals, and percussion rattle inside Olan's car as we drive to Vincent and Kent's condo on the west side of the peninsula. Since we had plans in the city, Olan scheduled an office day and I took advantage of the time to prepare for the next week while waiting for him to pick me up at school.

Olan takes my hand and holds it on the center console. His fingers gently caress my palm, their light touch sending a tingling sensation through my skin.

'Everyone thinks the Marvin Gaye version is the original, but technically, Gladys Knight and the Pips released it first,' he says.

'Oh, I definitely didn't know that.' The Pips, singing behind their leader's rich alto, fill the cabin of the car with smooth harmonies.

'Technically, The Miracles were the first to record the song. Marvin was the second to record it. Marvin Gaye. Not you.'

'Yeah, I figured.'

'Gladys Knight was the third to record it. But they released hers first. At the time, it was the biggest selling Motown single. Until Marvin released his version.'

'Gaye. Not me.'

Olan cocks his head.

'Marvin Gaye. Not me. I'm gay. Most definitely.'

'Thank goodness. Otherwise, you'd have some serious explaining to do.' Olan chuckles at his joke, his eyes sparkling with amusement. His ability to recall every single fact about certain things is nothing short of enchanting.

'How do you know so much about Motown, anyway?' I ask.

We pass a small bookstore, and I admire the colorful display of children's books in the window.

'My parents always had it playing when I was little and, well, I'm inquisitive. I had questions. And when they didn't have answers, I did my own research. You can find almost anything in a book. And the public library was my best friend.'

I've seen a few photos of Olan as a small child. His cute afro cut much shorter, close to his head, with a pensive grin as he waves to the camera. I try to imagine the Stone house, with his parents clamoring to keep tabs on three active boys.

'I love that. And I bet you regaled them with all the facts you learned.'

He nods, and his mouth pulls into a thin line. I know that face.

'What is it?'

We pull onto Vincent's tree-lined street. The west end of town is full of large, older homes. Many, like Vincent and Kent's, have been converted to apartments and condos.

'My parents. My mom. Remember when she called me?'

'In Mexico?'

'Yes, well, it was about Liam.'

The moment Olan's brother's name comes out of his mouth, my stomach flips. I know he struggles with addiction, but Olan never says much about it. Only 'it's his path to follow' and how Olan's recovery could be impacted if he was too involved. That's all I need to know.

'Is he okay?' My chest tightens, and I push through it, forcing a deep breath.

'Unfortunately, no. He's back in rehab. Well, detox specifically. In the rehab.'

My mind races, trying to remember all the details about Liam's last time in a treatment facility. He was there for a few months with his girlfriend. Olan helped his parents find a center where they could stay together.

'Oh.'

'Yeah. He's back, and, well, it's worse this time.'

'Worse? How could it be worse?'

Besides his one time in college, Olan has never been back to rehab. Between his meetings, sponsors and sponsees, and all his daily readings and rituals, he's stayed sober, except for the small relapse that brought him to Maine. But Olan explained that not everyone is so lucky. I knew Liam had been in and out, but the last Olan mentioned, he was working at a grocery stocking shelves.

'I thought he was better.'

'Babe. Alcoholics and addicts are never better. Recovery is a process. Folks go in and out all the time. Sometimes, we slip up, and it's easy to get back on track. You miss a meeting or two, and you come back. But sometimes, it's more of a major fall. The meetings become memories. Liam keeps falling off. Hard.'

'And your mom is upset?'

'Yes. The burden is substantial for them . . .' Olan's voice trails off, and then he perks up. 'There's a spot. Monumental spot.'

'Yeah,' I say as Olan parallel parks only a house down from our destination. My stomach turns with my head, wondering if there's anything I can do to support Olan more. I'm grateful he's opened up to me more about his family, but I can see how it's troubling him.

As we approach their front door, Olan takes my hand, and I stop him before we reach the buzzer.

'Olan.' As the chilly March air nips at our skin, I pull him into a hug, squeezing him tightly, desperate to establish a connection. 'You know, I'm always here for you. If you ever need anything. Or to talk. About your family. Your brother. Anything. I'm here.'

Olan pulls back and kisses my chin, my nose, and finally

my mouth. He's used extra ChapStick, and the scent lingers even after he pulls back.

'Thank you. I appreciate that.'

'I love you.' The need for him to know just how deeply I care consumes me. Despite Olan's stoic nature, I yearn for him to open up and show more of his vulnerable side to me.

'I love you too.'

We step up, hand in hand, and press the buzzer.

10

'Snacks. I'm surrounded by snacks.'

Ruth grabs Regina's shoulder and takes a quick bite through her purple sweater as her braids click and clack, adding a rhythmic sound to the room. Regina seems unfazed by her girlfriend's temporary transformation into a vampire.

'First, this one comes into the picture.' Ruth nods toward Vincent. 'And now you bring me these two?' Her focus lands on Olan and me. 'There are only twelve Black folks in Maine, and you found one of them.'

Olan allows a crinkle of a smile and I'm not sure how he feels about the enthusiasm of Ruth Parrish, but he seems to take her in stride.

'Of course I'm joking. There are more than twelve of us in the entire state. Maybe fifteen?' A loud laugh escapes her lips. 'No, no, I just like teasing.' Ruth winks at Olan, and the small lines around his eyes reveal he's a Ruth fan.

Vincent has been trying to make this dinner party

happen for almost a year, but with all our schedules and commitments, it took some time. Sweetums, Kent's enormous Maine Coon cat, lies on the back of the sofa, tail flicking, seemingly happy to be watching the action from a distance.

The spread on the dining-room table would be at home in a lifestyle magazine. Vincent doesn't cook, so I'm assuming Kent handled the roasted chicken and various side dishes.

'Kosher snack,' I say as I spoon some fresh coleslaw onto my plate. 'Me. Not him.'

'Oh, you're part of the mishpocha. Nice job, Kent. You brought me another mensch.'

'You'll have to excuse Ruth,' Kent says. 'She wants so badly to be one of us.'

'Hey, conversion isn't off the table.' Ruth nibbles Regina's shoulder. 'If we get married, it would make things easier.'

'My mother would love that,' Regina says. Just like Vincent, her bald head gleams under the soft glow of the paper pendant hanging above the table. Her lack of hair accentuates Regina's beautiful face – the entire focus on her striking features and olive skin.

'But it's not required. I mean, Olan's not converting.' I squeeze his hand under the table.

'Have you considered it?' Vincent asks. He takes a small scoop of mashed potatoes and carefully places them on his plate, making sure not to touch the chicken or Ruth's bean casserole.

'I haven't. Wait, it's not imperative, is it?' Olan turns to me, his beautiful eyes searching.

'Olan. No. No. No.' I shake my head. 'My mother is

84

fully aware you're not Jewish. She stopped asking after about six months.' I pull his hand up and kiss his knuckles. 'Trust me, she's thrilled I'm getting married. There are zero expectations about you converting.'

I give Olan's cheek a quick peck, doing my best to reassure him.

'Well, you two are utterly adorable,' Regina says.

'Completely,' Ruth adds. 'If you looked up "adorable" in the dictionary, there'd be a photo of you two – right next to a picture of a kitten trying to climb into a teacup.'

'They are,' Kent says. 'I'm still trying to steal Marvin from Pelletier, but Tori would never speak to me again.'

'Please,' Ruth says. 'Come to Lear. We need more queers. Can we replace the entire staff with homos? Olan, do you teach?'

Olan shakes his head, wipes his mouth, and says, 'No. I'm an aerospace engineer.'

'Of course you are,' she replies.

'Dr Knorse would survive,' I say. 'But honestly, I'm very happy at Pelletier. My bestie Jill would be more likely to take issue with my leaving.'

'Oh, is she your work wife?' Ruth asks. 'I'm Kent's.'

Vincent takes a tiny bite of chicken, and the light over the table hits the spices coating it. He laughs and wipes his clean face with a napkin folded within an inch of its life. 'Oh yeah,' he says. 'Ruth certainly is Kent's work wife. I had to get her approval.'

'Not technically,' Kent says. 'I knew she'd love you.'

'And I did. Do,' Ruth says. 'I mean, look at him. You know I have a thing for bald heads.' Ruth runs her palm over Regina's dome.

'And what do you do, Regina?' I ask.

'I'm a school social worker at Otis.'

'Otis? Do you know Kristi Brody? We used to work together at Pelletier.'

'Love Kristi,' Regina says. 'Salt of the earth. Although she's a little too fond of running for my taste.' She takes a bite of beans. 'Sweetie, these are your best yet.'

Ruth gives her a wink. 'It's the lemon pepper.'

'Right?' I ask. 'The woman loves her races. Anyway, yeah, we were friendly before Kristi was transferred to Otis. Please say hello to her for me.'

'Of course. Happy to.'

Like tiny buds on a tree, the elementary schools in Portland dot the map. The city has managed to keep the community school atmosphere by not merging into one or two larger, centrally located buildings as they did with the middle and high schools. Unfortunately, resources are stretched thin, and schools such as Otis desperately need additional support. In education, we all know fair isn't equal, but sometimes making that a reality, especially when it comes to funding, can be tricky.

'Vincent says you have a daughter?' Ruth asks Olan.

'Illona is part of the reason I decided the STEM position would work for me,' Vincent says before Olan can reply. 'She's one in a million.' Vincent beams because Illona has a special place in his heart. When I met him, he was not a fan of children or pets and now he teaches and lives with what has to be the largest domesticated cat on the eastern seaboard.

'She has that ability,' Olan says, resting his arm behind me. 'Our Illona has a way with people.'

He massages my shoulder when he says this, and I blink a few extra times. *Our Illona.* The closer that comes to becoming a reality, the more my emotions swell.

'Well, we need to meet her sometime,' Regina says. 'Maybe we can have you all over? We have a basset hound. Does she like dogs?'

'Cats, dogs, ponies, unicorns, Komodo dragons,' I say. 'Anything with four legs.'

'I'll get your number,' Ruth says. 'Let's make it happen before the wedding.'

Olan nods, and his lips pull into a smile. I know being around new people can sometimes overwhelm him, but Ruth seems to put him at ease. I'm really glad we came.

'And how is the planning going?' Vincent asks. 'August will be here before you know it.'

'We have the venue!' I say, maybe a little too enthusiastically. 'The Ocean Inn.'

'Oh, out near the edge of town. Right on the water . . . okay, Mr Fancy Pants,' Ruth says.

'Mr and Mr Fancy Pants,' Kent says. 'Well, soon enough.'

'A venue is a good start, but you realize there's so much more to planning a wedding, right?' Ruth asks.

'I found a blog post about it. We're going to keep things . . . simple,' Olan says.

'A blog post? Simple?' Ruth laughs. 'Oh, my sweet, sweet, naïve baby. You're getting married. A gay wedding.'

'Actually, Olan's . . .' I begin, still not sure exactly what label he wants to use with other people.

'He was married before,' Kent says. 'To a woman.'

'Bi?' Regina asks.

Despite blinking, Olan remains silent.

87

'Pan? Demi? Ace? Questioning? Something else?'

'Olan doesn't like labels,' I say, resting my hand on his knee.

'I respect that.' Ruth winks at Olan. 'But you're two men,' she says. 'Two gorgeous men getting married. There are expectations. Flowers. Chairs. Drinks. Favors. Seating plans. Cake.'

'Cake. Yes, the most important part,' I say. 'We can handle the cake.'

'You need help. A planner.' Ruth's serious tone catches me off guard.

Our eyes meet, and in that fleeting moment, Olan and I silently acknowledge the high probability of Ruth being right.

'You know, there's a teacher at Lear who might be able to help,' Kent says.

Vincent looks at Kent. Kent looks at Ruth. They all shift their focus to Olan and me, and in unison, say, 'Sheldon.'

'Wait, the first-grade teacher?' I ask. Visions of snow-covered trees and lights, so many lights, at the park by the water, come flooding back.

'We met him at the Lights Festival,' Olan says. 'He was with a much taller, quiet man.'

Again, the Lear Bunch glance at each other and, in unison, say, 'Theo.'

'Didn't he offer to help?' Olan asks. 'With the wedding.'

'Theo?' Kent asks. 'Doubtful. Unless with the menu planning. That might interest him.'

'No, Sheldon,' I say. 'When I told him we were engaged, he offered to help. Said if I needed anything to text him. Do I still have his number?' I take out my cell and begin scrolling, searching among the techno landfill that is my phone.

'I'll connect you,' Kent says. 'And he and Theo live together now. They're engaged.'

With the table cleared and cleaned, Vincent, Kent, Regina, and I gather in the kitchen. Sweetums sits on the counter, the center of attention with many hands reaching out to him, as we chat. The last ferry departs at ten-thirty and we need to leave time to drive and park. Ruth has taken Olan onto the sofa. With her elbows propped on her knees, she leans into him, their proximity allowing for a quiet conversation.

Regina's explaining her and Ruth's reconciliation – something about boats and being lost at sea, and I'm fairly certain she's using metaphors, but I'm only half listening, so maybe there was actual sailing. My attention is focused on Olan and Ruth. Even though I can't hear them, I'm watching their faces, trying to decipher body language.

Olan's shoulders are back. Resting against the back of the couch, legs slightly open, his gaze remains fixed on Ruth, who tilts forward with a serious expression. I can't make out what they're saying over the conversation I should be listening to, but it appears to be something important.

At a certain point, Olan wraps his arms around Ruth. She holds the back of his head and whispers something into his ear. Of course, I'm curious, but mostly, elation spreads through my chest seeing Olan make this new connection.

We say our goodbyes, and again, Ruth hugs Olan. There's a small kiss on his cheek, and his eyes dart down quickly. Damn, he's sexy when he's blushing.

'Text. Call,' Ruth says to Olan when they pull apart.

'I will.' The half smile on Olan's face melts my heart.

'I mean it.'

With a slight chin dip, her braids sway in rhythm, as she gives him a stern gaze.

Olan's quiet as we walk back to his car. Once we're inside, he takes my hand, weaving his fingers with mine.

'That was quite enjoyable.'

'Yeah? You and Ruth seemed to hit it off.'

'She's amazing. I like her. A considerable amount.' Olan nods and takes a deep, cleansing breath. 'I'm pleased we went.' He nods, still holding my hand on the console.

As we drive toward the parking garage, Olan's excitement about the evening is palpable; his eyes sparkle, and his smile is wide and contagious. Seeing him like this, my heart surges with profound joy. It's in these moments that I realize how much I treasure his happiness, how it lights up my world and makes everything else fade into the background. I close my eyes and soak in the moment.

The piano lightly sets the rhythm, joined by Diana's angelic, honeyed crooning. When I crack an eye open, I see Olan's head resting on his pillow, his wide-open eyes fixed on me.

'Hey,' I say, eyeing the alarm clock on his nightstand. It's just after five. We don't need to get up for at least another half hour.

'What?' I attempt to nod to the speaker, where the full band and an entire string section have joined in, as 'Touch Me in the Morning' fills our room. Olan loves Diana Ross and thankfully all her early albums were on Motown.

I roll toward him, wrapping my arm around his torso, and he kisses my bedhead before gently taking my hand and moving it down his body.

'Good morning,' I say. 'Someone is . . .'

'Horny.'

'What about . . .' I nod toward the door and Olan knows exactly what I'm worried about.

91

'I got up to use the bathroom. Door is secured. She's out like a light.'

Isabella brought Illona back last night and stayed for dinner. Given we have plans after school, Olan is working at the office. Today will be one of those Mondays when the three of us commute together.

'Well then,' I say.

With a slow and deliberate motion, I stroke as his cock pulses in the palm of my hand, eliciting an immediate response as Olan thrusts into my grip.

This rarely happens – morning sex, but with work, Illona, and the general over-scheduling that comes with adulting, sometimes you have to strike when the iron is hot. And right now, Olan's dick scorches my skin like smoldering embers.

He tightens his grip around my shoulder, pulling me near. There's a desire in his body, a need to be closer, and my lips sprinkle his chest with kisses, finishing on his nipple, where I suck and flick my tongue. This drives him wild.

'Babe. I love you so much.' His head's thrown back on the pillow, taking it all in, and I do everything in my power to help him get lost in the moment. A new song begins, and there's an ache to the way the bass guitar thumps over the driving piano. Smokey Robinson's voice comes in, and a smile flashes on my face when the song's title pops into my head. Without thinking, I blurt it out.

'"You've Really Got a Hold on Me."'

'Literally,' he says. 'Fuck, Marvin. C'mere.' Olan pulls my face up toward his, no worries about morning breath, and captures my lips. My hand pauses, but I don't let go.

'Are you okay?'

He nods quickly and returns his lips to mine. I know when something's bothering him. He'll tell me when he's ready. Right now, he seems to want this.

'Are you sure?' I hold his cock up, making sure this is what he needs in this moment.

He plunges himself into my fist, fucking my hand as his tongue darts into my mouth. I become lost in the moment as soft moans escape Olan's lips. I know how much he loves kissing while he comes, but I also know there are other things I can do to heighten the experience for him.

'Olan.' He opens his eyes. They're giant, damp, yearning ebony pools. 'I love you.' I kiss the bridge of his nose. The tip. His lips. Chin. And then glide down between his legs.

Knowing what I'm after, he lifts his hips, allowing me access to my target. His sweet, musky smell, perfectly Olan, overtakes my senses, and my tongue laps under his balls, sliding down to his ass as I resume jerking his cock, now surging as he fucks into my fist.

'You taste like heaven,' I say.

My lips kiss around the perimeter before my tongue dives in, sending Olan's hips higher. He wants more, so I cram my face into him, plunging deeper inside his sweet, warm hole. I've figured out how to turn my face at the right angle so my nose doesn't get in the way. How's that for ingenuity? When I pull out, he swings his legs in the air, desperate for more. We still have some time and I'm in no rush for him to finish.

I haven't shaved in a few days, and there's a good amount of stubble. With my incredibly coarse hair, my beard could cosplay as a Brillo pad, so I'm careful when I kiss and rub my face up and down his taint.

'Oh, Jesus,' Olan says.

'He can't help you now.'

'Fuck. I need you inside me. Please.'

I glance up, and his fingers are wrapped around my hand as I stroke him. There's a small bead of precum dripping down the tip – he's so aroused, and knowing I'm doing this to him, my dick swells against my boxers.

We have about ten minutes before we need to get Illona up and kick our morning routine into high gear. I'm not sure how long he was up before he woke me with his raging boner, but Olan's clearly ready. In the interest of time, my mouth and fingers will have to do.

'Stay like this,' I say. I take my hand off his cock and make sure he continues jerking himself.

Olan does as I ask, his sexy toes pointing toward the headboard, and I use both hands to spread him wide. He takes a heavy breath, relaxing on the exhale, and he opens even more, allowing my tongue deep inside. My index finger joins in the fun, pushing inside, assisting to keep Olan open while I devour him.

He rocks his pelvis, attempting to push back and provide more friction, and we find a steady rhythm, matching the drums in the song. Between his cock leaking more precum and the increasing frequency and volume of his moans, I know he's close.

'Marvin. That.' He's panting. 'Keep doing that.'

Shaking my head, I rub my chin up to the base of his dick, licking and lapping, and when his whimpers crescendo, I slide back down, tongue-fucking his hole while my thumb massages his taint.

The contractions around my tongue are my first clue, chased by his hips jerking up and blasts of warm cum showering my mug as he aims it toward me. He knows how much I love when he paints my face with it. When he lowers his hips, and I know he's finished, my tongue licks up toward the base of his shaft, lapping up his warm seed. I pop him in my mouth for a quick cleanup, and his powerful hands reach down, urging me on top of him.

'Your turn.' Olan uses his thumb to wipe a ribbon of cum off my cheek and pops it into his mouth.

'Daddy!' My eyes shoot open, and Olan lets out a little laugh. 'Marvin? Are you up?' A loud tapping on our door follows Illona's voice. Even though I know the door is locked, my heart pounds in my chest like an angry gorilla.

'One second, princess.' Olan nods toward the bathroom, and I leap from the bed, close the door behind me, and start the shower. I glance in the mirror as I wait for the water to warm up, and my face resembles a freshly glazed donut. Taking my thumb, I wipe a drop that's about to drip down my chin and pop it into my mouth. While it may not be as sweet as a strawberry donut, the salty tanginess carries the distinct flavor of Olan, and I can't help but break into a massive grin, knowing that we kicked off our days with a bang.

'Have you thought about chairs?' Sheldon has an open notebook covered in purple shaggy fur, with a pen poised and ready.

Finally realizing that Olan and I were out of our depth, I contacted Sheldon, who was more than willing to meet. Sitting on soft patchwork chairs around the heavy wood table at Branch Booch, a favorite kombucha spot, Theo and Olan look like small boys being dragged into the lingerie shop with their moms. Theo, in his school janitor's outfit, grips his Beach Break hard booch like a life preserver, and he and Olan do a lot of forced smiling and nodding. There are random grunts that resemble 'Hey' or ''Sup' but no actual words or sentences yet. They're two uncomfortable peas in a pod.

'The Ocean Inn has chairs,' I say. 'I mean, they said we can use the ones they have.'

'What kind of chairs? Folding chairs? Are they metal? Plastic? What color? What are your colors anyway? Did you bring any photos? Fabric swatches?' Sheldon scribbles something in his purple Muppet notebook.

'Um.' My head spins. 'Olan?'

Olan replies by gulping his non-alcoholic pineapple jalapeño booch. When he pulls the frosty mug away from his beautiful lips, he lets out a small burp.

'Okay, no colors. No swatches.' Sheldon jots more. 'And the chairs at the venue are . . .'

'Chairs?' I ask, not sure what the correct answer is.

'Marvin. Bubuleh.' Sheldon winks at Theo, who offers a small smile. 'You can't have folding chairs at your wedding.'

'We can't?'

'Why not?' Olan asks.

Hearing him finally speak, I choke a little on my kombucha, coughing to clear my throat.

'Yeah, why not?' Theo adds, and suddenly, the two of them are on my side.

'Because your wedding is on the beach. All of your friends and family will be there. Some of them are traveling from far away. They'll be sitting for a long time. Pre-ceremony. Ceremony. Post-ceremony while they wait to exit for the cocktail hour. And you want comfortable, elegant chairs, don't you?' Olan and I share a confused look. Before either of us can answer, Sheldon continues. 'Trust me. You do.' There's more frantic writing. 'Now, have you picked a signature drink?'

'Signature drink?' Lightheadedness joins the spinning in my skull.

'We don't drink,' Olan says.

'A mocktail then. They're very in now. Do you want a dry wedding, or are you okay with your guests drinking alcohol? Did you want to give out drink tickets or have an open bar? An open bar will increase the expense considerably, but it's a game changer. Did you bring your budget? I can whip up a spreadsheet.'

'Budget?' I lean back on Olan, wishing I could crawl inside him and disappear.

'No budget.' Olan wraps his free arm around me and kisses my temple. 'Take a deep breath,' he whispers. 'People get married every day. This will be fine.'

'No budget. I can make that work.' Sheldon sits up and pulls at his pink and yellow color-block sweater, straightening his shoulders. 'We will figure this all out.' There's more writing. 'We can rent chairs . . . once we know your colors.'

'Sheldon, come here.' Theo grabs him, pulling him

away from his notebook and hugging him close. 'I know you're excited, but let's try not to scare the guys. Relax for a minute.'

'I'm only trying to help,' Sheldon says.

'You are helping but take a breath.' Theo kisses the top of Sheldon's head. 'He's practicing his wedding planning skills – for ours.'

'When is the big day?' I ask, wondering how someone could possibly plan two weddings simultaneously.

'No date yet. But I'm already collecting ideas.' Sheldon taps his notebook. 'And helping you is fantastic experience.'

'And we appreciate your assistance,' Olan says.

'We'll pay you,' I say.

'No, no. This will be my gift to you.' Sheldon pulls his notebook into his lap and starts petting it softly. 'I enjoy it. Plus, it's like a dry run.' He turns toward Theo and plants a sweet kiss on his cheek. These two couldn't be more different or more perfect for each other.

'Are you sure?' Olan asks. 'We're more than happy to compensate you for your services.'

'Hush.' Sheldon shakes his head and extends his hand, palm out, fingers upward. 'I don't want to hear any more about it. Now, let's talk colors.'

We spend another half hour talking about various hues and pigments. We land on blues and browns, which Sheldon approves of. 'Very boho-beachy-chic. Ocean. Sand. I love it.'

Theo has another kombucha, but either the amount of alcohol is low or he just has a high tolerance, because he never seems even the slightest bit tipsy. Sheldon concedes that simply landing on colors is a win and we agree to meet again in a week or two. Oy.

On the ferry home, snuggled up in a booth, avoiding the frigid ocean breeze, Olan wraps me in his arms and his strong muscles squeeze me through his wool peacoat.

'That was . . .' I begin.

'A lot,' he says.

'Yeah. Who knew?' I lean into him, grateful for more contact.

'Apparently, Sheldon.'

We sit quietly, the hum of the ferry surrounding us, and a flickering of lights from the island in the distance summons us home. Isabella and Illona have gone to Boston for a girls' weekend of shopping and to catch a show. Olan and I have the house to ourselves for the weekend. I'll see Illona at school Monday morning when she waits in my classroom until the bell rings. The peace of our weekend together rushes into our bubble, creating a serene atmosphere around us – two days of lying naked in bed until Gonzo insists I get up and feed him and then not getting dressed because there aren't any little eyes around, and then straight back to bed for as long as we like.

'Marvin.'

Like a lullaby, the sound of Olan's voice makes my eyes grow heavy.

'Mmmh. Wake me up when we dock.'

'Liam is in trouble. My parents are doing their best, but . . . he needs me. They need me. I need to fly back. Soon.'

12

'Soon? How soon? What's wrong? Do you need me to go with you?'

A quietness takes over as I rest on Olan's chest. The powerful roar of the ferry's engine becomes a quiet hum in my head as this new reality sinks in. My stomach flips like a pancake on a hot griddle – filled with tiny bubbles. This is what's been eating at Olan. I don't know what I thought was wrong, but it wasn't this. My worries never seem to align with reality. Erika told me to remember that – before she retired. Usually, I over-worry. In this case, maybe I should have worried more. Great. Now I'm worrying about worrying. My head races, wondering if I can get a few days off on short notice – even if I need to take them unpaid.

'Monday. I'm going to book a flight when we get home.'

My stomach drops. Monday. This Monday? That's in two days.

'For how long?' I sit up and face him. He leans toward me, tilting his head and blinking more frequently than usual.

'I'm not sure. Probably a couple of weeks. Perhaps longer. It all depends on what awaits me when I arrive.'

My stomach shifts from dropping to flipping. Maybe I need to take a leave of absence. Is this one of the circumstances where they're permitted? Olan and I aren't married yet. Does it matter? Is there paperwork? A process? How long would it take to approve? Would Dr Knorse be able to secure a long-term sub or would my class have to endure someone new daily?

Olan pushes out a long, deep breath, his lips pulling my focus back to him.

'What's going on?' I ask.

I know Olan, and I suspect he said nothing sooner because he didn't want to put a dampener on things. Or make me worry. But this is no time to wait for more information from him. This is a time to lay the cards on the table so we know what we're playing with.

Olan takes my hands, and I draw small circles in his palm, my go-to for soothing him.

'It's another relapse. He's still in detox in a rehabilitation facility. My parents are understandably distressed. It's been a week, and he's still vomiting and having tremors. They wouldn't typically ask for me to come home. There's more happening than they're telling me – I can hear it in my mother's voice. I'm needed there.'

I know Liam struggles with addiction, but Olan hasn't really gone into details, and I didn't want to push him. Detox. Rehab. Vomiting. Tremors. The words splash in my head, trying to tread water, as I attempt to make sense of what I'm hearing.

'Okay. Do you want me to . . .'

Olan pulls his lips in and gently shakes his head. 'Marvin, I always want to be with you, but I'm going to be busy. Occupied. Liam needs me to be a point person at rehab. My parents are strained. We'll text. Call. Video chat. I promise.' Olan flips my palm over and returns the massaging, comforting me in his time of need.

This would be my time to step up. Be a mature, understanding adult. I lift my chin and pull my shoulders back. 'But I'll miss you.'

Operation Mature Adult failed.

'Babe.' He leans over. His lips brush my cheek, and my heart speeds up, desperately desiring we stay this close forever. 'I'll miss you too. But we'll be fine. I promise.'

Seeking solace, Olan pulls me close and envelops me in a warm embrace. With my eyes closed, I relish the last moments on the ferry before we dock, preparing myself for the harsh reality of Olan's revelation.

In bed, spooning Olan, I nuzzle into his neck, taking in the slightly sweet smell of his skin, trying to commit it to memory before he leaves for Chicago. Sometimes my yearning for Olan almost overtakes me, and right now all I desire is to be naked, clutching his chest and plastering him as close as possible.

It's clear Olan's sharing what he knows about Liam's current situation with me, but there's an uneasiness in my stomach. I wonder if there's more to the story he either doesn't know or hasn't divulged yet, and with him flying out Monday, I'm unsure when those pieces will fall into place.

We lie quietly in each other's arms, the sounds of the house murmuring, and then it happens. A pounce. At my feet.

'What the?' Olan lifts his head, searching.

'Gonzo.' I spy his black and white fur at the foot of the bed. 'He thinks our feet are . . .'

'Prey.' Olan sits up and snatches Gonzo, pulling him between us, his purr vibrating through the room the moment he's on his back, covered by our hands.

'Who's the hunted now?' Olan asks, burying his face into Gonzo's back.

Although he's never had pets, Olan's quickly become fast friends with Gonzo. He's unable to resist the magical draw of a sweet ball of fur that simply wants to play, eat, and receive an infinite amount of affection.

'Gonzo's going to miss you,' I say, rubbing Gonzo's favorite spot under his chin.

'Well, I'm going to miss him too.' Olan picks the willing kitty up, holding him under his front legs, so they're eye to eye. 'Now listen to me, Gonzo. I want you to take care of your dad. And Illona. Make sure everyone gets lots of attention and snuggles and if you could do me an extra favor' – he lowers his voice to a whisper – 'please make sure your father remembers to pay the electric bill.'

'Gonzo, tell your other dad that I will pay the electric bill when it comes.'

'They don't mail anything, it's all online. I'll leave you a document with all the usernames and passwords.'

As I nod, I can't help but reflect on how Olan has

seamlessly shouldered all the household responsibilities that I once struggled with. He almost seems happy to do it and both me and my ADHD couldn't be more pleased.

'And the gas. Water. Cable and internet.' Olan kisses my forehead. 'It's all on the list.'

'Thank you.'

'With checkboxes. I know you love checking things off.'

'I really do.'

As my index finger traces the contours of his chest, I can sense the rhythmic thumping beneath my touch and I check an imaginary box, right where his heart beats. I'm determined to etch the sensation of his skin beneath my fingertips into my memory and savor every precious moment before he leaves.

'For how long?' Illona asks.

Isabella, Olan, and I meet in our living room on Sunday night, a unified force, to explain to Illona her father's impending absence. The severity of the situation distracts me from my usual Sunday scaries about the looming week. Typically, I'm simply worried about the bombardment of activity and responsibilities that come with teaching, but now, knowing Olan is leaving and I'll be left to my own devices, the usual worries are dwarfed by the prospect of being without him for an indeterminate amount of time.

'I'm not sure, princess.' Olan's arm wraps around her shoulder. She's sandwiched between Isabella and her father and I'm parked in the chair across from them, with Gonzo blissfully unaware of the situation as he lies belly up on my lap purring away.

'But why aren't you sure? When you and Marvin went

to Mexico, you knew exactly when you were coming back. And when Mommy went skiing in Colorado, she told me when she was coming back.'

'I know, sweetie.' Isabella places her hand on Illona's knee. Sitting across from them, watching the delicate moment, my throat tightens. Olan insisted I be included in their chat, but I can't shake the feeling I'm imposing on an intimate family conversation. 'But this is different.'

'Why?' Illona leans into her father's shoulder.

'Your Uncle Liam is sick.' Olan's voice is quiet, and I search his face for any signs of distress. My gut tells me to move next to him, but I don't want to disrupt the dialogue.

'What's wrong with him?'

I know about Olan's family from little pieces of information he drops here and there. Illona has seen her grandparents once in the two years since we've been together. Rebecca and Erik came for a weekend last fall and spent most of it driving up the coast leaf-peeping. I know she's met Gabe's children, her cousins, once, before I was in the picture. I'm not sure if she's ever met Liam or only heard about him from Olan. Isabella once told me, 'Olan's relationship with his family is complicated. Just love him through it.'

'He uses substances that are hurting his body and he needs help to get better. While there are doctors, nurses, and other individuals supporting him, he needs me, too. I'm going to help him.' Olan kisses the top of his daughter's head.

'Like drugs?' Illona asks.

'Yes, sweetie.' Isabella smooths over Illona's yellow sweatshirt. It's one of her favorites. Illona and I put the laundry away together last night and I showed her how to fold it so the hood was tucked underneath. 'Some drugs help us,' Isabella continues. 'And some can actually hurt us. Doctors tell us what the good drugs are and give them to us when we're sick. Like when you have a fever, and we give you medicine.'

'And Liam has a fever?'

'No, princess. That's the problem. He's taking medicine when he doesn't need it.'

'Why would he do that?'

'Because he's sick. And he needs help. And he needs me to help him.' Olan glances at me, and a chill runs up my arms, overtaking my chest.

'Okay. Can I still stay here with you?' Now, Illona's beautiful brown eyes are on me. I assumed she'd want to stay with her mother.

'You can stay wherever you like,' I say.

Feeling left out of what he perceives as attention, Gonzo leaps from my lap to Illona, immediately headbutting her chin.

'If you want to spend more time with me, that's fine too,' Isabella says. 'Whatever you want, sweetie.' She gives me a soft smile and I nod in agreement.

'Of course. Whatever you want. Your mom and I will make it happen.' I smile at her, my body vibrating with worry.

Olan's leaving. For an undetermined amount of time. My whole world feels unsteady, like tectonic plates shifting and struggling to find their balance.

And then Illona Stone, the sweetest angel, comes over, crawls next to me, instantly enveloping me in a warm hug, grounding me.

My eyes close, keeping the tears in, and I wrap my arms around her and sigh, taking in the smell of her mango and coconut hair cream.

'I want to stay here,' she says into my chest. 'I mean, like I usually do.'

Gonzo, sensing my mood veering into anxiety, jumps up and pushes his head in between us.

'Gonzo agrees,' Isabella says. 'We'll keep our regular schedule. And if Marvin needs any backup, he'll let me know.'

My eyes open, and I gaze at Isabella as she eases closer to the edge of the couch, our eye contact full of understanding. With Olan gone, it will be just us responsible for Illona's day-to-day care. Two years ago, that thought would have had me trying every home remedy and power walking to ease my anxiety. But now, in the turmoil of the current situation, it's the only thing calming my nerves.

'And I'll call as much as I can,' Olan says, as he moves to the chair. There's no room for him, but he sits on the edge and leans into our huddle. Before I close my eyes, Isabella's up, standing next to him and I realize, maybe even when things get tough, incredibly tough, there are always people by our side, offering their unwavering love and support.

13

Olan: At the gate. Missing you already. I love you.

Marvin: ILU 2! Please text when you land

Olan: 👍

'Monday, you're a cruel . . .' Jill says.

She's sitting at her kidney table, stacks of paper before her, collating, stapling, and organizing for her day, when I catch her gaze and quickly dart my eyes to Illona, standing beside me.

'Witch.'

'Sweetie, do you want to stay in here with me this morning?' I ask.

Illona's been stoic about her dad leaving, and I'm trying my best to be supportive and let her know I'm here if she wants to talk while not projecting my anxiety about Olan being gone for an indeterminate amount of time on her.

'No, I'm good. I'll be in your classroom.' She taps her

backpack and heads over. I know her journal might be the best friend she has right now.

'Well, I'm fit to be tied. The daycare was closed today because of a burst pipe, so Nick is working from home, which means the house will look like a tornado hit it when I get home. Sometimes I wonder if he thinks having a child means he can simply toss trash on the floor without me noticing.'

I pull my lips into the best smile facsimile I can muster, but Jill knows me well and sees right through it.

'Someone woke up on the wrong side of the bed? Or was it too much' – Jill lowers her voice to a whisper – 'ex-say with your hunky fiancé over the weekend?'

I open my mouth to tell her, but only a small puff of air escapes. My chest thumps so loudly I can feel my heartbeat in my throat, and I lean against the St Patrick's Day bulletin board for support.

Staccato beats and acoustic strumming swirl in my head before the deep bass thumps. Usher's heavy breathing joins in and 'You Make Me Wanna' has me closing my eyes and gently bobbing along to the sweet rhythm. A flash of choreo from the video blazes behind my eyelids, Usher wearing a deep burgundy silk shirt, completely open, exposing his beautiful chest as he dances with a row of chairs. Oh, Usher, you handsome devil – you make me wanna indeed.

'Marvin? Marvin?'

Jill takes the bag from my shoulder, places it on the floor, and guides me to a tiny chair. She shuts the classroom door and plants herself next to me, taking my hand in hers. A few years ago, songs often permeated my head when anything overwhelmed me. But between Olan and therapy, my brain has been mostly music-free lately.

'That hasn't happened in a while. What song?' she asks.

'"You Make Me Wanna."' A vision of Usher, reaching out to strum that lucky guitar in the video, pops into my head and yeah, I don't really do celebrity crushes, but if I did, Usher would top the list.

'Usher. A total snack.' Jill continues rubbing my fingers as we both take a moment to daydream about his total deliciousness.

Shaking the vision away, she asks, 'Now tell me, what's going on?'

'It's Olan. He's . . . gone.'

My heart flutters again — saying it aloud somehow makes it more real.

'Gone? Wait what? Where?' Jill scoots her chair closer and starts rubbing my back. 'Do I need to call Dr Knorse? Do we need subs?'

'No, it's fine. He's in Chicago. It's not fine. I mean, it will be. I mean, we're fine. His family needs him is all.'

A loud Jill Kim sigh fills the room, followed by, 'Baruch Hashem.' Even in my spiral, a small laugh escapes my lips. 'You scared the shit out of me. Why'd you go and do that?' She slaps my back, hard, but immediately resumes rubbing. 'He's going home for a visit — that's what this is all about?'

'No, not a visit. His younger brother is in rehab. Or detox. I think the detox is in the rehab center? Olan explained this to me.' My fingers pinch at my forehead. 'Sometimes the detox is in a hospital. Sometimes it's in rehab. It depends on the facility. I think Liam is in the rehab. In detox.' I take my phone out. 'Let me text him and ask.'

'Marvin.' Jill puts her hand on mine, stopping me. 'Take a deep breath.'

She dips her chin and gives me her patented teacher stare – now supercharged with mommy powers – reminding me I need to ramp up my teacher-look game.

I do as I'm told, taking in a long drawn breath through my nose, and pushing it out through my mouth like my therapist showed me.

'Olan's in Chicago with his brother?' Jill asks, her voice slow and calm.

I check my watch. 'He's on a plane, but yes. I guess it's worse than before, and his parents are overwhelmed so he went to help.'

'Before?'

Olan didn't give me a play-by-play, but he told me a little. I also know the anonymous part of AA is super important, but the door is closed and I have to talk to someone. And Jill is part of our inner circle. Olan is aware of the extent of our conversations and has given me permission to share everything with her.

'It's not the first time. In rehab. Detox. All of it. I know he's struggled for . . .' I've only known Olan for two years, but I know it's been longer than that. A lot longer. 'A long time. Maybe since they were kids? I'm not really sure.'

'Oh, I, um,' Jill stammers. 'I didn't realize.'

'Yeah, he doesn't really talk about him much – Liam. That's his brother. Or his family. You know how he is.'

'Quiet. Pensive. Hunky?'

'All of the above.'

'How long will he be there?' Jill moves close enough that she's almost on my chair, which is a feat as my ass takes up much more surface area than a five-year-old's.

'That's the thing. He doesn't know. He bought a one-way ticket.' My throat tightens and I do my best to swallow past it.

'Oh, fuck. Fuck, fuck, fuck.' Jill's eyes double in size and she wraps her arm around me, leaning her head on my shoulder.

'Thank you.'

'For what?'

'For validating the severity of the situation by giving so many fucks.'

'Mr Block!' Andrew slams into my thighs, squeezing me like a three-and-a-half-foot-tall boa constrictor. I move my hand to his back, doing my best to stay upright.

'Andrew, I'm happy to see you, too.'

He doesn't reply, but simply glances up, his giant blue eyes peering at me, as a huge grin overtakes his face and he darts into the classroom.

Audrey walks down the hallway, and when she notices me, she lowers her gaze. She's holding something in her palm, but she clearly doesn't want me to see it.

'Good morning, Audrey.'

Without making eye contact, she extends her hand, opens her palm, and a single soft lilac crocus stares up at me. It's tiny and smooshed, and seen better days, but right now, it's Audrey's gift to me, and my job as her teacher is to act like she's just handed over the Hope Diamond.

'For me?'

Audrey nods and I carefully take the plucked bloom from her. Even in early March, crocuses will pop up on the walkways leading to the school entrance, and this poor one, catching Audrey's gaze, was extracted from its home in the soil just for me.

'I love it. I'll put it right near my laptop and then take it home with me.'

Take it home with me is teacher code for throw it away after you've left and won't have a clue what's happened to it. But in their minds, my house is decorated with their drawings, doodles, love notes, random toy pieces, trading cards, and yes, dead flowers.

Monday mornings are typically filled with extra smiles, hugs, grabs to hold my hand, and all the typical affection found in a kindergarten classroom. Sometimes, a tinge of claustrophobia creeps in with the constant barrage of tiny hands, but this morning, as Olan flies to Chicago, I'm grateful for the distraction.

During Morning Meeting, I'm sandwiched between Eddie and Riley. Eddie's a leaner. He's tiny, even for a kindergartner, and he plasters his hobbit-like body up to mine, grounding me with all of his thirty-five pounds.

Riley likes to pet my shoes. Today I'm sporting green sneakers with faux suede, and her fingers brush over them like she's discovered the world's softest kitten.

Doing my best to focus, I go through the motions of our meeting, and when we share about our weekends, Brian, with a serious look on his face, says, 'Petunia ran away.'

Gasps and oh nos fill the carpet area and I do my best to hide the confused and slightly amused look on my face. Petunia is Brian's pet turtle.

'Oh,' I say with a straight face. 'Where did she go?'

'We don't know.' Understandably distraught, Brian's doing his best to hold back the tears and I'm suddenly reminded that my presence, right here, right now, is imperative to my student's trust and sense of belonging. This isn't about a pet turtle's perilous escape, but about honoring Brian's feelings.

'Where did she run to?' Danny asks.

'We don't know.' Brian looks around the circle, perhaps for help, or hoping Petunia crawls out from behind a classmate.

'Don't you keep her in a cage?' Riley asks, sitting up and momentarily pausing giving my shoe a spa treatment.

'In an aquarium. It's a fish tank. But not filled with water. Well, a little water, but mostly not. There's a heat lamp and rocks. And there's one main rock she loves to sleep on with the light heating her shell.'

'Sounds nice,' Aaron says.

'Yeah, why would she want to run away from that?' Michael asks.

'How do I know?' Brian shrugs. The tears seem to have retreated for the time being. 'I'm not a turtle.'

Giggles erupt from the circle, and I take them as my cue.

'Well, Brian,' I say. 'I'm sorry Petunia's missing, but I'm sure you'll find her soon. You asked your parents to help?'

Brian nods and then says, 'And Hugo.'

Hugo is Brian's dog, and I have a hunch he might know something about Petunia's disappearance. But I'll leave that detective work to Brian's parents – they've got more experience in getting the truth out of a dog than I do.

114

'Well then, you have everyone on the case. Keep us posted,' I say, and nod to Austin to take his turn.

There's a lot I love about teaching kindergarten, but right near the top of the list is the way it demands my attention. Especially when my mind would rather spiral. Instead of moping about Olan leaving (there will be plenty of time for that later), my students require me to be fully present in the moment. And even though I try to hide my sadness and uneasiness, sensing something is off, they shower me with extra love. Not bad for a job most people think isn't much more than making glitter-covered macaroni necklaces (for the record, we craft those and they're fucking fabulous).

14

Even without Olan here to tether me to solid ground, the week somehow churns on. Between my days teaching and evenings with Illona, my heart barely has time to wallow in sorrow. Olan's texts are brief. The phone calls even more so. Typically, around Illona's bedtime, he calls to say good night, tells us he loves us, and then rushes off. I know he's back home for his brother. His family. I swallow my sadness and pat myself on the back for being a mature, understanding partner. Go me!

On Friday, with the looming weekend, loneliness creeps in like an unwelcome houseguest, refusing to leave.

'Any big plans for the weekend?' Jill asks.

She's finishing her salad, and the box of leftover donuts from the morning awaits. Because life is all about balance.

'No. Nothing.' I shrug.

'Is Illona with you?'

'No, Isabella is picking her up after school. Just me and the Gonzmeister.'

Jill pulls her lips in, opens her mouth, and then quickly shuts it.

'What?' I ask. 'I know that face.'

'Well, remember when you offered to take Maria for a weekend?'

'You mean before my fiancé flew to Chicago without a return ticket, leaving me abandoned and sad with nothing but strawberry ice cream and an endless queue of romcoms to soothe me?'

Jill exposes her teeth, giving me her best impression of the grimacing emoji.

'Nick has been bugging me for a date night. Not a weekend. One night out. Dinner. You could come to our place. Maria goes to bed by seven and you can watch TV or mindlessly scroll on your phone. We won't be late. I promise.'

Pleading eyes add to her urgent energy, and I'm unable to say no to my friend.

I let out an enormous sigh. My ice cream and movie date with Gonzo can wait.

'Sure. It will be a nice distraction.'

'Marvin Block, I could kiss you.' She's up, squeezing me while I attempt to choke down Olan's leftover beef stew. She pecks my cheek, and before pulling back, whispers, 'You are simply the best.' She grabs her phone and begins texting. 'Nick will kiss you, too. I promise.'

A smile skates across my face. 'How about two from him. One for each cheek.'

'Yes! He'll do it. He loves you.' Her face freezes for a moment. 'Wait, which cheeks are we talking about?'

I raise my eyebrows suggestively and we erupt into giggles.

*

'Sweetie, did you have a good day?'

Isabella stands at my classroom door, while Illona packs up her journal.

'It was fine,' I say. 'Marley scraped his knee at lunch recess, and that was a bit of an ordeal, but we managed to get him bandaged up.'

Isabella's smirk spurs a huge grin across my face, and I can't help but burst into a loud, hearty cackle.

'Marvin, you meshuggener.' Illona stands and slings her backpack over her shoulder. 'She was talking to me.'

'I was,' Isabella says. 'But I'm happy to hear Marley's knee won't require further medical attention.'

This friendship between us makes little sense on paper. She's Olan's ex-wife. Illona's mom. A healthy diet of TV movies of the week has taught me I should be on guard. But sometimes real life isn't quite as dramatic as the entertainment industry would like us to believe. And in this case, I'm grateful for the simplicity. It makes everything easier. Especially with Olan away. There's nothing uncomfortable about knowing Isabella and I are the only two taking care of Illona until he returns.

'Sweetie,' Isabella says, running her palm on Illona's back. 'Why don't you run to the bathroom before we go? We're stopping at the store on the way home.'

'Pizza night?' Illona asks.

'Yes, I'm all out of dough.'

Illona nods and skips off.

'Are you doing okay?' Isabella asks me.

She doesn't say more, but we both know what she means. *Without Olan.*

'Surprisingly, I am,' I say, willing it into existence. 'Do I miss him? Of course. Do I wish we could talk more? Also, yes. But the kids' – I gesture toward the classroom – 'and your kid' – I nod toward the hallway – 'they're keeping me occupied, and right now, staying busy is exactly what I need.'

'Good.' Isabella places her hand on my forearm. I'm not sure I've ever seen a more beautiful woman in person. She always looks like a movie star hoping to dodge the paparazzi, but also dresses impeccably because she knows they'll find her.

'Remember, I'm only a text or phone call away. You and I are . . .' She pauses, her brow crinkles, searching for the right word.

'I know,' I say. 'And thank you.'

'Ready!' Illona bursts into the room, holding her hands up. 'I remembered to wash, so you don't have to ask.'

'Good, okay, well, remember,' Isabella says, nodding toward my cell on the table.

'I will.'

Illona wraps her arms around my waist and I lift her, doing my best to hold and hug her the way her father does. She kisses my cheek and asks, 'Are you sure you don't want me to come help with Maria?'

I dip my chin and take her beautiful face in.

'You are the sweetest child in the world, do you know that? But no, I'll be okay. You have fun with your mom. We'll take her another time when you're with me, I promise.'

'Okay. Well, I'll see you Monday morning. Have fun.'

I plant a soft kiss on her cheek, then switch to the other side, playfully teasing, 'That one's from your dad.'

*

Marvin: Heading to Jill's to babysit.
Hope you're doing okay.

Olan: How lovely! Maria snuggles. I'm jealous.

Marvin: Of Maria or me?

Olan: Both?

Marvin: I miss you.

Olan: I miss you too. We'll talk this weekend.

'Marvin Block. I could kiss you.'

Nick Evans stands in the doorway wearing a blue button-down and khakis. I've never seen him so dressed up. Nick is more of a sweatshirt and jeans guy. He looks so damn handsome. Tall. Hunky. The exact type of guy I'd have a crush on if I crushed on straight men. Thankfully, I learned that was fruitless in high school.

Jill and Nick live off the peninsula, in an area of Portland that resembles more of one of the outlying towns, but still requires them to pay city taxes. Jill refuses to leave the city – higher tax rates be damned. And here they have a yard, sidewalks, and all the family-friendly features of the suburbs.

'Actually, your wife promised me two. One on each cheek.' I point to my right cheek, giving Nick a target to start with.

'Wait, which cheeks? Because honestly, for a night out alone with my wife, I'd kiss all four.' Nick guffaws and his deep voice echoes in the entryway.

'See? I told you.' Jill appears in the doorway. 'Drop trou and bend over. He'll totally do it.'

Heat flushes my face at the thought of Nick's lips on my ass and when I don't reply, Jill shouts, 'Come in, already. You're letting the heat out. Nick can kiss every inch of your body inside.'

A quick rush of blood shudders through me because – straight, married or not – Nick is a total dreamboat and the mere thought of his lips coursing over me sends my nervous system into a tizzy. One week without Olan and I'm getting flushed thinking about a peck from my best friend's husband. Oy.

'Seriously, though,' Nick says, taking my coat from me, 'you're a lifesaver. We haven't found a new sitter since Julia went to college and I fear your work wife might implode if she doesn't get a night out.'

'I told you, you could stay home with Maria, and I'd go out on my own. Or with Marvin. He'd take me for karaoke. Unlike you, he'd sing "Grease" with me.'

'As your gay best friend, it's my civic duty,' I say with a salute.

Jill's at the highchair in the kitchen, wiping Maria's sweet face. They've put her in the cutest fleece pajamas with little rainbows all over them.

Jill's wearing a dress. Unlike her school ensembles that resemble jumpers, this one is a true dress. The neckline is low, and she's showing some cleavage – something she never does at school.

'You look beautiful,' I say. 'Wow.'

'Thank you.' She gives me a peck on the cheek. 'This took almost an hour. Nick throws on a shirt and pants that don't have holes in them and voilà, he's ready for a modeling gig.'

'Beauty and the Beef.' Nick laughs at his own joke, while Jill rolls her eyes.

The kitchen and living room occupy the entire first floor open space, allowing them to monitor Maria while they're working or cooking.

'Daddy needs a night out too,' Nick says, kissing my cheek.

'Yes, Daddy,' I say and Nick's neck turns bright red.

'Yes, Daddy,' Jill says, pulling Maria from the chair and handing her to me.

'She can have one cookie, Guncle Marvin,' Jill says. 'One.'

'Daddy!' Chicken and rice waft from Maria's mouth as she adjusts to my hold.

'Not Daddy. Marvin,' Jill says. 'Your Guncle Marvin is going to watch you tonight. You're wearing your rainbow pajamas for him.'

'Daddy?' Maria asks.

'I'm Daddy.' Nick boops her nose.

'She's two,' Jill says. 'She thinks every man is her daddy.'

'Relatable,' I say.

'One cookie, then brush your teeth, sweetie,' Nick says. He kisses Maria on the forehead and she leans up to plant one on his lips. As he looks at his daughter, it's as if he sees the entire universe encapsulated within her tiny body.

Yeah, doting dads are definitely my kryptonite.

Jill glances at her watch. 'One cookie. One.' She puts up her index finger. 'Then bed. We have to go if we're going to make our reservation. Kellaria is squeezing us in.'

'A fancy new Greek restaurant.' Nick shrugs. 'I wanted

to go to The Olive Garden, but this one' – he nods toward his wife – 'wants fancy hummus.'

'Listen. We're going out. We're dressed up. I'm not having casual Italian at reasonable prices.'

'But they bring you endless breadsticks. Endless. Bread-sticks,' Nick says.

'And bottomless salad,' I add.

Nick makes puppy dog eyes at Jill and she smacks his ass.

'I'll give you bottomless. Let's go!'

'Marvin, text us if you need anything.' Nick winks at me. 'We'll be home by ten.'

Jill and Nick grab their coats and leave me holding Maria. She's calm for a moment, and then squirms, reaching for the closed door.

'Daddy?'

'No, I'm Marvin. Your daddy will be home soon.'

Maria glances at me, then the door, and bursts into tears.

15

After three cookies, Maria and I head upstairs to brush her teeth. Who are they trying to fool with these toddler cookies? They're tiny. Half a bite at best. Denying Maria more would be almost inhumane, especially when she stared at me with her giant, pleading puppy dog eyes. She was missing her parents. They were a good distraction. I tried one, and they weren't bad. I ate six.

'Daddy want teeth?' With jet black hair escaping her mini-ponytail, Maria stands near the bathroom sink, pointing.

'Remember, I'm your Uncle Marvin?' I ask and realize, nope, for tonight, like the gays on the hookup apps, I'm just another daddy to her.

'Daddy wants you to brush your teeth.' I take her small purple toothbrush and squeeze a small dot of toothpaste. 'And Mommy too.'

'Mommy?'

Maria's eyes begin to bulge, the lower lids become puffy,

and oh crap, I mentioned she who shall not be named when she's not within grabbing distance.

'Let's brush your teeth!' I say and scoop her up and place her on the edge of the vanity.

Maria lets out an enormous sigh and opens her mouth like one of the Hungry, Hungry, Hippos. This is the part where I'm supposed to brush her teeth. It can't be that different from brushing my own. Or Gonzo's. I tried once with chicken-flavored toothpaste and he kept chewing on the brush, making it almost impossible to get any actual brushing done.

'Okay, let's start in the back,' I say.

I maneuver the brush carefully, making slow circles on her back teeth before moving toward the front. The brush slips onto her gums and she pulls back, her small mouth erupting into giggles.

'Tickles!'

'Oh sweetheart, I didn't mean to tickle you. But you know, you really should brush your gums too! Gum health is the root of tooth health. If your gums are sad, your teeth are basically like, "We're just trees without roots."'

Maria looks at me like I've got two heads, but opens her mouth wide again. When I resume brushing, I try to keep the bristles on her teeth and only scrub near her gumline.

'You're so patient,' I say, remembering to praise her. 'Letting your Uncle Marvin brush your teeth.'

After what feels close to two minutes, I pull the toothbrush out and Maria spits into the sink.

'Water please,' she says, and I fill the small plastic cup halfway and hand it to her. She takes a tiny sip, rinses her mouth, swallows, and then smiles.

'I'm pretty sure you're not supposed to drink that, but we'll let it slide.'

Maria lifts her arms and, taking the hint, I pick her up and carry her into her bedroom.

'You've gotten so big,' I say. 'I bet you weigh as much as a turkey now.'

'Tookey?'

'Yeah, like for Thanksgiving. I'd say you're at least twenty pounds. Maybe twenty-five. You could feed a lot of people.'

Maria's eyebrows scrunch up like a tiny caterpillar attempting to sprint, and I realize I'm probably confusing her.

'Anyway, let's get you tucked in and I'll read you a story.'

I carefully place Maria on her bed, and she crawls right under the covers, slams her head on the pillow, and shouts, 'Gorilla!'

There's a copy of *Good Night, Gorilla* on the bedside table and I'm aware of Maria's current obsession with the book from Jill's many stories at school.

'Ah, a classic. I know it well.'

The story, about a tired zookeeper who whispers good night to every animal in the zoo, is told with minimal words. A cheeky monkey steals the keys and lets all the animals out of their cages. They all follow the zookeeper home, attempting to climb into bed with him and his unamused wife.

I sidle next to Maria, and she leans on my stomach, pats gently, and says, 'Soft.'

Yeah, no washboard abs here. But Olan never objects. He grabs on to my belly when he's spooning me, rubbing me like a magic lamp. Olan – my brain quickly whisks

126

away to his face. His smile. His lips. The tooth gap my tongue adores nesting in. I let out a sigh, open the book, and begin telling the story, pausing for Maria to take part.

She knows all the animals' names and whispers good night to each of them, while I point and narrate the action. Honestly, she couldn't be more adorable. She giggles at the naughty monkey, stealing the zookeeper's keys and assisting his friends to escape their incarceration.

When the story ends and the monkey sneaks back into bed with the zookeeper and his wife, Maria shouts, 'Again!'

I dip my chin and give her my best teacher look, but she doesn't budge.

'Again! Gorilla, Daddy!'

I'm not sure if she's calling me a gorilla daddy, confusing me with Nick, or simply asking for another reread. I'm going with the latter.

Glancing at my watch, I notice it's almost eight – way past Maria's bedtime. I need to get her off to dreamland, stat.

'One more time and then you've got to go to sleep, okay?'

'Again! Gorilla, Daddy!'

I know sleepy children, and Maria appears to have just mainlined a flight of espresso. She crawls out from under the covers and climbs me like a tree. Her hands grab my shoulders, then face, and this must be what it feels like to be attacked by an alien.

'Sweetie, it's your bedtime.'

'Gorilla!' Maria shouts and then makes what I think are supposed to be gorilla noises. Grunts, grumbles, and the occasional 'ooo-ooo' leave her mouth and shoot right into my ear as her face contorts, and she does her best monkey impression.

'Oy vey.'

My stomach flutters and I have visions of her scaling the walls as Jill and Nick arrive home, gape in horror, and present me with a Worst Babysitter in Human History sash. I need to get her to sleep, but I'm not sure how. My years of experience in kindergarten have sadly left me painfully unprepared for a night with a two-year-old. I grab my phone from my pocket.

> Marvin: Past Maria's bedtime and she's wired. Did this ever happen with Illona?
>
> Any tips?

With my phone on the nightstand, I wait for Olan's reply. Maria springs from my arms onto the bed and jumps, attempting to leap as high as possible while continuing her primate calls, and yeah, this is officially the end of my career babysitting toddlers.

'Do you want to read the book again?' I hold it up, hoping to lure her back under the covers.

'I want a banana!' she yells and I'm almost tempted to get her one, but realize there's no way she's hungry after dinner and three cookies. Three cookies. Wait. Jill was adamant I only give her one. She's probably had too much sugar. Oops. But they were so tiny – just like her.

I pick up my phone and stare at it, willing Olan to reply, but there's nothing. At this point, I'm not sure she will ever sleep again. How did two extra cookies transform her into the Energizer Bunny? I'm tempted to text Jill, but that would defeat the entire purpose of my being here. I'm a responsible adult. I manage a class of five-year-olds daily. Surely I can handle a two-year-old for a night.

Maria hops and lands in my lap. A surge of pain overtakes my groin as she crushes my most precious jewels.

'Doh!'

I close my eyes and stars fan over my field of vision, as the aching pulsates and slowly begins to retreat.

'Desperate times,' I eke out and grab my phone.

> Marvin: Hey! I know it's late, but I'm babysitting Maria and she's had too much sugar and won't go to sleep. Any tips?

Maria resumes jumping on the bed, and I stand, removing myself as a landing pad. My feet walk in slow circles, willing the dull soreness to go away. There's no time for distractions now. I have a tiny frog that won't stop jumping and should be asleep already on my hands. Dear God in Heaven, hear my prayer – please calm this child and help me put her to bed.

Maria doesn't stop, but when 'Poker Face' plays from my phone, I take it as a sign, maybe my lord and savior, Mother Monster heard my prayer.

'Marvin? Sorry, I was tucking Illona in. What's up?'

Never in a million years did I think the sound of Isabella's voice would bring such relief.

'I gave Maria three cookies.' I wince, knowing Isabella will clock the size of my misstep. 'They were tiny. Toddler cookies. There was a cute cartoon bunny on the bag. And now she's hopping on the bed like one.'

'Gorilla!' Maria shouts.

'Sorry, like a gorilla,' I say.

'Okay, first, take a breath.'

I do as I'm told, taking a deep sigh.

'Good,' she says. 'Deep breaths. It sounds like a simple sugar rush. Get her a glass of water. Hydration will help offset the sugar. And expect a crash.'

On cue, Maria plops face-first on her bed.

'Wait, she stopped,' I say.

'Good. Get a small glass of water. Not too much.'

'Okay, water. Then what?' I move toward the bathroom door and fill the plastic cup.

'Lie with her. Be still. She'll fall asleep. I promise.'

Sitting on the edge of the bed, I catch Maria's gaze as she glances at me. With her breath rushing out, she lays her head sideways. She's crashing.

'I think we're good,' I say into the phone. 'You're a lifesaver.'

Another sentence I never thought would come out of my mouth.

'I told you, I'm here if you need anything. It takes a village.'

'Good night, Isabella. I owe you.'

'The next coffee is on you,' she says, and I can almost hear her grinning. 'Bye, Marvin.'

Relief shrouds me as I rest my head on Maria's pillows and she squirms up, cuddling into my chest.

'Is my little gorilla sleepy now?'

She answers by yawning, wrapping her tiny arm around my torso, and closing her eyes.

Before I overthink it, I start softly singing 'Shallow',

and when I finish the opening verse, I wonder if Maria might take over singing Gaga's part. Nope. Her breath has become deep, and small bursts of air hit my shirt as she exhales. By the time I get to the bridge where the song erupts, I pause. She doesn't move. Praise Gaga, she's asleep.

Nick gently wakes me after eleven, and I leave a sound-asleep Maria in her bed.

'Thank you again,' Jill says, handing me a pillow and blanket for the couch. 'I hope she wasn't too much trouble.'

'Nope, we had a blast,' I say, giving my best smile.

'You're a wonderful guncle, Marvin.' She walks behind the couch and kisses the top of my head. 'And an even better friend.'

It's well past my bedtime, and I should be exhausted, but the brief nap with Maria has left me wide awake. I retrieve my phone from my pocket to put it on the coffee table for the night and see a notification.

> Olan: I'm guessing she's asleep by now? Sometimes you have to ride it out. I'm sorry I missed you. I've been getting back to my folks place late. I will call you tomorrow. Miss and love you.

The text came through an hour ago and, not wanting to wake him, I give his message a heart tap. The house hums with the noises of night, and I take deep breaths, praying for sleep.

March in Maine means unpredictable weather. We could have a cold snap and a massive snowstorm, or it could be shorts weather. Of course, Mainers will wear shorts when it hits forty-five, so it's all relative. The sun is bright and warm when I catch the nine-thirty ferry back to the island, so I find a bench on the deck.

I watch the tall buildings and working waterfront of the city fade and Maria's small face flashes in my head. Last night wasn't a total disaster. It was only two extra cookies. The sugar rush was temporary, and Isabella came to the rescue. Of course she knew what to do.

As much as I adore my students, I love sending them home at the end of the day. Illona was an exceptional kindergartner and having her as my soon-to-be step-daughter makes my heart overflow with joy. I never really considered being a parent. I'm still coming to terms with my childhood – an alcoholic mother, abandoned by my father, all dusted with an extra helping of generational Jewish trauma. With Olan's support, I am learning to be the best stepparent possible, and thankfully, Illona makes it relatively easy.

Once again, the pop perfection of 'Poker Face' rings through my pants pocket and my heart jumps in my chest. Olan. Shaking my shoulders, I smile and push a rogue curl behind my ear. Pulling my phone out, I glance at the screen and my heart drops. I really should learn how to assign different ringtones to specific people. Sarah Block lights up the screen. My mother. Oy.

16

Just when I thought life couldn't get more overwhelming, and exactly when I have limited patience to deal with her, my mother saunters into the frame.

In the span of the eight bars of Gaga's pop perfection, my brain runs through my options. Don't pick up. What if Olan calls? Keep the line open. You don't want to miss his call just because you're stuck listening to Sarah Block ramble on about her latest water aerobics routine and the bizarre collection of tiny lizards she's discovered on her lanai. I mean, unless you've always dreamed of hearing about synchronized swimming with reptiles. Pick up, you haven't spoken to your mother in weeks. She's lonely. I'm lonely. She's your mother. Maybe we can find some solace in each other. Yes, pick up. That's the right decision.

'Mom, how are you?'

'I'm fine. I haven't heard from you in almost a month, and I was starting to wonder if you died.'

Or maybe not.

'No, Mother. I'm not dead. Just busy with school. Life is . . . busy. Planning a wedding.'

My eyes slam shut and I wince the moment the *W* word comes out of my mouth.

'That's why I called,' she says. 'Well, that and to make sure you're not dead in a ditch.'

Portland becomes even smaller as we approach the island and I'm eager for the short walk home from the dock and some alone time with Gonzo. Two days of snuggling with my kitty boyfriend, eating sugary snacks (with some chips thrown in for variety), and binging whatever drivel tickles my fancy.

'I know it's months away, but flights book up. I've been watching prices. And wondering if I should come early. Maybe a week. Or two. I know you're going to be overwhelmed with everything and you might need some help with last-minute details. Unexpected things can pop up.'

I hear her shift, the plastic of her outdoor chair crinkling under her.

'Amy's daughter's dress didn't fit, and they didn't realize until the morning of the ceremony. Turns out not having carbs two weeks before the wedding worked better than she expected and she'd lost too much weight. Do you know how hard it is to find a seamstress at the last minute? We had to sew her into the dress. Good luck using the bathroom. I'm bringing my sewing kit.'

'Mom, we're not wearing dresses.'

'I can hem your pants if they're too short. Or too long. Olan's too. And let's be honest, you never know when a button will pop off and go flying like it's making a desperate dash to be a runaway bride. Or groom. Grooms?'

And she's up. The clanking of rummaging crackles in the phone. 'There. My sewing kit is ready.'

'Mom. It's March. We're not getting married until August.'

'First things first – that's what my sponsor says. Mostly about putting recovery first, but it works here too.'

I take a deep breath and close my eyes. Hearing my mother talk about her sponsor is a subtle reminder of her continued sobriety. It's been over fifteen years since she hit bottom and began her recovery journey. We're finally approaching a good place – which is helped by her living across the country in Arizona.

'Anyway, how are you?' I ask, attempting to change the subject.

'The same, I'm alive. You'd know that if you called. I found a new meeting. They call themselves The Wacky Women, which is a silly name if you ask me, but the ladies are wonderful. Most of them are older, like me, and we take turns with snacks. Their rule is homemade, no store-bought cookies. You know I love a Milano, but these women want Martha-Stewart-level treats. Wait, strike that. Martha's friendship with that pot-smoking rapper prob-ably doesn't make her a good role model anymore.'

My head spins and my body jerks as the ferry makes contact with the dock. I gather myself and wait with the small group of Saturday morning folks to disembark. Even though March is early for summer tourists, the rela-tively warm forecast means people are here for a day of exploring and enjoying the beauty of Peaks.

Sometimes I can't believe I live here. Two years ago, Gonzo and I were cramped in a tiny, barely one-bedroom apartment with radiators that only worked if I banged them with an old pot. Thing is, I wasn't unhappy. I was too busy and distracted by life. But there's a difference between contentment and genuine happiness. Being with Olan has taught me that.

'Marvin? Are you there? Did I lose you? Hello?'

'Yeah, I'm here. Home. I mean, I'm just walking home from the ferry.'

'On a Saturday morning? Where were you? Where's Olan?'

My eyes snap shut and my nose crinkles. Fuck.

I hadn't planned on telling her about Olan being away. At least not now. For a while. Too many questions. And she'll want to talk . . . more.

'He's home.'

'Why isn't he with you?'

'No, back in Chicago, with his family.'

Double fuck. Why can't my mouth behave?

'Oh, how nice that he went to see his parents. He's a good son. Why didn't you come visit me while he's away?'

'I'm working, Mom.'

'Yes, yes, of course. When will he be back?'

My brain scurries to think of a lie. 'He's not sure.'

'He's not sure? When is his flight home?'

The wobble in my legs prompts me to sit on a bench overlooking a pebble beach. Between Olan's absence and explaining it to my mother, my body craves stillness for a moment.

'It's his brother, Mom. Olan needed to go back to . . . help.'

'Wait, which one? Doesn't he have two?'

'Liam. His younger brother. He's in rehab.'

The line goes quiet, and my mother's soft breathing mingles with the sounds of the waves lapping the rocks.

My senior year of high school. Her final bender. The car accident. Me sobbing at the edge of her bed, pleading for her to get help. A year later, while going through her twelve steps, she admitted to me that was what alcoholics call their bottom. In any other context, I would've giggled at the term, but her vulnerability and honesty forced my mischievous side to take a sabbatical.

'Oh. Well, it's good he's there. Olan, I mean, not his brother. I mean, it's good he's in rehab. If that's what he needs. Not that . . .'

'I knew what you meant, Mom.'

'I didn't realize Olan's brother was a friend of Bill. Isn't he married with kids?'

'That's Gabe, his older brother. Liam is younger.'

'Well, it's good he's in rehab. As you know, it really can help.'

'I know.' A wild hare hops into view from the bushes. It spots me, twitches its nose, and quickly leaps away.

'It's not the first time, though. There's been a pattern. And Olan's parents are overwhelmed. So, he went to help.'

'Good. They need Olan now. He understands.'

But I need him. The thought floats into my head, but my pride keeps me from saying it.

'And he's not sure how long he'll need to stay.'

'Of course,' she says. 'Detox can take a week or longer. Then he's going to need to attend support groups – with Liam and probably on his own. Talk to his sponsor on the phone.'

'And his parents,' I say, not sure what their role is.

'They'll do the same. If they're willing. Olan's a mensch. He'll know what to do.'

A smile creeps onto my face, hearing my mother gush over Olan. They've only met over video, but Sarah Block instantly fawned over him. *He's so handsome. He's so smart. He's such a good father.* Yes, Mother, I know. Why do you think I'm so enamored with him? She always wanted me to find someone, and I don't think she could be more pleased with the prospect of Olan Stone as her son-in-law.

And she's right. Olan will know what to do. He always knows what to do. When my anxiety spirals and it feels like a giant boulder has tumbled onto my chest, Olan holds my hands. Tells me to breathe. Rubs my shoulders. Talks to me in his soft, low voice. And I do feel better. The anxiety doesn't disappear, but having him near somehow lightens the load enough to know everything will be okay.

'And you're good there by yourself?'

I bite my lower lip, unsure how to reply. 'I am. Mostly. I miss him. But Illona's here during the week and every other weekend. And Gonzo has reclaimed his spot on the pillow next to me in bed. I'll be okay.'

'Are you sure? Is there anything I can do?'

'Thank you, but no. I just have to get through this on my own.'

'If you need me, honey, for anything, you call me. The wedding. Olan. You call me.'

'I will. I'm almost home, Mom. Gonzo's got to be starving. I love you.'

'I love you too, sweetie.'

I pocket my phone and stand, stretching as the sun

peeks out from behind a cloud. The rest of my week-end awaits me. I miss Olan so much it hurts, but I'm also looking forward to getting into bed and not leaving until Monday morning. Gonzo will appreciate that. Maybe I'll take a bath and light a candle. He can sit on the edge of the tub and swat at the water. I take a deep inhale, smelling the ocean and nearby beach roses, and head toward home.

17

'There's my handsome boy.'

Gonzo sits on the buffet near the entryway, staring at me with no expression. It's hard to read his chubby kitty face. He's either pleased to see me or pissed I left him alone all night. Or maybe a little of both.

I hang my coat up, place my keys in the ceramic bowl, and pick him up. His little motor immediately revs up as he buries his head in the crook of my neck.

'I missed you too, buddy.' My lips brush the top of his head and I take a seat on the sofa to give him a proper cuddle.

'It's just us the rest of the weekend.' He flops over, presenting his belly.

'Illona's with her mother. Olan's in Chicago. Boys' weekend.' He slams his head into my lap, and I take my cue and begin petting under his chin.

Glancing around our kitchen and living area, I'm once again reminded of how far I've come since meeting Olan.

Not just by moving out to the island, but also as a person. My anxiety will never disappear, but I'm learning strategies for managing it. Meditation. Deep breathing. Sometimes meditation feels like my brain's way of hosting a never-ending infomercial for problems I'd rather ignore, but Olan insists it just takes practice.

Living with Olan has grounded me in a way I never thought possible. His calmness is so infectious it seeps right through my bubble of worry.

My phone vibrates in my pocket and I hold Gonzo in place with one hand while retrieving it with the other.

Vincent: How's bachelor life treating you?

Marvin: Hanging in there. I babysat Maria last night. It was . . . interesting.

Vincent: I can only imagine the messes.

Marvin: Mostly lots of jumping.

Vincent: Call me if you get bored.

Marvin: Will do. Thanks.

My chest expands with a deep inhale. I'm so grateful for Vincent's friendship. He's busy with Kent, Lia, and his LEGO builds – he's working on a replica of the Sydney Opera House that takes up most of their dining-room table – but he always finds time to check in. Truly a sweet friend.

'Well, Gonzo. It's only eleven, but I say we put on our pajamas and get into bed. Sound good?'

He headbutts my chest, smashing the top of his head into me.

'I thought so.'

With Gonzo cradled in my arms, we head upstairs to start our weekend of cuddling and watching brainless television.

Gaga's staccato vocals wake me from a deep sleep, and I grab for my phone in a stupor. How long was I out for? Was it fifteen minutes, or three hours. I'm not really sure. Squinting, my eyes quickly focus on the beautiful photo illuminating the screen. I took it while he wasn't watching, reading a nonfiction book about the universe. Or the ocean. Something sciency. He was studying a diagram or working out the mysteries of the universe, and the way the sunlight streamed in and hit his face took my breath away.

It's Olan. Finally.

I prop my pillow and sit up, willing myself awake.

'Olan?'

'There's my sweet guy.' Olan's deep tone acts like a shot of mood booster, instantly making my body a smidge lighter. 'I've missed your voice. And you.'

'Olan. I miss you too. So much.' I try my hardest to sound alert and not like I've just been woken from a twenty-year slumber.

'Were you asleep?'

And I've failed miserably.

'Just a catnap. Literally. Gonzo insisted.' Hearing his name, Gonzo crawls onto my lap and nudges my fingers, holding the phone. 'He misses you too.'

'Please give him a big kiss on the head from me.'

I crane my neck, holding Gonzo in place with my free hand, and smother the top of his head with my lips.

'There. Done. How are things there?' It takes every ounce of restraint to not scream, *And when are you coming home?*

'They're . . . progressing. I'm spending more time at the rehab than I thought. Liam needs a lot of support.'

'Isn't that what the rehab is for?'

'Yes, but friends and family are part of the process, and my parents can only do so much.'

My heart skips, thinking about Olan in the rehab. What it might mean for him. Wondering if it might be helpful for me to be there, for when he's not with Liam.

'Are you okay?' I ask and hope he understands I mean his heart.

'Yeah, I'm fine,' Olan says and there's some noise, rustling. It sounds like talking, but he's covered the phone and I can't make out who's speaking or what they're saying.

'Olan?'

'Marvin, babe. I have to run.'

My stomach drops. I've been waiting for the call for days and it's ending already.

'Oh.' It slips out and I hope he doesn't register my complete disappointment.

'I'm sorry. I'll be back at my parents' late and know you'll be asleep.'

'It's okay,' I say, hoping he can't tell I'm faking it. 'Go, I'll be here.'

'I love you, Marvin.'

'I know. I love you too.'

And he's gone.

I let out a heavy sigh and return my phone to the

nightstand. Gonzo balances on my chest as I shimmy back and lay my head on the pillow. Talk about anti-climactic.

I know Olan's in Chicago to support his brother and parents, and this process is unpredictable and emotional for family members, especially if they're in recovery. My brain understands why Olan needs to be there – away from me. But my heart isn't having it. My heart is having a temper tantrum like a big ol' immature crybaby.

I close my eyes and try to imagine Olan next to me. Naps on Saturdays when Illona is with her mom are his favorite. The cuddling leads to kissing, which leads to sex, which ultimately leads to an amazing nap.

Gonzo kneads my stomach and I rub my thumbs over his face, blinking back the tears. Instead of putting some drivel on the TV to numb my mind, I grab my phone and cue up Olan's Motown playlist. The opening synths lead to the thumping bass which vibrates in my chest over the fancy high-tech sound system Olan installed. The music engulfs me from speakers around the room and when the strings of 'I Wanna Be Where You Are' enter the mix, I roll over, clutch Gonzo near, and lose myself in a young Michael Jackson's crooning about missing his love.

When I wake up, once again I'm not sure if I've been sleeping for five minutes or five hours. I check my phone and I think it's been closer to an hour. I'm not a repeat playlist girlie, so the music has ended and Gonzo has left me, probably in search of a prime sunbathing spot. Even I have to admit defeat against the afternoon sun – it's like trying to outshine a spotlight with a matchstick.

My head feels slightly less dramatic about Olan being away for an undetermined amount of time. As I shift to get comfortable, I realize my dick hasn't received the memo that Olan is out of town. The quietness of the house. The solitude of the bed. I slip off my boxers and palm myself, letting the heat of my cock soothe my hand, providing a welcome momentary distraction.

Here's the thing about jerking off. When you're single, you do it all the time because it's the only release you have. But when you're in a relationship, having as much sex as you want, your body craves it even more. Then you're jerking off in between sex with your gorgeous fiancé. My math skills may be lacking, but there's no arguing with the male masturbation algorithm.

I fling the comforter off to give myself a little more room, and hold my cock up, giving it a quick study. For sure, it's pretty. Olan says it's gorgeous. I giggled the first time he said it, but objectively, it is an attractive dick. Olan does this thing with his tongue, where he licks up the shaft, swirls just over the tip, then goes back down and flicks his tongue right under my balls. My eyes roll back, imagining his beautiful lips gliding up and down my cock, and blood surges south, intensifying my arousal.

With a little help from the lube in the nightstand, everything speeds up, and I attempt to replicate Olan's signature move with my fingers. Eyes closed, I imagine he's here, on all fours, face between my legs, ass in the air, getting me hard enough to fuck him silly. After two years, muscle memory has my cock pulsing at the thought of plunging inside his hole.

The longer we're together, the more vers things seem to get, and flip-fucking has become one of Olan's favorite activities. With each stroke, I visualize what would happen next. Me on my knees, fucking his face while I lean over and spread his beautiful ass cheeks. There's the lightest fuzz, which tickles my lips when I'm kissing across them, getting ready to plunge my tongue deep inside him. Fuck.

My fingers, slick with lube, get him ready, applying a generous amount. I start with my index finger, slowly exploring while he bobs on my cock, devouring me with slurping and sucking noises. Reaching under, I stroke Olan's cock. He's rock hard, wanting to be fucked into the ocean. Returning to his ass, I work my way up to two, then three fingers, his hole open and ready for me.

My orgasm knocks as I think about moving behind him. He drops his head to the bed, arching his back, creating the most beautiful, perfect acute angle (I remember some things from high school math). When I position my cock at his hole, Olan pushes back gently – he's so fucking horny for it, and I watch as his ass slowly swallows me to the base.

And that's it. Olan's ass gripping my dick, watching it plunge in and out of him as the muscles in his back twitch with pleasure . . . my waist tightens in anticipation and then my entire body spasms with pleasure as cum blasts over my torso, the first hit to my chin, taking me right out of my fantasy as I laugh at the force of it on my face.

Olan would lick it off. Moan with pleasure as he tastes me and kisses my nose, calling me 'Adorable'. He'd hold me after, gently brushing the back of my neck with his lips while telling me he loves me. He'd flip over and let me hold him, my cock getting hard again against his ass, but the exhaustion lulling us both to sleep.

My feet shuffle under the covers and I can't decide if I stay in bed hoping for another adventure in dreamland, or get up and make something to eat. And by 'make something to eat', I mean a strawberry donut from the half dozen I grabbed before catching the ferry this morning.

The grumble in my stomach decides it.

Jill: Have you recovered from your night with Maria?

Marvin: I've slept most of the day.

I spare my friend the gory details of my phenomenal jerk-off session.

Jill: Now imagine having her all the time.

Marvin: I don't know how you do it.

Jill: Nick helps more than I let on.

Marvin: He's a wonderful dad.

Jill: He is.

Marvin: I'm about to demolish a strawberry donut.

Jill: Atta boy. Love you.

Marvin: Love you too. Give Maria a kiss from me. And Nick.

Jill hearts my message as I sit at the kitchen island, overlooking Casco Bay. Boats dot the water, keeping Portland's working waterfront in business. I close my eyes and take in a deep breath. Gonzo leaps onto the counter and immediately begins rubbing the back half of his body against me.

'Yeah, I agree, buddy.' I pick him up and kiss his nose. One from me, and another from Olan.

'Back to bed for us.'

After a Sunday of polishing off the donuts in bed while binging an old season of *Drag Race*, I wake up Monday with the sun peeking through the clouds over the water. Sometimes I pull the shades, but mostly, I want to wake up to the gorgeous view afforded me by living here. People pay thousands of dollars to spend a week here in the summer, and I get to savor it every day.

Gonzo's snuggled into me and I do my best not to disturb his sleep as I reach for my phone.

There's a message from Olan from the middle of the night.

> Olan: Good morning sunshine. I love you.
> Check your email. 😊

An email from Olan? Shortly after we moved in together, Olan set up private emails using a domain he purchased . . . solely for us. He said it's more secure and we don't need the Portland School Department and/or GreenSpace monitoring our correspondence. We don't email often, but I forward him my monthly phone bill and he occasionally sends me cute articles about teaching or recipes he might like to try. It's all very sweet.

When I open the email app on my phone, this isn't

about the phone bill. Or teaching. Or lasagna soup. He's written a letter. And it's long. A tingling sensation creeps up the back of my neck. Tiny electric pulses warn me that something important – or possibly unsettling – is about to unfold as I read his message.

18

To: MrAdorable@StonyBlock.com
From: OnlyStone4U@StonyBlock.com
Sent: 3/18 at 1:45 A.M.
Subject: My Guy

Dear Marvin,

At this hour, you're most likely asleep, which is why I'm emailing you instead of calling or texting. My beautiful guy needs his beauty sleep.

Plus, there's a unique aspect to writing my thoughts that allows me to delve deeper. It's almost meditative. I hope you don't mind.

Again, I apologize for needing to cut our earlier phone call short. Things here are hectic, to say the least. In addition to being with Liam at the center, my parents are in over their heads. They're proud, stoic people who dislike asking for assistance. And I have a propensity to forget to offer. My mother is beside herself that

Liam's landed in such trouble. She doesn't enjoy talking about drinking or addiction. Of course, I understand these aren't the most pleasurable topics to discuss, but like it or not, they're a part of our family's dynamics.

There's more to share about the current situation, but I'll save that for a phone call. And I'd like to write to you more. It's almost like you're here with me in my childhood bedroom, which my mother has redecorated to create a more palatable, neutral guest room.

Being away from you makes my heart ache in a way that's new for me. I'm caught up in the situation's chaos here, but when there's a lull, a moment of quiet, and my thoughts wander to you, my chest pounds. I quickly realized it's a product of us being apart. I'm a ship, lost at sea, searching for the lighthouse to bring me home . . . to you.

But my presence here is necessary. I need you to know why it's imperative I'm here. For Liam. For my parents.

Step Nine.

We haven't spoken about the steps in depth, but I also know you have a basic understanding of them from your mother's recovery. Step Nine asks that we make direct amends to those we've harmed through our addiction – unless doing so would cause them further suffering.

After I completed my stint in rehab, I knew I had to speak with my parents. My sponsor at the time, a kind older gentleman named Fred, helped me write a script to assist me with speaking to them. But when I invited them to visit me in rehab, only my father came. He apologized profusely for my mother's absence, but I quickly understood that my amends would have to be delivered individually – and differently for each of them.

The conversation with Dad went well. He was receptive and loving. He's a quiet man, so his lack of words didn't trouble me. His eyes told me he was listening, taking my apology to heart. He gave me one of his patented bear hugs and whispered in my ear, 'I love you, son. Be patient with your mother.'

When I departed rehab and went to visit her, I had a new script my sponsor helped me craft. Apprehensive at her reaction, the nerves in my stomach bubbled and churned, but like all aspects of recovery, the only way through was one step at a time.

I arrived for lunch on a day I knew Dad would be volunteering at the library. He reads to a blind man he met on the bus. Phil took Dad's bus every day for years, and they struck up a friendship that lasted long after Dad's retirement.

Mom made her famous meatloaf. The secret ingredient is cornflakes, but if it ever comes up, please don't tell her I've told you. Let the woman have her secret. Her recipe calls for vodka, but she informed me she could replace it with tonic water, which she thought would have the same impact. With my script memorized, I anxiously sat at the kitchen table, eyeing the steaming meatloaf as I waited for the perfect moment to speak.

When Mom dished out coleslaw and asked if I wanted one or two biscuits, I took it as my opportunity to speak. But as soon as I began, she interrupted me.

'I don't want to talk about it.'

'It' being the disease of alcoholism.

By this time, Liam had already gotten into trouble a few times in high school for drinking. Caught with empty bottles under his bed. Skipping school to party with his buddies. Mom's brother, Uncle Danny, was an alcoholic his entire life and never got help before he passed. Alcoholism hits a raw nerve with Mom – it was too much to discuss. I savored each bite of my meal, knowing this was one way my mother expressed her love. When we finished, I pulled her into a tight hug, uncertain how I would ever make proper amends.

I called my sponsor immediately. Fred asked how the lunch had gone, and when I told him how Mom had shut me down, he reminded me that Step Nine isn't about one speech. One lunch. One interaction. It's a continual occurrence. He reminded me there are two definitions of amends: one is to repair, and the other is to change. It wasn't only my job to restore what I'd taken from my mother – her peace of mind about her son – but also to change my behavior.

At that moment, my higher power spoke to me and told me exactly what I needed to do: be the best son I could be for my mom. Since then, I have strived to do that, honoring the path she offered. Being home now, not only for Liam and my dad but also for Mom, who is struggling the most, is part of my living amends. It wouldn't happen in a single speech, but would be a lifelong journey for us.

I hope this helps you understand why I need to be here. Again, there's much more to say, but my fingers and body need a rest.

Being away from you and Illona crushes me. She's growing up so fast, but will always be my little girl.

And you're my guy – not so little. You will always be mine. Always.

Now, my guy, I should get some sleep. But here's a quick lesson for you first.

'My Guy' by Mary Wells. Did you know Smokey Robinson wrote Mary's signature hit? Yes, he wasn't only The Miracle's lead singer, but an accomplished songwriter. Can you imagine the royalties?

If you listen carefully to the lyrics, you'll hear the song isn't a simple platitude toward her man, but she's rejecting an advance from someone else in an affirmation of her fidelity to her true love. He's her soulmate, despite others thinking he may be simply average. There's nothing average about him. Or you.

Now, my most adorable guy, I'm off to sleep.

I love you. I love you. I love you.

Olan

19

Marvin: Good morning, handsome.
That was some email. Thank you. I love you.

Olan: My pleasure. Expect more. My guy. ♥

'My Marvin pillow.' Illona's sweet face smooshes against my side on the bus to school.

From the first day she took my hand in class over two years ago, she's been affectionate with me. Living together has only increased her warmth, but now, with Olan gone, something has shifted. It might be in a different capacity, but she misses her father as much as I do. Children need their mothers, but they also need their fathers. This is especially true when that father is one of the sweetest, most loving dads on the planet.

That email from Olan gutted me in the best possible way. Like his father, Olan's not a man of many words. He talks to me when we're alone, often avoiding eye contact when he's spilling his most vulnerable feelings. But his past, his family, and his addiction are topics he doesn't bring up often. What I know is culled together from small bits and pieces he's shared and information from Isabella, who tries her hardest to remember she's Olan's ex first and my friend second but often blurs the line.

I knew Olan's relationship with his parents was complicated, especially with his mother, but he never told me about the time he tried to make amends or her reaction. The pieces of Olan Stone are slowly revealing themselves. In time, with more information, maybe I can understand more about his relationship with his family – and more about him.

My arm wraps around Illona, pulling her close. Having her near, a piece of her father, really does comfort my soul. We're bonding over missing him.

'Your dad told me to give you this,' I say, leaning over and kissing the top of her head.

Isabella texted early this morning. Illona wanted to meet at the ferry dock so we could take the bus to school together. Isabella braided her hair over the weekend, and I've located a smooth spot to plant a kiss.

'Well, this is from him to you,' she says.

Illona turns her head and plants a smooch right on my lips. I close my eyes and let the pure love from Olan's daughter ground me. Vincent calls her 'the sweetest angel', and he couldn't be more correct.

'When did you talk to him?' I ask.

'Over the weekend. It was quick. But he told me to give both Mommy and you a kiss.'

I squeeze her a little tighter, thankful she remembered.

'But, you know, even if he hadn't asked me to, I would have.'

The smile that blooms on my face could melt the polar ice caps. Illona's face mirrors mine, and I give the top of her head another peck.

When we arrive at Pelletier, I leave Illona in my classroom with her journal and a variety of pens and markers and head over to check in with my work wife.

'The cat is away,' Jill says, counting out construction paper for one of her infamous craftivities. 'Did the mouse play?'

'If by play you mean staying in bed most of the weekend snuggling with Gonzo, then yes. The mouse had a fucking fiesta.'

'Did Maria wear your ass out that much?' Jill pinches her face, waiting for my reply.

There's no way I'm admitting how over my head I was. And I figured it out with a little help. Plus, I know she'll ask again, and I want to be there for her. I've learned my lesson. No matter what little lost lamb cuteness Maria attempts, one cookie. Period.

'No, no. It wasn't that at all,' I say. 'I just felt . . . meh. Like when you've been waiting the entire episode for the lip sync on *Drag Race* and neither queen knows the words.'

'Gosh, if Nick took Maria away for the weekend, I'd be in heaven. The entire house to myself? I'd order takeout, take a bath, and binge regency romances with hunky men dressed in tailcoats. Wait, I'd eat the takeout in the bath while binging dreamy historical men on my laptop. I've yet to see a single episode of any of the new shows. Maria prefers Bluey.'

'You know, I'm happy to watch her anytime,' I say. I puff my chest out a little, reminding myself I actually enjoyed myself once she settled down from the cookie fiasco.

'I know. And I will definitely take you up on that. Nick and I needed that night out.' Jill raises her eyebrows and smirks.

'Hell yeah, you did,' I say, pleased my babysitting allowed my friend to get some.

'You've missed the baby and toddler stages with Illona,' she says. 'You're always busy doing something for them – getting a snack, cleaning up from a snack, laundry from the mess the snacks create. So much fucking laundry. Sometimes I feel like I work in a laundromat. And not the cute kind where kinky antics happen in the back room. The kind where you simply have an endless mountain of clothes to wash and fold. I swear she's so small. And one child. I'm not sure how she produces so much laundry. But she does.'

'Yeah, Illona is fairly independent. She's been like that since kindergarten. I think she gets that from Olan. She wants her bedtime story. To be tucked in. She needs to eat, obviously, but she's not picky. And she helps me fold the laundry.' I smile, showing all my teeth, waiting for Jill to smack me.

'Well, I have something to look forward to.'

'And you have Nick to help,' I offer.

'Yeah, he barely knows how to use the washing machine. He ruined Maria's favorite blanket by washing it on the regular cycle. With bleach. Part of me wonders if he did it on purpose, so he'd get out of helping with the laundry.'

'Just show him how to do it correctly.'

Jill snaps her head back, giving me her patented 'Are you fucking serious?' look I know all too well.

'I've gotten him to stop throwing his own clothes on the floor. I'm taking the wins where I can.'

'Fair. Very fair,' I say. 'Well, I'm here for you. Always. I better get myself ready for the day. See you at lunch.'

Monday mornings are always a reentry in kindergarten. Even after a regular weekend, being away for two days can throw some kids off.

When Marley comes down the hallway looking like someone stole his favorite stuffy, I sense a little extra TLC may be in order.

'Morning, Marley. Happy Monday to you!' I give him my biggest smile, hoping it helps his downcast face.

He lifts his head just enough so his giant brown eyes peer into my soul. Something's got Marley down.

Kneeling, I put my hands out, and he takes them.

'What's up, buddy?' I ask.

He lets out a tremendous sigh. The aroma of his breakfast blows over me – something magically delicious.

'My mommy is away.'

That'll do it.

'Oh. Where is she?'

'On a work trip. For the entire week.'

Now, a week isn't that long. If Olan told me he'd be back on Friday, I'd be over the moon. But I'm not five. And he's not my parent.

'I'm so sorry, Marley. I can tell how tough that is for you. Is there anything I can do to help?'

'Maybe a hug?'

'Now that I can do.'

Marley wraps his arms around me. His orange puffy coat cushions against my neck as he squeezes and lets out a tiny groan from the exertion of hugging his kindergarten teacher. There's a lot wrong in the world, and hugs might not solve everything, but they're a good place to start.

Our embrace doesn't solve Marley's problem. His mom is still away for the week. But he knows he's got me in his corner and if he needs a little extra attention this week, Mr Block will be more than happy to provide it. And if focusing on Marley and the rest of my students helps me forget how much I'm missing Olan, that's simply icing on the cake.

'That burrito looks like it's seen better days.' At one of my tables, Jill sits across from me, her face flushed from the steam rising off her leftover lasagna.

'I mean, it's been in the freezer for . . . ever? I'm sure if there was an expiration date on it, I'd be second-guessing eating it.' I poke at the stiff tortilla. 'I'm not sure if the microwave heated it up or simply pushed it along its way to complete fossilization.'

'Want some lasagna?' Jill holds up her plastic container. It smells amazing.

'No thanks. I'll just eat the insides.' I pry the tortilla away to reveal the remnants of what once was supposed to be tofu, cheese, and some unidentifiable vegetables. My fork brings a bite up to my mouth and something smells off.

'Maybe I'll just have an energy bar. I bought some new ones. They have tons of protein, but are supposed to taste like fudgey brownies.'

'Suit yourself,' Jill says as I open the bottom drawer of the filing cabinet where I stash emergency snacks.

I retrieve a bar, unwrap it, and take a bite. The chocolate flavor fills my mouth, but the consistency is all wrong. It's less like eating fudge and more like munching on an old gym sock.

'What's the verdict?' Jill asks with a raised eyebrow.

'Thoughtful, but dry,' I manage to say, grabbing my water bottle.

A text flashes across my phone on the table and my heart skips, hoping it's Olan.

'Awe, he misses you,' Jill says. 'I remember those days.'

'No, it's my mom.'

> Sarah: What time will you be home?
> I need to talk to you.

'She needs to talk to me,' I say.

'About what?'

'She didn't say. That's her M.O. Specificity isn't in her repertoire.'

I return my phone to the table and take another bite of my sock brownie.

'Aren't you going to reply? Your mother needs to talk . . . dark clouds are forming.' Jill motions to the ceiling.

'Nah. I'll call her when I'm home. She probably forgot how to set her DVR to record *Walker, Texas Ranger.*'

'Critical information. We don't want to miss out on Chuck Norris fighting for justice with his amazing martial arts skills.'

'And that sexy beard.'

'Marvin. No.'

'Meh,' I say, holding up my bar. 'The cat is away. I gotta get my rocks off somehow.'

The rest of the afternoon passes without incident, and with the warm March sun paying us a visit, Illona and I sit on the top deck as we sail back to the island. Not knowing when Olan will return creates a tiny crater in my heart, but having Illona with me helps fill it a bit. We'll distract each other from missing her dad by making dinner and listening to pre-teen pop music. When she goes to sleep, Gonzo will take over with kitty snuggles.

I've saved Olan's email in a folder I created and named 'Husband of the Year'. Each time I open it, I'm reminded of how he shared a little more about himself with me. I plan on rereading it before bed, letting his sweet words wash over me as I wind down for the night. Maybe he'll write more letters that capture his thoughts and feelings, adding to this little collection of joy.

Walking back to the house, Illona takes my hand, our arms swinging between us, and really, I have nothing to be down about. Olan needs to be with his family back in Chicago. Despite the uncertainty of his return, I know his absence is temporary. I've got the 'sweetest angel' to keep me company, and a cat thrilled to have me to himself in bed for the foreseeable future.

'What should we make for dinner? Pizza or tacos?' I ask.

'That's like asking me to decide between purple and pink as my favorite color.'

'Oh. Yeah, that would be impossible,' I reply.

At the giant oak tree, we turn down the street to our house, and I pull Illona's hand close enough to give it a peck.

'How about pizza tonight and tacos tomorrow?'

'Or we could make both,' she suggests.

'Too much work. I barely have one meal in me, and pizza and tacos are fairly simple.'

'I'll help.' Illona stops, but doesn't let go of my hand.

'I know you will. You're an amazing helper.'

I tug at her hand to move, but she doesn't budge.

'What's wrong, sweetie?'

'Who's that?' She nods toward our house at the end of the street. 'At our door?'

My heart races, climbing to the top of the roller coaster in my throat before plunging down my torso and falling right through a trapdoor in my bootyhole.

I gulp and remind my body to cooperate. Stay upright. Breathe. And also, please don't soil yourself.

'That's Sarah Block. My mother.'

20

'Mom.' I do my best to muster up some enthusiasm, but the word flops out of my mouth like a huge turd. 'What . . . Why . . . How . . . How did you get here?'

She's standing on our front porch. There are chairs for sitting – lovely chairs Olan and I picked out online. They came wrapped in so much paper and Bubble Wrap, it took almost as long to excavate them from the packing material as to put them together. We sat outside in the summer sun and assembled them without arguing once, mainly because my job was to read the directions, and Olan's job was everything else – another perk of being with an engineer.

Alas, my mother is not resting in a weatherproof chocolate wicker chair with striped cushions in muted earth tones. She's standing, hand on hip, foot tapping, glasses sliding down the bridge of her nose, and loose curls blowing in the ocean breeze. Sarah Block has no time or patience for sitting. She's ready to pounce.

I force a smile. Fake it until you make it. She'll never know.

'I walked. From Arizona. My legs are killing me.' She throws her head back and lets out a sharp laugh.

'Mother.'

'I flew here, you silly goose. All the way from Arizona . . . and boy, are my arms tired.'

Another piercing cackle.

Illona gives me a confused look, not quite sure about the strange creature taking up residence outside our front door.

My mother and Illona have only met on a video call. I've only seen Sarah once in the almost two years since we've lived together. I flew back last summer. Alone. Olan offered to join me, but I wasn't ready to introduce him to the whirling dervish energy of Sarah Block. I barely wanted to go. Asking him to come along didn't feel like the best way to promote Olan's faith in marrying me. My mom can be . . . a lot. For me. It was better to brave it alone.

'No, here.' I gesture to the house. 'To the island. Why didn't you tell me you were coming? I could have met you at the airport. Wait, why didn't you tell me you were coming? Where were you when you texted me earlier? Why are you here, Mom?'

'I had a layover in Chicago. That airport is a zoo.' She's digging in her enormous purse, searching. 'Popcorn for sale every fifty feet. Do people in Chicago have a thing for popcorn nobody is talking about?' She yanks a bag of caramel popcorn out. 'I took a taxi to the ferry. Charlie from Saco drove me.' Her pronunciation of Saco with a long *a* instead of the proper short vowel sends a chill down my spine. 'Those ride-share apps are taking over, but I'll stick to licensed taxis with trained drivers and proper insurance, thank you very much. Have you seen the *Dateline* about what some of those drivers do?' She dips her chin and gives me her no-way-in-hell look over the top of her tortoiseshell frames. 'I preferred arriving in one piece.'

Illona dances over, her feet barely touching the ground, and as I scan her face, I recall that she urgently requires the restroom.

'Mom, let's go inside. Illona needs the bathroom.'

'Illona.' Sarah takes Illona's face in her hands, ignoring the pee-pee dance I know all too well. 'Such a shaina madel. More beautiful in person than on the video chat or those pictures you sent me.'

I open the door and Illona darts inside, both to escape my mother and to the bathroom. My mom's suitcase is enormous. An adult human could fit inside. Sarah Block doesn't travel light. She brings clothes for every type of weather, every season, and any potential event. I'm not a betting man, but twenty bucks says there's an evening gown in there.

'The walk from the ferry was easy.' She holds up her cell. 'The man at the phone store showed me a map in here that will show you how to get anywhere.'

'How long were you planning on staying?' I ask with probably a smidge too much sarcasm as I drop her bag in the foyer.

'I bought an open-ended ticket.'

The kitchen counter is about ten feet away, and my feet move on autopilot. I need to lean . . . preferably sit and pour a cool drink of water. Over my head.

'Before you say anything . . .' Sarah pulls a stool out and climbs on. She tucks a loose curl behind her ear, and I notice her hair is shorter than the last time I saw her. 'You sounded . . . lonely on the phone. You need help. A mother knows. When you were little, you were so tiny, maybe four, when you got scared or worried about something, you would crawl into the space my legs made when I took a nap on the couch. You called it your "nest", and you'd curl up and sleep with me. Consider this' – she aims both thumbs at herself – 'your nest. Plus, I figured you could use a distraction while Olan's away.'

I let out a quiet sigh, attempting to keep the dramatics at bay.

'Plus . . .' She opens her purse, takes out a small mirror, readjusts her glasses, and checks her face. 'I knew you'd never ask for help.' She removes a tube of lipstick – Flamenco Red, her signature color, and the only hue bold enough for Sarah Block. 'If I'd offered, you'd only have said no, so . . .' Sarah puts her mirror away and gives me enthusiastic jazz hands. 'Here I am.'

Illona skips into the room, a big smile on her face. 'Yes, I washed my hands.' She holds them up.

'Plus,' Sarah says, opening her arms as Illona approaches, 'I wanted to get to know my future granddaughter. I'm finally going to be a bubbe.'

'A what?' Illona asks, letting my mother hug her.

Sarah pinches one of Illona's cheeks. 'A bubbe. Grand-mother. I've been waiting a long time. This one's entire life.' She nods toward me. 'When Marvin was little like you, I'd imagine his wedding. Standing under the chuppah – that's a canopy – and then, well, grandchildren would come.'

Sarah squeezes Illona close, her voice softer, and says, 'And here you are.'

I'm not sure when my mother realized I was gay. Sure, there were clues. Maybe it was when I asked for another Big Jim doll, so my original one would have a friend to bunk with inside the Big Jim Camper. Or maybe in first grade, when I had a terrible crush on Asher Stevens, and Mrs Cooper had to call Mom and ask her to talk to me about kissing at school. In this conversation with Illona, she never mentioned the gender of the person she imagined me marrying. She simply wants grandchildren.

'Mother, be careful, you'll hurt Gonzo's feelings,' I say.

Never one to miss out on a commotion or attention, Gonzo strolls into the room and rubs against both Illona's and Mom's legs.

'He will always be my first grand-kitty,' Mom says, scooping Gonzo up and tossing him over her shoulder, where he balances like a stole. Thrilled for the attention, his purring immediately permeates the room. 'But now, a granddaughter.' She takes Illona's face in her hands again, rubbing her thumb across her cheek. 'I'm kvelling over this face.' Without taking her gaze off Illona, she asks, 'Are you going to offer me a drink?'

My eyes pop open. It's a simple reflex.

Before I can say anything, Sarah clarifies, 'Water, dear. Still sober. No plans for that to change. One day at a time.'

I knew that's what she meant. Plus, she knows about Olan, and we don't keep alcohol in the house. But when I hear 'a drink', my mind immediately goes to booze. Thank you, society, for the constant barrage of alcohol in advertising, TV shows, movies, and social media.

'Water. Of course. Regular or seltzer? Ice or no ice?' I ask, grabbing two glasses and some milk for Illona. 'Grab a snack from the pantry,' I say to Illona, and she darts off.

'Regular. When did you get so fancy?' She lowers Gonzo to the floor and scans the first floor of the house, and yes, it's a complete left turn from my apartment. 'And ice, please,' Mom says, 'I worked up a thirst walking from the ferry.'

Over the past few years, I've worked really hard to let my guard down with my mother. She's been working hard to earn my trust, and I'm trying to let her in more. Our relationship is a journey, and we're both putting in the work to strengthen it. Typically, that happens over the phone. Or via text. Not with her flying here on an open-ended ticket with no clue about her departure.

But her heart is in the right place. That's what Olan would say. Fuck, I miss him. I didn't think it was possible to miss him more than I already did, but with my mother here and him absent as a buffer, the ache for him feels sharper and more profound. It's like I've unlocked a new level of longing I didn't know existed.

'Do you want me to make dinner?' Sarah is up, poking in the fridge. 'What does Illona like? Does she have any allergies? Martha's grandson can't come within ten feet of a peanut. Can you imagine?'

'I'm not picky.' Illona returns from the pantry with three single-sized bags of chips. 'No allergies. And I like almost everything.' She hands one to me and one to Sarah, and says, 'Have a nosh.'

My mother's eyes open wide and a giant grin lights up her face. She wraps her arm around Illona's shoulder and squeezes. Illona opens her bag of chips, and the satisfying crunch of her first bite fills the room.

'Hmmm.' Sarah sets her bag down and opens cabinets and the freezer, lifting things, reading labels, and formulating a plan.

'This mustard expired two months ago,' she says.

'It's mustard. It doesn't expire.' I take the bottle from her and read the date, and of course, she's correct.

'Until you're trapped on the toilet from bad mustard.'

I throw the mustard in the trash, pop open my chips, and begin munching.

'How about hamburgers, a salad, and . . .' She pulls a bag from the freezer. 'Tator tots. Gosh, I haven't had these in years.'

'Mom, I can make dinner. You've been traveling all day.'

'Marvin,' she says. 'I came here to help. Let me.' With ground meat in hand, she says, 'Plus, I slept on the plane. Now let's see . . . yes, still good. At least we won't get worms from expired meat.'

'Worms?' Illona asks mid-chip.

'Rotten meat is no joke. I'm going to teach you how to read the expiration dates while I'm here. Your dads need a little help.' Sarah sets the ground beef and salad fixings on the island and begins searching for the various bowls, cutlery, and supplies to make dinner.

'Mom, I can do it.'

'No, sir. Go change. Relax. Watch some TV. Take a little nap. Do whatever you like. Dinner will be ready in one hour. Maybe sooner. I'll call you.' Before I can reply, she adds, 'Illona, do you want to stay and help? No pressure. You can go unwind too, if you like.'

I squint my eyes, attempting to tell Illona 'run for the hills' with only my face, but she doesn't look at me. She's opening a drawer and pulling out the cutting board.

'I can make the salad,' Illona says. 'My dad taught me how to chop carefully.'

'Of course he did,' Mom says. 'Well, I'm right here if you need anything. And we can chat. Girl talk. Shoo, Mister Block. Leave us ladies to make dinner.'

'How nineteen-fifties of you,' I murmur. 'What's for dessert? A Jell-O mold?'

And with a wave of her hand, I'm a child again as my mother sends me to my room.

I wasn't expecting an hour of free time, but I do as I'm told. Out of my work clothes and resting on the bed, I'm almost at a loss at what to do with my free hour. Maybe I can close my eyes for a few minutes. Power naps are like nature's energy drinks. Sadly, knowing my mother is downstairs poking in every drawer has my brain spinning like a DJ at a club. Or a wedding. Crap, we probably need a DJ. I better mention that to Sheldon.

Taking his shot to snuggle, Gonzo leaps up and lies right on my groin – insuring I'll have to pee in five minutes. Why is that his favorite spot?

Marvin: My mother is here.

Olan: Here as in where?

Marvin: Our house. She's downstairs making dinner with Illona.

Olan: What is she making?

171

Marvin: Hamburgers. But I think you're burying the lede. My. Mother. Is. Here. 😟

Olan: Take deep breaths. Let Illona be a buffer. She's a wonderful diversion. You got this. And remember, I love you more than apple pie.

Marvin: With or without ice cream?

Olan: With ice cream. And whipped cream. And caramel sauce.

Marvin: Now I'm hungry.

Olan: Enjoy your hamburger. And look for an email from me in the morning.

Marvin: I can't wait. I love you more than a private concert from Lady Gaga.

Olan: No you don't.

Marvin: Equally then.

Olan: I'll take it. 💜

Mom's hamburgers are delicious. She does this thing where the outside is almost burned, but the inside is still pink and juicy. Illona seemed to enjoy making dinner with her. Mom insists she calls her Sarah, but deep down, I know she wishes she'd call her bubbe, or anything resembling grandma. When Illona and I both turn down seconds, Sarah packs them up for our lunches.

'I'm going to make you Happy Meals,' she says. 'I only

let Marvin have them for very special occasions when he was little, but he loved them.'

'Mom, I don't think Illona wants leftovers for her lunch at school.' I motion to the food.

Illona nods. 'No, actually, it was delicious. I bet it will be even better tomorrow.'

'Perfect.' Mom claps her hands together and shoos Illona and me away while she cleans up.

After dinner, we play Uno, and my mother lets Illona win. Mom's usual Uno strategy is to crush all hopes and dreams, so this is a little like seeing a unicorn in our living room. But she seems more than willing to lose to Illona.

After I tuck Illona in, I'm ready for my own early bedtime. It's been a long day, and after a few hours with Sarah, I need a little alone time with Gonzo.

'Good night, Mom.'

'Going to bed so early?' She pulls her sweatshirt around her neck and shivers a little. 'I'm not used to this arctic air.'

'Maine isn't arctic.'

'Compared to Arizona, it is.'

Touché.

'Here,' I say, grabbing a throw from the sofa.

'Thank you.' She wraps the blue knitted blanket around her shoulders like a shawl. 'Sleep well.'

I wrap my arms around her, pulling her close. As I envelop her in a warm embrace, I let out a contented sigh, savoring the comfort of her presence. The soft fabric of the shawl blends with the warmth of her body, creating a cocoon of coziness.

'I'm glad you're here, Mom.'

'Me too.'

She kisses me on the cheek, and I grab Gonzo and head upstairs to bed.

With the morning sunlight filtering into the room, I'm stirred from sleep by the gentle pressure of Gonzo, once again lying on my bladder. Although I desperately need to use the bathroom, I grab my phone and check my email before attempting to get out of bed.

My heart leaps in my chest when I see the message from Olan. I bring Gonzo close to my face, feeling his warmth as we snuggle, give him a few good morning kisses, and open the letter.

21

To: MrAdorable@StonyBlock.com
From: OnlyStone4U@StonyBlock.com
Sent: 3/19 at 1:45 A.M.
Subject: Ribbon in the Sky

Dear Marvin,

Breathe. Wherever you are, pause and take a deep breath.

Okay, now another.

One more.

That's my guy. Gosh, I miss your face. Your head. Your curls.
Your dick. Your ass.

The whole ass, by the way. Sometimes, when you're wearing
pajamas, they slip a little, and I get a glimpse of the top, like a
way sexier plumber's crack. I know you're not trying to tease me,
but when I see it, I can't help but smile, wishing I could yank
them down, bury my face in it, and ravage you. Your cheeks, the

way they curve under right where they meet your leg. And then there's my favorite part – your beautiful hole. Often, when you're waiting for me to fuck you, I just want to study it. Admire it. Give it the reverence it deserves. Marvin, a portrait of your hole should be in the Louvre.

Now I'm all worked up. We should arrange a video chat sometime. So I can see your masterpiece of an ass. But I digress.

I know having your mother there is a lot, and I'm sorry I can't be there to be a buffer, but you're working during the week, and Illona will help in the evenings. If you want to keep her for any of her Isabella weekends, let me know and I can reach out to her. I know she'd understand and be flexible.

Has Sarah informed you how long she plans to stay? I know this is challenging for you. Me being away. Your mother being there – while I'm not. But remember who you are. You're Marvin Block. Maine's Teacher of the Year. Your caring nature, strength, and adorableness make you the most exceptional man I know. I try not to preach my AA jargon to you, but perhaps taking this one day at a time would help. Focus on today. Get through today. That's your goal. If you're feeling frustrated or need to vent, text me. Even if I'm unable to reply, text me. Know I'm thinking about you. Always.

I'm not sure when I'll be back. The situation here is too complex to explain fully in an email, but there are important details I need to share with you. Liam's detox was longer and more uncomfortable than anyone expected. Besides alcohol, he used narcotics. Opioids. He and his girlfriend, Abby, were in serious trouble.

Drugs and alcohol are dangerous enough on their own, but combining the two can be lethal – Abby overdosed about six months ago. Liam was with her but had blacked out and wasn't able to intervene or call for assistance. Tragically, Abby passed away. Liam has immense guilt about what happened and my parents are struggling to cope with the overwhelming nature of the situation. There's more to explain, but I'd prefer to speak on the phone.

I understand I'm dumping a lot of information on you. Please know things are strained here, and I miss you. So fucking much, Marvin. I know I'm needed here and I know you understand, but I miss every cell in your body. Every atom making up those cells.

Even when we're apart, you're with me. In my heart. My body. My soul. Loving you is the best gift I've ever been lucky enough to receive. I've never told you this, but after Isabella and I split, I used to pray I'd meet someone who would wake me up. Show me love in a way I hadn't experienced yet. Accept me wholeheartedly, embracing every quirk and idiosyncrasy that I bring to the table. And I realize there are many.

Then I walked into Pelletier Elementary on Illona's first day. I'd had too much coffee and needed the bathroom. Never in a million years did I expect to see an adorable man experiencing an epic battle with the automatic sinks. But the moment I laid eyes on you, something shifted inside me. I couldn't name it, but it was like God poked my soul and said, 'Hey, you. Pay attention. All that praying you do? This one. Here. With the wet pants. That's him.'

And God was right. It's no accident that I relocated to Portland, that you were in the bathroom struggling with the sinks, or that you were assigned to be Illona's kindergarten teacher. I truly believe there are no accidents in life. The universe has a way of making things happen, and by the grace of God, it made us happen.

Remember who you are when you're feeling anxious, lonely, or frustrated with your mom. When you're missing me. You're Marvin Block. My blue rose. My person – we share a 'Ribbon in the Sky.'

And here's your lesson about, in my humble opinion, one of Stevie Wonder's finest songs. The abstract lyrics of the 1982 hit add to its unique appeal. Most people agree the song describes a deep and abiding love that transcends time and space. He's not singing about a literal ribbon, but rather a representation of a boundless and unbroken connection, much like a band stretching infinitely across the sky. It's a bond that cannot be broken, a love that will endure for all eternity. It's almost like Stevie wrote the song about us. You were guided my way, and I will never stop being grateful to have you in my life.

But also, it's simply an extremely beautiful, romantic song.

Let's schedule a call soon. Perhaps that video chat? I miss your face. Maybe on Thursday night during Illona's bedtime? Then we can speak alone once she's asleep.

All my love,

Olan

22

'Lunches, coats, bags . . .' My mother taps both Illona's and my gear as we stand near the door, literally checking things off.

As a child of an alcoholic, there were days I put myself on the bus without seeing my mother. Times I came home, gave myself a snack, and watched TV until it was time for me to make dinner. Over the past two years, I've put in a lot of effort working closely with Erika, and also independently, to cultivate a stronger and more stable relationship with her. But I also know the trauma of being raised by an alcoholic can't simply be swept under the rug. As much as I wish it didn't, her attempt at cosplaying as June Cleaver plays games with my head.

'Mom, we're good. Thank you for the lunches.' I hold up my brown paper bag.

'Now yours,' she says, cradling Illona's face, 'has a surprise in it. A girl toy. For a little girl.'

'There's no such thing as boy toys and girl toys,' Illona

says, and the piece of me that was her kindergarten teacher two years ago beams with pride. 'Toys are toys. Anyone can play with them.'

'Well, this toy is for you. How about that?'

Illona shrugs and backs away toward the door. Smart kid.

'I wish I'd known you were coming,' I say. 'I could have taken a day or two. Arranged sub plans. What are you going to do all day?'

'Marvin Isadore Block.'

Her use of my full name sends a slight chill up my spine.

'Isadore?' Illona's face contorts into the cutest state of confusion.

'My middle name.'

'After my great Aunt Ida.' Sarah grabs my shoulders, and I brace myself. 'Now, Marvin Isadore.' She winks at Illona. 'I know you have to work. Your students need you. I am perfectly capable of entertaining myself. There are meals to plan. Shop for. Prep. Is there a store on the island, or do I need to take the boat back downtown?'

'Hannigan's. It's about two blocks from the dock where the ferry left you off. Here, let me write the directions down.'

I grab a pen and pad from the drawer next to the fridge and start drawing a map.

'Sweetie, I can put it into the Google on my phone. Maps! I'm good.'

'Are you sure?' I ask.

Mom pokes at her phone and then shows me Hannigan's on a map with directions from our house. 'Right as rain. I need to move my legs, anyway. I'll find it. And I have my book.' She grabs a worn book from the counter and holds up *Jewish Wisdom for Growing Older: You Know*

Bubkis with a smile. 'I think I'm going to make meatloaf for dinner.' She puts a hand up. 'Before you say we had hamburgers last night and you're having hamburgers for lunch, protein is essential for growing bodies.'

'I'm good, Mom.' I pat my stomach.

'Not you.' She smiles at Illona and gives another wink. 'Plus, my meatloaf isn't only beef. You know that.'

'What is it then?' Illona asks from the door.

'Bubbe's secret. I'll tell you after school.' Another wink. 'And there's wedding planning to be had. I know Olan is paying, but I told you, as the mother of the bride, I'm buying the flowers. And the welcome mocktails are on me. I'll hear nothing else about it. I have investigating to do.'

'Mom, I told you, I'm not the bride.'

'Mother of the groom then.' She gestures toward me.

'My friend Sheldon is helping with the planning. And by helping, I mean doing it. I'm sure he has some ideas.'

'Perfect. Text me his number,' she says.

There's no way in hell I'm giving her Sheldon's number. 'Okay.'

'I have plenty to keep me busy until you two get home. And Gonzo will keep me company.' Gonzo lies by the window, unaware his feline alone time is about to be severely interrupted. 'Now go, don't be late for school.'

I give her a quick hug and kiss on the cheek, and Illona and I rush for the ferry.

'Your mom is . . .' Illona stares at the clouds in the cool March sky from our seats on the upper deck. Even with our light jackets, we're snuggled close to keep warm. 'Interesting.'

'You could say that. She means well.'

'I like her,' Illona says. 'Her hamburgers are amazing. I've never had them with onions cooked inside it like that.'

'Yeah, my mom puts onions in everything. I used to joke if someone made onion ice cream she'd devour it.'

'Onion ice cream?' Illona shakes her head.

'Hey, Jews and onions – it's a love story with many layers.'

Illona laughs and rests her head on my shoulder, cuddling against me.

Time is funny. In the grand scheme of things, two years isn't really that long. When you consider the history of the universe, two years is a blip. The tiniest dot. But it's almost one-third of Illona's seven years of life. She's going to be my stepdaughter – me, her stepfather. Not the evil robot kind who wants to murder her like poor Buffy had to deal with in Season Two. More like Mike Brady, where you couldn't quite tell who was whose biological child because everyone was just part of the bunch. Yeah, definitely more of a Mike Brady.

I take out my phone and play 'Ribbon in the Sky' softly over the hum of the ferry's engine.

'One of Daddy's favorite songs,' Illona murmurs.

Of course she knows.

I close my eyes, thoughts of Olan's latest email swirling in my head.

His brother's situation. Rehab being more difficult than expected. I never really gave much thought to what rehab was like, but I can't imagine it's fun for anyone. For Olan to write it's harder than he thought, it must be grueling. And Liam's girlfriend. I wonder how long they were together. Did Illona know about her? I'm guessing no, since Olan only had brief contact with Liam beyond the occasional text. How does someone overdose? I mean, obviously it's by consuming too many drugs and/or alcohol, but what exactly happens? And Liam was there. With her. Surely that contributed to his current situation.

My heart aches for Olan's brother. A man I've never met, my knowledge of him limited to a lone photograph Olan keeps in his office. The picture is the only one I've ever seen of all three of them together. On a dock near some lake, with their beautiful smiles, Gabe and Liam surround Olan, who stands out with his lucky tooth gap. I think Olan told me he was twenty-one in the picture, which means Liam would've been almost nineteen. Babies.

Sarah's arrival has only exacerbated my longing for Olan, and the thought of him navigating a strained family situation without my presence makes my stomach twist and knot with unease. My brain knows he needs to be there alone. My heart, not so much.

The beginning of Olan's email floats into my head, and a smile skates across my face, remembering his words. A portrait of my hole in the Louvre. Would people line up to see it like the *Mona Lisa*? The Hole-a Lisa. A chuckle spills out of my lips, catching Illona's attention.

'What's so funny?'

'Oh, nothing. Just thinking about something your dad said to me.'

'What?' She sits up, eager for a morsel of her father's words.

'That he loved you more than apple pie with ice cream.'

'What about whipped cream?' She cocks her head, apparently offended by the omission.

'Sweetheart, your father loves you more than apple pie with ice cream, whipped cream, sprinkles, chocolate sauce, with a cherry on top.'

'Two cherries?'

'All the cherries in the world.'

Illona smiles and wraps her arms around my torso. 'Yeah, that sounds about right.'

23

'Your mother is here?'

Jill halts mid-sentence, her pen frozen in midair, and whirls around to face Illona and me standing in her classroom doorway. Her eyes are so wide, they look like they're about to leap off her face.

'Sweetie, I'll be over in a few,' I say to Illona.

'She packed us Happy Meals!' Illona lifts her paper bag and then skips off to my classroom.

'Here as in Maine?' Jill dips her chin, her jaw locked in shock.

'Yes, at my house. Hence the homemade Happy Meals. I have one too.' I lift my brown paper bag. 'Apparently, she's now a one-woman McDonald's.'

'But why?' Jill sits on a table, pulls out a chair, and rests her feet on it.

'She thought I sounded lonely.'

'You do.'

'Whose side are you on?' I leave my backpack at the

door and carefully lower myself onto a kindergarten-sized chair. It's the closest I'll ever come to doing a squat.

'Your side. Always. But you are lonely. Still, that's no reason for her to show up unannounced. Why didn't she tell you she was coming?'

'I think she knew I'd tell her not to.'

'Of course you would have.' Jill leans forward, placing a hand on my forearm.

'But it's moot. She's here. In my house. Cleaning and poking around.'

'And finding your . . . things.'

'Please. Don't say that.' An image of my mother rummaging around my bedroom flashes in my head. Riffling through my dresser. The second drawer. Behind the socks. My stomach flips.

'What is she going to do all day while you're at work?'

'She's making meatloaf.'

'That can't take her all day.'

'She wants to take a walk around the island.' I shrug. The island is just large enough for her to get lost, but she has her phone. 'And she has a book.'

'You better hope it's a long one. War and motherfucking Peace.'

'It's fine. What is she going to do?'

'Besides find your sex toys? If my mother was in my house alone, I would lock my bedroom door and bring the key with me. No, wait, burn the house down. Without her in it, of course.'

'Jill Kim, what kinky antics are you and Nick up to?'

'Straight people can have fun in the bedroom, too.'

'I don't doubt it.'

186

'I'll have to fill you in at our next donut date. One word spoiler. Pegging.'

'No way. Stop.'

'Way. And I will not. He loves it.'

'Nick?'

Jill nods, a sheepish grin radiating in the room.

'Wow. I didn't see that coming.'

'Neither did I. But when you're married, you have a choice. Allow the grapes on the vines of your relationship to wither, shrivel into raisins, or nurture them until they flourish into succulent, plump fruits.'

'So you can peg them?'

'Exactly.'

Jill lets out an enormous sigh, stands, and returns to writing her morning message on the whiteboard easel near the front of the classroom.

'Olan emailed me. Again.'

'Mr Romantic.' She turns back toward me, her entire face shifting. I'm fairly certain she has a major crush on Olan. She's a sucker for beautiful men. 'I'm loving this whole letter writing fantasy you're having. Very *Shakespeare in Love*.'

'Fuck, Joseph Fiennes was sexy in that movie.'

'I almost slid off my couch when I saw it for the first time in college.'

We both stare into space, picturing the dreamy face of Mr Fiennes as Mr Shakespeare. That pretty-boy beard and mustache stirred something in me, even at seven. I wasn't sure what I was feeling, but something about him, that facial hair, that face, I knew at a minimum I needed to read everything Shakespeare wrote.

'But yeah. He's spending a lot of time with his family during the day and by the time he's home and ready to chat, I'm in bed. So, he's emailing me in the middle of the night. It's kind of amazing to wake up to. Almost beats that first cup of coffee. Almost.'

'How are things? With his family?' She signs her name at the bottom of the message.

'I think his brother is having a harder time with rehab than Olan had hoped.'

'I'm no expert on recovery, but if Sandra Bullock in *28 Days* has taught me anything, rehab isn't all bad. Your hair still looks fantastic, and most importantly, you get to have sex with Viggo Mortensen. Also, the world was sleeping on Viggo way before he made everyone horny in *Lord of the Rings*.'

'Return of the Schwing.' I gesture to my pelvis as I give a little thrust.

'There's my Marvin,' Jill says, patting my shoulder.

'Well, between missing Olan and talking about Shakespeare and King Aragorn, my engine is revving.' I stand to prepare for departure. 'And I have a full day of teaching kindergarten ahead of me so . . .' My eyes briefly flicker downward, toward my crotch. 'Settle down.'

'Joe and Viggo. I'd watch that movie,' Jill says.

'With popcorn and Junior Mints.' I smile and head for the door to prepare my classroom for the day.

'Friends, I want you to think about the story.' I hold the bright orange hardcover up. A picture of a pensive purple dog is splashed across the cover. 'George had a lot of trouble in the first part of the book. So many things went wrong for him when his human left him home alone. Who can tell me some mistakes he made?'

'He chased the poor cat!' Alex shouts.

'He ate the entire cake on the counter,' Andrew adds.

'Who leaves an entire cake out when you leave?' Amanda's pigtails sway as she shakes her head.

'Who eats an entire cake?' Andrew asks and the A-Team are on fire this morning.

'George!' the entire class calls.

'He dug the dirt in the plant pot,' Eddie says.

'He was kind of a bad boy.' Danny dips his head, possibly from relating a little too much to George.

'Not kind of. He was a very bad boy,' Katherine says.

'But then he felt really awful about it,' Amanda says.

'Right, he sure did. But what did he do? To make it better?' I've turned to the page in the book where George is on a walk in the park with his owner.

'He did better!' Marley yells and my chest puffs. They're almost there.

'How did he do better?' I ask.

'He didn't chase the cat in the park. Or eat the cake of those people on a picnic,' Marley says.

'I love picnics,' Audrey says. She often shares about her picnics on the Eastern Prom with her family. 'And cake. But I've never brought a fancy cake on a picnic like that.'

'He didn't dig up the flowers,' Danny says.

'He made better choices!' Brian yells.

My head nods as they call out, and with the last declaration from Brian, a big smile springs up on my face.

Children process and learn by talking. Sure, shouting out may not be everyone's cup of tea, but I know they're engaged. They're taking turns and not talking over each other. It's productive talk and with Brian's summary, they've uncovered the kernel of wisdom I've hoped to share with them for this lesson.

'Yes! He made better choices. When you make a mistake, you can make a better choice the next time a similar situation arises – when you know better, you do better.'

The entire class leans toward me, eyes open, tracking my every word. They're in this with me – eager to learn. It's one of the things I love most about kindergarten. Their complete enthusiasm for whatever I teach.

'Have you ever made a mistake and then decided to make a better choice?' I ask.

They look at me, then at each other, and I slowly see a few light bulbs go off over their small heads.

'Let's turn and talk to our partners about a time we made a mistake and then did better. One time I made a mistake and did better was . . .'

Given a prompt, like clockwork, each child turns and talks. A gentle hum of focused conversation permeates from the carpet as they chat. But instead of listening in as I should, my mind wanders to Olan.

He mentioned doing better by his parents. His family. His mother. Living amends. Changing his behavior to show his mother he's sorry. Changed. And it's been years, but he's still doing it. And he'll never stop. He said it was a lifelong process he continually needed to show up for.

Just like my mother showed up on my doorstep. Sure, unexpectedly. Unannounced. Uninvited. But she's here – shopping at Hannigan's, packing Happy Meals, and making meatloaf. She's probably cleaning the oven. Who cleans their oven? Sarah Block. And, yes, she's possibly finding the sex toys Olan bought for us, but I'm not focusing on that right now.

When she started her recovery, she told me she was sorry, but I also remember her saying she would show me she was sorry by changing her behavior. Cold chills scatter up my arms. Time after time, my mother shows up and tries. Maybe it's about time I stop shutting her out.

'Mr Block? Are you okay?'

Marley's squeaky voice brings me back to the task at hand and a momentary pang of guilt slaps at my chest. I should have been listening for a few nuggets to share. Usually, I'm much better about being present with my students and I shake my head, hoping to center myself in the moment.

'Yes, all good. I just got distracted for a minute.'

'Happens to me all the time,' Marley says with a quick nod.

Marley's face softens with relief and he stares up at me with the rest of the class, waiting for my instructions.

'How was your day?'

Illona sits next to me on the bus as it heads down the hill toward the ferry.

'Fine. The "toy" your mother gave me in my "Happy Meal" was interesting.'

'Oh no. What was it?' I wince, afraid of what she's going to say.

Illona reaches into her backpack and pulls out a small,

banged-up compact. Opening it, she flashes the mirror toward me.

'It came with a note.'

She unfolds a small piece of paper, and there, in my mother's chicken scratch, it says: Look at how beautiful you are! Inside and out.

'That's sweet,' I say.

'Yeah, but it's no toy.'

'Fair.'

Illona plugs herself in to watch an episode of her new favorite show about a tween witch and I pull out my phone to a barrage of missed notifications.

> Sarah: Do you want mashed potatoes or macaroni and cheese with your meatloaf?

> Sarah: Bruce at Hannigan's was very helpful and friendly. Nice man.

> Sarah: Do you have a loaf pan? Casserole dish? A bundt pan? I can make it work.

> Sarah: Sorry, I know you're working. Found a loaf pan by poking around.

> Sarah: What time do you expect to be home? For dinner, I mean? Same time as yesterday? You didn't mention any meetings after school, but I know you have them sometimes.

> Sarah: Did you see my note in your lunch? If not, it read: Reach for the stars, Marvin!

> Sarah: OK, no more texting. I'll see you soon. Love you!

> Sheldon: I know Olan is away, but we should probably meet anyway. Tick, tock. We don't want to lose momentum. How about Saturday morning at Schmear and Far? I hear you love their bagels.

> Sarah: One more text. Your house smells like my meatloaf. Bye!

Oy. My mother never texted me this much from Arizona. Apparently, being here has opened the floodgates on communication. Deep breaths. I remind myself to stay open to her overtures. In a moment of weakness, overconfidence, delusion, or perhaps a mix of all three, I create a new group text.

> Marvin: Sarah, this is Sheldon. Sheldon, this is Sarah Block, my mom. I'm going to bring her on Saturday to our wedding planning session. We'll see you at 10. 😊

24

'Daddy!'

Illona's face lights up like the moon when she discovers Olan on my phone's screen. To ensure he could be a part of her tuck-in routine, we scheduled our chat to coincide with her bedtime, and he asked me to not tell her — he wasn't positive the timing would work out and also wanted to surprise her.

The pure joy on her face makes my heart melt and I hand over my phone so she can have him close.

'Princess. There's that beautiful face I miss. Are you keeping Marvin and Gonzo in line for me?'

'Of course I am,' she says. 'And Sarah too. I helped her make dinner tonight.'

My mother leans over Illona's shoulders and waves at Olan.

'Olan! How lovely to see you. I hope you're doing okay. Your daughter is well taken care of. We made lasagna. I know you're not vegetarians, but I used turkey meat anyway.'

Illona squints her eyes and tilts her head in confusion, but my mother is too focused on Olan to notice.

'It's a little healthier,' Sarah continues. 'Illona made the salad all by herself. She's got amazing knife skills.' Mom wraps her arm around Illona's shoulder and squeezes her.

'That's my little chef,' Olan says.

I can't see Olan's face from my view by the kitchen island, but I'm fairly certain he's smiling, and having him here, even only virtually, and for a short time, settles my soul.

'Are you enjoying your visit, Sarah?' Olan asks.

'I am. The highlight is spending time with this one.' She kisses the top of Illona's head. 'And my son, of course. I never tire of his face.'

'It's a good face.' Olan lets out a small laugh. 'Well, thank you for coming. I know it's hard with me being away and it sounds like you're offering much needed assistance.'

'Anything for my family,' Sarah says, and she shoots me a wink and a soft smile.

'Well, we need to be getting you to bed, young lady,' I say, knowing Olan has a limited amount of time.

'I can put myself to bed, thank you very much,' Sarah says. 'But thanks for noticing the new beauty cream I've been using. Look, less fine lines.' She pulls at the skin around her eyes.

'Not you, silly,' Illona says. 'Me. I'm already in my pajamas!'

'Oh my goodness.' My mother laughs and gives Illona a wink.

'Why don't you go upstairs and I'll be right up,' I say.

'Okay! Good night, Sarah.' Illona clutches her around

the waist, and she reaches down and strokes Illona's head. I can't recall the last time my mother was this happy.

'Good night, Sarah,' Olan says as Illona skips upstairs to bed with my phone in hand.

'Good night!' Mom yells back, but I'm not sure he's heard her, as Illona has him at the top of the landing already.

'I'm going to help tuck her in and then chat a little with him in the bedroom before I hit the hay,' I say.

'Sounds good, sweetie.' Sarah sits on the couch and pulls her legs underneath herself. 'I'm going to stay up and read a little. I'm dying to find out who the killer is.'

She holds up a new book.

'Where did you get that?'

'Hannigan's. Bruce and I were talking about thrillers and he recommended this one. They sell books, right next to the aspirin. You truly never need to leave the island if you don't want to.'

I walk over and kiss the top of her head.

'Love you,' she says.

'I love you too, Mom. Thanks again for dinner. The lasagna was fantastic.'

'Illona made the salad all by herself. I can see why you adore her so much.' She grabs the throw from the back of the couch and blankets her legs. 'And you're welcome. It's what moms do.'

I pull my lips in and nod. Yeah, it is what moms do.

Upstairs in Illona's bedroom, I sit on the edge of her bed, the pink comforter bunched up around her. Illona lies with my phone propped up against an extra pillow on her stomach. Her room always smells like bubble gum and lavender to me, which is strange since she doesn't chew gum or have any lavender products I know of. Olan says some of her stuffies came with the fragrance infused into their DNA, but I prefer to just think of it as Illona's scent. Simple, calming, and sweet.

She's quiet, and I hear the low tone of Olan's voice coming from the tiny speaker.

'And your mom was convinced she had all the time in the world before your arrival, so she insisted on taking a shower, putting on makeup, and checking her hospital bag for her favorite slippers.'

'The yellow fuzzy ones,' Illona says.

In the two years since we've lived together, I've heard this story many times. I can't decide who derives more joy – Illona from hearing her birth story or Olan from recounting it.

'Yes, the yellow fuzzy ones.' Olan laughs. Even though the sound from the phone is minimal, its impact is magnified in the peacefulness of bedtime, as his deep chuckle reverberates through the room.

'She still has them.' The smile on Illona's face is priceless and I'm deeply grateful they're on video and Olan can enjoy it.

'She does.'

Now, Isabella has confided in me the fuzzy yellow slippers in question are actually a new pair that replaced the original 'birth story' pair, but we're not telling Olan or Illona that. Let them maintain the magic of their story.

'So, after a couple of hours, your mom told me she was finally ready, and we got in the car to head to the hospital.'

Illona cuddles in with Noelle, her favorite stuffed kitty, while Gonzo makes a spot near her feet. She's told me this

197

is her favorite part of the story and I'm eager to watch her reaction.

'When we finally got there, the nurse put your mom into a wheelchair and started pushing her to the room where we'd wait, but then –'

Illona's eyes burst open. She knows the story by heart, and she's too excited to not interrupt her father. 'I came early! Before you made it to the room, there I was. Born in the hospital hallway. The nurse did most of the work, 'cause nurses can do anything, and the doctor ran up when I was already born.'

'Yes, princess. You couldn't wait to see us. And we were over the moon – we finally got to meet you.'

'And Mommy says that's when she knew I wasn't going to be someone to wait around for things to happen.'

'That's right. And that you'd always be early. Which you are.'

'It shows you care.' She kisses Noelle's ear.

'You were the sweetest angel. You still are.'

'And then you sang to me.'

'I did.'

Olan sings the first verse of 'Isn't She Lovely,' and Illona's face beams with pure joy. Her dad's voice is . . . not great. Okay, not even serviceable. His soft, monotone bass doesn't land on any of the actual notes in the song, but Illona doesn't care. And why would she? He's singing to her. Crooning that she's lovely, wonderful, precious, a genuine gift from God, made from love.

The sound of the man I love singing to his daughter stirs something within me, like a dormant parental clock coming to life. Having my own children may not have been something I saw for myself, but being Illona's step-father is the perfect fit for my parenting abilities, and I am eagerly embracing the opportunity.

Olan finishes the chorus, pauses, and says, 'I love you, princess.'

'I love you too, Daddy.'

She puts the screen up to her face and gives it a soft kiss and I hear Olan do the same. Yeah, his fathering prowess floods my basement.

Illona hands me the phone and I see Olan's face, full of love for his daughter, and I'm beyond grateful video call technology allows us to feel almost like we're together. I miss his body, though – his thick arms, his beefy thighs, his delicious dick.

'One second,' I tell him and put the phone on the bed-side table.

'You sleep well, sweetheart,' I whisper. 'It made your daddy's day, seeing your beautiful face and talking to you.'

Illona's already pulled the covers up to her chin and turned on her side, clutching Noelle for dear life. I kiss the top of her head and turn her light off.

'Good night, Marvin.' Her voice, tired and soft, is barely audible, but I'm careful to take in every syllable.

Phone in hand, I walk toward our bedroom, the soft-ness of Illona's carpet cushioning each step. Anticipation bubbles within me, knowing that the moment to chat with Olan alone has finally arrived.

25

'There's my adorable fiancé.' Olan's voice wraps around me like a warm embrace, easing the tension in my shoulders and bringing a serene calm to my entire body. It's low. Deep. Rich. Hearing him makes me miss him more than I thought possible, but I'm so grateful he's able to carve out some time for us tonight. 'It looks like things are going well on the home front?'

'Honestly, yes. I know she misses you terribly, but Illona is being a trooper. And keeping her typical routine is helping me as much as her.'

Illona acts as a tether, constantly connecting me to Olan, even more so when he is not around.

Lying on our bed, with Olan's handsome face in front of me, my arm instinctively reaches toward the vacant side of the bed, wishing he was there. Wishing I could touch him.

'Good. I hoped that would occur. Isabella is more than happy to pick up any extra slack, but it appears that won't be necessary. Illona doesn't just adore you. She loves you.

You're going to be her stepfather soon. Nobody is more pleased about that than me.'

'Well, she might beat you.' Carefully, I position a throw pillow on my stomach, using it as a makeshift stand for my phone.

'Fair. And I'm more than content to let her win the title of Most Pleased at Marvin Being Illona's Stepfather. A little long for a sash, but we can figure something out.'

I smile at his silly dad joke, but also at his face. Those beautiful, deep brown eyes. Even on the phone's small screen, they tempt me. That damn tooth gap, which still makes my insides simmer after two years. When I first met him, I wasn't sure it was possible for him to be more sexy, but falling in love with him has somehow made him even more handsome.

'And things with your mom seem to be well, too?' Olan's left eye winces slightly, waiting for my reply.

'Yeah.' When the word comes out of my mouth, I'm both surprised and relieved at the revelation. 'She's been amazing. Cooking. Cleaning. Doing the laundry. Grocery shopping. I think Bruce might be flirting with her.'

'From Hannigan's?'

'Yes. She bought a thriller on his recommendation.'

'Well, good for her. And him.'

'It's been surprisingly easy having her here. Besides the first day I left her alone. She rearranged the living room furniture, but I quickly moved it back and told her we didn't need her playing Nate Berkus for us.'

Olan chuckles. 'Wait, what?'

'Yeah, she moved the couch so it was facing the sitting chairs. She said it was more conducive to conversation.'

'She moved the couch by herself?'

'Don't underestimate my mother's upper arm strength. She may look small, but with all those water aerobics classes she takes three times a week, she could lift an elephant.'

'Noted. Do not piss off your mother.'

'Please, she adores you. Sometimes I wonder if she loves you more than me.'

'That's ridiculous. Of course she doesn't.'

'Olan, her lock screen is a photo of us.'

'Us. You're in it too.'

'Yeah, but half my face is cropped off.'

'Oh my gosh, really?' Olan lets out a loud laugh and quickly covers his mouth. 'I'm sorry, but that's hilarious.'

I purse my lips and nod. 'Laugh it up, pretty boy.'

'Hey, I can't help it. This is the mug God gave me.' He moves his hand away, revealing his million-dollar smile. I glance at the closed door and wonder if I might convince him to get naked with me.

'And I thank the Lord every day for that punim.'

'I wouldn't take the cropped photo personally. Your mom knows very little about technology. She calls you for help to record shows on her DVR. Plus, it's simpler for her with me. I'm not her son. We don't have the same history you have.'

'Oh, I don't mind at all. I'm happy she worships you. It makes my life easier.'

'I miss you,' Olan says. He lets out a slow sigh and maybe knowing his heart aches as much as mine should console me, but it doesn't. 'Speaking of family, there's more I need to tell you.' Olan stands, and I can see he's in a small room, but the video shakes as he walks and it's hard to make out any details beyond the light gray walls. 'There. Just wanted to shut the door.'

He's back on a chair, or maybe on a bed, I'm not sure. He's sitting with the phone close enough that I can't make out much else, and I'm perfectly fine with that.

'I know I wrote to you about what's going on here with Liam,' he says. 'But there's more.'

More? What more could there be than Liam's girlfriend passing away from an overdose? I take a deep breath, the electricity from finally having some private time with Olan evaporating into trepidation about what he's about to tell me.

'What is it?' I ask.

'I'm going to ask you to just listen. Is that okay?'

I nod.

'Abby overdosed six months ago. It's what caused Liam to come back and live with my parents. They tried an outpatient program, but with . . . everything else, it wasn't working. Not for Liam, but also not for my folks.'

I bob my head slowly, listening, and doing my best to focus and not let my mind wander to what I might want to say. Olan never asks me to be quiet and listen, and I want to respect his wishes. His chin quivers and I wish I could reach through the phone to comfort him.

'There's more. A baby.'

Chills march in formation, running down my spine and causing my mouth to hang open in silence. Olan asked me to just listen and as luck would have it, I'm unable to speak. A baby?

'Gregory was born a few weeks before . . . everything.'

Gregory. The name echoes in my head like a promise.

'When the paramedics arrived, they discovered him sleeping near Liam. He's been with my parents ever since. I wasn't told about him until I got home. Imagine my surprise. Walking into my parents' home with my dad holding a baby. My mother didn't want me to worry. Part of me wonders if she thought I wouldn't come. Which is ridiculous. She knows I adore babies.'

I smile and wonder, did I know Olan loves babies?

'We're not sure if Abby was using when she was pregnant, but the doctors seem to think not. Which could explain her overdose. Her body couldn't handle it after months of being clean. So far, it appears Gregory is okay – he's hitting all the milestones. Babbling. So much babbling. Grasping and reaching for toys. People. Me. And the crawling has commenced. My parents raised three boys, so they have experience with babies, but it's been a long time. And they're older.'

Olan smiles, and I return a grin, still quiet and nodding, taking it all in. His face lights up when he mentions Gregory. It's reminiscent of the way he appears while discussing Illona.

'Liam has expressed an awareness that he's in no place to be a parent right now. He's hoping my folks will take custody. I brought up foster care, and my parents said it's not an option. Once he's entered the system, removing him would be extremely difficult.'

I nod in agreement.

'He's a beautiful baby. Sweet. Snuggly. He's part of why I've been so distracted. I'm trying to balance helping my parents with their emotions around rehab, caring for a six-month-old, and going to the center for Liam. I postponed sharing about him because it didn't seem appropriate to convey through a text, email, or a quick phone call. But Marvin, he's a light. An angel. He gives the most amazing side-eye. My father says, "He's a Stone all right with that look." He didn't ask to be born into this situation, and as his uncle, I owe it to him, to Liam, and to my parents, to help however I'm able. It's hard for me not to see Illona in him. He's just so incredible. I'll text you a photo when we get off the call.'

I open my mouth, but wait, making sure Olan's finished and ready for me to talk.

'Go ahead,' he says. 'That's it.'

'I . . .' My brain treads water, trying to stay afloat. 'I'm not sure what to say. It's a relief to know that you're there. I can't even imagine what it's like for your parents. For Liam. For the baby – Gregory – to not have his mother . . . or his father. Oy.'

'He's doing better than anyone expected. There's a lot of love coming his way and so far, he appears to be thriving. He'll be okay.'

'Is there anything I can do to help?'

'Just keep things calm there.' Olan scratches his chin and I focus on his mouth for a moment. Fuck, I wish I could kiss him.

'Isabella knows. We'll tell Illona she has a new cousin when the time is right. I'll definitely keep you posted about that.'

'Of course. Whatever you need.'

'Thank you,' he says.

'For what?'

'For understanding. For listening. For being the love of my life.'

'I love you.' As the words escape my lips, I realize their inadequacy in expressing the intensity of my feelings. I bring the phone to my face and kiss near the camera. 'So much. Be safe and text me soon.'

'Of course. And I'll email more, as well.'

'I love them. So much. I made a folder to save them.'

'Speaking of, I almost forgot your Motown lesson.'

'Ready.' I sit up straight, doing my best star student impression.

'I know I massacred it, but "Isn't She Lovely" has such a special place in my heart. Stevie wrote it for his daughter, Aisha. That's a real baby crying in the song. They recorded it during childbirth, although not Aisha's. There are sounds of Stevie bathing her toward the end of the song. It's a love letter from a father to his child, and that's why I sing it to Illona.'

'She loves it. The song and you singing it to her.'

'Luckily, she's not critical of my less-than-radio-ready voice.'

'She's no Simon Cowell. And you're her dad. She's enamored with everything you do.'

Olan smiles and nods. 'Okay, I should probably go,' he says. 'We're transitioning Greggie to baby food, but he still gets a few bottles, and I've been taking the middle of the night shift for my parents while I'm here.'

'Greggie?' The nickname makes my heart melt like butter on warm toast.

'My mom came up with it. It's small and cute. Just like him.'

'I love it. Completely adorable.'

'Just like you,' Olan says with a grin, his eyes twinkling mischievously. 'Okay, my love. Sleep well.'

'You too. And Olan, I'm proud of you. For doing all this for your family. Just more proof of what a good man you are. Good night.'

Olan kisses near his phone's camera and then ends the call.

I take a deep breath, yearning to experience the warmth of his presence in the same room. Touch his skin. Kiss his lips. Hold him tight. There's so much more happening than Liam being in rehab, which is big enough on its own. But a baby. Olan's nephew. Illona's cousin. The open-ended ticket suddenly appears to be a much wiser choice given the circumstances. Olan is committed to supporting his parents as they adapt to having a new addition to the family. But he can't stay forever.

I slide under the covers and turn the bedside light off, hoping all this new input doesn't keep sleep at bay too long. As I place my phone on the nightstand, a text comes through.

> Olan: So good to see your face. ILY! Here's Greggie. Mom took the pic during his bath tonight.

A photo comes through of a baby boy in a blue plastic tub on a table. One of Olan's hands cradles him while the other holds a washcloth to his chest. Greggie has chubby cheeks and a smile as he peers off camera, presumably at his uncle washing him. His hair resembles Olan's, but it's shorter and cropped much closer to his head.

There's a sudden spark in my core, something I've never felt before, and I'm not sure I can name it. But I have an overwhelming desire to make sure this child is cared for. I'm beyond grateful Olan is with him. I may have won Teacher of the Year, but Olan's the Father of the Year every year, and I have zero doubts he's also cinching Uncle of the Year with Greggie.

Marvin: He looks so much like Illona.

Olan: His mother was white too.

Marvin: I meant they look like they could be siblings.

Olan: Well, they're cousins.

Marvin: He's perfect.

Olan: He is. ♥

26

Olan: Happy Saturday sunshine! I love and miss you.

Marvin: Sarah and I are headed in to meet Sheldon for some wedding planning. Why are you up so early?

Olan: Greggie was hungry. And needed some snuggles.

Marvin: Tell him his Uncle Marvin feels that.

Olan: Roger. Have fun and be safe. ♥

Sarah joins me on the nine o'clock ferry to meet Sheldon in town. The realization of being alone with my mother all weekend came crashing down on me like a boulder when Isabella picked Illona up after school yesterday. This meeting with Sheldon could've been an escape for a few hours. A lifeline. Instead, Sarah sits across from me, wearing a maroon 'Mother of the Groom' T-shirt as the wind blows both our curls. Much to her chagrin, I refused to wear the matching 'Groom #1' shirt she had made for me. She assured me Olan would wear his 'Groom #2' shirt if he were here, and much to *my* chagrin, she's probably right.

'This Schmear and Far place – are the owners Jewish?' Mom asks.

'I'm not sure. With that name, I'm guessing so, but I don't really know,' I say.

'I'll know. After one bite. I'll know.'

'Mother, you can't tell if the owners are Jewish from one bite of their bagels.'

'Can't I? You'll see. I'll ask before we leave.'

'You will not.'

'Won't I?'

She most certainly will. Oy.

I decided not to tell my mother about Greggie. The mere mention of children sends the bubbe portion of her brain into overdrive, and I fear what bringing up a baby might do. But I can't stop thinking about him. Olan holding him. Olan feeding him. Olan playing with him. Right from the start, Olan's exceptional parenting skills with Illona were a total turn-on. Keep your dark and broody, morally gray men – I'll take an exemplary father any day, please, and thank you very much.

There was something in Olan's eyes when he talked about Greggie. I wonder if that's what he was like when Illona was a baby. I'll ask Isabella. Apparently, Olan loves babies. How did I not know this about him? But also, the way he dotes on Illona, this wouldn't be earth-shattering news. *News Flash: Amazing Father Also Loves Babies.*

'Marvin? Where did your mind wander off to?'

'Sorry, Mom. Just thinking about the wedding,' I lie.

I'll tell her. Just not now.

'I brought my notebook.' She pulls a small black-and-white composition notebook out of her handbag. As a child, I used to imagine her purse was like Mary Poppins's bag – filled to the brim with the entire contents of a pharmacy along with assorted knick-knacks and snacks. One time she asked me to find her lipstick and I went spelunking, scouring through hidden pockets and compartments, finally finding it at the bottom under half a bag of cashews. My mother could pull a machete out of her purse and I wouldn't be shocked.

'Good,' I say. 'It will be helpful to take notes. Sheldon is very . . . passionate. There will be lots to write down.'

When we walk into Schmear and Far, Sheldon waits at a table with Theo, who once again looks like a small boy dragged into the lingerie section of the department store with his mother.

'Which one is Sheldon?' Mom whispers by the door, but before I can answer, Sheldon stands, wearing a maroon shirt with the words 'Wedding Planner' sprawled across his chest in bright purple, bordered by rainbow glitter.

'Mother, how did you two . . .'

'Sarah!' Sheldon shouts. He runs over and embraces her. 'I'm so happy to meet you in person. I hope I matched the color and fonts correctly. I was going strictly off your photo.'

'You did! But this glitter.' She motions to Sheldon's chest.

'Glitter makes everything better,' he says, raising his chin.

'It sure does. This one' – she nods toward me – 'refused to wear his shirt.'

'Are you being a grumpy pants about wedding planning?'

Sheldon hugs me and then lowers his voice to a whisper in my ear. 'You'll have to sit at the grumpy pants' table with Theo.'

'I heard that,' Theo says from his seat. He looks, well, grumpier than usual. 'And I'm not grumpy. I'm hungry. You said we couldn't order until they got here. They're here. Can we please eat now?'

'This is Theo?' Sarah asks.

Sheldon nods and says, 'He hasn't had breakfast, and, well . . .'

'I totally understand,' Sarah says. 'I get cranky when my blood sugar is low, too. Let's get our food, then we can chat about the wedding.' She holds her notebook up and Sheldon's eyes go wide.

'A notebook! How precious. I've got my planner in my bag. I can't wait to show you, but first, bagels. Theo, let's order!'

When we're all seated with bagels piled high with fixings, Sheldon reaches for his backpack.

'Theo, you were right about the pastrami lox,' Sarah says. 'I never knew how much I needed this in my life.' She takes a bite and emits a noise to convey her complete pleasure. 'Can I date this bagel? Is that a thing now? I'm bagel-sexual.' She laughs at her own joke and Theo, mouth full, shoots me a perplexed look. 'And the owner is Jewish. Or at least whoever makes the bagels.'

Sheldon pulls his planner from his bag. It's the Miss Universe of Planners to Mom's Regional Third Place Notebook. It's a massive, purple, and sparkly spiral-bound affair. He moves his plate over toward Theo and plops the planner down.

'You don't want your bagel?' Theo asks.

'Maybe half. I had a yogurt before we left.'

Theo raises his eyebrows.

'You can have the other half, baby.'

This sends a smile shooting across Theo's face and he promptly moves half of Sheldon's bagel and lox onto his plate.

'Now, I've done some preliminary work.' Sheldon opens the giant book and flips pages. There are mood boards with photos. Fabrics. One page seems to have what appears to be a twig glued to it. Oy. 'Based on what Marvin told me, I was thinking we could go with blue hydrangeas. They're native to Maine, inexpensive, and classic.' Sheldon pulls what I think is a flower petal from a page. It's sad and limp between his fingers.

'Very nice,' Sarah says, tilting her head down and peering over her glasses. 'And if we need a complementary flower, delphinium are pretty.' She holds up her notebook and reveals a photo of a blue flower in a field. Unlike Sheldon's live one, the flower in the picture is erect and full of life.

'Love.' Sheldon holds his pitiful petal next to Sarah's photo. 'What do you think?' Sheldon asks.

Before I can speak, Theo, with a full mouth, mumbles, 'I like blue.'

'Yes, my cream puff, I know you love blue, but I need to know what Marvin prefers.'

Theo's eyes narrow at Sheldon's term of endearment, his expression turning into a mix of annoyance and amusement. These two could not be any cuter if they tried.

'Oh, yeah, blue flowers. These are both beautiful, but

it's actually blue roses.' I open my mouth and grin, showing all my teeth.

'Blue roses?' Sarah asks. 'What kind of mishigas is this? There's no such thing as a blue rose. Yellow, white, orange, even green. Red, of course, but blue? Not a thing.'

'We'd have to buy white,' Sheldon says. 'And then have them dyed blue. It's totally possible. There's a guy in Kennebunk who did it for one of the Kennedys' weddings a few years ago.'

'Hmmm, that would work,' Sarah says. 'It's a little unusual.' She shrugs.

'Strange or not.' Sheldon writes something in his planner. 'We want the grooms to be happy. And we'll say . . . unique.'

'What does Olan want?' Theo wipes a smidge of cream cheese from his face and then picks up Sheldon's half bagel and takes a bite.

Sarah and Sheldon both look at me, waiting for an answer.

'I don't think Olan cares. He'd probably be fine with carnations.'

Sarah and Sheldon share a synchronized gasp, their astonishment echoing through the seating area.

Sheldon clutches his shirt near the collar, careful to avoid the glittered lettering.

'As if.'

'No carnations,' I say. 'Noted.'

'Let me call the guy in Kennebunk and see what we can do.' Another page flip, and more scribbling.

'Holy cow, this pastrami lox – I'm plotzing. I'm going to buy some to bring home with us, sweetie.' Mom taps my arm and heads for the counter.

'Told ya!' Theo shouts after her.

'I love your mom,' Sheldon says softly. I'm fairly certain Sarah can hear him from the counter ten feet away, but she's engrossed in conversation with the poor mensch helping her.

'Yeah, she's a hoot,' I say. 'Listen, I know she has lots of ideas, and I appreciate you acting interested, but you don't have to . . .'

'Marvin, no.' Sheldon flips open his planner and points to a printed page. 'She's got wonderful concepts. Look at the drink list she sent me. We need to pick a signature drink for your cocktail – sorry, mocktail hour. All these drinks feature blue Curacao syrup, adding both flavor and vibrant color, without any alcohol. We'll have a mixing and tasting party at our place. I'll make the drinks and Theo will make hors d'oeuvres.'

'I'll do what?' Hearing his name, Theo looks up from his phone.

'Noshes, for a mocktail tasting party, baby. The drinks will be sweet.'

'Got it,' Theo says, returning to his phone with new enthusiasm.

'Don't worry, Marvin, it will be fun. And relax, your mom is fantastic. She's just . . . overly enthusiastic. Better than not interested at all.'

Sheldon's lips curl downward and I'm reminded of his family situation. It's just him and his twin sister. Theo's parents have taken them all in, but he has no contact with the rest of his family. I should be more grateful for my mom's interference. For God's sake, she flew to Maine (yes, unannounced, but still) because she wanted to help.

'I got half a pound.' Sarah returns, holding up her prize, a package crisply wrapped in white butcher paper stamped with illustrated red salmon. 'And I was right.' She sits and leans toward the center of the table and lowers her voice. 'The owner is Jewish. Bernie Stein. You went to preschool together. Do you remember Ada and Joel Stein? From Brooklyn. Those are his parents. Such a nice boy.'

I don't remember Bernie. Preschool. Or the Steins, but I'm not telling her that.

'Of course. You called it, Mom,' I say.

With my arm around her shoulder, I feel a sense of comfort as I pull her close. With each act of love from my mother, the tiny fractures in my heart from childhood carefully stitch together, creating a new, stronger seam. Over time, I realize, wounds have a way of healing, not just through time but through love – the kind that reassures you, that reminds you of your worth, that makes you believe in the beauty of second chances. In her embrace, I find not only solace but a profound sense of belonging, a reminder that even the most broken hearts can become whole again.

27

To: MrAdorable@StonyBlock.com
From: OnlyStone4U@StonyBlock.com
Sent: 3/25 at 2:33 A.M.
Subject: Reach Out (I'll Be There)

Dear Marvin,

I miss you. I miss kissing your face. Holding you in bed. Being
held by you. You do this thing where you wrap your arm around
my chest and your palm floats between my torso and stomach.
When you touch me, I'm instantly calmed and lulled into a state
of blissful sleep. How do you make me feel so incredibly loved?

My parents are asking about you. That's a good sign. After
two years, I think they finally understand me being with a man
isn't a phase, nor an indicator of their success as parents. My
mom loves that you're a teacher. It's a connection point for
her. They're not sure about making it for the wedding, only
because of everything going on here. Even though it's hard for

my mother to talk about, I know she feels responsible for Liam. Barring another crisis, he should be in a sober house within a few weeks, but we don't know if he'll be in a place to travel by August and I'm not sure they'd leave Chicago without him. All things that will work themselves out.

As I type this, your soon-to-be nephew is plastered to my chest in a sling. The pediatrician advises against letting him sleep in this position for extended periods, but since he's still waking up at least once during the night to eat, putting him in the sling after a bottle is the fastest way to get him back to sleep. An added bonus – I love it. Having his head on my chest. His sweet baby smell. Feeling his tiny heartbeat. He's been through so much and he seems to be bonding with me. After being Illona's dad, being Gregory's uncle might be my next greatest achievement.

There's a magic that happens when you hold a baby, Marvin. I remember when Illona was this small. All she wanted to do was cuddle. Nothing made her happier than being snuggled up with the two of us in bed. Isabella coined the term 'cuddle bubble' for our cherished spot, where we would spend hours snugly intertwined like puzzle pieces that had finally discovered their perfect match. There's a coziness, a warmth, a complete feeling of serenity when a baby sleeps with you – I think you'd love it.

Greggie weighs eighteen pounds. When I'm holding him, every atom of his body depends on me. There's no feeling more perfect than the warmth of a baby snuggled close. He's completely trusting and vulnerable and did I mention the baby smell? Sometimes, when he's in his highchair, I catch my father sniffing the curls on his head and the biggest grin overtakes my face because I understand completely. Right now, he's making

218

the tiniest little rumbling, or maybe it's a gurgling while he sleeps. I wish you could hear it. I'm not sure my phone would pick it up, but I can try recording it. I'm pretty confident this is what angels sound like when they slumber.

My parents and I have been talking more about the situation. Liam. Greggie. It's stirring up emotions for my parents and adding to the tension here. Marvin, I need you to know more about my family's history with alcoholism and recovery.

Liam began drinking when I was away at college. My parents didn't want me to worry, but they also couldn't hide the situation for long. I was having issues with drinking and when I went into rehab, my parents decided it was too much to share about Liam's struggles. Addiction is a family disease. The impact of its use extends beyond just the individual; it affects the entire family, who must bear the consequences.

Liam was a senior and missing classes. He'd been an excellent student until then, but his grades plummeted. My mother's brother had died from the disease, and having not one, but two sons afflicted was too much for her to handle. She was convinced alcoholism was a psychological problem. She wondered if a therapist could help Liam. Coming out of rehab, I knew a therapist wasn't the only answer, but my mother didn't want to talk about it. And my father wanted to protect her. So I retreated into my shell. I not only avoided the topic with my parents, but I also kept my distance from Liam, hardly speaking to him. I knew he was spiraling and instead of running toward him to help, I bolted away. Looking back, I understand my actions were a defense mechanism, and I'm not proud of how I handled the situation.

But I can't run away now. Not from my parents. Not from Liam. And certainly not from this precious baby.

I spoke to Gabe last night. He's worried about the situation, but not in a place to offer more than emotional support. His work demands that he spend three weeks out of every month traveling, leaving him with only one precious week to spend with his own family back in Anaheim. Thankfully, the alcoholic gene skipped Gabe in our family. His understanding of things falls short compared to mine.

Mom and Dad have agreed to take custody. This way Greggie stays with family and can see and know his father. I know it's challenging for Liam, but he seems to understand that, with his track record, he may never be capable of being solely responsible for his son. I told him this was the most loving act he could perform. It was a tough conversation. I held my little brother while he sobbed. It was probably both his darkest hour, but also the most loving thing he'll ever do for his son. And I've never felt closer to him. I told him I was sorry for not being there when he was struggling. For not trying to slap some sense into him. For not being the big brother he needed.

This is my chance to do right by Liam.

I swore to do everything I could to make sure his son was taken care of. Of course, I'll help financially. I offered to pay for a nanny, but my parents won't hear of it. They're proud. They'd never have anyone in their house helping. My father always teased me about Cindy. 'You and that wife have all that money in the world, but can't take care of one little girl.' They're just of a different mindset. We've talked about maybe having Greggie come stay with us in Maine for a month during the summers.

Don't worry, I can take time off. This way, he can stay connected to his uncles and cousin. I've already talked to Isabella and she'll do whatever we need to help.

That's probably a few years away, but something for you to think about.

Okay, I should put this little peanut in his crib and try to get a few hours of sleep myself.

But not before a quick lesson.

'Reach Out (I'll Be There)', sometimes written without the parentheses, was not only the biggest hit of the Four Tops' career but widely considered one of the best songs of all time. Did you know after they recorded it, the band disliked the song so much, they begged the label not to release it as a single? Of course, the all-knowing head of Motown, Mr Berry Gordy, insisted it was a hit, and the rest is history.

Take a listen to the song. Listen to the words. This is what a living amends is all about. We don't have to speak about it, but my family knows whatever they need, all they need to do is reach out, and I'm there. I need this baby to know I'm here for him, too. To shelter him. Love him. Protect him. Even from far away.

I love you, Marvin Block. You make me want to be a better man – that's not something to take lightly. Please be safe and know I'm thinking of you. Always.

We'll talk soon.

All my love,

Olan

28

'A surprise baby? Whoa. I didn't see that coming.'

Jill pulls her head back, recoiling in surprise.

'Neither did I. But Olan is committed to helping his family and, well, Greggie is his nephew.'

'Greggie?' Her face softens and her forehead wrinkles. 'That might be the cutest name I've ever heard.'

'Right? Short for Gregory. You should hear Olan say it. It's adorable.'

Olan's email has my head and heart in a whirlwind of emotions. He's always been a kind, loving partner, but reading these letters peels back new layers and once again, I find myself falling deeper in love with Olan Stone. Or maybe I'm just missing him. Or horny for him. Or all of the above.

Olan's email only cemented his connection to his nephew. The way he was writing about Greggie, pouring out his feelings and emotions, left my head spinning by the end of the letter. I wasn't able to chat with Isabella about it because she had Illona. We texted a few times, and she assured me everything would work out. Olan brings a sense of peace and calm to everything he touches, and Isabella reminded me he would carry that energy over to his family's current situation.

I almost told my mother. This morning, she was cradling Gonzo, making baby noises at him and it practically slipped out. But I need Jill's counsel first. Witnessing my mother's reaction to Illona has been very sweet, but I fear she'll become unhinged at the mention of a baby. The dormant bubbe inside her will spring to life like a volcano stirring from its slumber, ready to erupt after years of quiet stillness. I need to be ready for that energy.

'And Olan's parents are taking custody?' Perched across from me on a student table, Jill pulls her legs up and crosses them, leaning forward.

My lips form a thin line, and I nod.

'Good. That's smart. Makes perfect sense.' Jill's eyebrows collide in the center of her forehead. Perhaps the gravity of the situation has tampered with her quips. 'Does all this family talk have your uterus catching baby fever?'

Or maybe not.

'Contrary to what you may believe, Ms Kim, I do not, in fact, have a uterus. And baby fever? No ma'am. The thought of being Illona's stepfather is enough to send my anxiety into overdrive. And she's seven.'

'Going on twenty-seven.'

'Exactly. Illona, I can handle. Or she can handle me is more like it. But a baby? No way. I'd break it.'

'You watched Maria on your own. And you had fun.'

My mind replays little Maria leaping on the bed uncontrollably from the extra sweets I gave her. The dread curdling in my stomach from knowing I didn't follow Jill's directions. The guilt about my misstep comes crawling up like bile, and I blurt out the truth.

'Even though you said only to give her one cookie, I gave her three. Okay, three and a half, she ate half of one of mine. So almost four cookies.' I bow my head in shame. 'Those cookies were . . . interesting. Something was off. Don't get me wrong, I still ate a bunch. But do they think toddlers don't enjoy a quality chocolate-chip cookie? What's in those things?'

'Beets.' Jill pinches her face and shrugs. 'It's a way to sneak more vegetables into her diet.'

'In cookies? The goyim have lost their damn minds.'

'Very true,' Jill says, nodding.

'Anyway, I'm sorry, but she was jumping on her bed and I couldn't get her to settle down and I didn't want to bother you during your night out with Nick so I called Isabella and she talked me down from the ledge.'

Jill's face shows little emotion, and I rush to finish my confession.

'Maria crashed after maybe fifteen minutes and, well, you saw, she fell asleep on me. I am so not cut out to be a parent. No way. I'd give Greggie all the cookies and send him into a sugar rush tailspin.'

'Marvin, breathe.' Jill reaches across the table, taking my hand. Her skin is always so soft and the light floral scent of her lotion soothes me. 'Do you think you're the first person to question their ability to parent? Look at me and Nick. How they let us take Maria home from the hospital is still a mystery to me. Do you know why I told you to only give her one cookie?'

Jill removes her hand from mine, readjusting herself on the table.

'Because the first time I bought them, I let her have six. Six. And she didn't crash after fifteen minutes. She was up all night. Dancing. Screaming. Jumping. I thought we were going to have to perform an exorcism.' Her hands re-enact a wild Maria. 'And then there's Nick. He still leaves his towel on the floor after a shower. He still forgets to flush when he takes a dump. But you know what he's terrific at? Being Maria's dad. When he bathes her, he tells her to hang up her towel. We're potty training Maria and her favorite part about it all? Flushing the damn toilet. Because her dad made a game out of it. He can't remember to flush himself, but he created a flushing song for his daughter. *Flush, flush, flush away, all the pee and poo, merrily, merrily, merrily, watch them go adieu.*'

'Adieu?'

'Right? He made that up. It includes French, for fuck's sake.'

'Je suis impressionné,' I say, proud of remembering something from the two years of French I took in high school.

'Marvin, here's the thing about being a parent – kids don't come with instructions. And all the parenting books and mommy blogs in the world aren't going to tell you what's right for your kid – because each one is unique. You love your child, do the best you can, and understand from time to time you're going to royally mess up. But they're built to survive. Maria is doing just fine – even with all the extra cookies.'

'More than fine, if you ask me,' I say. 'And thank you. I honestly didn't think fatherhood was in the cards for me, but with Illona, I don't know, it just feels . . .'

'Natural,' Jill says. 'That's what happens when you love them. You figure it out.'

'Well, thankfully, Olan's parents are taking on that role with his nephew. And they've raised three boys so . . .'

'Yeah, you're right.' Jill stands and gives a firm nod. 'Totally for the best.'

She raises an eyebrow and turns toward her easel to finish writing her message.

'Okay, friends, let's get ready to share something we did over the weekend.'

I'm sitting on the floor, sandwiched between Michael and Marley. I've privately asked both boys to sit next to me on the carpet. They both tend to be squirrelly, chatty, and have trouble focusing. It makes everyone's lives easier if they're next to me. Like many children, Michael finds solace in plastering his entire body against my side, and this is enough to settle him. All Marley needs is a quiet hand on his shoulder to remind him of the rules. During the first few months of the school year, the other children would ask if they could sit next to me, but now they understand this is what these boys need. It's what's best for them and the entire class.

'When you share, it might sound like "this weekend I . . ." and remember it doesn't have to be anything particularly exciting like a birthday party – although yay if you went to one. It can just be something simple, like going to the store or playing a game with your family.'

There are lots of nods.

'I'll go first,' I say. 'This weekend I had breakfast with my mother.' I leave out the details about Sheldon, Theo, and the wedding planning to keep my share short.

'You're so lucky your mom is here,' Andrew says. His top lip quivers and I pray to Kelly Clarkson he doesn't have a crying relapse. The first two weeks of school, he cried. Every. Single. Day.

'When I'm grown up, I want my mom to live with me, too,' Amanda says. Andrew perks up at the possibility of this.

'My mom doesn't live with me,' I clarify.

'So she can take care of me,' Amanda continues, ignoring me.

'And my husband . . . or wife,' Riley says. My shoulders pull back with pride.

'And your baby, too. Moms are fantastic with babies,' Austin says. He would know. He's got six siblings.

'Daddies too,' Amanda says. She shoots me a wink, and it takes every ounce of restraint for me to hold back my laugh.

As usual, my short, simple share has completely derailed us. Instead of fighting it, I let them chat, doing my best to guide the conversation.

'Yes, most parents are good with babies,' I say. 'But when you grow up, usually, your parents don't live with you. My mom is only visiting.'

'Maybe she'll stay forever!' Andrew shouts and my heart does a little flip in my chest. Andrew would probably love it if his mother flew across the country to stay with him without a plan to leave.

'No, no, she's just helping while Olan is away. She's definitely not staying forever.'

I'm saying it for them, but also me. Truth is, I really haven't minded having her around. Even though I'm sure Illona and I would've been fine on our own, it's nice having the support. And let's be real, my meals are no competition for hers. I smile, thinking about the leftover chicken and rice she packed for our lunches today.

'But if you and Olan had a baby, maybe she could stay and help more?' Austin asks.

If Olan and I had a baby? Clearly, I'm not about to delve into the intricacies of reproduction and discuss the birds and bees with my class.

'We have Illona,' I remind them.

'She's not a baby,' Amanda says.

'But maybe she wants a little sister?' Ben asks. He often talks about wanting a sibling, but his parents confided during their parent conference, they have no plans to expand their family.

'Or brother?' Austin says.

My chest feels tight with all this family planning talk from my kindergarteners, and I decide it's time for me to get the train back on the tracks.

'I'm pretty sure Illona is very happy with Gonzo,' I assure them. 'Now, let's hear about your weekends.'

Olan informs me he has a baby nephew, and suddenly my world is screaming about babies. If she knew about Greggie, I'd think my mother had something to do with this.

But I meant what I told Jill – Illona is more than enough. She's the perfect child. Why would we want to play the slots and risk it with another? I remember all Olan's talk about Greggie. How caring for him is the most amazing feeling as a parent. The baby smells. The baby babbling. Baby this. Baby that. Reminiscing about Illona at that age. But Olan doesn't want another child. Or does he?

29

'Two handsome men without their partners. How did I get so lucky?'

Ruth sits next to Vincent at a round table inside East End Espresso. It's closer to my school than theirs, but the casual, clean vibe inside and access to easy off-street parking has made it Vincent and my usual meetup spot. Illona occupies the fourth chair and has her headphones on while she writes in her journal.

'Because Regina convinced Kent to be her pickleball partner,' Vincent says.

'You don't play?' I ask Ruth.

'Not with Regina. Mixing sports and' – she glances toward Illona – 'ex-say isn't a good idea.'

'She can't hear you,' I say. 'Plus, I'm pretty sure she's mostly figured out pig Latin by now.'

'Oh. Well, as long as you're sure she can't hear us.' Ruth purses her lips and glances at Illona.

'Illona,' I say. 'We're taking the rest of the week off and flying to Disney.'

Illona's concentrated face never leaves her notebook. Her purple pen flies as she records the sordid details of her day in second grade.

'See?'

'Yeah, but maybe just in case we should,' Vincent says as his lips curl into a sweet smile.

He's got a napkin in his lap and another rests folded on the table. With all his insecurities, Vincent has always been open to help. He's wanted advice and (mostly) listened and tried. Of course, he'll never be 'cured' of his OCD – that's not how it works. But he's learning to live with it, and most importantly, not beat himself up. He's come so far since I met him. I'd hoped we would stay in touch and become friends, and here he is, one of my closest confidants.

'You love pig Latin, don't you?' I ask.

'Up-yay. It's way more un-fay to talk about ex-say,' Vincent says and then covers his mouth as he giggles.

'When I met this one,' Ruth says with a nod toward Vincent, 'he wasn't this . . . orny-hay, but apparently living with a hot Jaddy will do this to you.'

'Uilty-gay,' Vincent says. 'I'm sure Olan would agree.'

Another burst of laughter from Vincent and I'm not sure I've ever seen him so giddy. His amusement is contagious, and I'm unable to stop my face from bursting into a massive smile.

'How is Mr Handsome?' Ruth asks. 'We've texted a few times since he's been back in Chicago, but I haven't heard from him in almost a week. I know family can be intense and I don't want to bother him, but you remind him Auntie Ruth is always here for him.'

Since they first met at Kent and Vincent's, I knew Olan and Ruth had been in touch, but I didn't realize he'd been texting with her while back home. My insides warm knowing he has a new friend as supportive as Ruth.

'He's good. Just dealing with a lot. It's not just his brother . . .'

'Greggie, his nephew. Have they made any decisions?' Ruth asks.

Olan told her and a zip of curiosity rushes through me, wondering if Ruth knew about Greggie before I did.

'Wait, he has a new nephew?' Vincent sips his black coffee and dabs at the corner of his mouth with a napkin.

'Yes,' I say, unsure how to explain the situation quickly and without diving into the details, especially with Illona so close.

'He's only six months old,' Ruth says, saving me. 'Olan's brother isn't in a place to take care of him and the family is trying to figure out the best course of action.'

Ruth winks at me and I wonder if it might be inappropriate to scoop her up in a giant bear hug. There's no mention of rehab, which I've already told Vincent about, but also no mention of Greggie's mother.

'I think their parents are going to take custody,' I say.

'That seems wise,' Ruth says. 'But, boy, is Olan fond of that baby.'

'And there's no way . . .' Vincent says but doesn't complete his thought.

'No way what?' I ask.

'You and Olan . . .' Vincent smirks and wipes his mouth again.

I shrug. 'He hasn't mentioned it.'

'Mentioned what?' Ruth asks. 'You two taking him?'

'I mean, he hasn't brought it up.' I take a sip of my espresso tonic, the bitterness mixing with sweetness from the quinine as the bubbles tickle my nose.

'Have you?' Ruth cocks her head and gives me what I'm assuming is her teacher look. Being a PE teacher, there's an athleticism to it.

Vincent joins her by tilting his head and raising his eyebrows as he glares at me.

'Me?' I pull my head back, attempting to avoid their dual eyeball interrogation.

'Yes, you.' Ruth dips her head and gives me what I'm going to call her Teacher Look Version 2.0: The Mid Boss.

'No. I mean, I haven't brought it up because I had no clue that was an option. Or that he'd want that. Or that we'd . . .' I nod to the side, indicating Illona. 'Be in a place to have a . . . ittle-lay other-bray in the ouse-hay.'

'Marvin, sometimes people tell you things without actually saying anything,' Ruth says. 'It's called an inference.'

'Like when I need another napkin, you just know. I don't have to ask anymore.' Vincent holds up the extra napkin near his coffee. 'All the talking about the . . . aby-bay. Maybe Olan's trying to feel you out. Gauge your reaction. Test the waters. See if you mention the possibility of custody.'

'Oh.' A dryness crackles through my mouth and it takes effort to swallow past the lump in my throat.

'Oh? Oh?' Ruth's stare evolves to its penultimate form – Teacher Look Version 3.0: The Final Boss.

Vincent places his hand on my forearm and offers a half smile. 'How do you feel about it?'

'I don't know. I hadn't really . . . I mean, she . . .' I nod at Illona. 'This is more than I ever thought I'd be parenting. And she's easy.'

'Yeah, this girl is the dream.' Ruth chuckles. 'Drinking her chocolate milk and writing her deep dark secrets while the adults kibbitz.'

'You never thought you wanted to be a father, and Illona's changed that.' Vincent moves his hand to Illona's shoulder. She looks up at him and smiles, then returns to her notebook. 'Maybe Olan's nephew might change how you feel about being an uncle.'

'Vincent's right,' Ruth says. 'Talk to your man.'

'Think about it.' Vincent tips his cup back, carefully swallowing the last sip of his coffee. 'You've always told me communication is key.'

'Damnit,' I say. 'I hate when my advice comes back to bite me in the ass.'

'At least something's biting your ass,' Ruth says.

'Munch, munch.' Vincent uses his hand as a makeshift puppet and pretends to chomp at my bum.

Vincent and Ruth flash a look at each other and burst out howling.

Illona, hearing the commotion, takes her headphones off, rolls her eyes. 'Adults. Oy.'

Her statement, delivered in a deadpan tone my mother

would adore, tickles my insides and I join my friends in their chorus of laughter.

> Marvin: Can we meet on the playground today? I'd love to chat for a min if you have time.

Isabella: Of course. See you soon. ☺

Under the late March sun, Illona sprints over to her mother and they share a long embrace. We typically do the Friday handoff in the classroom, but with the warmer weather, and me needing to talk, the playground allows us a little privacy while Illona plays with other kids whose parents are in no rush to leave school.

'Marvin and I need a few minutes, sweetie,' Isabella says. 'Leave your bag and go play.'

'Have fun kibbitzing!' she shouts and darts off toward the other children on the play structure.

'She really is learning so much from you.' Isabella pushes a loose strand of hair behind her right ear. It's such a simple gesture, but when she does it, there's such grace and beauty to her movement. I find myself lost in the moment. Her fingernails are painted a bright red, but there's some soft pink near the tips and I wonder how long it takes for someone to make that happen.

We're standing near the parking lot, away from the school building where the other parents have congregated. It's the only way to have a modicum of privacy and where Isabella and I had our first one-on-one chat over two years ago. I thought she was swooping in to obliterate me, but turned out she wasn't the evil ex after all. A small puff of air escapes my nose, the faintest seedling of a laugh, remembering how petrified of her I was.

'So . . . you wanted to talk? Is everything okay?'

Oh right, I asked her to chat. Focus, Marvin. Focus!

'Yeah, she's a sponge. Illona. Not literally, of course, she's much bigger, and talks, and much less absorbent.'

'Marvin.' Isabella hooks her arm in mine and pulls me closer. Her soft late spring sweater feels like a cloud against my skin. It's probably cashmere. 'Relax. You can talk to me. Remember, we're all on the same team.'

'You know I don't play sports ball,' I say.

'Neither do I. Pilates and water. That's my routine.'

'Sure, that's what's responsible for all *this*.' I motion toward her.

We share a laugh, and I get a whiff of her sweet perfume and my body relaxes into hers.

'It's Olan.' I dip my head, unsure how to ask her what I've been wondering about since Olan and I talked just over a week ago. What my brain has been turning over and over since coffee with Vincent and Ruth at the beginning of the week.

'And Greggie,' Isabella says.

'Yes, how did you know?'

'I spoke to him a few days after you and, well, he has baby on the brain, so I figured, maybe it was that.'

'Was he like this with Illona?' I run my hand up and down Isabella's arm, unable to resist the softness of her sweater.

'Oh yeah. Babies are magical, I can admit that, but for some people, it's next level. They're just smitten with that stage.'

'So this is temporary? For Olan?'

'I don't think so. I think he just loves children. Family. The newness of having a daughter has worn off, but he's no less infatuated with Illona than the day she was born. I realized quickly those two would share a special bond and a lot of that has to do with Olan. He's just that kind of father. I used to wonder if it would be different had Illona been a boy, but now I see how it is with his nephew, and nope – gender has nothing to do with it. He just loves taking care of them.'

'I mean, that's one of the things I love about him.' The minute it comes out of my mouth I worry I've crossed a line.

'Me too,' she says. 'There's nothing more attractive than a man doting on his children.'

'Oh thank goodness,' I say. 'I was worried you'd think it was strange.'

'No. Not at all. There's a reason I love *Modern Family* and his name is Phil Dunphy.'

'Right? They try to play him off as an awkward nerd, but, I mean, that's my kryptonite.'

'That tracks.' Isabella brushes a piece of lint off my hoodie that I wasn't aware was there.

'Did he tell you Liam is giving up custody?' I ask.

'To Olan's parents, yes.'

'Do you think Olan is okay with that or . . .'

'Do I think Olan wants him?'

'Yeah.'

Isabella rests her head on my shoulder and speaks in a quieter voice. 'You should probably ask him.'

'I will. But what do you think?'

Isabella has known Olan longer than anyone else I'm able to talk to about this and she has to have at least some gut feeling about it.

She lifts her head and faces me. 'Given the circumstances, I think Olan would love to bring Greggie home and be his legal guardian. But I also know he would never ask that of you.'

'Oh. So what should I do?' Once again, I'm standing on Pelletier's playground, seeking advice from the ex-wife of the man I'm head over heels for – just like a soap opera but with fewer dramatic cliffhangers.

'What do you want to do?'

My stomach churns like a tempestuous sea, as if a massive vessel were capsizing within me.

'I know that's not what you asked,' she continues. 'But you need to figure out what you want before you talk to Olan, because I think we both know what he wants.'

A boulder-sized lump appears in my throat, and I attempt to swallow it.

Isabella pats my arm, leans over, and gives me a soft kiss on the cheek. 'But I also know Olan loves you. Very much. And he'd never do anything to jeopardize what you have. Think about it.'

She's probably left a lipstick mark, but I don't even consider wiping it away.

What do I want? I would like someone to tell me what to do. How to feel. Make all difficult life decisions for me. And maybe do all the housework while I snooze with Gonzo. That's what I'd like.

But that's about as likely as Gonzo giving up napping to run a marathon.

30

To: MrAdorable@StonyBlock.com
From: OnlyStone4U@StonyBlock.com
Sent: 3/30 at 2:12 A.M.
Subject: Every Little Bit Hurts

Dear Marvin,

As I type this, your nephew peacefully slumbers in a sling
on my chest. At dinner, we gave him a little taste of Mom's
mashed potatoes, and Marvin, his face lit up like it was
Christmas morning. The sound of his contagious laughter and
giggles clarifies he is genuinely happy. Of course, he had more
potatoes on his face than in his mouth, but that was part of the
experience. Getting to witness him discovering additional aspects
of his world, and even himself, is such a gift, and I'm grateful to
be here, even temporarily. I can't wait for you to meet him. As
I get to know him better, I can't help but think that you and he
will become great friends.

Liam has been rather cranky the last few days. Detox is always an unpleasant experience, but this time it seems to be affecting him more intensely. He's finally making headway in the program. When an addict admits they're powerless over drugs and alcohol, it's their first step toward sobriety, and therefore, the most important one. I'm cautiously optimistic and determined to support him through it.

Yesterday I accompanied him to an AA meeting in one of the on-site meeting rooms. Two kind men in recovery came to talk about their experiences. Liam slept through most of it. The other rehab patients weren't much more attentive. I did my best to be alert and nod, giving the speakers some positive non-verbal feedback. My inclination is to be frustrated or annoyed with Liam, but there are signs his body is breaking the physical dependence on drugs and alcohol, and I'm holding on to that knowledge as a win for him. He's receiving around-the-clock monitoring and they've weaned him off IV therapy for hydration, which is another positive sign. Please keep him in your thoughts.

We have a court appearance next week where my parents will officially gain legal custody of Greggie. Liam insists he wants to give up his full parental rights, but the attorney I've hired says most judges won't allow that as an initial step. If, after a year, he still feels this way, he can make that decision, and my folks could adopt Gregory. One step at a time.

Mom and Dad are slowly warming up to the idea of being primary caregivers again in their sixties. I think Dad is more receptive to it, but honestly, Mom will bear the brunt of the work, so that makes sense. At this stage of their lives, it's not ideal, but it's the only viable solution other than foster care, which we've agreed as a family isn't on the table.

I've told them we'll take Greggie in the summers. Not until you're done with school, of course. Illona and Isabella will help, I promise. I hope that's okay. We can chat more about it on our next call. I promise you'll love having him around. Marvin, this boy needs me in his life. I didn't expect it, but there's a strong connection between us. My mother has taken to calling us Buzz and Woody – and yes, I'm Woody. I thought you'd be amused by that. My mom says it's because I'm 'tall and lanky' and Greggie is 'short and stout,' but of course, there's another reason Woody fits me. And you know it well. Fuck, now my body misses you as much as my heart.

Which leads me to your lesson. 'Every Little Bit Hurts' by Brenda Halloway might be the song that encapsulates how much my soul longs for you. Recorded in 1964 for Motown, Brenda actually released the song a few years earlier on a different label before signing with Motown and was initially against rerecording it. Of course, Mr Gordy convinced her and, with a new arrangement and performance, she had the biggest hit of her career. If you're able, please listen to the song and know every word, all the emotion in Brenda's voice – that is how much my heart aches for you.

Can we please talk soon? Video or regular chat, I don't care. I crave to hear your voice. And I miss your face. Maybe a video chat would be better. I know this is tough for both of us, but please understand the immense love and longing I have for you. Every day, I pray for our peace of mind, hoping that my prayers are making a difference. We'll be back together soon. I can feel it in my soul.

Love always,

Olan

31

Olan: How is my adorable fiancé? Did you get my email?

Marvin: Yes. Come back to me. I'm missing you. A lot.

Olan: Let's chat tomorrow night to distract you from the Sunday scaries.

Marvin: I'd love that. Maybe a video call? I'd love to see your face, Woody.

Olan: Wait, do you want to see my face or my woody?

Marvin: Both. Face first, please. Woodster.

Olan: I'm never going to live that down, am I?

Marvin: Nope! I'm ready to see McWoody. 😊

On Saturday morning, after I've read Olan's email and we've exchanged a few suggestive texts, I drift back to

242

sleep and awaken with my cock rock hard, gnashing into the bed. When I hear coffee grinding downstairs, for a second, in my haze, I think it's Olan, and my dick almost explodes through my boxers into the mattress. But then I remember his email. The texts. His family. He's still away. It's Sarah, making coffee and passive-aggressively waking me up – the very definition of Boner Killer.

I procure my pajamas from the chair in the corner of the room that mostly serves to hold my pajamas, scoop Gonzo up from Olan's side of the bed, and head downstairs. It's almost been two weeks since my mother arrived and while it's been more pleasant than I'd imagined, I also know if I don't have a conversation with her about her visit and timeline for departure, she may never leave.

And while I'm at it, I probably need to tell her about the baby. The mere thought of her reaction makes my face instinctively contort into a wince.

'Morning, sweetie!' Sarah shouts from the kitchen island, pouring a cup of coffee for both of us.

Gonzo lies near the mugs, his tail slapping the counter.

'I hope I didn't wake you.'

'With what? The blaring sound of coffee beans grinding? Putting the dishes, pots, and pans away like you're assaulting them? Maybe you could whip us up some smoothies in the blender? Burn some toast and get the smoke alarm going?'

'Don't be fresh.' She dips her chin and gives me her serious mom glare over the top of her glasses, the inspiration for my teacher look.

And suddenly, I'm six again.

'I'm sorry, I just need some . . .'

'Coffee.' She hands me my favorite mug and Gonzo darts away. A student gave it to me a few years ago as an end-of-year gift. It's bright orange and says 'Mr Block. He sings nice and loves kids.' Someday that phrase will go on my tombstone.

'Yes. Thank you.'

I take a sip, and of course, Mom knows just how I like it. Three sugars. Extra cream.

'So, what's on our docket for the day?' She sips her coffee from my 'You're Strong, You're a Kelly Clarkson Song' mug.

I don't need to go to the grocery. Or clean. Or do laundry. She's done it all.

'Mom, I'm so happy you're here, and I appreciate all you're doing, but you don't have to stay . . .' I can't even say the word – forever.

'Of course, I don't have to stay. I want to be here. I'm enjoying helping. And there's Illona. And you, of course. Plus, that Bruce smiles every time I go into the store.' A brief look of joy blossoms on her face, and then just as quickly, it vanishes. 'What do I have back in Arizona waiting for me? Dry heat and water aerobics.'

'You have friends.'

'But they don't need me.'

'You take Lanie to her doctor's appointments.'

'She can't drive when they have to dilate her pupils. It's zany. She looks like one of those little, oh, what are they called . . . they have giant eyes. Primates, I think. Big saucer eyeballs.'

'Lemurs?'

'Yes, lemurs. She looks like a lemur in a kaftan. Would

244

you want to drive behind a lemur in a kaftan? Of course not. They probably couldn't reach the wheel, let alone see much. And their arms would get lost in all that flowing fabric. Or maybe they have incredible vision with those giant peepers.'

'Actually, they have terrible eyesight,' I say. 'They don't see in color either, but they have excellent night vision.' Sarah cocks her head at me. 'My class studied them a few years ago and, of course, I remember the most random facts.'

'Well, that's Lanie. She can take a taxi.'

'Of course she can. But I'm sure she'd rather have her friend take her.'

'And you're my son.'

'I am. But I'm an adult. And as much as I love having you here, I'm okay, Mom.'

The corner of her mouth turns up at my confession.

'But Olan's not here.'

'Mom, he's coming back. Soon, I hope.'

'Aren't you lonely? Without him here?'

'Of course, but I have Illona. My friends. And honestly, sometimes a little alone time isn't a bad thing. I enjoy it. And I always have my boyfriend to keep me company.'

Sarah's eyes perk up and I quickly reach for Gonzo, who lies on the counter, waiting for attention. Cradling my kitty reminds me of the other topic I need to broach. I puff my chest and steady myself.

'Mom, I need to tell you something. And I don't want you to get worked up about it.'

She puts her mug down and takes a breath. I notice the rapid blinking, a sure sign of my mother's worry, so

I quickly blurt out the words, barely pausing to catch my breath.

She sits still and listens. I tell her everything about Liam. Abby. The overdose. Greggie. The Stones taking custody. Olan's closeness and connection with him.

Finally, when I'm done, I purse my lips and wait for her reply.

'Is he Jewish?'

'Mother, I've told you a million times, Olan isn't Jewish.'

'Not Olan, the baby.'

My head juts forward, and I open my mouth, but my mother's words leave me utterly speechless.

'Maybe the mother was Jewish,' she says. 'You know it comes through the mother. If the mother was Jewish – God rest her soul – the baby is Jewish.'

'I don't think so. And really? That's what you want to know? That's where your mind went first?'

'Just curious.'

I inhale a deep breath through my nose and blow slowly out of my mouth. Dear Lord, give me patience.

'Addiction is a nasty beast,' she says. Her voice does that thing where it's lower, softer, almost like she's changing her tone to make sure I'm paying attention. 'Not everyone follows the same path toward recovery and many are consumed by it.' There's a sparkle in her eyes, and she places her hand on my forearm. 'Olan and I are the lucky ones. We learned to love ourselves more than drinking. That's how you stay sober. Be patient as Olan navigates the situation with his family. He's going to need you more than ever.'

And once again, without knowing it, my mother has gotten to the very core of what's been eating away at me.

Olan needs me to step up to the plate and be there for him. For his parents. For his brother. His nephew.

'The thing is, even though Olan's folks are taking custody, I feel like Olan might wish he were. We were.' I close my eyes, waiting for her reaction.

'Did he say that?'

'Not exactly. But he's gaga for Greggie. And he's already offered for us to take him in the summers.'

'Have you talked to him about this? About taking full custody?'

I shake my head and shrug.

'Marvin, you need to talk to your fiancé. And soon.'

'He's calling tomorrow night. I was going to then.'

'How do you feel about it?'

'I'm not sure I'm cut out for it.'

'For what? Being a parent?'

'Yeah. A dad. I mean, I don't really have a role model of a good father.'

'Marvin, your dad was a complete shmendrik. He has no idea what he missed. Is missing. And listen to me . . .' She scoots a little closer and takes my hand. 'You would be the most amazing father in the world. Look at Illona. I know, I know, it's only been two years and technically you're going to be her stepfather, but labels mean nothing. This.' She pokes my chest, right near my heart. 'This is what matters. This makes family. You don't have to worry about being a good father – you already are one. I can see it with my own eyes.'

'Thanks, Mom. I appreciate that.' I know she's right, but a nagging worry still pokes inside my chest. 'Illona is easy. And she's seven. This is a baby. A tiny, helpless baby.'

'And you don't have to do it alone.' Mom smiles and then shakes her head. 'No, not me.' She lifts her chin and takes a deep breath. She nods, her lips pressed together firmly. I know that nod well. Her confident stance means she's deciding something important – I sense a shift. 'I'm going home on Monday. I'll call the airline and reserve a seat today. You don't need me here anymore.' She looks around the kitchen, nodding slowly. 'Even with a baby coming home. You have Olan. And all your friends. You've built quite a support system here. People love you. You're easy to love. Remember . . .' She pokes my chest again. 'This makes family.'

'You don't have to leave so soon,' I say as a fluttering sweeps through my stomach.

'No, I do. Lanie has an eye appointment next Friday, and you know those taxi drivers can't be trusted. Have you seen *Dateline*?'

'Yes, Mom. I have. With you.'

'Come here,' she says, opening her arms.

I fall into her chest and squeeze her. I'm beyond grateful she came.

'Thank you again,' I whisper in her ear.

'For what?' She pulls back. 'I'm your mother. I'd do anything for you.'

'I know you would.'

My mother has made it one of her life missions to be the best mom she can be – her living amends. Just like Olan with his family. Two weeks of her staying with me. Without Olan. And it was . . . pleasant. I didn't anticipate that. Maybe she needed to come and see I'm okay. Or maybe she was just missing me. The reason doesn't matter. Her presence made the past two weeks without Olan feel less burdensome.

'And Mom,' I say, as she turns to put her mug in the dishwasher. 'Let's plan another visit for you soon.'

'I'd like that,' she says. 'There may be a baby for me to spoil.'

'Maybe.'

I'm mentally preparing myself for Olan's call tomorrow night. Maybe he has no desire to take custody. Maybe he's simply a doting uncle and having Greggie with us for summers is all he wants. Or maybe he's afraid to tell me how he feels. Of my reaction. Of how I'll be as a parent. Does he worry about me with Illona? He left her with me. At least Mondays through Fridays and every other weekend. I take a deep breath, close my eyes, and lower my shoulders. I will not spiral about this. This is Olan and me. We communicate. We talk about our feelings. We're getting married. It's time for us to have this conversation.

32

'There's my adorable babe.'

Olan's face fills the screen of my phone and my chest instantly calms at his presence. He's alone. It's not quite nine and I'm guessing Greggie is sleeping. Olan isn't in the same room he was in last time. He's on a bed. I'm presuming his bed and all I can make out is the wood headboard behind him. He's wearing a white tank top – the one he loves to put on under his dress shirts – and the sight of his beautiful skin sends a wave of lust shooting to my groin. And then my body quickly remembers the topic I need to bring up and I hope Olan can't hear my heart thumping like a bass drum.

'Here I am. And there you are. You look good. Really good.' My tongue quickly coats my lips. 'How is everything?'

'Surprisingly well. Liam is finally on the other side of his detox. We went to a meeting today, and he was alert. Interested. Curious. Afterward, he thanked me for being here. For all I'm doing with Mom and Dad. With Gregory.

There was a deep sincerity in his voice that moved me.' Olan pulls his lips in and pauses. 'I know this is hard for you and Illona, but also, I'm grateful I'm able to be here. So, thank you. For being so understanding.'

Me? Understanding? About him being away for so long. Didn't see that on my bingo card.

'Of course. Illona's been the best distraction. And you won't be surprised to hear Gonzo's been sleeping on your pillow most nights. My mom's been an immense help, too. It's actually been really nice having her here.'

'Good. I'm glad to hear that.'

'She's leaving. Monday.'

Olan nods and asks, 'How do you feel about that?'

'It's time. We're already planning another visit. When you're here. She wants to see her son-in-law just as much as her son.'

'That sounds like a solid plan.'

'It's not only Sarah. Isabella. Jill. Vincent. Honestly, everyone's been rallying around me while you're gone. It's been . . . eye-opening.'

This spawns a smile on Olan's beautiful lips, and our gazes lock with an unspoken understanding. 'Marvin. People adore you. Almost as much as me. Of course, they want to step up if you need help. You have an amazing support system.'

'I do. We do. They're all here for us. No matter what. I've been told that many times lately.'

'That's lovely to hear. And even better to feel. We're lucky. We have each other, and they've all got us. That's why I needed to be here for my family. I'm not sure my folks could handle this on their own. My mother never wants to bother Gabe or me with anything, but this wasn't something she could pretend didn't exist. Given my recovery, and how successful I've been, it makes sense I'm here. I regret not being more attentive to Liam years ago, but dwelling on it won't alter the past. My focus right now is supporting him in his recovery and the custodial situation.'

And there it is. My opening.

'I've always known you're an amazing father. But you're an amazing son. Brother. Uncle.'

'I'm trying to be.'

'You are.' My lips curl into a soft smile, and I take a deep inhale. 'How is Greggie?'

'Currently sleeping in his crib like a sweet angel.' He angles the phone toward the bedside table and a small white plastic baby monitor comes into view. 'Silent as a lamb. Hence why you get me solo.' He winks, and a zip of excitement flutters through my core.

'Happy to hear he's sleeping well. And more than happy to get you all to myself.'

I shift on the chair in our bedroom, giving it a purpose beyond holding clothes and pull my legs under me. Years of sitting on the floor in the classroom have my body fooled into thinking sitting crisscross applesauce is comfortable for an adult man approaching his mid-thirties.

'Are you?' Olan's eyebrows jut up and he places the phone against something. I can see into the room. I know it's Olan's childhood bedroom, but there's no actual evidence he grew up there. His parents have transformed it into a generic guest room with beige walls, cream curtains, and taupe bedding. It's like the neutral threw up and passed out from boredom. He pops off the bed and is suddenly off-screen.

'There's something I wanted to ask you about.' I raise my voice, hoping he hears me.

'Hang on a sec.'

Olan's back, but he's standing in front of the phone, yanking off his tank. 'Just wanted to lock the door. Now, what did you want to ask me?'

He's standing in front of me. Well, on his phone. Shirtless. His firm pecs and dark nipples taunt me. I'm staring. My mouth waters, thinking about nibbling on his chest while he moans under me. Fuck.

There's a very serious conversation about a very serious topic I need to have with Olan. Having him put on a striptease for me over video while I salivate at his gorgeous body will not help that happen. It's also been over two weeks since I've seen anything more than his face and am getting a little tired of recalling images of him from memory for my spank bank. The conversation can wait ten minutes. Twelve, if I'm lucky.

'Um, it can wait. I mean, if you're wanting to remove more clothing.'

'I thought you liked my gray sweatpants?' He snaps the waistband and then glides his thumb under it, pulling slightly. I jut my face toward my screen, squinting. There's a faint outline toward his right leg. Or is it his left? Does the phone reverse the image? Who cares? He's totally getting hard.

'Woody appears to be getting a woody.' My tongue grazes my lips and the complete need to have him near overtakes me. I'm drowning in open waters and he's my oxygen.

'Babe. It's you. That face. You. You do this to me.'

He tugs his pants and briefs around his thick thighs and Olan's cock pops up, pointing directly at the camera. My mouth drops open and my tongue falls out. Why hasn't anyone developed technology allowing me to lick my phone's screen and taste his delicious dick?

I firmly return my tongue to its home inside my mouth and prepare to speak.

'You're rock hard.'

'For you. Listen. How about we share a little mutual gratification? Do you have time?'

'Do I have time? For . . . this?' I gesture toward the camera. Him. His perfect Goldi-cock. 'Olan, I'd fly to that atomic clock you told me about, blow it to bits, and stop time for this.'

'The US Naval Observatory Master Clock in DC. I'm fairly certain they have impeccable security.' He's palming himself, slowly stroking and – without a word – my joggers and boxers come sliding off and are tossed on the floor like yesterday's news. Sayonara, pants!

Olan pops an earbud into his left ear, and the sound coming from the phone shifts. 'Can you hear me?'

I nod quickly and pull at the hem of my T-shirt.

'Stop. Keep your shirt on.' Olan's voice is low, and much clearer. 'I love how you look in nothing but a T-shirt – your cock and ass the focus.'

My eyes widen at his confession and I run my palms over my 'Teaching is My Cardio' shirt.

'Listen to me,' Olan says. 'Are you okay if I give you some directions? Will you do what I ask?'

My cock stands at attention, off-screen, and when I grip myself, precum leaks from the tip. That's what this man does to me. Right now, Olan could tell me to take a run around the island naked and I'd do it.

A small nod is my only response, silently acknowledging my understanding.

'Good. Put your earbuds in.'

I grab the case from my nightstand and pop them in, and the sound of Olan's breath in my ear sends more blood rushing to my groin.

'Take your phone and prop it up on the light on your nightstand. Face it toward the chair.'

Olan's rich voice fills my ears, and I'm so fucking turned on I worry I'll explode in ten seconds. Deep breaths, Marvin. I follow his command and make sure the phone is angled so he can view the chair in the corner of the room.

'Take the toy out of my nightstand drawer. Don't forget the lube.'

I know where this is going and my ass pulses in anticipation. I haven't used the dildo while Olan's been away. It just felt like too much work and I've been so wrapped up with my mother, Illona, and trying not to miss Olan that when I've gotten myself off it's been quick, like a chore my body needs to complete.

'Do you have it?'

'Yeah,' I say off camera, holding up both items in my hands.

'Good, babe. You're listening well. You're going to earn a gold star.'

I snicker at Olan's attempt at playing naughty professor as my cock grows firmer.

'Now, please head to the chair.'

He's always so damn polite. Even when he's taking

control and bossing me around from his childhood bedroom halfway across the country. I'm so ready to comply.

When I glance back at my phone, Olan's sitting on the edge of his bed with one foot on the floor and the other on the bed. He's stroking himself and I'm tempted to abandon my post at the chair and sprint back and glue my eyes to the phone's screen.

'Get yourself ready.'

His voice, deep in my ears, reverberating through my head, guides me.

I open the lube and apply a generous amount, sliding the tip of my index finger in and realizing that hearing Olan's voice, seeing him jerk his mouthwatering dick, I'm open and ready for this.

'Now the toy,' he says. 'Use a generous amount of lube. I want this to feel amazing for you, babe.'

I take a moment to hold the blue dildo, applying lube to it with care. Why is it blue? I have no idea. Did the person who designed it have a Smurf fetish? One will never know. My eyes shut, and gliding my slick fingers around the shaft, coating it with lube, I can't help but imagine it's Olan's cock I'm preparing.

'Lean back on the chair, lift your legs and show me you're ready.'

I shimmy down and hoist my legs up, doing my best to expose myself, and I hear Olan's moan and growl echo in my ear.

'Mmmh. That's my Marvin. So hot. So good. Look at your pretty hole.'

I can't see him from this angle, but his voice spurs me on.

'Tease yourself with the tip. Right around the perimeter. That's good, babe. So good. Look at you. Fuck, I wish I was there . . . gliding my tongue around you, getting your sweet ass ready to take my cock.'

'Me too.' It escapes my lips like a reflex and I point my toes toward the ceiling slightly, raising my hips, hoping he gets a better view.

'Slowly, guide it in. Take a deep breath with me.'

Olan's intense inhale fills my ear, and I mirror my breathing to his.

'Not too fast. Let's take our time.'

I do as I'm told, pushing the tip in only a tiny bit, and when I clench around the toy, I quickly remove it.

'Easy, babe. Easy. Fuck, your hole looks so beautiful. I'd say I want to take a picture, but you're literally giving me a live feed video.'

A tiny laugh bubbles up from my throat and I take a deep breath.

'That's it. Deep breaths. I know it's been a few weeks. We're in no rush.'

With each gulp of air and the sound of his voice, Olan fills my head, creating a sense of tranquility.

'Do you know how much I love you? More than all the stars in the universe. Which astronomers estimate to be about two hundred billion trillion. It's a massive amount.'

Olan knows how his nerd speak turns me on and I let out a big exhale.

'Ready to try again?'

I nod, unsure if he can see it from the phone, but he replies, 'Just the tip.'

The dildo slides right to where I stopped it last time and I wait for Olan's direction.

'Now a deep breath and give a little more pressure.'

My mouth makes a circle and I push the air out as I apply gentle pressure, and the dildo glides past my tight ring of muscle and fills me up.

'There we go,' Olan says slowly. 'Now hold please.'

The cool silicone of the toy presses against the inside of my ass, pleasure radiating outward as I steady my breath while Olan's sexy voice spills into my ear.

'You've got me rock hard, babe. My entire life, my dick has never been a jealous fellow, but right now, it's so damn envious of that toy. Filling you up. Feeling all the warmth of your body. If I could blink and be there, holding your legs up, thrusting my cock into your gorgeous ass, there's nothing I desire more right now. I can't tell you how fucking beautiful you look like this.'

As Olan urges me on, my hand slowly pulls and pushes the toy, opening up with the motion and sound of his voice.

'Fuck, Marvin. Does it feel good?'

'Uh huh,' I eke out, lost in the sensation. His breathing. His voice.

'Good. Now, I'm interested in seeing you leaning over the chair. Your ass up. Is that okay?'

Without answering, I lower my feet to the floor and stand, removing the toy. Before I turn around, I catch a glimpse of Olan on the screen. He's leaning back, staring at his phone, jerking his cock faster.

Bending over the chair, I spread my legs, arch my back, and shake my ass at the camera.

'How do you make even that adorable?' he asks. 'When I get home, I'm going to kiss every inch of your ass. Would you like that?'

I nod and return the dildo to my entrance. This time it slips right in and my cock pulses as I fuck myself with it.

Encouraged by Olan, I find myself swept away, completely absorbed in the experience.

'There we go. Your hole is so horny, babe. Wait until I'm home. Wait until I get my dick up in there. And then you can fuck me. We can have a marathon flip-fuck session. Would you like that?'

'Fuck, yes.'

'I'm close.' There's a growly breathlessness to his voice and I know it won't be long.

I turn my head toward the phone but only get a tiny glimpse of him in my peripheral vision. He's stroking faster.

'Imagining that's my cock fucking you. Wishing I could pound my cum inside you. Marvin, damn I miss you. All of you. So much. Oh fuck, fuck. Fuuuuck.'

Olan's breathing becomes heavier in my ear and there are multiple gasps and deep moans as he unloads hundreds of miles away from me. When his breath steadies, I head over to the nightstand and bend over, peering at my phone to get a closer look.

He's drenched. Milky liquid covers his stomach and chest and the phone shakes in his hand.

'Damn, that was a lot,' I say. 'You needed that.'

'I did. It's been . . . since I left you.'

'Olan, that's not healthy. You'll explode.'

His deep bass laugh rumbles in my ear.

'God, I wish I could lick you right now.'

'Me, or this?' He angles his phone down and I get a closer look at the glorious mess covering him.

'Both. You. All of you.'

'I'd love that.' Olan puts his phone down and I see him wiping himself with a washcloth. 'Now, let's have you back on the chair to finish. I need to see you blasting all over your stomach while you fuck yourself with the dildo.'

'Yes, sir.' My shoulders fall back and I scurry over to the chair. 'How do you want me?'

'Sit, legs up. I can see well from here.'

I do as I'm told. As I thrust the toy inside as far as I can, and the suction of my ass holds it in place at the ring around the base. I hold my dick up, ensuring Olan gets the best view as I jerk myself.

'That's my adorable boy. Fuck, I can't wait to get my hands all over you.'

With my head tilted back, I say, 'Keep talking to me. I'm so close. I'm imagining you over me, pounding me.'

'That's it, stroke yourself. Faster. I want to see your fat cock shoot all over.'

With Olan's voice inside my head, and the dildo in my ass, the tiniest scratch of my orgasm appears. Using both hands now, my fingers glide up and down my shaft, and then, like an unexpected downpour, the pleasure cascades over me, from the inside out as thick ribbons of warm cum gush over my stomach and land on my rolled-up shirt.

'That's my sweet guy,' Olan purrs in my ear. My feet fall to the ground and I pull my shirt off to wipe myself.

'Did you enjoy that?' I ask, returning to the bed and retrieving my phone.

'What do you think?'

'I think that was almost as much fun as having you here in the flesh. Almost.'

'I'm coming home soon.' Olan slides his sweats on, his dick disappearing behind the fabric. 'Liam is rounding a corner. He's going to need a few more weeks of rehab, but I don't need to stay until he's out. And I can fly back. Once we have the hearing this week and I make sure my parents are settled with everything they need, I'll be in a better place to return.'

The important conversation we were supposed to be having. How did I forget that? Oh, right. Olan in a tank top is like that device in *Men in Black* that wipes your memory.

I take a deep breath.

'That's what I wanted to ask you about.'

'Coming home?'

'No. I mean, sort of. Not really. I know it's all decided and your parents are on board, but have you considered, well . . . you? Us. I mean, as his uncle, you'd be the legal guardian, but you're with me, so it would be us. I think. Right? I'm not sure how all that works. But is it something you've thought about? Or talked about with Liam? Or your parents? Wait, do you even want that?' My face pinches with the realization I've gone too far. 'Is that out of line for me to ask? Sorry, I'm rambling . . .'

'You'd do that?' A light sparkles in Olan's eyes. He's put his left arm behind his head and I do my best to focus on his face and not his sexy, lickable armpit.

'Of course. Olan, I'd do anything for you.'

'But do you understand what that means? To have a six-month-old in the house? Full-time.'

'No. Not really. Jill says at that age they're not much different than a cat. They take two to three naps a day and then sleep ten to twelve hours a night.'

'Greggie still gets up in the middle of the night. Sometimes he's hungry, but other times he simply wants to cuddle. Otherwise, that's about right. But he's not going to stay this age for long. Soon he'll be a toddler. His tiny hands will be on everything. We'd have to figure out daycare. And it would be a big adjustment for Illona. And Gonzo. He wouldn't be the only baby in the house.'

'We can figure all that out . . . if this is what you want. Is it?'

'Marvin, I know it's only been a few weeks, but I've been praying about this and I know all this suffering my family is experiencing, the way addiction has challenged us, it's not an accident. There's a reason my parents begged me to come home. Liam's path to recovery differs from mine and if this is something I can do to help him, and my parents, it seems it would be wise to make that decision. But only if you're all in because you come first. Us. And it's crucial we're on the same page.'

'Olan, when it comes to you, I'm always all in. Always.'

I lean over my knees, getting my face as close to the screen as possible.

A noise interrupts us. It's the baby monitor.

'He's babbling,' Olan says. 'I think we know his opinion on the matter.'

'So is that a yes? You want this?' I cock an eyebrow.

'Marvin, I'm not sure I've ever wanted anything more.'

'Then please bring your nephew home.'

262

A serene tranquility washes over me, and I experience weightlessness as if I could effortlessly float. I'm not accustomed to this sensation – all the anxiety and worry magically vanishes from my body. I take it as a sign. The universe is whispering its approval.

33

Sitting on the carpet Monday morning, surrounded by my students, I'm not sure I've been this at ease since Olan left. He's coming home. With his nephew. Our nephew. Gregory. They'll be here soon. With a deep sigh, my soul settles, knowing we'll all be together. Our home will be complete.

'I have another fun book to share with you,' I say, holding it up. 'This one is about a rhino and a porcupine who want to play outside, but there's a problem. Let's read it and see what happens.'

The children are attentive, eager even, as I do my best to infuse the story with emotion and humor. The characters make plans for a glorious day of outdoor fun, but then it rains. As animals, they have no house to play in, although they can stand upright and speak (thank you, children's books).

'Look at the porcupine's face.' I point to the somber creature on the page. 'How do you think she's feeling?'

'Sad!' Eddie shouts.

'Yeah, definitely sad,' Amanda agrees.

One of the biggest reading comprehension hurdles kindergarten students face is understanding emotions beyond happy and sad. If you read something and ask them how a character is feeling, ninety percent of the time it's going to be 'happy' or 'sad.' To tackle this, we analyze intricate emotions and record them on a chart for better understanding.

'Well, I can see why you'd say sad. Look at her face. She's looking down at the ground. What else about her face and body makes you think she's sad?'

'She's not smiling,' Michael says.

'She's frowning. That's a sad face,' Ben says.

'She is frowning.' I shift onto my knees, putting the book down so they can focus on me. 'But let's think about what's happening. The porcupine really wants to do something – play outside. And because it's raining, their plans are ruined. There's a name for that emotion. It's called disappointed.'

'I've heard of that,' Austin shouts.

'When you're disappointed, you feel let down,' I explain.

Lots of nodding in agreement. I love when they acknowledge what I'm teaching them.

'Let's see what happens next.'

I continue reading, and two tiny frogs appear. They're dancing. They're singing. They're frolicking and playing in the rain. Rhino points out how much fun they're having and wonders if he and Porcupine might have fun too.

'What do you notice about Porcupine's face now?'

'It's changed!' Danny says.

'Her eyes are open wide,' Brian says.

'Her lips are open a little bit,' Aaron adds. 'Maybe she's wondering if Rhino is right.'

'Yes, her emotions have changed now!' I close the book momentarily, using my finger as a bookmark. 'She's not disappointed anymore. She's feeling like it might be possible for them to have fun. Even in the rain. There's a name for that emotion too! When you feel hopeful, like something is worth trying and it will probably work out, that's called optimism. Can you say that with me?'

The entire class calls back, and the room is filled with 'Optimism'.

There are moments in the classroom when I wonder who's teaching who. Sure, I'm the adult with the teaching certificate, master's degree, and years of classroom experience, but the stories we share and the lessons I plan – I'm often learning right along with my tiny charges. The wide grin on my face speaks volumes. For the first time in weeks, I actually feel optimistic.

'I knew it.'

Jill sits across from me, poking at her salad while she chews.

'How exactly did you know?'

'Babies have this magical power over people. You don't think you want one, and then poof! You see one, smell one, hold one, and all your I-don't-want-a-baby resolve washes away like my high school infatuation with the Backstreet Boys.'

'Say it isn't so. You don't want it that way anymore?'

'Nope. I've moved on. My lust for Nick Carter has been replaced with my Nick.'

'Would you say he's "Larger than Life"?'

'Good one. But yes.' Jill pushes a strand of hair behind her ear. 'You'll see. Baby magic is deep and real.'

'Well, I've only seen him on the phone. I haven't smelled him. Or held him. And I've done all those things with Maria.'

'Ah, but you're forgetting the special ingredient . . . watching your man do those things. That's the secret sauce. The first time Nick took his shirt off and held Maria, I almost tossed her into her crib so I could jump him right there.'

'Really?'

'Yes. But then I remembered where she just came from a few days earlier . . .' She nods down. 'And I cooled off. The point is, Olan is doing all those things and conveying all that to you and you're done for. Welcome to Baby-ville, population . . . exhausted.'

My fingers rub the back of my neck and I let out a little laugh.

'Don't worry, you'll catch up on sleep,' Jill says. 'When he goes to college.'

I muster up a bigger chuckle as my stomach churns the leftover veggie burrito my mother packed. Her last lunch for me.

'I'm pretty sure my mother slept fine while I was home,' I say.

'That's because she was drinking. Sober parenting is a whole different ball game.'

'Right,' I say.

'And actually, I take that back. Once your kids go to college, you still worry enough to impact sleep. So, basic-ally, your entire sleep cycle is fucked until you die.'

'Awesome.'

'But it's worth it. You'll see. I mean, look how much Illona's enriched your life in two years. Now you'll get to experience the whole thing from a much younger age.' Jill stands, moves to the chair next to me and wraps her arm around my shoulder. 'I'm so happy for you, Marvin. You're getting married. You're going to be a full-time parent.' She leans her head on my shoulder and I take a deep breath, the scent of her vanilla shampoo soothing me. 'Now, if you'd just do something a little wild before Olan returns.'

'Excuse me?'

'Your fiancé has been away for weeks. And he's coming back. With a baby. Have you done anything fun for yourself? Let loose?'

'I stayed up all night last Saturday and binged the latest season of *Drag Race*.'

'Oh, let me alert the authorities.' Jill's back at her salad, poking, excavating the chicken. 'I mean, I'm not suggesting you have a torrid affair. We don't condone cheating. But we could go to a strip show in Boston this weekend. Or at least have a solo date night. Take yourself out to dinner and a movie. Go to a spa. Get your hair done. Have a massage.'

'I have been meaning to get a trim.' I run a hand through my thick, unruly curls. 'My mother offered to do it, but I'm not keen on her using sharp objects so close to my face.'

'Well, do something. Trust me, once the baby is here, you'll wish you had time to yourself.' She purses her lips, raises her eyebrows and gives me her trust-me-I-know look. 'And are you prepared?'

'For the baby?'

'No, for the Backstreet Boys reunion tour. Yes, the baby.'

'I mean, I think so. Olan's been taking care of him for weeks now. And he's raised Illona. He's got the dad thing down. I'll just follow his lead.'

'That's all wonderful, but I mean literally – is your house ready for a baby? Do you have a crib? Baby gates? Safety latches? Outlet covers? Diapers? A diaper pail?' She's on her phone, pecking away, no doubt making a list. 'You'd be surprised how dangerous our homes are for little ones – every corner poses another potential death trap.'

My mind does a quick scan of our house. The cords. The plugs. Gonzo's toys scattered all over the premises. A tingling takes over my chest and my heartbeat suddenly ramps up.

'You need to babyproof.' She's back to typing on her cell. 'I'm coming over Saturday morning. Nick can take Maria to the library solo.'

'You don't have to do that.'

'Yes, I do. It's my duty as your best friend, best woman, and most likely the godmother of this new bundle of joy. Nobody fancies an electrocuted baby.'

'Gosh, no. And, thank you.'

Jill has this extraordinary way of both ramping my anxiety up to eleven and then simmering it back down to a tolerable level. Before Greggie's arrival, there's bound to be a multitude of things that need to be taken care of. I'm also sure I have no idea what those things are. Jill has a baby. Well, she's more of a toddler now, but she was a baby not that long ago. And besides too many chocolate-chip beet cookies, she hasn't lost or severely injured Maria yet. Saturday morning. We'll get the house ready. Olan's counting on me. We've got to be prepared.

And I do need a trim. Maybe I'll go wild and have them give me a shampoo too. Why not? This is my last hurrah before everything changes.

34

To: MrAdorable@StonyBlock.com
From: OnlyStone4U@StonyBlock.com
Sent: 4/4 at 1:53 A.M.
Subject: Ain't No Mountain High Enough

Dear Marvin,

Next Monday will be a month since I've seen your adorable face in person. Touched you. Kissed you. I'm coming home and our nephew, Gregory Stone, will be strapped to my chest.

I can't wait to see you. Hold you. Kiss you. And I can't wait for you to experience Greggie's magic. It's been a tumultuous few days and I still have a few items to cross off my list before I return, but I'm confident in the decisions and plans I'm setting in place before my departure.

Liam's team at the center has planned his next steps. That's a highly promising sign. I visit him daily and we pray before attending a meeting together. My first step in bringing Greggie home was talking to Liam. Marvin, he cried when I told him. He told me it was what he wanted, but was afraid to ask. It's not that our folks aren't capable or willing, but they've had their turn raising kids and he, like me, was worried about their stamina and ability to keep up with a soon-to-be toddler. He knows how well Illona is thriving and he wants that for his son. This decision has me positively elated.

Right now, Liam doesn't want contact. I think it's too painful. Greggie reminds him of Abby and what happened. His guilt is overwhelming and it will take him time in therapy to come to terms with what happened. I've worked with his team here to line up a bed in a recovery residence. It's about forty-five minutes from Mom and Dad's and he'll reside in a structured and supportive environment as he transitions from rehab to independent sober living.

We've talked about a few of his wishes for Greggie. He'd like him to call us both 'uncle' – so get ready, Uncle Marvin. Liam is and always will be his father. We're going to modify the way those roles are traditionally viewed in our family for Greggie.

My parents were deeply emotional when I broke the news. I'm fairly certain it was a mix of disappointment and relief. They were gearing up to take on this massive responsibility, but I know in my heart it was a considerable ask. My parents would do anything for their children or grandchildren, but they agreed we're better suited to take him.

Dad has come with me to visit Liam. He's in a better place than Mom with everything, but of course, he doesn't have the same baggage she does. I'm optimistic she'll be able to visit him soon, if not here, then in the sober house.

I've scheduled a chat with Illona this weekend when she's with Isabella. I'm confident she'll be over the moon to have a baby nephew around, but I think she should be with her mom for questions and any big emotions afterward. If you don't mind, I would greatly appreciate it if both of them could accompany you to the airport on Monday evening. Isabella is excited to help in any way she can. When I told her she said, 'Olan, we once said for better or worse to each other. We've been through a lot, but even if we're not married, I meant it. Even now.'

We've worked hard to be a team raising Illona, and she is excited to include Greggie in that equation now. I'm profoundly grateful for her and for the effort both of you have invested in building a friendship. It means the world to me.

One thing I know is, if nothing else, you and I are an amazing team. There's nothing we can't do together. You've proven what a wonderful parent you are with Illona and now your nephew will get to experience the same Marvin Block charm. There are lots of details to figure out. We'll need to think about making the home safe for Greggie. I've talked with my team at GreenSpace and they're letting me take six weeks of paternity leave and will be flexible with my work-from-home vs. in-office schedule. All details we'll figure out in time. Right now, Greggie and I are coming home.

Before I sign off, your lesson. Did you think I forgot?

'Ain't No Mountain High Enough' might be my favorite Motown song. It also happens to have a very interesting recording history, so buckle up!

The track was written by Ashford and Simpson. Before they broke out as recording artists, they were extremely successful songwriters. Originally recorded by Marvin Gaye and Tammi Terrell in 1967, the song was a modest hit but didn't quite reach the heights of Marvin's solo work. The playful back and forth between the singers, the joyous jubilation of the chorus, and the yearning in Marvin's voice approach musical perfection in my book.

A year later, Diana Ross & the Supremes recorded a duet version with The Temptations, which was quite faithful to the original version. That version was an album track on the superstar combination album *Diana Ross & the Supremes Join the Temptations*. Here's where it becomes really interesting.

Two years later, after Diana left the Supremes and found success as a solo artist, Ashford and Simpson convinced her to rerecord the song on her own. This version was a complete reworking of the track with a more gospel style and elements of classical music with strings and horns. Even though the new version was a massive number-one hit for Diana, the original Marvin and Tammi version will always hold a special place in my heart.

You've been so patient and understanding while I've been away. My love for you has only grown while we're apart. The day I become your husband will be one I'll never forget. I can't wait to be married to you. Parent with you. Grow old with you.

Nothing can keep me from you now, Marvin.

All my love (and see you soon),

Olan

35

'What. Did. You. Do?'

With the April sun shining on her, Jill stands at my front door, shopping bags in both hands, mouth agape. The gentle ocean breeze blows her hair, but she has no time to be distracted by the strands blowing in her face.

Sheldon appears behind her, followed by Theo, who carries a large toolbox in one hand and a small cooler in the other. Walter, Theo's service dog, sits at his feet, waiting for his owner to move.

'Oh. My. Gaga.' Sheldon pauses after each word for an extra dramatic effect.

'What?' I run my hand over my head. Except for the tiniest hint of one trying to return near the front, my curls are gone. I'm like a shorn sheep.

'What did you do?' Jill repeats, this time shaking her head.

'I got a trim.'

'Trim?' Sheldon joins Jill, slicing his head sharply to the left and then to the right.

'Wait, what are you all doing here?' I ask.

'Babyproofing. Remember?' Jill lifts the cluster of bags.

I look at Sheldon and cock an eyebrow.

'Your mom texted me and told me everything. We are shifting from Operation Wedding Planning to Operation Baby Preparation.' Sheldon holds up a hand. 'Only temporarily.'

My eyes land on Theo and he says, 'I'm here to help.' He holds up the toolbox, and Walter stands.

'He's not only handsome,' Sheldon says. 'He's tall. And strong. He knows how to fix things. We need him.' Sheldon pats Theo's thick biceps.

'Speaking of fixing things, what the fuck did you do with your curls? And how are we going to get them back before Olan returns?' Jill asks.

'I got a trim.' I shake my shoulders and stick my chest out. 'I like it.'

'You got it chopped.' Sheldon moves toward me, inspecting.

'Massacred is more like it.' Jill sets her bags down and pokes a finger in my hair. 'Does Olan know?'

'Not yet. He'll see it Monday.'

'You should've waited. Without the curls, I'm not sure he's going to be as enthusiastic about the whole till death do us part thing.'

'Olan is marrying *me*.' I scratch at the fuzz on the back of my head. 'Not my hair.'

'Whatever you say.' Jill picks her bags up and walks inside.

'I'm sure he won't mind.' Sheldon walks past me, turns to Theo, and whispers, 'Please never cut your curls off, baby.'

'No chance,' Theo says as he comes inside, followed by Walter.

'Wait.' I close the door and my stomach flips, worrying about a dog entering Gonzo's territory.

Before anyone can intervene, Gonzo pounces into the entryway and approaches Walter with his head toward the floor. His ears flatten against his skull while his tail flicks back and forth.

'He's never met a dog before,' I say.

'Oh, Walter's not a regular dog,' Sheldon says.

'He's a service dog.' Theo pets Walter's side. 'Nothing fazes him.'

'It's not Walter I'm worried about.'

I move to save Gonzo, and before I can pick him up, he stands upright, ears perked up, and smooshes his face on Walter's neck.

'See, they're friends already,' Sheldon says. 'Everybody loves Walter. He's like the Freddie Mercury of dogs. Maybe we should've changed his name to Freddie?' Sheldon looks toward Theo.

'No, he's a Walter. And he wouldn't hurt a fly.' Theo bends down and removes Walter's service harness, and he immediately trots over to Gonzo's water bowl and begins lapping.

Gonzo follows, waiting to see where his new buddy will settle.

'Okay, okay, Garfield isn't going to scratch Odie's eyes out. Kumbaya, and all that jazz. We have work to do.' Jill hoists her bags onto the counter.

She removes various devices, doodads, and paraphernalia I've never seen.

'What is all this?'

'Babyproofing gear.' Jill plops what appears to be some sort of padding on the counter.

'So the baby doesn't accidentally get electrocuted, impaled, drown, or poke an eye out.'

'Locked and loaded.' Theo holds up a drill in one hand and a hammer in the other.

'But this is all your stuff,' I say. 'I can't take it.'

'You're not,' Jill says. 'My mother sent so much baby gear when Maria was born that we'd need a mansion to fit it all – and since my teacher's salary doesn't quite cover that, I tossed the overflow in the basement. I knew someone would need them at some point. Nick has been bugging me to clean it out, so, really, you're saving me from having to audition for an episode of *Hoarders: Baby Edition.*'

'Happy to help,' I say.

'There's a crib and changing table en route. You should be set with the basics by Monday.'

'Wow. Thank you. I guess I didn't know what I didn't know,' I say.

'This is what we do, Marvin. Take care of each other. When Gregory outgrows all this, save it for your next baby or pass it on to someone else.' She wiggles her eyebrows at Sheldon.

'Oh, no babies for us,' Sheldon says. 'We have Janice and Walter. We're good.'

Theo nods in agreement. 'Fur babies are plenty.' He smiles and Sheldon gives him a quick peck on the cheek.

'Okay, we need to focus.' Sheldon takes his phone from his pocket and begins flipping.

'I made a list. A long list.' He glances around the great room. 'And this place is a baby minefield. Let's get to it.'

Jill and Theo nod and the three of them huddle around Sheldon's phone as he gives orders. It's all a jumble to me – a symphony of table corners, outlet covers, safety latches, window guards, and stairs.

By the time we break a few hours later for the gourmet lunch Theo's packed in his cooler, the house seems ready.

'You're ready for an army of babies,' Jill says, taking a bite of quiche. 'Holy shit balls, Batman, what is this?'

A massive smile overtakes Theo's face as he puffs his broad chest out.

'It's a roasted tomato, basil, and parmesan quiche. The secret is roasting the tomatoes myself.'

'And he grates the cheese, too,' Sheldon says.

'I'm not buying pre-grated "cheese" in the plastic canister. I'm not a heathen,' Theo says.

'He also makes the crust from scratch.' Sheldon rubs his hand up and down Theo's arm. 'No cutting corners.'

'Would you be interested in moving in with me and my husband?' Jill wipes her mouth. 'He's really cute.'

'Not cute. Gorgeous,' I say.

'I'm all set.' Theo leans over and kisses the top of Sheldon's head. 'But thank you.'

'Wait until you taste the potato salad,' Sheldon says. 'New potatoes with fresh radishes, red onions, and cucumber.'

'And fennel,' Theo adds.

'Damn,' Jill says. 'You're lucky.'

'I am.' Sheldon beams.

'We both are.' Theo pulls Sheldon onto his lap and the

stool wobbles under him, but he steadies himself by grabbing the counter.

'I need a gay husband,' Jill says.

'Excuse me. You have one,' I say.

'One that can cook.'

Theo coughs, but it swiftly evolves into an infectious chortle, causing all of us to burst into laughter alongside him.

'Marvin, hello, you . . . , um . . . what . . .' Isabella stands at her front door, eyes agape. 'Marvin!'

Illona's arms wrap around me. Her face buries into my stomach and even though it's only been two days since I saw her, having her so close still melts my heart.

Isabella invited me to her condo so we could talk to Illona about Gregory together. Despite his initial plan to call in, Olan's preparations to fly back tomorrow and all the final loose ends he needs to tie up with his family left him unable to do so. He assured me Isabella and I could do this without him, and honestly, I'm so damn excited he's coming home, I didn't argue.

'You cut your curls off.' Isabella motions me inside from the hallway.

Illona's grip finally loosens, and she catches a glimpse of my head. 'You look completely different. Has Daddy seen?'

'Not yet. He'll see it tomorrow when he comes home.' Butterflies swarm in my belly. Tomorrow. Attempting to change the subject, I ask, 'Are you excited to see him?'

Illona nods eagerly, and her eyes widen.

'You've missed your dad, a lot,' Isabella says, taking a

seat on the long white sofa in the living room portion of the open concept room.

More nodding from Illona, who joins her mom and I move to her other side.

'We all have,' I say, putting my arm around her shoulder. She does that thing where she melts into me, and I'm beyond grateful we've had each other for the past month while Olan's been away.

'Can we make a sign for him?' Illona looks toward her mother.

'Of course, sweetie, you can work on it while I make dinner. But Marvin came here because we wanted to talk to you about something important.'

Illona's eyebrows scatter up her forehead and I wonder if something similar occurred when they told her about their separation and eventual divorce a few years ago.

'It's nothing bad,' I say, squeezing her close.

'No, it's actually amazing.' Isabella's face lights up and I'm not sure if she's acting or not, but I recognize this from the classroom. Fake it until you make it. We might be feeling a bit anxious about the new addition to our lives, but we should focus on showing Illona how excited we are. We need to present this like it's a brand-new kitten, full of joy and promise.

'It's about your new baby cousin,' Isabella says.

'Greggie?' Illona sits up and leans back against the oversized cushions.

'Yes,' I say. 'It turns out he's going to be coming home with your dad tomorrow.'

'He is?' Illona's jaw drops open.

'Yes, he's going to stay with you and your dad and

Marvin.' Isabella moves a throw pillow to the side, giving us a little more room.

'A baby cousin visit? Oh my gosh, this is going to be epic.' Illona sits up and her face illuminates with excitement.

'Well, that's the thing,' I say. 'He's not just coming for a visit. He's staying . . .'

'For a while.' Isabella looks at me, her lips pursed.

'For how long?'

'We don't know,' I say, taking her small hand in mine. 'But probably for a long time.'

'But what about his mom and dad?'

Isabella and I lock eyes, communicating our thoughts without saying a word.

'Right now, they want him to come live with you,' Isabella says.

Another knowing look and it becomes clear. Now isn't the right time or place to share the details with Illona. There will be an occasion for that, but that time isn't now.

'How do you feel about that, sweetie?' I place my hand on her shoulder and she falls back into me.

'Where will he stay?'

'Your dad and I haven't talked about that yet, but we have quite a few extra rooms. And he's so small. We'll figure it out,' I say.

'He can stay in my room,' she says with bright eyes. 'I can pack some of my toys away to make room.'

'That's so thoughtful.' Isabella pats her daughter's knee. 'But you don't have to share your room. You've got lots of space in that house.'

'What about weekends when I come here?' Illona looks at her mom. 'Can he come too?'

Isabella and I share another glance. We're in undiscussed, uncharted territory.

'We'll see sweetie. Maybe sometimes. Don't worry. We're all going to be helping. Just like with you. Your dad and Marvin and I are all a team.'

Illona flops into her mother's arms, and Isabella brushes her hand over her hair. Isabella's eyes meet mine, and her lips curl into a warm, kind smile. She nods gently and a lump forms in my throat. She means it. And who'd have thought the three of us would make such a great team?

'That's what family means,' I say. 'We all support each other.'

Illona leans back from Isabella's chest and says, 'Can I add Greggie's name to the sign?'

'Of course,' Isabella says.

Illona leans back into her and Isabella reaches over, grabs my forearm, and pulls me into their cluster. As I find myself nestled among them, the reality of being here with my fiancé's ex-wife and my soon-to-be stepdaughter hits me. It's an unexpected twist, one I never could have envisioned, yet the moment is imbued with a deep joy. A serene wave of contentment washes over me, filling me with a sense of fulfillment and gratitude that surpasses anything I could have imagined. The bonds we've formed continue to evolve and grow, and in this moment, everything seems to align perfectly.

36

Olan: At the gate. I cannot wait to see you. ♥

Marvin: Me too. I am so ready for you to be home.

Olan: Thank you again for being so understanding.

Marvin: Of course. Like you said, we make a fantastic team.

Olan: I love you Marvin Block.

Marvin: I love you too, and I cannot wait to see you and meet Greggie. Safe travels. ♥

Olan: ♥😊♥

The knowledge of Olan's return makes Monday at school the least Mondayest Monday in a long time. When I tell my students about my plans after school to pick Olan up at the airport with our baby nephew, their excitement snowballs into a massive avalanche of kindergarten baby fever.

At choice time, it seems everyone has Greggie on the brain. At the Art Center, they're painting pictures for him. The Writing Center crafts notes welcoming him to Maine. Even at the Building Center, they make little models of his room for me. When I head to the Dramatic Play Center, Eddie and Alex use a doll to demonstrate how to change a diaper. Alex has a baby sister and has taught almost everyone in the class who wants to learn.

'When you finish,' he says, 'you gotta hold the baby and give her a kiss.'

He demonstrates with the plastic doll.

'But use some hanitizer first,' Eddie adds. 'And be gentle. Babies are delicate.'

I listen and nod. The realization that in a few hours, this dramatic play scenario will be a reality in my home crashes over me. Instead of nervous butterflies swarming in my stomach, a sense of excitement bubbles inside me.

At our Closing Circle, instead of telling me something they're proud of, or something they're going to do at home, they ask me questions about Greggie, most of which I don't know the answer to.

How big is he? How old is he? How much does he weigh? Will he have his own room? How does Illona feel about him coming to stay? How does Gonzo feel about him coming to stay? Can he talk? Can he walk? What is his favorite food? Favorite color? Favorite TV show? Song?

'We'll all get to learn about him together,' I say, and the class departs with excitement building around the new addition to our collective family.

After school, Illona and I meet Isabella in the parking lot and head to the airport. It's only a ten-minute drive, and we're quiet in the car, not something typical for us. Isabella has the new car seat buckled in and ready. Illona snacks on a pack of peanut butter crackers in the backseat her mother brought for her and when I glance back to smile at her and she catches me eyeing them, she offers me two. As I munch on them, wishing I had a glass of milk to wash them down, I realize the cast of *High School Musical* was on to something. We really are all in this together.

We pull into the arrivals parking lot, and before anyone can speak, the familiar sound of my phone dinging with a text alert fills the car.

'Daddy?' Illona asks.

I pull my phone from my pocket to check.

> Olan: Just landed. We'll be out shortly.

'Yup, they're here,' I say. 'Well, will be. Soon. They have to deplane. And walk outside. But it won't be long.'

'Why don't we get out so we can greet them,' Isabella says.

'And they can see my sign.' Illona unclicks herself from her booster seat and wrangles the posterboard sign next to her.

Mother Nature has gifted us with a sunny afternoon, accented by a few fluffy clouds scattered across the sky. A perfect Maine spring day. Illona holds up her poster and her handwriting, so much better than when I met her back in kindergarten, says it all: *Welcome Home Daddy and Greggie. We love you!*

There are hearts and flowers and a large orange truck near the bottom.

As I study her work, tears prickle the corners of my eyes. At her growth. Her love for her father. Her willingness to share him with her cousin.

'I don't think I've ever seen you draw a truck before,' I say.

'It's for Greggie. I figured being a boy, he might like trucks.'

'Maybe.' Isabella rests her hand on Illona's shoulder. 'But he probably loves hearts and flowers, too.' She winks at me. And how did I ever think Olan's ex-wife was going to be the villain in our story?

'I know, there aren't girl things and boy things,' Illona says, looking at me, and I'm quite certain she remembers those conversations and lessons from kindergarten. 'But a lot of boys I know love trucks. That's all I'm saying.'

'Fair.' I squat down and hug her, taking her all in, knowing this will be the last time, at least for a while, it's just her.

With my arms wrapped around her, Illona does her best to hold her sign, and then it happens. I feel her heartbeat race against my chest, and her voice, louder than I've heard it since we told her she could be the flower girl at our wedding, screams, 'Daddy!'

As I stand and turn, my eyes meet his, and a wave of relief crashes over me. With Greggie strapped to his chest, a backpack on his back, a duffel bag in one hand, and a folded stroller in the other, Olan swiftly walks toward us. He's home.

My brain tells me to run to him, but my legs feel weak. Numb. My skin tingles and my chest tightens. The past month has been a constant ache, as if a vital part of me had been lost. But now that he's back, it's as if the missing piece has finally been found. I'm lightheaded. My ears ring. Breathe, Marvin, I tell myself. Breathe.

Illona jumps up and down screaming, 'Daddy!'

When my bottom lip quivers, Isabella's hand lands on my back and rubs slow circles. She leans over and whispers, 'It's okay. He's home.'

And then Olan's here. Right here. Illona cries. The emotional impact of having her father back after a month overwhelms her, and she grabs on to his waist. Olan opens his arms, leans into me, and I do my best to embrace him without squishing the baby.

'Here, let Auntie hold this little nugget,' Isabella says. We move apart and she reaches behind Olan's neck and I hear a click. She's holding Greggie, who's either sleeping or simply confused by all the commotion and hasn't made a peep.

'Thank you,' Olan says to her, and then he grabs me, and holds me, Illona still attached to his middle, as he kisses my cheek, then my lips. He clasps my chin with his thumb and finger, keeping my mouth near his, then pulls away just enough to say under his heavy breath, 'I love you.'

'I love you too.'

'You cut your hair.' His eyes scan my head. I bite my lower lip and glance toward the pavement. 'I like it.' Olan combs his fingers through my short hair, quickly giving my scalp a scratch.

Another kiss, this one slightly deeper, and then Olan pulls back and lifts his daughter, almost too big for this, but they make it work. Illona's legs wrap around her dad and he kisses the top of her head, and then her lips, and I realize, now more than ever, this experience of missing

Olan Stone in such a deep and visceral way is something Illona and I have shared. It's another check on the list of items that bring us closer. I'm more than ready to be her stepfather.

'And thank you. Again. For everything.' Olan reaches over and pulls Isabella into the embrace.

'Remember. I got you. Always,' she says with a wink. Olan gives her a peck on the cheek, and I look at the sky and close my eyes. Grateful for the day.

Watching them interact, it dawns on me. Sometimes, even when a marriage ends, especially when children are involved, it doesn't mean the relationship does. It can morph. Change. Evolve. These two started as friends and they've found their way back to that. Perhaps Isabella never anticipated me as an addition to their family, but we have surpassed mere tolerance and understanding to develop our own unique bond.

Isabella. Illona. Olan. Me. We've created our own family. Our own way.

'Now, meet your nephew,' Isabella says.

As soon as she hands him to me, I can feel the weight of his presence in my arms, and a powerful surge of emotion takes hold of me. He's so small. But the weight of him, not just his physical presence, but the significance of him being here, with us, overwhelms me.

And between Olan's return and holding Greggie, my eyes are unable to hold back the tears anymore.

'Hey there, little guy.'

He's awake, but barely. When I run my fingers through his tiny afro, I can't help but be amazed by how incredibly soft it feels, almost like the touch of a heavenly halo. Olan was right, he smells like a combination of soap, milk, and freshly baked bread. They should bottle the scent up and sell it. He moves his mouth, his lips pursing, and Olan quickly retrieves a pacifier from his backpack and hands it to me.

Without thinking, I place it near Greggie's mouth and he latches right on, sucking and closing his eyes, happy as a seagull with a french fry.

'See, you're a natural,' Olan says.

'Now, why don't we get you all home?' Isabella asks.

'Sounds good to me,' Olan says with a heavy sigh. 'Home.'

37

The next few days pass in a haze, with everything blurring together. My body relishes having Olan home. In my arms each night. His energy in the house makes it complete. Illona has a spring in her step, skipping from point A to point B as her smile shines a little brighter with her father back. The addition of a baby to our family unit happens rather seamlessly, and much of that is due to Olan's ability to calmly juggle everything thrown at him.

True to Olan's word, Greggie sleeps a lot. In addition to a three-hour nap during the day while I'm at school, he sleeps through the night, except for waking for a bottle and/or snuggling like clockwork between one and two. Even though I offer, Olan gets up every single night. He's home, working a few hours a day, and I'm still back at school. Dr Knorse offered me a week of unpaid leave, but Olan and I agreed that sticking to our typical routine is best for Illona and me, given all the recent changes.

When Illona and I commute to school, we're quieter, often closing our eyes, nodding off, and doing our best to catch our collective breath from the seismic shift in our world. My friends, true to form, come together as a united front, offering their unwavering support.

Vincent: How is everyone holding up?

Marvin: So far, so good.

Vincent: Kent says babies are exhausting.
I say they're filthy.

Marvin: You're both correct.

Vincent: Well, we're here if you need anything.
Even babysitting. For you, I'd do it. With Kent.

Marvin: Thank you. I appreciate that.

'Are you taking a trip somewhere?' Jill asks when I arrive at school on Wednesday morning.

'Excuse me?'

I plop my backpack down and sink into one of the tiny student chairs.

'Those bags under your eyes are packed and ready for takeoff.' She lets out a loud cackle and even though she's wearing a plaid jumper ripe for a clapback, I'm too tired to think of one.

'Are they that bad?' I eye the mirror over the water fountain/sink combo in the corner of the room, but I'm too spent to walk over and check.

'You're going through an adjustment period. When Nick and I brought Maria home from the hospital, I don't think I slept more than two or three hours at a time. For weeks. But I was on leave, so I could adjust my sleep schedule to hers. Or try to, anyway.'

'Yeah, Greggie sleeps fairly well, or that's what Olan says. It's this middle of the night wake-up. It's like clockwork.' I run my fingers through my hair, feeling the small curls starting to return on top.

'He'll grow out of it.' Jill walks behind me and places a hand on my shoulder. 'Eventually.'

'From your mouth to God's ears.'

By Thursday night, or technically Friday morning, when the soft cooing and whines crackle from the baby monitor, I'm determined to take my turn. Olan has gotten up all week and, surprisingly, my body almost expects the 2 a.m. wake-up call. I'm awake and ready.

I stir under the covers, willing myself up as Gonzo makes a beeline for Illona's room. Smart kitty.

'I'll be right back,' Olan whispers.

'No, let me,' I say. 'Please.'

'Marv, babe, I've got it.'

'I know you do, but let me take a turn.'

Olan yawns and the taut muscles of his stomach flex. 'I'll be right here if you need anything.'

With a warm bottle from the kitchen in hand, I slowly poke open the door to Greggie's room. We quickly decided the guest room, which has a pullout loveseat and a few small pieces of furniture, would be the easiest to transform into a nursery. With Maria's crib, changing table, and the colorful mobile Jill bought because even though she's two, Maria still loves hers, we have enough to get us started and plenty of time to add items as he grows.

'Hey, little sprout.'

When he hears my voice, the cooing, which was bordering on crying, ceases. I peek over the crib's railing and see his giant, saucer-like brown eyes staring up at me. His right hand extends, tiny fingers wiggling in anticipation, and I reach in to scoop him up and carry him to the sofa.

'Are you hungry?'

Cradled in my lap, on the animal-themed baby blanket my mother sent, I move the bottle to his face and his hands attempt to hold it in place. He doesn't quite have the fine motor strength yet, so we do it together.

'There we go.'

As he drinks, his eyes flutter, and then close.

'You don't know if you're hungry or tired. Wait, maybe both.' I let out an enormous yawn. 'Hashtag relatable.'

As I cradle him in my arms, his weight resting on my lap, I am struck by the pure bliss radiating from his tiny, angelic face. He already trusts me with his entire existence. And then it hits me like the most fabulous ton of bricks. I love him.

He's been here less than a week and managed to weasel his way straight into my heart. I think I loved him before this moment but was too wrapped up in the minutia of adding a baby to our routine to notice. Amid the complete chaos of my life and the world around us, we somehow found each other. With a deep sigh, my eyes well up with tears as Greggie looks up at me, blinking.

But because I'm me, and nothing can be pleasant or simple for long, my brain immediately begins to worry. I'm now going to be a parent to not one, but two children. My heart thumps against my chest with the weight of the responsibility, but then I remember Olan. And Isabella. Jill and Nick. Sheldon and Theo. Kent and even Vincent. My mother would drop everything and fly here permanently if I asked. I'm not in this alone.

Greggie finishes his bottle and I quickly burp him. The noise that comes out of him vibrates through my torso, and I'm unable to suppress a giggle.

'You were starving.'

By the time I maneuver him back to my lap, he's managed to fall asleep. I know I'm supposed to return him to his crib and head back to bed, but I want just another minute with him. Holding him carefully, I extend my legs and turn on my side with Greggie between me and the back of the loveseat. He makes a few gurgling noises but quickly snuggles into my chest. As I close my eyes, I am immediately embraced by his comforting warmth and sweet fragrance that swiftly lulls me into a deep slumber.

'Marvin?'

There's a soft pressure on my shoulder.

'Babe?'

I crack an eye and see Olan standing before me. He's holding a sleeping Greggie.

'You dozed off for a few minutes.' Olan heads toward the crib. 'Let's get the baby back to bed.'

After placing Greggie in the crib, he returns to me and takes my hand.

'And now, you.'

Back in our bed, Olan spoons me, and his mouth lands on my shoulder blade.

'You did an awesome job.' Even though we're alone, Olan's voice is a low, rough whisper.

'You were right. About everything. About him. It's only been a few days and I already love him. So deeply. Is that strange?'

'Nope, not at all. I loved him the first time I held him.'

I push back against his firm chest, and Olan kisses the crook of my neck.

'Marvin, this paternal side of you is so fucking hot.'

Olan pushes his entire body against mine and there it is, his raging hard-on poking at my ass.

'Olan, it's almost two.'

'I know. I'm sorry, I've just missed you. This.' He thrusts into me.

The night Olan returned, by the time we unpacked, got Illona to bed, and Greggie was settled in his new space, we didn't have energy for much. We wanted to do more, I could feel it from both of us, but exhaustion took over and we settled for a hot, quick mutual jerk-off session. We kissed the entire time and there were absolutely no complaints. Our bodies were simply too spent for anything more.

As our new routine begins to take shape, it seems this might be our new normal. It's time to seize the moment. Illona is fast asleep. Greggie's been fed and won't stir for hours. And right now, Olan's skin sizzles against mine.

'Hang on,' I say, and quickly slide my boxers down. 'Now . . .' I turn around to face him. 'We need to fuck.'

Olan's eyes pop open.

'Please.' I draw us close, enveloping him in an embrace, and he melts into me with a sigh of pure passion.

38

There's a distinct energy when you have sex in the middle of the night. Even though both tiny humans are sleeping and the door is locked, there's an urgency. Or maybe it's because we haven't been this connected in over a month.

Returning from a quick trip to the bathroom after me, Olan lies on top of the blanket, applying a generous portion of lube to his hard dick. In the dim moonlight coming in the windows, I'm just able to make out his face. When he spots me, he makes a show of holding his cock up, stroking slowly, his thumb and index finger lingering over the tip as he wiggles his eyebrows at me.

Fuck. I want to start at his toes and bite my way up to his nose.

When I join him, Olan plants a soft kiss on my lips and then leans over and taps his bedside table lamp on. A warm light illuminates the space. Now I'm able to see him more clearly, his deep brown eyes sparkle with lust and his arms envelop me, pawing at my back as he grinds against me.

His lips trot over my skin, kissing, nibbling, licking like a switch has been flipped. He's in sex mode and even though I need to get up in a few hours for work, my brain easily succumbs. Olan does the thing where he mashes our hard cocks together, almost wishing there was a way to connect with our dicks. He gets such a kick out of it, glancing down and watching our swords crossing, trying to become one.

'What do you want . . .' I say, and before I can finish, Olan interrupts.

'You. This.' He reaches a hand around and buries his fingers in the muscle of my ass. 'And this.' His other hand grips my cock, and a soft moan escapes my lips. 'Both. Let me fuck you first. Please. Is that okay?'

Instead of replying, I flip over, arch my back, and stick my butt in the air, wagging it at him.

'That's my adorable babe.'

'First, an appetizer,' he says as he moves behind me.

Strong hands spread me wide and Olan's tongue skates around the perimeter of my hole. There's low, gravelly moaning, and finally, he utters, 'Fuck, I missed this.'

And with that, his tongue enters me, and my knees spread to give him better access. When he's rimming me, Olan mumbles and murmurs, like he's burying his face in the most delicious dessert, too busy enjoying himself and lost in the moment to breathe. In this case, the confection in question is cake. My cake. And having Olan inside me again opens me right up. My body instinctively pushes back against him, urging him to plunge deeper.

'Fuck, Olan. You and that tongue.'

He's unable to speak, and the combination of his light stubble and the vibrations from his groans sends a jolt of heat to my cock, which throbs in anticipation. When I reach under to palm myself, Olan seizes my dick from my hand, pulls it down and begins sucking. Never one to leave anything unattended, he slips his thumb into my hole while his mouth gives my cock attention. The sensation of being filled and sucked at the same time sends my eyes rolling back in my head, and I'm not sure how much longer I can wait.

'Olan, I'm ready. Now. Please. Please.'

'You wanna be fucked?' He's asking permission, but there's a playfulness, a teasing in his tone. He knows damn well what I want, but I thrust my ass against his face, anyway.

'Yes. Now.' I arch my back, doing my best to expose myself to him, showing him exactly how willing I am.

'Okay, babe. Okay.'

With my head resting on the pillow, Olan applies a generous amount of lube. There's something caring in the way he warms it up between his palms and carefully applies it. He values my pleasure just as much as his own. Another thing that makes him incredibly sexy. Just when I think he's done, he adds a little extra squirt.

'Never enough,' he says as his thumb gently enters me, spreading the lube.

When he finishes, I hear the tube drop next to me and he stands, positioning himself behind me. His weight pushes the end of the mattress down, and he wobbles back and forth a few times, finding his balance. Determined hands grasp just below my waist, and the tip of his cock slides into place. But being the gentleman he is, Olan waits.

'Ready?'

I nod and quickly realize between the low light and my head jammed against my pillow, he probably can't see.

'Yeah, so ready. Plow me.'

And with that, Olan carefully enters me, fusing us in the deepest, most glorious manner. He's slow at first, and I know he's worrying about my comfort, but like my heart, my ass has missed him. It's eager to be fucked.

'Olan, I'm good. You opened me right up with your tongue. You can fuck me. Hard. Fast. Deep. Please.'

With permission granted, he does exactly what I ask – speeding up, plunging further, sending ripples of pleasure through my body. The room is quiet except for the sound of our heavy breathing and Olan's hips slapping against my ass. The noise adds to the heat in the room and I grasp my cock. It's wet with precum. As he continues to thrust, it becomes more and more slick.

With a loud grunt and final drive, Olan pulls out and flops onto his back. The soft light reveals beads of sweat on his forehead, shimmering like tiny diamonds.

'Do you need a break?'

'Come here.' Olan pulls me close, my head resting on his beautiful chest, and while he catches his breath, I nibble on his torso. With the attention being paid to his chest, his cock pulses as I stroke him, keeping him hard for round two.

Fingers graze my chin, lifting my head, and Olan's mouth finds mine. I continue to jerk him with long strokes, taking breaks to massage his balls and taint. The ever subtle lift of his hips offers a hint that his ass craves some attention too. Olan's tongue parts my lips and, never breaking the kiss, I shift on top of him and guide his cock to its target.

He has to lift a little more and I'm tempted to pause and grab a pillow to place under him, but I don't, because right now, in this moment, I'm not breaking this kiss. Olan thrusts up, fucking deep inside, as our tongues tangle and I nip at his lips.

My legs widen, and Olan grasps my ass, spreading me wide, and I'm fairly certain he's trying to feel his cock enter me, but while kissing, he simply can't reach.

I sit up and move my feet under me, using his firm pecs to balance. Without hesitation, he swiftly removes his hand from behind and slips it under my balls, teasing and exploring the spot where we connect.

'Babe, you look so hot right now, bouncing up and down on my cock.' Olan takes his free hand and grips my dick. There's no movement. He's simply holding on. It's clear he's not ready for me to come yet.

'I need to have this in my mouth.' His thumb rubs the tip. 'Soon. Please. I've been patient.'

'Okay. Fair.' As I lean forward, Olan's cock slips out, but when his lips find mine, I'm appeased for the moment. With his fingers still wrapped around my raging boner, I'm ready to have my turn.

I move to the end of the bed, my feet float to the floor, the softness of the plush area rug under my toes. I lean back on my elbows, and my dick sticks straight out.

'Suck me like this.'

'Yes, sir.' Olan's up, moving to the floor, on all fours, quicker than I've seen him move in a long time.

'There's that beautiful fat cock. Fuck, I missed it.' He swallows me, taking me almost to the base. A slight gagging noise breaks free from his lips, wrapped tightly around me.

'You okay?' I ask, but Olan simply bobs up and down, saliva dripping from the corner of his mouth.

When he arches his back, his plump ass taunting me, I reach over and grab the lube. He's in the perfect position to apply it and I'm fairly certain his ass in the air is Olan's way of hinting at it.

Leaning over, I apply a liberal amount, using two fingers to spread it around and then one to gently dip into his hole. He's more open and ready than I expected after over a month apart, and before I'm able to say anything, he pulls off.

'I bought a toy. After our hot video chat, I needed it.'

He smiles, his inviting tooth gap on full display, and a dab of saliva dots the corner of his mouth.

'Excuse me, Mr Stone. You brought a dildo into your parents' house?'

'My bedroom door has a lock. And I thought about you every time I used it.'

'Every time? How many times did you fuck yourself with a dildo in Chicago?'

He glances at the ceiling in thought. 'Maybe three times?'

'Fuck, Olan.' My dick hardens at the thought of him using it. 'Well, good for you. And me.'

With that, Olan slides back, my finger gliding easily into his inviting hole. He returns to sucking and my cock becomes more rigid as his tongue slides over the tip and my finger gets a preview of what's coming.

'Do you want to do it like this?' I ask and Olan pulls off again, catching his breath.

'Yeah, get right behind me. Is that okay?'

'I think we can make it work.'

Standing, I move behind him, kneel, and kiss his left butt cheek.

'You really have a spectacular ass,' I say.

'Thank you. I'm glad you appreciate the squats. Now if you're ready . . .'

Olan reaches back and pulls his cheeks apart, and my heartbeat accelerates. Moving into position, I place the head of my dick near his opening, and before I can push in, he moves back, his hole starving for me.

'There we go,' Olan murmurs.

He's bracing himself against the bed, with his forehead down. As soon as I find a rhythm, Olan reaches under and starts stroking himself. This is his favorite way to have an orgasm and at this point, we're both keen to come.

'Don't move for a minute,' he says.

When I pause, Olan thrusts back and forth, fucking my cock with his magnificent hole. Allowing me to simply stare down and enjoy the view of my dick stretching him wide as it glides in and out of him.

'Olan, you're going to make me come like this. It's too perfect. You. This.'

'I'm close. Go back to fucking me, please.'

I do as I'm told, grabbing his waist and pounding myself into him while he strokes harder and faster.

'Harder.' Olan's voice becomes even lower, more raspy. 'Fuck the cum out of me.' My body slams against his. 'Please.'

He needs this. I need this. I pull back, my cock almost completely out before plunging back in deeper, harder. I repeat this and notice Olan's hand moving quicker, and his ass begins to pulse around my dick. He's so close.

I lean over, wrap an arm around his torso, and my fingers land on his chest, squeezing, massaging, pinching, and flicking his nipple as I rail him.

What starts as a low hum evolves into a deep moan and Olan's hole convulses around my cock. Shots of warm cum blast my forearm underneath him as he shakes with pleasure.

'There's my sweet guy,' I whisper into his ear. I'm bent over him, our bodies stacked like the sweetest warm pancakes. 'I love you.'

Olan cranes his neck, reaching back for a kiss and before my mouth lands on his, he says, 'I love you, too. So damn much.'

In one swift movement, I'm on my feet and plop down onto the bed, my legs hanging over the side. When I palm myself, I'm still raging hard, but a yawn stretches across my face. It's late – already Friday morning, and I have to be at school in a few hours.

'Don't move,' Olan says.

'I'm too tired to move.'

'Good.'

He's next to me, kissing my neck, moving his way to my ear, stroking me. Slowly at first, but picking up speed. When Olan's lips land in that spot right behind my ear, I swear there's a magical button that sends a message right to my cock. He kisses and sucks right there and yup, my orgasm knocks within seconds.

'I'm close.' My fingers swaddle Olan's neck, keeping him in place.

In between biting and slurping, he pauses to reply. 'I know.'

And that's it. My dick can't hold back as he jerks me faster and frissons of pleasure crisscross over me as I shoot all over my chest – a few rogue drops landing on my chin.

'Oh, babe. You got me.'

And I'm pretty sure Olan's cheek.

When I glance at him, a mischievous smile forms on his face, followed by a low, enticing giggle.

'You needed that,' he says.

'We both did.'

Olan retrieves a washcloth from the bedside table and begins wiping us.

'Thank you again,' he says as he brushes the rag over my chest.

'No, thank you. That was amazing. I think I'll sleep like a baby now.'

'I meant for all you've done while I was away. For suggesting I bring Greggie home. For being amazing with Illona. For the friendship you've cultivated with Isabella. You've somehow managed to jockey yourself for Husband of the Year before we're even married.'

'I'm pretty sure you're winning that,' I say as we get under the covers.

'Or maybe' – Olan pulls me close and wraps his arm around me, replicating the spooning position that started all this – 'we can share the title.'

'That sounds perfect.'

I close my eyes and take it all in. My life has only gotten better in the short time we've been together, and now I'm more than ready to be married. There's nothing quite like drifting off to sleep with your limbs intertwined, knowing you're meant to be together forever.

39

Sheldon: I've left you alone all week to enjoy your man being home, but we need to get cracking.

Marvin: Cracking on what?

Sheldon: Hello? Your WEDDING. There are decisions, deadlines, and deposits to make.

Marvin: Don't we still have four months?

Sheldon: Four months is like four minutes in Wedding Planning Land.

Marvin: Is that an actual place?

Sheldon: Yes. And don't forget to pack snacks, you might be there for a while. We're coming to you tomorrow morning. Theo will pack bagels and schmears. Do you eat lox?

Marvin: Does RuPaul love quirky comedy queens?

Sheldon: Amen. We'll be on the 9:15 ferry.

Amidst the chaos of the past month, planning the wedding has been put on the back burner. Apart from the meeting with my mother and Sheldon, I have given little thought to the specifics of the day. Olan's absence has prevented me from making decisions that should involve him and now that he's home, we've been a little preoccupied.

Sheldon and Theo arrive Sunday morning, both carrying various bags and boards, and I nearly miss Walter standing behind Theo's cooler.

'Come in, guys,' I say. Greggie's lulling between alertness and a nap in the sling against my chest. It's only a matter of time before he dozes off. 'Gonzo will be happy to see Walter again.'

Theo bends over and removes Walter's harness and he scuttles inside, searching for his kitty playmate.

'How was the ferry?'

'Perfect day for it,' Sheldon says, walking past me with full arms.

'I didn't realize you were bringing so much . . . stuff. We could've come to you.'

'Marvin, you have a baby now.' Sheldon pats Greggie, who is doing his best to take in the whirling dervish that is Sheldon Soleskin.

'Having a baby doesn't preclude us from leaving the house,' Olan says.

He's on the stairs, freshly showered, wearing his favorite cream T-shirt and navy joggers. One sign of the warming spring days – Olan's bare feet. When it's not freezing outside, he enjoys going sockless, and there's an undeniable allure to the extra flash of skin as he approaches us in the foyer.

'I told him that,' Theo says.

'He hasn't even been here a week.' Sheldon rubs the back of his fingers on Greggie's chubby cheek, eliciting a soft smile. 'Next time you can come to us.'

Sheldon drops his assortment of boards and bags onto the dining-room table, then starts unfolding, unpacking, and arranging what looks like a rather elaborate setup.

'Next time?' The words come out without thinking, and I cringe as soon as I say them.

'Marvin, planning a wedding this size is a marathon, not a sprint. The meeting we had with your mother was just the kick-off. The amuse-bouche.' Sheldon winks at Theo, and then assembles some sort of stand from one of the bags and places a large board on it.

There are photos and fabric swatches, more sticks and twigs, and a large seating chart. My head spins and I pull a dining-room chair out from the table to sit. Olan moves behind me, the scent of freshly applied cherry ChapStick soothing me as he rests a hand on my shoulder.

'Here's your seating chart.' Sheldon points to a diagram of tables and chairs. 'You'll notice it's empty.' He taps the board with his finger. 'The Ocean Inn provides tables, but we'll need to discuss linens. Once you finalize the invite list, we can start working on seating. And speaking of, we need to order the invitations soon. Like yesterday. I have some samples here.' With a swift flip of the board, a fresh sight emerges – stationery of various hues and delicate tissue paper dance in the air, stirred by the gentle breeze caused by Sheldon's movement.

'Do you want plain or printed vellum inserts? Printed are slightly more, but worth it in my opinion. It says "We care about the details. Also, we're not cheap." Technically, this will be a destination wedding for some of your guests. We should probably include an information card with places to stay, eat, sightseeing spots, maybe arrange some tours.'

More flipping, this time a giant collage of photos is displayed.

'What about seating?' Sheldon points to a section with pictures of various chairs. 'The venue only provides folding chairs.' He sticks his finger in his mouth and pretends to gag. 'We'll have to rent chairs. Totally worth the extra expense. But there are options.'

'Rent chairs?' I ask.

'Yes. I've got it all. You just pick which ones.' Sheldon motions to the choices. There's at least five and they all look very similar to me.

'This seems like a lot,' Olan says.

'I told him that too,' Theo says. He's unpacking his cooler, taking only a small corner of the table to display the plate of bagels, what looks like three different cream cheese options, and lox with all the fixings.

'Boys.' Sheldon pauses from his setup and turns toward us. 'You're inviting a hundred and fifty people to celebrate your union at a gorgeous seaside venue. We're not tossing them bagels and cream cheese and calling it a day. No offense, baby.'

'None taken.' Theo makes himself a plate and my stomach grumbles, watching him pile lox on a bagel.

Olan sighs and I sense bubbling tension. My hand brushes Greggie's hair. The complete softness of it on my fingers soothes me as a massive yawn appears on his cute face.

'Yes, Gregory,' Sheldon says. 'Weddings aren't for the faint of heart.'

'I think baby boy might be hinting at a nap,' Olan says. 'I'll take him.'

Olan lifts Greggie from the sling. His chunky arms attempt to grasp around Olan's neck, but his fingers land near his mouth instead.

'I'll come too. We'll be back in two minutes,' I say.

'I'll have all this' – Sheldon motions to his displays – 'ready when you're back.'

'Take your time,' Theo says between bites. Walter and Gonzo have taken a break from playing to sit at his feet, praying he drops something.

Upstairs in the nursery, Olan gently places Greggie in his crib and starts the mobile. The bright plinking of 'Twinkle, Twinkle, Little Star' plays, filling the room, and Greggie waves at the brightly colored orange fox and blue owl that appear to dance above him.

'Are you okay?' I ask.

'I'm fine. It's just . . . overwhelming.'

'I'm fairly certain if you looked up overwhelming in the dictionary, there would be a photo of Sheldon wearing his Wedding Planner shirt.'

'No, not him. I mean yes, him. But the paper samples and fabrics and seating arrangements. And now with . . .' Olan nods toward Greggie, who's closed his eyes and seems to enter the initial stages of a power nap.

'Between Sheldon and my mother, all we really need to do is make a few decisions. Or maybe many decisions.' I scratch my head. 'But they're going to do most of the heavy lifting. We can just show up and get married.'

Olan envelops me in an enormous embrace. With a deep sigh, his body melts into mine and he squeezes me tighter than he typically does. A quick flip in my stomach gives me pause.

'It will be okay. No, amazing,' I whisper into his ear.

Olan's lips kiss the side of my neck before moving to my cheek, and finally my mouth. His gaze avoids mine, but he responds with a deliberate nod as if lost in deep thought.

'We should go back down.' Olan gives me another soft peck on the lips. 'Sheldon's waiting.'

40

'Hey, Mom.' I do my best to keep my voice down. Luckily, this morning there are only two other passengers on the bus and they're sitting near the front.

'I only have a few minutes. We're almost at school.'

'I figured as much. It's just after five, but I wanted to catch you.' I hear her take a long sip, and I can almost smell the hazelnut creamer in her coffee.

'Wait, I thought you were three hours behind us?' My mind does somersaults, trying to do the mental math.

'Three in the summer and two in the winter. Remember, Arizona doesn't observe daylight savings. Who invented this fakakta time change? Were they just trying to confuse me more than usual?'

'I'm sure that wasn't their intention,' I say, swallowing the kernel of annoyance bubbling — it's simply not helpful. 'Anyway, what's up?'

'I spoke to Sheldon yesterday. He's really such a nice boy. And so cute. If he wasn't engaged to that custodian and you weren't with Olan, maybe you two could have dated.'

'Is that why you called? To play hypothetical match-maker in a universe where neither Sheldon nor I are single?'

'No, I'm just saying. He's adorable. And sweet.'

'He is. Theo,' I say his name sharply to remind her of it, 'thinks so, too. And I'm marrying Olan.'

'Yes, I know. Theo yes. He's a nice boy too.'

'Very nice. And they're engaged.'

'Engaged. Oh right, that's why I called. Lord, if my head weren't screwed on so tight, it'd be out there playing hide and seek with my socks!'

As I tilt my head, my gaze lands on the observatory, its grand silhouette piercing the sky, as the bus makes a turn toward Pelletier.

My mother doesn't continue, and knowing we're only a few minutes from school, I prod her along.

'And . . . The wedding? Sheldon?'

'Right, oy. He told me all about your meeting. And Theo with his bagels. Three types of cream cheese. Plain and veggie, yes, but I've never heard of horseradish cream cheese, and now, of course, I want some. Sheldon promised the next time I visit, they'll have me over and Theo will make a spread. Did you have lox? I know when you were little you didn't care for it, and I noticed you didn't have any when I was there, but really you should try it again. Loving lox is in your DNA. Don't deny your ancestors this mitzvah. And I bet Olan would love it. The smokiness. He's got sophisticated taste, I can tell.'

If there was any doubt about the genetic link to ADHD, my mother and I are living proof of it.

'Mom. I'm almost at school.'

'And?'

'And what?'

'Did you have the lox?' she asks.

'Yes, I love lox now.'

'Good. You can use all the protein you can get. It's good brain food. Anyway, Sheldon mentioned you have some work to do. Guest lists. Invitations. Seating plans. If you need any help, you tell me. I'm emailing you a few of my friends who'd like to come. This way I'll know some people. Marta and I can go dress shopping together – I have a few dresses in my closet, but I definitely need something new. You don't want the mother of the bride wearing a shmata.'

Deep breath.

'Mom, I'm not the bride.'

'Olan's the bride?'

'There is no bride. We're both the grooms. Remember?'

'Right, right. I'm sorry, sweetie. Well, the mother of the groom. Either way, you want me to look nice, right?'

'Yes, of course. My stop is coming up.' A beacon of hope, the bus approaches the school stop. 'I love you, Mom.'

'I love you too, honey.'

'What now?' Jill asks.

Like a penny thrown into a wishing well, I sink into the tiny kindergarten-sized chair, wishing the hard surface under my ass was my bed.

'It's just a lot.' I lean forward, letting my bag slide off my shoulder until it lands on the tile floor with a thud.

'Marvin, you went from having a seven-year-old – who

let's be real, is a dream – five days a week and every other weekend, to having a baby twenty-four seven. Having children means mourning the life you're losing, while also falling in love with the new life taking root. It took Nick and me months to get a night's sleep in bed together, let alone more than sleep.' She wiggles her eyebrows. 'There's going to be an adjustment period.'

'No, it's not that. We're fine there.'

'Of course you are.' She rolls her eyes. 'Men. You're never too tired for it.'

I shrug. 'Fact.' She shakes her head and joins me at the table. 'I mean, that's part of it,' I say. 'But honestly, so far, everyone's adjusting well.' I take the last sip of my coffee and regret not getting a refill before boarding the bus. 'It's the wedding. The planning.'

'Sheldon.'

'How did you know?'

'He emailed me on Friday.' She holds her phone up as evidence. 'And asked me to join them at your house. I declined. No offense. We took Maria on a hike up at Bradbury Mountain.'

'None taken. A beautiful hike over wedding planning – I would've done the same.'

'It was lovely. It's still cool enough the bugs aren't bad.'

'Wait, how does Sheldon have your email?'

'Marvin, the district website lists every school, every teacher, every contact.'

'Oh, right.'

'He was quite adamant I come. "Best woman duties" and all that jazz. I assured him you four could handle it without me.'

'Oy. I'm sorry.' I pull my lips in and shake my head. 'I didn't mean for you to get roped into this mishigas.'

'Don't apologize. Some people get carried away with weddings. It's a whole thing. There are entire shows dedicated to Bridezillas.'

'Well, Sheldon, no doubt egged on by my mother, might be cranked up to eleven about the wedding, but it's Olan I'm worried about.'

Jill's eyebrows dart up and she makes her oh-no-what-the-fuck-now face.

'You think he's having second thoughts?' She glances at the top of my head. 'It's the hair. I knew it. I told you it was a mistake to chop off your curls. They were your catnip.'

'Thanks.' I run my hand through my hair. Slowly, the curls are returning, but it could take months for me to regain the pre-cut level of Jewfro perfection.

'I don't think he's having second thoughts.' With a deep inhale, my stomach expands. 'He just doesn't seem that into it.'

'The wedding or getting married?' Jill asks. 'Because they are not the same thing.'

'The wedding. I think? Wait, what do you mean?'

Jill smiles and pulls her chair in closer, leaning her arms on the table. 'A huge, expensive, intricate wedding a marriage does not make. People elope. Las Vegas has built an entire tourist industry around it.'

'But he seemed so into it . . .'

'B.B.' Jill sits up and cocks her head. 'Before baby. Everything's different now. You better talk to him. Soon.'

I head to my classroom, wondering if Jill might be

on to something. Maybe with all the changes, with our additional responsibilities and busier schedule, with all Olan has going on not only with Greggie but helping his brother, and his parents, keeping his family afloat from halfway across the country, maybe he's changed his mind. My anxiety kicks up a notch and I immediately remind myself, Olan loves me. He's told me he can't wait for us to be married. Many times. Why am I so eager to fall back into a worry loop?

One thing Jill is right about for sure: I need to talk to Olan. Soon.

41

'That's right, disappointed is a really strong feeling word,' I reply to Amanda. 'Why do you think the mouse is disappointed?'

I hold the book up and point to the page where the little mouse sits with her face in her hands.

'She wanted to play in the big hockey game,' Amanda says.

'With her friends.' Eddie pops up on his knees, but he's in the back row, so I don't ask him to sit.

'And she hurt her foot, so she can't.' There's a melancholic tone in Katherine's voice.

'Right, so how is disappointed different from sad?' I ask. We've talked a lot about ranges of emotions and using more precise language, and Amanda recognized the opportunity, so I know they're grasping this concept.

'It's like you're sad,' Ben says. 'But really, really sad.'

'Like a sad sandwich.' Danny's face lights up. 'Take sad bread and add sad meat and sad mustard.'

A few of the other students look confused, not quite following Danny's sandwich metaphor.

'You're on the right track,' I say, hoping someone else can give a more succinct answer.

Austin's hand tentatively goes up and everyone turns toward him. I nod quickly, urging him to speak.

'When you want something and you can't have it, you might feel sad,' he says. 'But if you've been waiting a really long time and hoping and wishing and then you don't get it, that's more than sad.'

'Exactly. You're disappointed,' I say. 'Nice work, friends. Unpacking complicated emotions can be challenging. But when you consider sadness or happiness as the core of these other emotions,' I explain, gesturing toward our chart, 'you see how we can effectively express the feelings of our characters or ourselves more clearly.'

When I return from walking the last pickups to the cafe-gymatorium, Illona's sitting on the floor, writing in her journal, waiting for me. It was her first weekend with Isabella since Greggie came home and somehow my heart missed her more than usual. Despite the chaos of taking care of a baby and the drastic shift in our weekend, I can't help but feel a void in my heart when Illona is with her mother.

'There you are.' I plop down next to her and without pausing her writing, she wraps her free arm around me as I hug her.

'How was your day? Wait, your weekend? Did you have a snack? I have some crackers in the cabinet. Maybe some fruit snacks? How are you?' The words tumble out of my mouth, but Illona doesn't seem fazed. She understands me well.

'Day was okay. Frankie Sanderson told me he has a crush on Andrea Sterling.'

'I'm sorry. I didn't realize you liked him.'

'Ew. Gross. I don't. Mrs Day has to remind him to wash his hands after the bathroom.'

'Oh. Then what's the issue?'

'Andrea likes Ricky Shroeder. Anyway, I don't really care, it was just kind of annoying. I told Frankie he should keep that information to himself.'

A laugh erupts from my belly. 'That sounds like wise advice.'

'Weekend was fine. Mom and I baked an apple cake. I have two extra pieces in my lunch box for you and Daddy. I figured Greggie wasn't ready for apple cake.'

'That's a smart assumption,' I say, rubbing her back. Her writing abruptly comes to a halt, and her beautiful face takes on a melancholy expression, capturing my attention.

'I missed . . .' Illona's gaze meets mine. I give her a moment, but when she doesn't finish her sentence, I simply open my arms, and she melts into me.

'Sweetie, we missed you too,' I say into her hair. Isabella has braided it into an intricate geometrical design.

'We always miss you when you're not with us.' I move back, making eye contact. 'But we're only a ferry ride away. And you know, we can talk to your mom and dad. Maybe we can be more flexible with the days you're with us and her. Like maybe you spend some days during the week with her and more weekends with us.'

She nods and then bites her lower lip. 'Sometimes I just wish we could all be together.' Her voice breaks with emotion and I'm instantly aware of the tears forming in my eyes. What is this all about?

'Oh, sweetie. I know it's hard. That's why your mom moved here.'

We've had this arrangement for almost two years with no issue, and then Jill's words echo in my head: *Everything changes*.

'Does this have anything to do with your cousin?' I ask.

Illona pulls her lips in, and I spy the slightest tremble of her lower lip. 'I'm glad he's here. Honest. I can tell how much Daddy and you love him already. And I love him too. But he gets to be with you . . . all the time.'

And there it is.

'You feel left out?' I tilt my face toward hers and Illona dips her gaze and nods.

I'm overtaken by the realization this is probably a conversation we should have with Isabella and Olan. But they're not here. She needs to talk about it now. With me. Of course, I'll loop them in later, but right now, I have Illona's exposed heart before me and my biggest concern is treating her with care.

'Illona Marie Stone.' As soon as it comes out of my mouth, I realize I sound like my mother.

'Trust me, your mom and dad would love nothing more than to have you all the time. Me too. But your parents are divorced. And I know that isn't fair, but we all love you so much and want what's best for you. I know that doesn't make it better, but I have a feeling having Greggie here, we might all be doing things together a little more.'

'Really?'

'I mean, your dad and I need help. From your mom, yes, but we need you too.'

322

'When Mommy and Daddy needed help, they brought Cindy to live with us.'

Ah yes, the gorgeous nanny I was convinced Olan was having an affair with. How could I forget?

'But now, they want to do it with us. You're older.' My hand lands on her shoulder. 'I know this is a big change, but Greggie needs all of us. He needs you, too.'

She nods, and dear Lord in heaven, I hope this is helping.

'And there's me.' I stop, unsure if my words are coming out correctly. Anxiety taps at my door, and I fear I'm making a mess of the conversation.

'Three adults now,' she says.

Her eyes find mine. 'Plus, me.' A hint of a smile appears. 'So, actually better than with Cindy.'

'Exactly.' My chest tingles as she makes a case for our new family structure.

'But instead of a mom, dad, and nanny, now there's two dads.'

The lump that forms in my throat threatens my ability to breathe or swallow. I take a cleansing inhale and clear my throat, confirming my vocal cords still work.

'Nothing will bring me more joy than being your stepfather.'

'I mean, honestly, you already are.' She shrugs. 'Getting married just makes it official.'

'You're absolutely right.'

I pull Illona close, a smile lighting up my face as I give her a heartfelt hug, cherishing the moment.

'Now,' I say. 'Let's go home.'

42

Teaching tires me out like nothing else – even with my anxiety humming along at a slightly lower frequency. Mondays are always a smack of reality, and coming home to Olan is always a refresher – like an energy drink to propel me over the bedtime finish line.

Somehow, Olan's presence at home all day calms me. Sure, I'd like to be home with him, but the simple knowledge he'll be waiting for me brings a little extra sense of ease to my days.

Tonight, after we savor Olan's homemade meatloaf, I stand at the kitchen sink, the sound of running water filling the air, while Olan cradles Greggie and Illona concentrates on her math homework at the island. Second-grade math is no joke.

With the last plate loaded and the counters wiped down, I stand watching them. Olan sways slightly, keeping the baby content while he watches Illona's pencil move across the paper. Gonzo lies on the counter, his tail thwacking against the assignment. Just like his dad, fractions are not his cup of tea.

'Two-fifths. I can barely say it, let alone solve the problem.' Her tongue juts out the side of her mouth.

'Princess. Watch.' Olan takes her pencil and draws something, scribbling and shading. 'Understand?'

'Oh. Duh.' She rolls her eyes, takes her pencil back, and writes something. 'There. Done.' She pushes her homework away. 'Fractions. Oy.'

A mischievous smirk dances on my lips as I watch them, and a desire to stir up some cheer takes hold of me.

'I have a lesson for the class,' I say, grabbing my phone and quickly connecting to the wireless sound system Olan spent weeks teaching me how to use.

'A lesson?' Olan cocks his head.

'For all of you. Come here.' I motion to the open area of the kitchen beyond the island and press play on my phone.

The bright singing and xylophone intro pumps through the entire first floor, followed by the deep, funky bass line, and when Shanice's distinct, bright voice begins, Illona's face lights up like a sunrise.

I extend my hands to her, reaching out to bridge the distance between us.

She takes them and we sway, moving our shoulders to the music.

When the chorus hits and 'I Love Your Smile' blasts through our home, right on cue, Olan's face cracks into an enormous grin, and I'm not sure there's ever been a more perfect song to capture my admiration for him.

Illona lets go of one of my hands, extends it to her father, and he takes it.

'Your dad's knowledge extends beyond fractions.'

Olan's hips move to the rhythm of the music, gyrating with a confidence I've only seen in the bedroom, and a burst of laughter escapes me, catching me off guard.

'Go Daddy!'

Greggie's head bops, either from Olan's movement, the music, or both. This might just take the prize for the cutest thing I've ever witnessed. As we dance, Olan holds him tightly with one arm, ensuring his safety.

'Motown. 1991. Produced by Narada Michael Walden and featuring a sax solo by Branford Marsalis and laughter from Janet Jackson near the end of the song,' I say over the music.

'Color me impressed.' Olan winks and yeah, I may have studied up on the song while he was away.

'Your teaching skills are on par with your ability to be a student.'

'Marvin's an excellent teacher,' Illona says. 'I should know.'

'Thank you,' I say and hold her hand up so she can spin.

In the kitchen, the four of us are caught up in the infectious rhythm of Shanice's complete bop, moving and grooving with pure joy while Gonzo watches from the counter. The vibrant beats and catchy melody fill the air, igniting an undeniable energy that propels our bodies to sway and twirl effortlessly. Laughter and smiles adorn our faces as we're bound by the sheer euphoria that only music and dance can provide.

When both children are tucked in, Olan and I retreat to our bedroom. In the room's stillness, the baby monitor remains quiet. I sink into the chair, my pajamas casually tossed over the back, my feet propped up on the ottoman. My mind wanders perhaps more than it should, but I realize we need to have this conversation. The weight of the unspoken words hangs in the air.

'It's only eight-thirty. Did you want to watch something? Or read?' Olan sits on the bed, waiting for my answer before he commits to lying down.

'How about a chat?'

I move next to him and rub my palm up and down his thigh. The softness of his fleece pajama bottoms soothes my fingers, and he places his hand on mine.

'Always pleased to talk to my love.'

Monday night before bedtime might not be the ideal time to have this discussion, but when would be? For once in my life, I'd rather have the difficult conversation sooner rather than later. I have enough experience to know whatever the ramifications, eventually the dust will settle. Do the thing. Rip the bandage off. Get it done.

'It's about the wedding.'

'What about it?' Olan scoots back and leans against the large throw pillows he uses to make the bed. He likes a clean, simple look, and always a crisply made bed.

'Maybe I'm off base. I know I sometimes misread situations. And I tend to worry about things too much . . .'

'You? Worry too much?' A cheeky half smile flowers on Olan's face. Marvin Block, do not get distracted.

'Yes, me. Guilty. But instead of spiraling into a pit of anxiety, I figured I should ask you about it.'

'Okay, ask away.' He moves his hands behind his head and his biceps flex. I try really hard to focus on his face.

'I got a vibe. A feeling. When Sheldon and Theo were

here, when we came up to put Greggie down . . . all the planning was feeling . . . overwhelming was the word you used.'

'I mean, it is. Overwhelming. Considerable. It's not the money, it's just . . .'

Olan's eyes swivel toward the door and he pauses, pursing his lips.

'Tell me. Please.' I'm sitting next to him with my legs crossed and my hand on his thigh.

'It's just with the baby. My brother. Me being absent for a month. Handling my family back in Chicago. I'm going to need to fly back at some point. And here. We're a few weeks into this, and so far, everything seems to be going smoothly. Still, I can't help but consider how significant this transition is for Illona. I know she's adjusting well, but I want to be gentle with her. And with us. We're doing it. Skillfully, if I don't say so myself. But I'm concerned with all the pandemonium that accompanies a large-scale wedding, particularly the chaotic scene downstairs – the charts and diagrams and arrangements. Do we have unrealistic expectations of what we're asking from the universe? From Illona. Even Gregory.'

'Oh.'

It's not my most thoughtful reply, but I'm not exactly sure what to say. He's not wrong. And his focus is on his family. Both back in Chicago and here. Olan's thoughtfulness and unwavering concern for the people he cares about sets him apart. It's one of the qualities I love most about him.

'So, maybe we shouldn't get married?'

Wetness wells up in my eyes as I say the words, but I'm determined not to cry.

'No.' Olan sits up, leans toward me and brings his hand to my face. As his thumb brushes against my bottom lip, I feel a gentle tingle of electricity.

'Then what?'

'Maybe all that . . .' He nods toward the door. Downstairs. Sheldon's Wedding Central. 'Is too much.'

Too much. The words crackle in my ears, and I exhale, my breath skating over Olan's fingers.

'The wedding?'

'*That* wedding. Yes.'

My chest expands with air and the urge to be closer consumes me as I lean in and kiss him softly.

'Should we wait?' I ask. The August wedding begins fading away like residue on a washed chalkboard. 'I've waited my whole life for you. I can wait another year or two if you think that would make it better.'

Olan's other hand joins his first, and he cups my face, holding my gaze.

'Marvin, listen to me. I want nothing more than to be married to you. If we could go down to city hall right now, I'd pack the kids up and do it. The size of a wedding doesn't equate to the quality or success of a marriage. I think a wedding of that magnitude might be too much for our family right now.'

A heaviness overtakes my head, like I'm stuck in a fog, and I find solace by resting against his palms.

'I want to marry you, Marvin. Now. Maybe we don't have to wait a year or two for an elaborate wedding. We could do it sooner.' His eyes light up with that magic sparkle. 'Just us. Close friends and family. Would you be okay with that?'

The Ocean Inn. One hundred and fifty guests arriving from all over the country. My college friend Jenny flying from New Zealand. She took a vacation there after she became infatuated with the *Lord of the Rings* movies, fell in love with the country, a cute Kiwi, and never looked back.

But of course, he's right. The focus should be on the marriage itself, not an extravagant wedding.

I sit up, turn to face him, and offer a small nod. With a gentle tug, Olan pulls me closer, his lips pressing against mine.

Pulling back, he says, 'Let's do it. Next weekend. Simple. Quick. Easy. And then we'll be married.' He leans in, resting his forehead on mine. 'That's all I want. To be married to you.'

How am I supposed to argue with that?

Pressing my lips against my fiancé's, I am reminded that sometimes the unexpected can lead to the most beautiful moments. And then, like a lightning bolt, it hits me.

Oh my God.

This time next week, we'll be married.

43

Sheldon: Emergency meeting after school at Branch Booch.

Marvin: There's no emergency.

Jill: Have we alerted the National Guard?

Marvin: Don't encourage him.

Vincent: I'll be there.

Marvin: Really, we can just hop on a call.

Sheldon: Absolutely not. This is a code red. I will see you at three.

Jill: Lucky us.

Sheldon: I read that.

Jill: 😒

Olan agrees to handle the major wedding cancellations while Greggie naps. Unlike me, he has no issue making phone calls, talking to strangers, and letting them know we'll be abandoning all the hard work they've already banked. It's like ordering a cheese pizza for him. My job is to handle Sheldon. And my mother. Oy. One thing at a time.

Isabella picks Illona up after school for 'emergency dress shopping' while I meet with the crew at Branch Booch. I'm not sure if Olan's idea has eliminated the whirlwind of planning or simply truncated it to a few days. Regardless, I remind myself we'll be married soon.

'All right, Operation Wedding is now Operation Getting Hitched.' Sheldon slams down his purple notebook on the table and Jill and Vincent watch their drinks tremble at the impact.

'Nice to see you, too,' Jill says.

'Sorry, there's no time for pleasantries. We have three days to pull this off.' Sheldon sits in a large wooden chair with a high back that dwarfs him.

'Sheldon, there's nothing to pull off,' I say. 'I texted you the plan. We're going to city hall and then dinner. That's it.'

'City hall?' Sheldon opens his notebook, scratches something out and then takes a dramatic sigh as he braces himself on the heavy oak table. 'They're not open on Saturday. And the last appointment to get married is Friday at four. Three days! Oy.' His palm smacks his freckled forehead.

Jill shrugs and says, 'So we'll go after school.'

Vincent and I nod as Sheldon rolls his eyes.

'An after-school wedding,' he says. 'How romantic. Okay, fine.'

There's more scribbling, and I make an attempt to shift Sheldon's mood. 'Where's Theo?'

As I hoped, Sheldon's expression softens at the mere mention of his fiancé's name, and the tension in his shoulders eases.

'He's playing mini-golf with Brodie. Today's their Big Brother's Day.'

'Brodie talked about it while he was helping in my class,' Vincent says. 'He's very excited. The two of them are quite the pair. I spied Brodie holding Theo's hand by the entry at dismissal.'

'Theo would never admit it, but he's just as excited as Brodie,' Sheldon says.

'Well, that's sweetest.' I offer a smile.

'Yes, Theo's the sweetest.' Sheldon's face mirrors my grin momentarily before he returns to the seriousness of his pre-Theo thoughts. 'Now, what are you wearing?'

I glance down at my green hoodie, brown corduroy pants, and white sneakers. 'Um, clothes?'

'No, you silly goose. To the wedding.'

'I don't know. Probably whatever I wear to school on Friday? Olan will probably wear a dress shirt and khakis.'

'His standard uniform,' Vincent says. 'I appreciate the predictability of his wardrobe.'

'Plus, his ass looks great in khakis.' Jill smiles. 'I'm allowed to say that. Best woman!'

Sheldon shakes his head. 'What about dinner? Have you thought about a restaurant? How many people are going? Do we have reservations?'

'We figured we'd go with the flow and see what folks

felt like.' I lift my chin because, at this point, I'm simply not going to allow myself to worry. 'Worst case, we could grab burgers at The Shake Shack.'

Sheldon's mouth drops open. My mom is right, he really is adorable.

'Go with the flow?' Sheldon slowly closes his notebook. 'Marvin, listen. As your friend . . .' Sheldon looks toward Jill. 'Your gay friend . . .' He glances at Vincent. 'Your gay friend with style, no offense . . .'

'None taken,' Vincent says.

Sheldon's lips curl up into a gentle smile. He really does mean well.

'It is my duty to give you the best possible experience. You can cancel the gorgeous invitations, the spectacular decorations, the chairs – jeesh, they were a deep burgundy velvet, oh well – but I cannot allow you to have your wedding dinner at –' Sheldon clears his throat, the slightest gagging noise escaping his mouth. 'The Shake Shack.'

'You know,' Jill says, 'Nick says you can't beat their Savory Sliders.'

Sheldon gives her a stare that could melt the polar ice caps.

'Marvin.' Sheldon places his hand on my forearm. 'Let me make a reservation someplace nice. Please.'

I steal a glance at Jill and Vincent, who both nod.

'Okay, dinner is up to you. Say five o'clock, so we have time to get there.'

'Dinner at five o'clock.' Sheldon writes in his journal. 'Got it.'

*

On my walk to the ferry, I pull out my phone and make the call I've been avoiding since Olan and I changed the wedding plans. Deep breaths. This will be fine.

'Mom, I only have a few minutes. I'm meeting Isabella to pick up Illona, but I wanted to tell you –'

'Sweetie, I already know.' The calmness in her voice makes me uneasy.

'Know what?'

'What you're calling to tell me.'

'Which is?'

'About the wedding.' She knows. And the tranquility remains. 'Olan called me. He said he was spending the baby's nap time canceling all the things and wanted to call me himself.'

Just when I think he can't be any more amazing, Olan goes and proves me wrong.

'Oh. Are you okay about it?'

'Marvin, I've told you from the beginning of all this, all I want is for my son to be happy. You're getting married. Soon. You're going to be a Sadie.'

Since I can remember, *Funny Girl* has been a comfort movie for my mother. The soundtrack was on repeat in our apartment for all of my formative years. She's right. I'm finally going to be a . . .

'Well, married . . . gentleman.' I'm determined to make her understand in this marriage equation, there are no brides.

'Doesn't quite have the same ring, though, does it?'

'How about we go with "lady"? Just for us.' It's the least I can do for her.

'Thank you.' I can almost hear the smile spread across her face.

'But you won't be here.'

'We can celebrate the next time I visit. I'm coming for a week this summer. Possibly ten days. Heck, maybe two weeks, we'll see. Olan and I already discussed it.'

'That sounds wonderful, Mom. Illona will be thrilled. We'll take lots of pictures on Friday. I promise.'

'You better.'

'Thanks for understanding.' I'm about a block away from the terminal and spot Isabella's Range Rover.

'Of course. And remember how much I love you.'

'I love you too, Mom.'

When I approach the car, Isabella and Illona pop out, with matching massive smiles.

'How did it go?' I ask.

They exchange a quick glance, then turn to me and burst into uncontrollable giggles.

I raise my eyebrows. 'What?'

Taking a deep breath, Isabella says, 'Illona and I agreed. I'm keeping the dress. You and Olan will see it Friday.'

Illona covers her mouth, concealing her beautiful grin, and nods.

'I'm going to pick her up at lunchtime on Friday. We ladies need a little extra time to prepare. We'll see you at city hall at three.'

'Sounds good. Maybe I should take the afternoon off.' I scratch my chin.

'You are getting married,' Illona says. 'I think it's allowed.'

Now I'm laughing, but also, holy crap, I'm getting married in three days.

'Okay, you two better get moving so you don't miss the

ferry.' Isabella kisses Illona and then pulls me into a warm, tight hug that lingers a little longer than usual.

Before she pulls away, she whispers into my ear, 'This feels right. Doing it now. I cannot wait for Friday.'

And yup, my damn eyes are leaking again. As I return Isabella's embrace, who will soon be my . . . what do you call your husband's ex-wife who's somehow become one of your closest friends and now your lives will be intertwined forever? Isabella.

'Thank you,' I say. 'For everything.'

'Marvin . . .' She pulls away, but still holds on to my arms. 'You've been good for my family. Look at this face.' She cradles Illona's chin in her hand.

'It's a good face,' I say.

'It really is,' Isabella replies. 'So happy. And you're a big part of that. We are so lucky to have you.' She glances at her watch. 'Now, go before you have to swim home.'

This apparently tickles Illona, and she bursts into laughter. 'Swim home. Good one.'

Illona grabs my hand and we jog toward the waiting ferry. Before we hop on, we both turn around and give Isabella a wave. Her perfectly manicured hand returns our gesture and my heart swells with warmth at how much has changed in the past two years. When you open yourself up to it, the universe has a way of working its magic.

44

'Friends, we've almost made it to the weekend!'

I'm on the carpet with my class as butterflies flutter in my stomach. Every single woman I work with has shared big personal news with their class without reproach. I spoke with Dr Knorse this morning and she was thrilled. She quickly asked one of the support techs, Ms Ball, to cover my class and was supportive of me telling the students why I'd be out. But, of course, being queer means always wondering if you're crossing a line and making others uncomfortable. In this case, the parents, not the children. But in all my years here, the community at Pelletier has been nothing but supportive. There's no reason to believe this will be different.

'I know on Fridays we usually share what our plans are for the weekend, and today, I have some news to tell you.'

Their little bodies lean in, eyes wide, chins down, waiting. Even Michael lifts his body from leaning against my side to listen and watch as I deliver my announcement.

'I'm going to be leaving at lunch today.' The sea of eye-balls grows slightly wider. 'Olan and I are getting married.'

'In August,' Audrey says. 'We have it on the calendar.' She points to the large summer months plastered on the wall where our wedding is listed along with all the summer holidays and birthdays. There was something less scary about it happening while we're not in school.

'No, actually, today,' I say.

Mouths drop open, and I quickly speak to explain.

'We were planning to have a big wedding in August, but we decided we didn't want to wait. Sometimes that happens. You make a plan and it changes.'

'That's called being flexible,' Ben says. 'When your original plan doesn't work out, you make a new one.'

I smile at him, remembering our lesson on flexibility from the beginning of the year. And of course, he's right.

'Exactly,' I say. 'Olan and I are being flexible. We're making a new plan.'

'Can we come?' Michael asks before leaning back in on my torso.

'Sadly, no. We're only having family there.'

'But what about Ms Kim?' Katherine asks. They know how close Jill and I are.

'Well, she'll be there, of course.'

'But she's not your family,' Alex says.

'You're right. We're not related. But she's still family.'

'Like how I call Aunt Kandy my aunt,' Brian says. 'Even though she's really not. She still is.'

'Exactly like that,' I say.

'We should celebrate,' Aaron says, sitting up a little taller.

I nod in agreement. 'How about a dance party?'

The class erupts in a chorus of 'yes!' as I rise from my seat and make my way toward my phone, eager to connect it to the wireless speaker resting on the chalk railing.

'I know just the song.'

With a few taps, the thumping bass and crisp horns of Martha and the Vandellas' 'Dancing in the Street' fills the room. Olan mentioned that Marvin Gaye was one of the songwriters, but I doubt my students have any interest in that detail. When the ladies' voices join in, the entire class takes their direction, swinging and swaying. I take Michael's and Audrey's hands, and before I know it, they're connecting with those beside them, creating a ripple effect that sweeps through the group. Soon, the entire class is linked together in a circle, dancing and celebrating the upcoming wedding of their kindergarten teacher.

> Olan: Which ferry are you catching?
>
> Marvin: 12:15. I'm on my way now.
>
> Olan: I can't wait to kiss your face. 💋
> We're getting married today.
>
> Marvin: ILU! 💜
>
> Olan: I know the ferry has one speed, but hurry.
>
> Marvin: I'll see what I can do.

The late April sun warms my head as I run my fingers through my short curls, attempting a revival, but still a few weeks away from a full comeback. Olan and I discussed our outfits last night. We're both wearing dress pants, shirts, and ties. The only contrast was in the color of our pants – mine are a bold blue, while Olan's are a neutral khaki. It was nice to pick something from clothes we already own and since we rarely dress up together, we'll still feel special.

Even though our time is limited, as we have to catch the 2:45 ferry to make it back before city hall closes for the weekend, I'm eagerly anticipating the precious moments of alone time with Olan. He'll have the baby dressed and ready, which will give me plenty of time to shower and change.

There's an extra pep in my step as I approach the house and skip up our front steps with a huge smile plastered on my face. As I reach for the door, it unexpectedly swings open before my hand touches the knob.

Olan swiftly joins me on the porch, closing the door behind him. He's all dressed, except for his tie, his body filling out the dress shirt deliciously, and I wonder if the baby's afternoon nap might help me convince him to undress and shower with me.

'Hey.' He kisses me, his cherry ChapStick sweetening his already tempting lips.

'Hey yourself,' I say.

'I have a couple of surprises for you.'

'Oh, really.' My fingers grab at the slick leather of his belt, doing their best to poke underneath his waistband.

'We're getting married in a few hours. Remember, that's what matters most.'

He's not taking the bait, and his thoughtful tone catches me off guard.

Olan opens the door and beyond the foyer, sitting on the sofa in our living room, is Sarah Block.

'There you are.' She stands with Greggie in her arms and approaches me.

'Surprise.' Olan's not winning any Oscars for his performance, but he gives it the college try.

'Mom. How? When? What are you doing here?'

'My son is getting married. I needed to meet my new grandson. So, I'm here!' She holds the baby up, kissing his forehead, and I get my first look at his outfit.

He's wearing a mini version of Olan's ensemble, with the cutest baby blue bow tie and matching newsboy hat. I'm not sure it's possible for him to be any cuter.

'Oh, my goodness. I didn't know he had this outfit.' I extend my arms and Sarah transfers him to me.

'Surprise number two. I thought he should coordinate with his uncles.'

'This boy could not be any sweeter.' My mother runs her hand behind Greggie's head. 'Look at that punim. I would eat those cheeks if I could.'

'Thankfully, that's not allowed,' I say. 'But I've thought about it myself.' My fingers graze Greggie's cheeks and he gives me the most precious smile.

Sarah leans into me, her head resting on my shoulder, as we both gaze at Greggie in my arms. Holding this precious baby boy with my mom here, close, on my wedding day, a warm sense of happiness surges over me and I take a deep breath, attempting to soak it all in.

'I'm glad you're here, Mom.' I turn and kiss her on the cheek. 'Thanks for coming.'

'Sweetie, I wouldn't miss it.' She moves back to the couch and places a large throw pillow on her lap. 'I wasn't sure the flights would work out, so I didn't tell you. I didn't want you to worry. Or be disappointed. I told Olan I'd do my best, and thankfully, the travel gods were with me. Now, let bubbe hold this tattele while you go get ready.'

She pats the cushion, and I hand Greggie back to her.

'Technically, we're his uncles,' Olan says. 'So, I'm not sure what that makes you.'

'His bubbe.' She leans down, whispering into Greggie's ear. 'Nobody will know.'

Olan shoots me a smile and I shrug.

'You look beautiful, Mom. I've never seen that dress.'

'This old thing.' Her dress is a sight to behold. A soft cream fabric that hits just above her ankles, it's covered in tiny blue flowers that add a touch of elegance. 'I've been saving it for a special occasion. I'd say this fits the bill.'

'Come.' Olan extends his hand. 'Your mother has the baby. Let's get you ready.'

As we head upstairs, my mother sings 'You Are My Sunshine' and lets out a deep sigh. Now that she's met Greggie, I wonder if she'll ever return to Arizona.

As the bedroom door swings open, I notice Olan has already taken the time to press my outfit and arrange it on the bed.

'You didn't have to do that,' I said.

'Wait, there's more.'

He opens the top drawer of the dresser and pulls out a pair of suspenders.

'Surprise three.'

The fabric on the suspenders matches my pants and the leather attachments coordinate with Olan's belt.

'Olan, when did you get these?'

'I still have a few tricks up my sleeve.' He hands them to me. 'I wanted something special. For my special guy.'

'I love them, but I didn't get you anything.'

'Babe. I've got you. That's all I need.'

He pulls me close, and as I embrace him, my lips find their way to the curve of his neck.

'Thank you,' I whisper into his ear.

'Wait, there's still more.'

My legs wobble, and I carefully take a seat on the edge of the bed, trying to steady myself.

'Olan, I'm not sure I can take more surprises.'

'Well, buckle up, buttercup, because there's more.'

'Excuse me, did you just call me buttercup?'

His head clips a quick nod, and a mischievous smile appears on his face.

'All that writing I did when I was home got my creative juices flowing and, well, I wrote something else.'

Olan pulls a small piece of paper from his pocket, unfolds it, and hands it to me.

'Surprise four.'

Adrenaline courses through my veins, my breath coming in quick gasps as I process the whirlwind of surprises.

'Go ahead.' Olan sits next to me. His strong hand wraps around my shoulder. 'Read it.'

The Blue Rose
This flower, in starry skies with lovers, weightless . . .
Like saying forever.
Rare and gorgeous,
Once in a lifetime,

I pluck the petal, place it in your palm,
and smile at how well it fits in your hand.

'You wrote this?'

He nods, a smile sneaking over his lips.

Before I'm able to say more, Olan opens my left palm, the soft petals touch my skin, and then my eyes see it – a blue rose.

'Surprise number five – the last one. Just so you know.'

'A blue rose?'

'For both of us.' He pulls another one from behind a throw pillow on the bed. 'Sheldon helped me with these. That man can locate anything.'

'He knows a guy in Kennebunk.'

'Of course he does.' Olan pins his flower to his shirt. 'Now, go get ready and we'll affix yours. My beautiful blue rose.'

As his lips touch my cheek, my eyelids instinctively flutter shut. I breathe deeply, Olan's scent and the flowers mixing as I attempt to process it all.

'It's too much. The poem. The flowers. Greggie's outfit. I thought this was supposed to be simple.'

'Marvin, this is simple. But we're getting married. Let me spoil you a little.'

'I love it.' I hold the poem up and kiss right in the middle of the paper. 'But I love you more. Most.' I lean over and hear a soft breath escape his lips as our mouths connect. There is a part of me that longs for us to remain in this moment, frozen in time. But my mom is downstairs and our friends are meeting us.

'Now, go. Get ready. We have a date at city hall.'

45

The trees on the street outside city hall are lush with fresh green leaves and burst into bloom, their delicate petals drifting on the breeze, carpeting the sidewalks. Olan finds a parking spot, and when I see Isabella and Illona standing by the entrance waiting, it takes me a minute to catch my breath.

'Look at them,' I say. I turn around toward the backseat. 'Mom, can you get Greggie out of his car seat?'

'You boys go ahead. I'll be right there with this little munchkin.'

As soon as Olan puts the car in park, we jump out, and when Illona spots us, her face lights up like a menorah on the eighth night and she dashes over.

The dress she's wearing is absolutely breathtaking, with its intricate lace and vibrant colors. It's white and covered in blue and pink flowers. The fabric gracefully flutters in the wind as she sprints toward us, enveloping us both in a tight, affectionate embrace.

'You look beautiful,' Olan says as he lifts her up.

Her hair has been braided into a giant bun that rests on top of her head like a crown. Today, she's truly her father's princess.

'Thank you, Daddy.' She shifts her gaze to me. 'Do you like it?'

'I love it. You always look beautiful, but I never imagined you'd look this perfect today.'

'We spent a lot of weekends searching for this dress.' Isabella joins us, the sound of her heels clacking against the sidewalk as she approaches. 'But the minute Illona saw it, she knew.'

'And you look gorgeous,' I say. 'As usual.'

'This old thing?' Isabella holds up the side of her baby blue pleated skirt. She's wearing a simple white blouse, with sheer sleeves, and her hair is also up, giving her a regal appearance.

'Thank you,' Olan says, leaning over and kissing her cheek.

'My pleasure.' Isabella now gives me a soft peck, being careful not to leave lipstick on my face. 'Plus, we had a blast.'

'We did,' Illona says as her dad sets her down. 'One shop had little cakes, and they kept giving them to us. I ate so many I got a tummy ache, but it was totally worth it. What were they called again, Mommy?'

'Petit fours.'

'Yeah, those. And they were so yummy. You would love them, Marvin.'

'Maybe we'll need to go back for another dress,' I say. 'I mean, you can never have too many dresses.'

'My sweet loves his sweets.' Olan nudges his shoulder against mine.

'I'm here!' Jill Kim, wearing the most stunning traditional dress with a red floral motif on light pink fabric, skips toward us. I can't help but be captivated by her beauty.

'You clean up nice.' I wrap my arms around her, holding her close. 'This is next level.'

'It's an áo dài – a traditional Vietnamese dress. I had Nick bring it to me after school and changed in the classroom.' She smooths her hands over the shiny fabric. 'Only for you, Marvin.'

'Let's go,' Isabella says, glancing at her watch. 'The clerk is waiting.'

We walk toward my mother, who is standing near the stairs to the entryway of city hall, with Greggie nestled in her arms, and then we head inside.

Our shoes echo on the massive marble staircase in the old building's entrance and when we reach the top, we walk to the door down the hallway with a sign that reads Marriage Licenses.

The room is simple. Sparse. There's a long low counter, with a few desks behind it and various signs displaying fees and other information. Turns out, you can also take care of a parking ticket here or obtain a fishing license.

A kind, middle-aged woman stands from her desk and approaches the counter.

'Can I help you?'

'We have an appointment to be married.' Olan takes my hand and we take a step forward from our family.

'Of course, names?'

'Marvin Block and Olan Stone,' Illona says before either of us can speak. 'Marvin was my kindergarten teacher. I'm in second grade now. But he and my dad fell in love and now they're getting married. He's going to be my stepdad now.'

The woman offers an amused look. Surely in her position she's seen it all before, including enthusiastic children watching their parents tie the knot.

'How lovely. And what's your name?'

'Illona Stone. This is my mom. That's Sarah, Marvin's mom, and Greggie, my baby cousin.'

'I'm Patti, the notary here, and I'll be issuing your license and then marrying you.'

I can only imagine the variety of blended families Patti has encountered, yet I wonder if she has ever come across one as unique and wonderful as ours.

After filling out some paperwork, and lots of checking boxes and stamping forms from Patti, our license is issued.

'Now, let's get you two married.'

Standing at the counter in city hall, with our family behind us, Olan and I listen as Patti reads off her paper, and it's all a blur as my head does its best to stay afloat. She asks us if we want to be each other's wedded husbands and we're told to exchange rings. Olan measured my finger weeks before he left for Chicago. Even before the change of plans, he wanted to be in charge of buying them. He takes out two boxes, hands me one, and winks, which sends my insides tumbling.

I flip the box open to a platinum ring. It's not too big, not too small, but the perfect Goldi-ring.

'Marvin, repeat after me . . .' Patti instructs.

I listen carefully, holding the ring, rubbing it between my fingers, the cool, smooth metal soothing my nerves.

'With this ring, I thee wed, as a token of my love, faith, and loyalty.'

I slide it onto his ring finger, and he gently squeezes my hand. My heart swells with an abundance of boundless love.

Olan repeats the same line and places his ring on my finger. Another grasp of my hand, and this time, he doesn't let go.

'By the love that has brought you here today,' Patti says, slowing down so everyone hears, 'and by the vows you have pledged, surrounded by your family, by the authority granted to me by the State of Maine, it is my extreme honor to now pronounce you . . . Husband and Husband.'

There's some light clapping from behind us, and I'm pretty sure I hear a few sniffles from my mother.

'Kiss!' Illona shouts. 'Now you kiss.'

Olan leans over and when his lips land on mine, my eyes close and I have a flash of our first kiss. In my old one-bedroom apartment. He took me home after babysitting Illona. When he made a pass at me in the car, I bolted upstairs like a shlemiel, forgetting my backpack in his car. He brought it up to me. He was adamant he wasn't leaving my apartment until he kissed me.

And now we're married. Husbands. Thank you, Lord, creator of the universe, for bringing this man and his family into my life.

When Olan and I turn toward our group, there's a flurry of congratulatory hugs and kisses from everyone. When a loud ding interrupts, Jill pulls her phone from her purse.

'Sheldon.' She rolls her eyes. 'They're waiting for us at the restaurant.'

46

When we arrive at The Ocean Inn Restaurant, our small group grows only slightly larger. They've put us in a cozy private room near the back of the building, which means we're overlooking the water. It may not be a huge wedding with burgundy chairs and over a hundred guests, but it's simply perfect.

Dressed in their finest attire, Theo, Vincent, Kent, Ruth, Regina, and Nick, holding Maria in his lap, gather around the oversized table. Sheldon stands near the end, wearing a huge smile.

'You're married!' He feigns wiping a tear from his eye. 'I thought since the wedding was supposed to be here, it might be nice to at least have dinner here. And' – he looks toward Olan – 'I was able to convince them to transfer the deposit to this celebratory dinner.'

Olan winks at him and says, 'Well, thank you. That was astute of you.'

'Sheldon,' Theo calls from the table. 'Let them breathe. Come sit.'

'Yes, let's sit. The mocktails are on the table.' Sheldon winks at my mother and then wraps his arm around her. 'I saved you a seat next to me, Sarah, I hope that's okay.'

'Of course. Greggie and I will be right there.'

Sheldon joins Theo, and my mother pulls me down for a quick hug.

'I'm so proud of you,' she says. 'You've grown into such an amazing man. I'm kvelling. And now, married to such a wonderful man.' She grabs my chin. 'I love you.'

'I love you too, Mom.'

When I break free from her embrace, she grabs Olan. 'And thank you for finally making my boy a Sadie.'

'Of course. And I promise not to gamble away all our money on a cruise, leaving him dejected and hopeless.'

My mother takes a step back, eyes bulging, and then I see the reference register.

'I may have made him watch *Funny Girl* a few times,' I say.

With Greggie in tow, Sarah takes her spot near Sheldon while Olan and I make the rounds, giving hugs to our friends.

'Congratulations,' Kent says, standing with Vincent. 'You two make a very handsome couple.'

Vincent snaps one of my suspenders. 'Aren't you glad our SWISH date was a disaster?'

He hugs me, and there's a genuine warmth as we embrace.

'But it wasn't,' I say, pulling back. 'I found a dear friend.'

Ruth stands. 'And now you're stuck with him,' she says. She's wearing a crimson dress shirt, and her braids are adorned with blue beads, matching the flowers on the table. 'And us.'

'Thank you for coming,' Olan says, hugging her and then Regina. 'And thanks for being there when I was in Chicago. I appreciate it.'

'Olan, Auntie Ruth's got you.' She kisses his cheek and his sheepish smile hints he's blushing.

'Mazel tov to you both,' Regina says. 'The only thing I love more than a wedding is a queer wedding.'

'Hear! Hear!' Ruth shouts.

Theo stands, holding his blue-tinted mocktail high. 'Cheers to queers!'

With everyone shouting 'cheers', we make our way to our seats.

Nick, handing Maria to Jill, catches my arm before we sit.

'Olavin. My boys. You did it. Sadly, now we can't run away together, Marvin.' He pats my arm and gives me a peck on the cheek.

'Oh, great. Now I'm stuck with him,' Jill calls from her seat.

'Really. I couldn't be happier for you guys.' Nick pulls Olan and me into a giant huddle.

The table is adorned with blue roses, matching the boutonnieres Olan provided. There are candles and blue and silver confetti sprinkled over the white linens.

'Sheldon, you outdid yourself,' I say.

'Hey, you can't have a party without a little glitter.' He reaches into his pocket and tosses more confetti in the air.

'My Sheldon loves his sparkles.' Theo wraps his arm around Sheldon, pulling him in for a kiss on the top of the head.

The waitstaff bring salads for everyone, but before we begin, Jill returns Maria to Nick, stands, and clinks her glass.

'Best woman speech incoming.' She claps her spoon against the glass so hard, I worry she'll break it. Which would actually be on-brand for her.

The room quiets, and Jill continues.

'Marvin, from the moment I saw you and Olan together, I knew. Like how you know about a good avocado. Sure, like everyone else, I was taken aback by the hot dad in the school office – sorry, honey, but hot dads are a crown jewel for us teachers. Why do you think I love you so much?'

Nick kisses the top of Maria's head, and she grabs at his chin.

'But I knew this wasn't only physical. Olan, you bring something out in my friend – something special, something I don't even think he knew was there. For all his insecurities, you've helped him love himself. And as RuPaul says, "If you can't love yourself, how the hell you gonna love someone else?"'

Sheldon raises both hands to the ceiling and shouts, 'Amen!'

'Marvin,' Jill continues, 'you finally learned to love yourself enough to receive love from someone else. And not just anyone. Olan. Who's kind, loving, a great parent, friend, and looks amazing in gray sweatpants – or at least that's what I'm told.'

Heat flashes across my face and I quickly cover it with my hand.

'Here's to Marvin and Olan. And Illona and Isabella

and baby Gregory. May you all be happy and healthy for many, many years.'

'Hear! Hear!' Ruth shouts and everyone toasts.

During dinner, Greggie gets passed around like a collection plate, everyone taking a turn holding him. When Theo holds him, the baby somehow appears even smaller, and when Greggie fusses, my mom hands Theo a bottle, and with no direction, he feeds him. As Sheldon watches his boyfriend feed the baby, a look of pure adoration lights up his face. I know that look. Perhaps their family might grow beyond fur babies someday?

When I notice Illona poking at her mashed potatoes, I lean down and whisper, 'Hey, can you come here for a second?'

She's going to be too big for laps soon, but right now, she gladly hops on, wrapping her arms around my neck.

'How are you?' I ask.

'Fine. I don't like the potatoes, though. They're spicy.'

'Yeah, I think it's wasabi. They're trying to be fancy.'

'Why can't potatoes just be potatoes?'

'I couldn't agree more.' I pull her closer, and she rests her head on my chest. 'But you're okay otherwise?'

She nods. 'I know I should be smiling more, but I am happy. I've been waiting for you and Daddy to get married forever and now you've finally done it and I guess I'm a little overwhelmed is all. Is that weird?'

'No, sweetie. It's not weird at all. I totally understand.' I pull her close and whisper into her ear, 'You just remember how loved you are. By everyone around this table.'

She grips me so tightly, I worry she'll crush me, but I

wouldn't even mind. I squeeze her back, holding the back of her neck.

'Okay, I'll just not eat the potatoes.'

'Totally fine,' I say.

'One more thing.' Her bright eyes peer up at me. How did I get so damn lucky to have the universe bring this child into my life? 'Now that you and Daddy are married, maybe I should call you something else . . . besides Marvin.'

As I utter the word, 'Oh,' I feel goose bumps spread across my skin and tears welling up. 'Well, what did you have in mind?'

'I've been making lists in my journal. But nothing seemed right.' That's why she's been so invested in her writing lately. 'Then I talked to Courtney on the playground this week. She has two dads too, and she calls one "daddy" and the other "papa" and maybe I could call you that?'

The words get stuck in my throat and I do my best to swallow past the massive lump.

'You want to call me Papa?'

'Only if you wanted.'

'Illona. Nothing would make me happier.'

She wraps her arms around my neck again, burying her face, and whispers, 'I love you, Papa.'

And now I'm crying. Not just a few tears, but full-on sobbing. This day has truly been filled with overwhelming emotions. Deep breaths. Hold it together.

'Why are you crying?' Illona pulls back, her eyes wide.

'I'm just on cloud nine.'

'Me too.'

She gives me a quick kiss on the cheek, hops off my lap, and returns to her seat next to her mother. I see her explaining our conversation and Isabella gives her an enormous hug. My God, I'm blessed.

As I take in the scene before me, I am overcome with emotion. All these people, here on a Friday night with only a few days' notice, are my family. Not only my mother. Not only Olan now, legally my family. But my friends. My husband's former spouse – now my friend. I've managed to surround myself with the most amazing, caring people. They're all my family now.

'Sarah,' Olan says. My mother is attempting to burp Greggie after the bottle Theo gave him. 'Would you mind if I took your son outside for a minute?'

'Go, go! Bubbe's here.' She kisses the side of Greggie's head while patting his back.

Exiting the restaurant, the sound of waves crashing on the shore fills the air as Olan gently takes my hand and guides me toward the beach. The sun has set, but twilight still allows us to take in the beautiful view (and not trip on random shells and driftwood in the sand). When we're about ten feet from the water, Olan lowers himself to the ground, and I join him.

'C'mere,' he says, patting his chest.

'My favorite place,' I say.

'The beach or my chest?'

'Both.'

As I rest against him, the firmness of his pecs supports my back, while the stars twinkle in the darkening sky.

Olan's arms envelop me, his embrace growing tighter as his warm breath caresses my hair with each deep exhale.

'You okay?' he asks.

I nod, my head buried in the crook of his arm.

'You're not disappointed we didn't have the big wedding?'

'Are you kidding? I couldn't have asked for a more perfect day. And now we're married. That's all I really care about.'

'How does it feel? Being married?'

I hold my left hand out, admiring the ring on my finger. 'It's like everything's changed, but also nothing's changed.'

'Exactly. Except, now you're mine.' He holds me a little tighter. 'Forever.'

I nod over the lump that apparently has taken up permanent residence in my throat.

'Look.' Olan points to the sky. There's a swirl of clouds, resembling cotton candy being pulled and twisted by invisible hands.

'A ribbon in the sky,' he says. 'Just for us.'

'I love you,' I say. 'So much.'

'Can you feel my heart?' As Olan holds me tightly against his chest, the comforting thumping on my back fills my entire body with affection.

'Yup.'

'You're doing that. Your love. You.'

As I gaze up at the darkening sky, the stars begin to emerge, their distant lights twinkling against the velvet backdrop of night. My heart synchs with his and a deep sense of peace washes over me, filling every corner of my being with tranquility. Under the vast, star-studded canopy, it's like the entire universe came out to celebrate us.

Me.

Olan.

My love.

My husband.

Epilogue

Fourteen Months Later

'Isn't this where you got married?' Illona shields her eyes from the bright June sun. It's warm, but thankfully there's no humidity and our collective curls aren't rendered into a mountain of frizz.

'Sort of.' We hold hands as we wait for the crosswalk. 'We're going across the street to the courthouse.'

'That's where the judge has a chamber.' Olan pushes Greggie's stroller, with a diaper bag strapped to his shoulder. 'A notary married us, but we need a judge today.'

'Got it.' Illona's hand lets go of mine and she turns around. 'Mommy!'

Isabella jogs to join us, her hair a few inches shorter, blowing in the breeze. I've decided it's her lot in life to always have her hair blowing in the wind like a pop diva.

'I'm sorry, I couldn't find parking,' she says, giving us each a quick hug.

'It's fine.' Olan checks his watch. 'You're right on time.'

Illona takes my hand, while her other grabs her mother's. Olan steers the stroller over a few bumps in the pavement, and Greggie lets out a sweet coo and then shouts 'Bella' and reaches for his aunt. Isabella leans over and kisses both of his cheeks.

'Auntie Bella is here, my handsome boy.'

Greggie smiles up at her and then grabs for her when she stands. He's almost two, and I wonder if he understands exactly what's happening as we head into the courthouse together.

'All right, let's get started.'

The judge, wearing a traditional robe, sits behind the bench. Her black hair and dark golden skin shine under the fluorescent lights and even though I've been told this is simply a formality, my heart races with nerves.

'What a beautiful family,' she says. 'I'm Judge Leigh. I'll be presiding today. I'm going to swear you in, ask you some questions, and then make a ruling. It shouldn't take long. Sound good?'

Olan's holding Greggie in his lap now, and we all nod.

She requests we rise, lift our hands, and collectively vow to speak nothing but the truth. We all agree and return to our seats.

'Who presents themself as the adoptive parents here today?'

'We do,' Olan and I say in unison.

'And who are you, young lady?' Judge Leigh asks Illona.

'I'm Illona. These are my dads. That's my mom. Greggie is my cousin.'

The judge nods, checking some papers in front of her. The attorney assured us she'd be aware of the situation, but would probably ask some simple questions.

Liam's still living in a sober house in Chicago. Olan talks to him about once a month and we keep him in the loop about his son. We all flew out for the holidays in December so Greggie could see his grandparents and father. I was nervous he might have second thoughts, but seeing him with Greggie actually made me worry less. It's just as Olan said, for Greggie, his father plays more of an uncle role while his actual uncles parent him.

Liam thanked us both for what we're doing and reiterated he knows his son is in the right place. After Greggie had lived with us for a year, Liam asked to sign over his full parental rights. It was a no-brainer for us and we planned the adoption as soon as possible. It may not be a traditional family arrangement, but it's working extremely well for us. Liam had one relapse last year, but he was able to return to the home quickly. Olan knows he has a long journey ahead, but he's optimistic about his brother's recovery.

'And do you understand that adoption is a lifelong commitment?' Judge Leigh asks.

Before Olan or I can answer, Illona says, 'Yup. After this, he's permanent. Like a marker.'

We all laugh, including the judge, who adds, 'And how about you, dads?'

'Yes, we understand,' I say.

'And you're willing to treat Gregory as a child born to you, having all rights to inheritance?'

'Of course,' Olan says.

'All right, I think I'm ready to rule.'

My heart thumps against my chest, knowing in a few moments, this will all be over. My mother asked if I wanted her to come out and when I told her it wasn't necessary, I assumed she'd probably hop on a plane and surprise us, anyway. But she didn't. She was here two months ago when she flew out for a week and she'll be back soon to help us transition back to our fall routine.

'Let's make this official.' Judge Leigh clasps her hands, leaning forward on the bench. 'I've reviewed the files, and there is no doubt in my mind that this adoption is in the best interest of Gregory. It is truly my honor to be able to grant the petition filed by Marvin Block and Olan Stone for the adoption of Gregory Antwone Stone. Congratulations, you are officially Gregory's parents.'

Unaware of the magnitude of the moment, Greggie smiles, probably from gas, as Olan hugs him and I lean in to join their embrace. Yup, definitely gas.

Illona snuggles up against her dad, and we create a small huddle as Isabella uses her phone to snap some photos of the moment.

'How about a picture?' Judge Leigh asks from the bench.

She steps down, and we all gather. The clerk uses Isabella's phone to take a photo.

'Thank you,' I say to the judge, as Olan gathers our things.

'No, thank you,' she replies. 'This is my favorite part of the job.'

Outside on the sidewalk, there are more hugs, and Illona asks, 'Now what?'

'Now, we go to lunch to celebrate,' Olan says.

'Come,' I say and extend my hand.

Illona holds my hand and swiftly reaches for Isabella's with her other, while Olan pushes Greggie in the stroller. As we walk toward the restaurant a few blocks away, the warmth of my family's presence surrounds me. Although we may not fit the mold of a conventional family, we are perfectly crafted by love.

From the bottom of my gay heart, thank you, universe. Thank you.

Acknowledgments

And now the fun part where I get to thank folks. I typically end my acknowledgments by thanking my husband, Dave, but given the title and theme of this book, I'm going to start with him. Marvin and Olan's story is about finding your person. The one who accepts you – warts and all – and makes you an even better version of yourself. I'm the luckiest guy on earth, and you're my person. The love we share is something for the ages . . . every time I sit down and write about the deep (and sometimes messy) connection between two people, I'm inspired by you. By us. Thank you for being you. For letting me love you. For loving me. For choosing us. For our family.

Next, I must thank you, dear reader – for picking up *Husband of the Year* and continuing this journey with me. It's never lost on me the honor it is to write and share queer love stories filled with joy. I'm eternally grateful you've given me that opportunity.

Even though they can't read or write, I must thank my cats. Every day, they help me understand the importance of patience and never underestimating the power of sweet furballs curled in your lap to make everything feel okay, even if only for the moment.

To the entire online book community, your support for my stories has buoyed me in ways I'm not sure I can fully express. Every post, meme, gif, comment, reel, etc., means the world to me. Thank you for lifting my stories and my spirits.

Writing can be a solitary profession, but I'm lucky to have a group of author friends who keep me entertained, supported, and (most importantly) help me procrastinate. Jay Leigh, A.J. Truman, A.M. Johnson, Kayla Grosse, Ashley Bennett, Clio Evans, Max Walker, Brian Kennedy, Falon Ballard, and Courtney Kae – I'm lucky to call each of you friends. If I've forgotten anyone, please know I love and adore you. To all my author buddies, you continue to inspire and amaze me. Please never stop sharing your stories with the world.

Manda Waller, you have been the best editing partner a guy could ask for. You have truly helped me become a better writer, and for that, I will never stop singing your praises.

To my fantastic sensitivity reader, Priscillah Bancy, thank you for your time, guidance, and kindness. Your input has made all the difference.

Having early readers has always been a massive blessing for my work. Thank you, Gillian, Zoe, and Dave for all your early support.

Kirt Graves, Mark Sanderlin, and Evan Parker – I will never stop thanking you for the voices you've given my guys.

Local bookstores have always been my favorite place to get lost. A massive thank you to all who've believed in me along the way, and a special shout out to everyone at Back Cove Books.

As a gay Jewish romance author, I've been in need of therapy my entire life, and no one has helped me like Erika. You've made a real difference in my life.

You gotta have friends, and I'm lucky to have some of the best: Karen (both of you!), Emily, Jillian, Deedee, Maggie, Nate, Sarah, Susan, Patti, Brandon, Ron, Derek, Landon, Elise, Liz, Fiona, and all my friends, your encouragement and love continue to buoy me.

To my dear Jeremy, I hope you know how loved and missed you are. Keep a seat warm for all your buddies. And please, have some warm biscuits waiting.

Having an agent who really understands not only your writing, but you, is something I never dreamed of, but Stevie Finnegan, you are the real deal. Thank you, from the bottom of my heart, for all you've done.

Alex Logan, Estelle Hallick, and the entire Forever Team, you're all the true dream team.

Hannah Smith and the entire Penguin team, thank you for helping my stories shine worldwide.

To my mother, you've always been my fiercest champion, standing by my side through every challenge and celebrating every success. Your unwavering belief in me has been a constant source of strength, and I am forever grateful for your love and support.

I hope you've enjoyed the conclusion of Marvin and Olan's story. Now, more than ever, the world needs more queer joy, and I'm honored to play a part in spreading it. Remember, you are worthy of love and acceptance, no matter what anyone tells you. Sing out loud – dance when nobody's watching. Dance when they *are* watching. Never stop being unabashedly, authentically you because you're amazing.

On a station platform, with nothing to read,
and a four-hour train journey stretching ahead of him...

That's where the story began for Penguin founder Allen Lane.
With only 'shabby reprints of shoddy novels' on offer,
he resolved to make better books for readers everywhere.

By the time his train pulled into London, the idea was formed.
He would bring the best writing, in stylish and affordable
formats, to everyone. His books would be sold in bookstores,
stationers and tobacconists, for no more than the price
of a ten-pack of cigarettes.

And on every book would be a Penguin, a bird with a certain
'dignified flippancy', and a friendly invitation to anyone who
wished to spend their time reading.

In 1935, the first ten Penguin paperbacks were published.
Just a year later, three million Penguins had made their
way onto our shelves.

Reading was changed forever.

—

A lot has changed since 1935, including Penguin, but in the
most important ways we're still the same. We still believe that
books and reading are for everyone. And we still believe that
whether you're seeking an afternoon's escape, a vigorous debate
or a soothing bedtime story, all possibilities open with a book.

Whoever you are, whatever you're looking for,
you can find it with Penguin.